The Valley of the Fallen

The Valley
of the Fallen
El Valle
de los Caídos

CARLOS ROJAS

TRANSLATED FROM THE SPANISH

BY EDITH GROSSMAN

YALE UNIVERSITY PRESS ■ NEW HAVEN AND LONDON

A MARGELLOS
WORLD REPUBLIC OF LETTERS BOOK

The Margellos World Republic of Letters is dedicated to making literary works from around the globe available in English through translation. It brings to the English-speaking world the work of leading poets, novelists, essayists, philosophers, and playwrights from Europe, Latin America, Africa, Asia, and the Middle East to stimulate international discourse and creative exchange.

Yale University Press books may be purchased in quantity for educational, business, or promotional use. For information, please e-mail sales.press@yale.edu (U.S. office) or sales@yaleup.co.uk (U.K. office).

Set in Electra and Nobel types by Tseng Information Systems, Inc.
Printed in the United States of America.

Library of Congress Control Number: 2017944084
ISBN 978-0-300-21796-4 (hardcover : alk. paper)

A catalogue record for this book is available from the British Library.

This paper meets the requirements of ANSI/NISO Z39.48-1992 (Permanence of Paper).

10 9 8 7 6 5 4 3 2 1

For María Dolores and Giovanni Cantieri

The English edition is dedicated to Marina,
and Sandro Vasari, as well as to Edith Grossman,
who translated their book

Comme un pâtre est d'une nature supérieure à celle de
son troupeau, les pasteurs d'hommes, qui sont leurs chefs,
sont aussi d'une nature supérieure à celle de leurs peuples.
Ainsi raisonnait, au rapport de *Philon*, l'empereur *Caligula*;
concluant assez bien de cette analogie que les rois étaient
des dieux, ou que les peuples étaient des bêtes.
—Jean-Jacques Rousseau, *Du contrat social*

CONTENTS

The Valley of the Fallen

THE ABSURDITIES

THE DREAM OF REASON

The Family of Carlos IV

In July 1800, Goya receives the fee for the most celebrated of his portraits, *The Family of Carlos IV*. According to the date payment was made, Josep Gudiol deduces that the artist would conclude his canvas that spring, the first of the century. Goya begins by making a sketch, a "rough," of each member of the royal family against a red-wash background. Those of Infanta Josefa and Infante Antonio Pascual, the king's sister and brother, are in the Prado. In these studies, which are authentic paintings, the painter leaves clear evidence of his moral purpose in portraying the entire ensemble. He will not idealize or caricature his models. He feels as far from mockery as he does from flattery. He limits himself to representing the monarchs and their kin as Velázquez painted court jesters: detailing their physical flaws in order to reveal their inner world. And yet the results achieved by Velázquez and Goya are completely antithetical. While Felipe IV's buffoons reveal their sensitivity and tragic sense of life through their deformities, Goya's royal imbeciles, as Aldous Huxley will call them in another century, lay bare in their features the stupidity, ambition, and duplicitous cunning that dwell within them.

Almost all the "roughs" contain a complete depiction of the subjects. The only exception is the sketch of the head of Prince Don Carlos María Isidro, who will ignite the so-called Carlist Wars in the next generation when he competes with his niece, Isabel II, for the throne. In the sketch a boy's head looks out at us, with blond eyebrows and a glance almost as obscure as that of his brother Fernando, the crown prince, though much more willful and devoid of the glint of sadness that in the eyes of the firstborn is mistaken for rancor. In the family portrait, however, Don Carlos, pale and half hidden behind Fernando, seems an extraordinarily and prematurely aged adolescent: almost a dwarf, mockingly invested with the blue-and-white sash of Carlos III, his features withered and arrested on the verge of puberty.

Although the king stands in the center of the painting, a step ahead of the others, the queen is the real protagonist in this grotesque tragedy. Wearing a low-cut dress, her bosom, wig, and ears heavily bejeweled, she smiles disagreeably with tight, almost invisible lips. At the time that Goya is painting *The Family of Carlos IV*, in March 1800, the French ambassador writes to Napoleon: "The Queen arises at eight, receives the nursemaids of the younger children, and arranges their outings. She writes every day to the Prince of Peace, telling him everything. After the King's breakfast, the Queen is served hers. She eats alone and has a special cuisine because she is missing all her teeth. Three experts continually retouch her false teeth. The entire royal family attends the bullfights. The Queen is so superstitious that she covers herself with relics during a storm." A great, ugly mythic bird from *The Caprices* seems to metamorphose into the head of María Luisa right in the middle of the canvas. Napoleon is enthusiastic about that august head when he conquers Madrid. "It is incredible! Never before seen!" he usually says and then laughs when he describes the canvas. The monarchs, on the other hand, are pleased with Goya's work. On June 9 of that year, María Luisa writes to Godoy: "Goya begins my portrait tomorrow. The rest, except for the King's, are already finished and show a great resemblance." Two weeks later she writes to him again: "Goya has done my portrait. He says it is the best of all. Now he is preparing the portrait of the King, in La Casita del Labrador."

In the center of the canvas, treated with a resinous solution and painted in oils as transparent as watercolors, María Luisa has her arm around Infanta María Isabel and holds the hand of Infante Francisco de Paula. Court gossip attributes their paternity to Godoy. At this time the infante is only eight years old. Antonina Vallentin notes on his face a tenacious, somber look, inexplicably perverse on the face of a child. His resemblance to the portrait of Godoy in his youth, the work of Esteve, is startling. Two years later, Infanta María Isabel will marry the prince of Naples. Her mother-in-law, Queen Carolina, confesses to Alquier, the French ambassador, that the Infanta is manifestly Godoy's daughter and has inherited his appearance and expressions. The Neapolitan sovereign does not think highly of her son-in-law, the prince of Asturias: "The Prince does nothing, he does not read, he does not write, he does not think, nothing. Nothing . . . And this is deliberate, for they wanted him to be an idiot. The vulgarities he commits constantly, with everyone, are mortifying. The same is true of Isabel. They were allowed to grow up in the greatest ignorance, and what was done to them is a disgrace. Since María Luisa rules despotically in Spain, she always fears that someone will want to meddle in politics or her affairs."

The king looks like a wax statue of himself. He is now fifty-two, two years younger than Goya, who portrays himself at the other end of the painting, like Velázquez in *The Ladies-in-Waiting*, painting it and painting himself. Yet one would say the monarch is much older than the man who immortalizes him in this portrait. He has put on weight and aged prematurely after having been very vigorous. His blue eyes, lost in vacancy like those of a blind man, are somewhat darker than those of his brother, Infante Antonio Pascual, who, peering out from behind His Majesty, resembles the caricature of a caricature. When Princess María Antonia of Naples, now Fernando's fiancée, eventually gives birth to a stillborn child, her only one, María Luisa again writes to Godoy: "The child was smaller than an anise seed. To see him the King had to put on his reading spectacles." María Antonia herself is found between Fernando and María Isabel, her head turned toward the paintings on the wall. She has not come yet from Naples, and Goya cannot complete her profile without seeing her. He will never paint her, and the portrait is still incomplete. Behind Fernando and María Antonia appears the head of the ancient Princess María Josefa, sister of the king and Infante Antonio Pascual. An observer would think that one of those mirrors in which Goya's old witches look at themselves, while winged time prepares to sweep them away, has brought the image of one of those sorceresses back to life. Adorned with long gold earrings and peacock feathers on her head, the apparition is smiling. She has a blemish on one temple and eyes as blue and glassy as those of her brothers.

Four beings crowd together at the right. We see only the profile of the monarchs' oldest daughter, Princess Carlota. She will be queen of Portugal, and one of her daughters, Isabel de Braganza, will rule in Spain, wed to her uncle Fernando VII, in his second marriage. The duchess of Abrantes says that Carlota is quite deformed: one leg is longer than the other, and she is hunchbacked as well. In front of Carlota we have her sister, María Luisa, holding a child in her arms. She has small features and an artless glance. Her face is pleasing without being beautiful. A pillow on which she holds her baby does not hide her twisted waist. She is accompanied by her husband Prince Luis de Borbón Parma, heir to the duchy of that name and María Luisa's nephew. A tall, blond boy with lively eyes and fleshy lips, in whom there is already a suggestion of obesity. He is also an epileptic.

In the background of the painting are two other paintings; as in the background of *The Ladies-in-Waiting*, there is a mirror, which perhaps is also a painting although it could be taken for a window. In *The Family of Carlos IV*, two large canvases hang on the wall behind the fourteen figures. Both are by Goya in Goya's canvas, though they do not appear in Gudiol's complete catalogue. One is a trivial blurred landscape, perhaps a work of his youth, when the painter believed he accepted the world as his time seemed to accept it, in the glow of the enlightenment and at the hour of *Blind Man's Bluff* and outings along the Manzanares. In the other, darkened by time, are three indistinct figures. Until 1967 no one paid very much attention to it. However, it contained the final moral key to *The Family of Carlos IV*.

In June 1967, the Prado decided to restore Goya's canvas. In December, the surprising results of that undertaking were made public. In the painting represented in the background, along with the landscape of the stream and birches in the glow of enlightened harmony, there appeared a confused orgy of giants. In that canvas within a canvas, with large brushstrokes that come from Velázquez and precede or at the same time invent impressionism and expressionism, Goya displays a naked titan frolicking with two half-naked women as enormous as he is. The male's face is undoubtedly Goya's, according to Xavier de Salas, director of the Prado. No one dares to contradict him.

When Goya paints *The Family of Carlos IV* in 1800, he has been almost completely deaf for eight years, and living on loans of life. In 1792, the syphilis that perhaps he hadn't known until then he had contracted in his early youth, infects his inner ear and has him at death's door for two long years. Malraux compares him then to one of those sick people who, saved in their death throes, become mediums. At the end of the crisis, imprisoned in his silence, Goya would have an aura of the next world. The truth is precisely the opposite, because Goya conjures living specters, not dead phantoms. This is why his monsters seems so *vraisemblables*, so believable, to Baudelaire. In his deafness he describes the dark night of the soul, where life hides its most terrible truth. Death will reveal itself to him from the outside, sixteen years later and on another principal date in his life, May 2, 1808, when the savage battle in the Puerta del Sol between the Spanish people and Murat's Mamelukes is recounted to him.

From his brush with death Goya has learned to judge so that he may be judged. Faced with reason, which, after all, dreams of hobgoblins and monsters in its nightmares, Goya proclaims the truth of man, inhabited by monsters, incapable of reconciling with the world if he does not reconcile first with himself. Like death, truth is common to everyone; like syphilis, it is also contagious. Nineteen years later, Goya, the old convert to enlightened harmony and the idealist of reason, will record all the demons of his people on the walls of his house, so that neither he nor history can forget them. His belief in truth as the only measure and synthesis of man is passed on to the monarchs, who willingly accept seeing themselves as Goya saw them, not as they believed they were. The only compromise between the painter and his models is reduced to hiding Princess Carlota's hump behind the Prince de Borbón Parma. But the deformed waist of her sister María Luisa is as visible as all the flaws of her kinfolk.

In the painting at the back of the room, Goya leaves his own confession. There, and in his orgy with the two prostitutes, this deaf man silently proclaims his condition as a man, since nothing human is alien to him. He does not condemn the flock of dressed-up caricatures he has just portrayed for posterity, because he does not imagine himself as better or worse than any of them. He knows very well that in a similar orgy he contracted the syphilis that gnaws at him, deafens him, and has destroyed four of his children. His guilt, the guilt of Saturn, presides over this last judgment, which is, at the same time, the noblest document of the eighteenth century. A last judgment of the living, more profound than Michelangelo's judgment of the dead, according to Ramón Gómez de la Serna. A century and a half later we read in a now forgotten book: "With Goya's eyes we are to see ourselves in his goblins and in his Monarchs, in the two waiting rooms of our destiny. Goya's ethical precept opens each day with the doors of the Museum. It is the first principle of an indispensable, even incomprehensible dialectic, in which he attempts to anticipate the final salvation of man: 'You will love your neighbor, the monster, as yourself.'"

March 16, 1828

And His Majesty the king said to me:
"What is your idea of happiness on earth?"
"Dying before my son Xavier," I replied immediately. "My wife

and I had already buried four others before I had to bury her too during the wartime famine. I don't want to lose this one."

He burst into laughter without letting go of the cigar he held between his teeth, as yellow as a lamb's. He was close to, or had already turned, forty. Only when I painted him, for the last time and at his request, did I become fully aware of how deformed his face was, large-jawed, fat-cheeked, asymmetrical beneath his long black eyebrows. And yet in his slightly crossed eyes gleamed a guile that was in no way dim-witted. He had been the most loved man and was the most despised in this country that always charges forward when it is time to kill or reproduce. I supposed that our hatred and our love made him equally proud. In fact, he almost confessed as much to me on the previous afternoon, when I finished his portrait. He said: "You were a traitor and pro-French during the invasion. I overlooked it then, twelve years ago now, as I have forgiven you this time when I learned you were returning from exile, because you are even greater than Velázquez. Tomorrow you return to the palace to dine alone with me.

"You're a cynic. You believe in nothing. Nothing at all. 'Nothing' says the paper that the skeleton brings back from death in one of your etchings. There was a time when you would have been burned at the stake for much less."

"I'm not going to believe in you and your divine right over all of us. We know each other too well."

The truth was that everybody knew him. Before the war, and at the trial in the Escorial, when he and his coterie were accused of conspiring against Godoy, our sausage-maker and Prince of Peace, he wrote incredible letters to his parents, the king and queen, which would be repeated afterward by all the gossipmongers. 'Mama, I regret the horrific crime I have committed against my dear parents and sovereigns and beg with the greatest humility that Your Majesty deign to intercede with Papa so that he will allow his grateful son to kiss his royal feet.' His mother shouted that he was a bastard, and to confirm his status he denounced all his accomplices. During the war and in the Castle of Valençay where, according to him, the French held him prisoner, he again betrayed those who had conspired to liberate him. At the same time, he congratulated Napoleon for his triumphs in Spain and asked that he make him his adoptive son by marrying him to a princess of the Imperial House. Then we also learned that in Valençay he received music and dance lessons when he wasn't hunting, fishing, or riding horses in the castle's parks, and dedicated his evenings to his favorite leisure activity, embroidery with beads and bugles. And yet, if we think about those times, perhaps it would be better not to recall him or any of us, for that matter. When remembering them, one could say that only murderers knew how to preserve their dignity in this unfortunate land of ours.

"We know each other too well. No doubt about that," he agreed with slow nods, suddenly pensive or regretful. "You didn't want to bury your children. I was never happier than when I learned my parents were dead. It's been almost seven years since my mother died in Rome, and ten days later, in Naples, my father followed her to hell. Only then, and for the first time in my life, did I feel free. Then I told myself no, to really be free, they would never have engendered me. Only those who have never lived are free, because even the dead suffer their punishment. The rest of it, including the crown, is a line in the water and the intrigues of courtiers." He paused for a moment, looking into my eyes, and belched. "It's a gift to speak to a deaf man: like confessing to a brick wall."

"Señor, you forget I can read your lips."

He was the deaf man then, or at least he wasn't listening to me. His legs crossed, inner thighs touching, he stretched out in his chair, contemplating the Tiepolo ceiling with half-closed eyes while he smoked, drawing slowly on his cigar. To one side of the cold fireplace, on an easel, was the portrait of him I had just painted. I looked at it with cold lethargy, as if someone else had done it, and felt satisfied. It was his legacy to men, not mine.

"The day my mother passed, my sister María Luisa wrote to me from Rome," he sighed suddenly, scratching his privates. "My mother had almost died in Godoy's arms, so to speak. For an entire week he watched over her constantly as she lay dying, the two of them alone in that room. The night before she died my mother called for María Luisa and said: 'I'm going to die. I recommend Manuel to you. You can have him and be certain that you and your brother Fernando will not find a more affectionate person.' He burst into strident laughter, shaking that head of his, too long and flattened at the temples, on his narrow shoulders. "When my sister saw that things were going badly, she removed the sausage-maker, who was crying like a penitent woman, from my mother's side, and summoned the priests. They gave her the viaticum, unction, and every spiritual aid. They would do her little good in the next world, I tell myself."

"Señor, you forget that I can read lips."

"What do I care what you read or what you hear, old man!" he screamed without warning, as red as a cider apple. "Have you forgotten that I'm the king and you'll rot in the grave, like my parents and your children?" In one of his typical sudden changes, which happened so often, he smiled at me disagreeably and placed a hand on my knee. "You won't be angry with me, will you? Remember how often you deserved the garrote and I pardoned you. You'd deserve it again now, for painting me as I am and not how I'd like men to see me. It's fitting that you're as deaf as a post, because when all is said and done, you look at the world and your fellow man with eyes more truthful than mirrors. I'm going to confess something that nobody else knows. My mother left her entire personal fortune to her lover, the sausage-maker. Naturally, I never allowed Godoy to see a penny of his inheritance. He'll end his days in Paris, rotting in poverty, I assure you of that."

He smiled and seemed to withdraw into the pleasure that paralyzed him. He crossed his hands, rubbed his palms, and cracked his knuckles. His hands were too short, puffy and plebeian, with thick nails and flattened fingers. Exactly like those of my son Xavier. Suddenly I was struck by the obvious revelation that His Majesty the king could also be my son. A son deformed in soul and body as he was, blemished in his flesh and his spirit by my blood, poisoned before he was born. The French disease, which I contracted at some brothel in my youth, and that thirty-four or thirty-five years ago had made me deaf, perhaps had made me conceive of him as he really was in life and in the portrait: a kind of potbellied, grotesque buffoon, his head and body too long, his arms and legs those of a small straw-filled dummy, illuminated by the malicious glance of his pale eyes, where one read as if in a book his betrayals, his cowardice, and his extreme cruelty. What then was his freedom, if in my own way I had condemned him by fathering him? Could it be frighteningly true, as the king himself declared, that only those who never existed are free, because even the dead suffer in hell for other people's crimes?

Back when I was young and beginning to paint for the Royal Tapestry Workshop, our son Vicente Anastasio was born. "He's a very handsome, robust kid," I wrote to my friend Zapater, "and his mother is in satisfactory condition." The next morning the boy was found dead in his cradle, already as yellow as a relic and with a thin line of blood on his lips. Hours before he had nursed hungrily, and as my wife recounted afterward, he even seemed to smile. Two years later Josefa gave birth to my María del Pilar Dionisia. She had a gigantic head, almost as large as a man's, though her forehead was sunken like a macaque's. As soon as she was born and had been washed, after an interminable delivery, I was told it was a misfortune because fluids were pressing on her brain in the huge skull. That was why I gave her a name as resonant as that of a duchess, in contradistinction to her deformity and above all her destiny. She was a sweet monster, all smiles, simpers, and affection. She horrified Josefa, but I spent hours bending over her little cradle, seeing myself in her eyes like a wounded fawn's. She died when she was a year old and also in silence, like Vicente Anastasio. Another daughter, Hermenegilda, was born dead and we had time only to baptize her before putting her in the ground. When my wife became pregnant with Francisco Xavier Pedro, after the sudden death of Francisco de Paula, I managed to arrange, through my brother-in-law Bayeu, for a physician from the Royal House, the same one who brought His Majesty into the world, to visit us and find the sickness in our seed. He discovered the disease in my blood. He said the affliction had no cure, because the only thing anyone knew about it was its origins. The conquistadors contracted it in Peru, fornicating with llamas when they wearied of raping Indian women. I was transmitting it to my babies in my semen, though it might happen, with heaven's help, that by dint of trying, we might conceive one who was healthy. Silently, just as my children always died, I decided to kill myself immediately if we lost the one we were expecting. It was the cold, unbreakable decision of an immovable Aragonese, which I would have carried out even against my own instincts, always thirsty for life. There was no need because we were successful with Xavier. He was so handsome and healthy that, as I wrote to Zapater, one would say all of Madrid doted on him because he was so beautiful.

I must have been lost in thought and my own chimeras because I almost jumped when His Majesty the king patted my knee. His dark brows frowning, he looked at me with an expression of curiosity mixed with commiseration. His breath smelled of tobacco and decay when he said to me:

"What's wrong, old man, are you asleep or distracted? You're as white as snow."

"Señor, years ago I built a house on the lowlands of the Manzanares, between Móstoles, Navalcarnero, and Alberche. In Madrid they called it the Deaf Man's Villa, and soon it will belong to Xavier, because I'm leaving it to him in a bequest. I closed it up two years ago, when I left this country, and it won't be opened again until after my death. I'd advise you to go and see it then, even in disguise and incognito, which they say you do occasionally at night. The house is my legacy, as I suppose the portrait I've just made of you will be yours. On its walls I've painted the examination of my own conscience turned into a nightmare, although perhaps you might believe I painted the demons inside me, demons that are beginning to be as familiar to me as your subjects must be to you, and as their jesters were to your forebears. If the walls displease you, don't go into the dining room, because Saturn is there devouring his children."

He burst into laughter again, with that laugh that sometimes resembled the laugh of a woman in heat and sometimes the laugh of a parrot imitating men. In Bordeaux, Moratín told me about a letter His Majesty's mother-in-law wrote when he was married to his first wife. "He is false, crafty, despicable, and almost impotent," said the queen of Naples about her son-in-law. "At the age of eighteen, my daughter feels absolutely nothing with him. Patience and cures are like sowing in sand; their efforts fail and give no pleasure." Then she described him as a hoax that did not reach the princess's shoulders, all body, almost no legs, and the head of a dwarf.

"Don't tempt fate, old man, you might end up with my benevolence," he replied, laughing. "I forgave your serving the French during the war and then I forgot about your chats and contacts with your liberal friends, the leprosy that is trying to destroy me. I even allowed you to go into exile, when you feared for your head, just as I gave you permission now to return. I can pardon your actions but not your sinful thoughts. I am your Saturn, devouring my people."

"In this case Your Majesty is mistaken. Saturn is my self-portrait, and I realized that only tonight. This was precisely the reason I told you that my idea of happiness on earth is to die before my son Xavier. I consumed the others when I gave them life, for the disease that is rotting me doomed them. I became aware of this speaking to Your Majesty, when I realized that because of your age, you could be my son too. Perhaps I'm not being clear. I'm deaf, and maybe I ought to be mute. Painting is enough for me to know I'm alive."

"You're very clear, and it pains me to understand you. I didn't know you were sick, because I always saw you as an oak. Besides: the viciousness you can do to yourself with that kind of thinking hurts me almost as much as the harm that could be done to me."

"Perhaps that's true, but I can't believe it because you always lived for the sake of hatred. I give credence only to the fact that I returned to Spain before I died, and in order to realize that I was Saturn and had to confess that to you. As for the rest, disposing of my goods after I died and revisiting the places where I lived my conscious life were an oblique excuse for my true purpose. It's strange that a man can live for eighty years and then see that his earlier actions had very different aims from the ones he thought they had. Perhaps no one in the world knows who he is, because he doesn't know for certain who he might have been."

"Perhaps it's too late to find out in your case and in mine," he interrupted with a shrug. "Take comfort in the thought that when you're gone, your art will remain."

"Michelangelo already said that, Señor: men pass, their art remains."

Suddenly he looked at me, and his expression changed. Without even being aware of it he hated me then because he envied me for everything: my paintings and my fame, which prevented him from garroting me or throwing me into a dungeon, as he liked to do to his enemies and would have done to his own mother if she had lived. He even envied me for my age, perhaps because he was afraid he wouldn't reach it, and for the French disease that had made me deaf and was devouring me, and even for my dead children because they weren't his.

"Your art is great but you're good for nothing! You were wicked enough to sell me and you even sold the French. During the invasion you painted the portrait of the Intruder King, and you offered to choose paintings for him to take to Paris. By any chance did you think, you doddering old coot, that I was in a perpetual daze? Then, to mock me even further, you painted *The Shootings on Príncipe Pío*

Hill and *The Second of May in the Puerta del Sol*, those gigantic canvases that adorned the triumphal arch prepared for my return in the Puerta de Alcalá, while the rabble cheered me, howling 'Long live our chains!' and 'Execute liberty against the wall!'"

"You don't have to yell that way! I've already told you I can read your lips!"

"I'll yell as much as I want to," he insisted. "You outlived your wife who was good only for giving birth to the children you destroyed with your syphilis; but I don't know how you could outlive your own duplicity and shamelessness. I mean, I do know, since your cowardice made you in the image and likeness of our people."

"The image and likeness of Your Majesty! In the Escorial you denounced your accomplices so your lies would be forgiven and even threw yourself into the arms of Godoy, pleading with him to save you from the wrath of your own father!"

"Also my image and likeness. So be it. You also betrayed out of fear. We're very similar, though in your pride you refuse to believe it. We both despise our fellow men, though, strangely enough, we fear them at the same time."

It was true, and against my will I found myself nodding in agreement. Then I remembered, as if I had painted it in my memory or was seeing it again with the eyes of half a century ago, the day Josefa and I were presented at court, before he was born. His grandfather, Carlos III, was still on the throne; I would paint his portrait a short time later. My brother-in-law had arranged the audience, which took place on a winter afternoon filled with light. The widowed king, with the face of a small-eared sheep and a gaze shining with intelligence tinged by sadness, received us, half sunk into the pillows of a couch, raising a lavender-scented handkerchief to his nose because the Sierra winds had given him a cold. The princess of Asturias ("I'm going to die. I recommend Manuel to you. You can have him and be certain that you and your brother Fernando will not find a more affectionate person") was sitting beside him. I met her then when she was young and still beautiful, tall and high-breasted, with the dark skin and sloe eyes of an Italian. Her husband, the prince, who ten years later would inherit the throne, remained standing next to the seat. He was the strongest man I've ever met and even then, in spite of my confusion, I was surprised by the width of his shoulders and the roots and branches of his muscles, visible at the edge of his ruff and under his silk stockings. His smile, which was always at the ready, though no one could forget the fury of his rages, half-closed his pinkish eyelids over eyes so blue they were almost transparent. Josefa's resigned timidity became reconciled to the grandeur of the moment. Prudently and moderately, she spoke to the king and his children as if they were blood relatives, distant, but very close in their respectful esteem. I, on the contrary, trembled with fear when I kneeled on the marquetry of the floor to kiss the august hands of that family. The prince obliged me to stand, taking me by the elbows. His palms were small, but hard and lined like those of an old blacksmith. It surprised me that, being who he was, they were so roughened, and that he was accustomed to working with his hands. His Majesty the king spoke a little of Mengs, of Tiépolo, and of my brother-in-law. The princess said something to me in Italian when she learned I had lived in Rome. She praised our manners, as if we were children, and smiled. *Saper fare e condursi a quel modo.* Then the monarch also intervened in Tuscan. He remarked on the light at that time of day, as one painter would to another. After having spent so many years in Naples, where the twilights are shorter, he marveled at dusk in Madrid. *Allora, appena il crepuscolo, il giorno comincia a scolrire e nel traspasso dei colori tutto rimane calmo.* Don Carlos, the prince of Asturias, put his arm around my shoulders to lead me to the door. I supposed this was his way of ending the audience; but I could still kiss the hands of the princess and His Majesty again, on my knees and very quickly. I hadn't taken ten steps when the prince almost broke my back with a huge slap on my shoulder that resounded like thunder throughout the room. At the age of thirty, I weighed 175 pounds and boasted of bending an iron bar with my hands and a coin, a *real*, with my fingers; but breathless and stumbling I fell flat on my face, while the prince said: "Well, well, my dear friend, I hope we'll see each other again very soon." Then he began to guffaw as he held out his hand and I, gasping and servile, echoed his loud laughter. The princess laughed too, although unwillingly, as if that farce, repeated so often, bored her by now. Josefa looked at us with the same withdrawn mystery as when she accepted infidelities and the births and deaths of her children. His Majesty the king sighed, closing his eyes and placing the handkerchief in his sleeve. "No one can resist a slap from me," the prince of Asturias gloated, "the hardest stablemen fall like ninepins. When you come back we'll fight with pikes in the stables and then I'll play the violin for you, if you like." I agreed to everything, like a scoundrel who'd been beaten with a cudgel. I would have sold my soul at any offense in order to be court painter. (Afterward I was, unexpectedly, thanks to Godoy, when I had almost lost all hope.) That same night I wrote to Zapater: "If I had more time, I'd tell you how the King, the Prince, and the Princess honored me. Through the grace of God I kissed their hands, I've never had such good fortune before." At that time I felt vulnerable and intimidated by men, in the double uncertainty of my youth and my destiny. But I wouldn't learn to really fear them until many years later, when I discovered the monsters that lived inside them.

"Why did you bring me to the palace? Why did you insist on my painting your portrait when they told you I was in Madrid?" I was overcome by a fit of rage against His Majesty for having obliged me to conjure up the dead. I was surprised to find myself shouting at him in that voice of mine that I would never hear again.

"You're a part of my past that I don't want to forget. From those years I value only your memory and that of my first wife in her final days. At the beginning of the century, when you painted our family, you looked us in the eye, one by one, and we all lowered our heads. 'This is the only man,' I said to myself then, 'whom you could truly respect.' Then I thought that in the final sessions we posed all together for you, like actors on a stage, and it seemed reasonable. The day you allowed us to see the finished painting, while my parents outdid themselves making up base compliments to please you, blind to the horror of that parade of ghosts and monsters reflected on the canvas as if in a mirror, I thought: 'It hardly matters now what we do or fail to do, action is worth as much as refraining from action, because this painting will outlive us. Here we are all judged and condemned, even the children, because any blind man would see that María Isabel and Francisco de Paula are not my father's children but Godoy's.'"

"Señor, leave the dead in peace."

"I didn't pass judgment on them, you did."

"I painted your August Family as I saw them at the time."

"You painted us as we were and now you've portrayed me again as I am. This is your own punishment, old man: to paint the truth." Enraged again, he crushed his cigar in a dish. "The dead, as you call them, made me what I am and turned my life into a shameful nightmare! Do you know the name the queen of Naples gave my sister Isabel when they married her to the queen's son? The epileptic bastard, yes sir, the epileptic bastard! Do you know what my sister Carlota replied shortly after her betrothal to the prince of Portugal, when she was reproached for her collection of lovers? 'I don't want a single favorite, because I'm not prepared to have him attached to me like Godoy was to my mother.' Do you know what it means for a boy of sixteen, exactly my age when you painted my family, to read the stolen copy of a memorandum from the French ambassador, where he says, with all the fairness in the world, that no drunken soldier would have dared to humiliate a prostitute in the way Godoy treated my mother? Do you want me to spell out my suffering back then, recalling that my father, the king, was incapable of buying a watch without seeking the advice of Godoy himself?"

"Your Majesty ought to forget the dead or at least be silent when you remember them."

"Can you forget the children you buried and your French disease?"

"No," I said, "no I can't."

"Then we're even, because nobody's more than anybody else."

Memories became entangled like cherries; they settled, and then suddenly a memory caught fire and blazed like a torch, at the back of time. Looking at his recently completed portrait, I saw the boy he had been so many years ago, when I painted the portrait of the family. He wore gray stockings, sky-blue breeches and coat, his chest crossed by the sash of Carlos III. Even then he had the prominent belly of a prematurely aged man beneath his narrow shoulders. In the presence of everyone the queen said to me: "We'll have to find a bodice for this boy. He's almost growing boobs like a girl." He controlled himself, not protesting and not blushing; but beneath his eyebrows, as long and thick then as they are now, I could see the gaze of a wounded fawn that my María del Pilar Dionisia had in her cradle. Then, in no time, the light in his eyes hardened into an expression of hatred mixed with hypocrisy. With the same rancor and shrewdness in his eyes, I painted him with his family. A few nights later, I dreamed he was looking at me in that way, as if he were confronting his mother, and I woke up shouting the useless howls of a deaf man. When I uncovered the painting, he was the only one who refrained from praising it. Standing apart from the others, it seemed he was smiling at the celebration of the portrait, and not its veracity. Yet in the eyes of his father, His Majesty the king, there were tears of joy. He hit me again on the back, guffawing and congratulating me at the same time.

More than a quarter of a century had passed since our first meeting, and his slap was no longer the blow that knocked me down that day, for the years had aged him very quickly. He had put on weight, his muscles had weakened beneath his skin, and his goiter spilled over onto his chest. Nonetheless, he still woke at five o'clock every day of the year, and never used wine, coffee, or tobacco. He slept alone, and they said he no longer visited the queen at night. It was rumored that after the queen lost the ability to become a mother, he feared being damned if he carried out his conjugal duties for pleasure. The king heard two masses every morning, read the lives of the saints, had breakfast, and went down to the palace workshops. There, in shirtsleeves, he worked as a blacksmith, a clockmaker, a carpenter, a locksmith, or a saddler. He was very skilled, and sometimes he offered foreign ambassadors a pair of shining boots that had recently left his hands. Then he would visit the stables and fight the stable boys with rods. At one time he could defeat them all, but later on they allowed him to win because he lost his breath before his strength. At eleven he received the royal family and the minister of state for a quarter of an hour. Then he ate lunch with great appetite, and always alone. He went hunting every afternoon if he wasn't leading a procession. He was escorted by the captain of the guard, the master of the horse, a gentleman-in-waiting, the beaters, a surgeon, and another physician. When he returned he dispatched with all his ministers in half an hour. Later he would offer a violin concert to some intimate friends, accompanied by the cellist Dupont. I was told that he played very badly, although he thought himself a virtuoso. He would skip entire lines of the staff, which Dupont in turn attempted to ignore. After the music there was a card game, during which the king tended to fall asleep holding his cards. He had supper at nine with the queen and went to bed at eleven sharp. I remember that I tried to kiss his hand to thank him for his compliments, but he hugged me to his chest. "Someday we'll see if you're as good at fighting with rods or at Leonese wrestling as you are at painting," he said to me, laughing. "Come back one morning and try it with me. Then I would play the violin for your pleasure, if you weren't deaf." By reading his lips and in a flash of conscience, I was surprised to find myself wondering: "God of heaven and divine Reason, why are we alive?"

"When he was young your father, Señor, was the strongest man

I knew. And he was always the one with the simplest soul and best heart. If he had been born a cobbler or a tanner, perhaps he would still be alive and happy."

"At his age. And if he had been born a tanner or a cobbler, he probably would have starved to death in the war, like your wife," His Majesty replied. "Thanks to you liberals, we're entering an era that exempts neither kings nor rabble. Now we're all made of the same ashes."

"You're probably right, although guilt for the times we live in lies with all of us. At times I fear being immortal, when I think of the horrors I have survived. During the war and the invasion, people died of starvation on the streets of Madrid. Twice a day they picked up the corpses in the gutter and took them away in creaking wagons, pulled by scrawny mules, from the parish churches. The very old and the very young were the first to die. Nursing infants with monstrously swollen bellies, and old people reduced to skin and bone, like mummies, who dragged themselves, trembling, away from the doors to their houses so they would not die in the presence of their families. They were followed by the men and then by the women, who were the strongest. They paid for loaves of onion and flour, moldy hardtack, and even scraps of garbage with their jewels. Then they traded entire houses for a handful of acorns. We ate rats and dead people, because there were many cases of cannibalism, not only on the Rastro but on the Prado as well. The rabble chewed on their dead, but so did some nobles whose blood was almost as pure as yours. In the meantime, Señor, you were taking music and dance lessons in Valençay."

"The Intruder King saved your life. I know that very well."

"King José baked in the palace, although it's obvious he was almost as destitute as we were. His servants would distribute part of that bread to the people, and on occasion he did that himself. Thanks to his kindness, Josefa did not die of hunger that fall. She succumbed the following spring, along with twenty thousand other Madrileños, but by then there was no more flour or wood, even in the palace. Once, unannounced, King José came to our house to bring us a brazier that was still warm. I gave him a glass of water, all that I could offer him, and he confessed his despair. The crown was a sentence he did not wish to serve at that price. '*Dans ce pays de Malheur, je reve toujours des peres et des frères aupres des cadavres de leurs femmes et de leurs enfants sur la chaussée.*' He had written to his brother, the emperor, to present him with his resignation. Napoleon did not even bother to respond."

"Stories of thieves and their lackeys," His Majesty said with a yawn.

Spots of yellowish spittle dried at the corners of his lips. He lit another cigar after biting off the end and spitting it on the floor.

"You ceded those thieves the crown when you returned it to your father, so that he in turn could hand it over to Bonaparte. If you, Señor, had remained steadfast and not given in to the demands of the emperor in Bayonne, the war would not have taken place. Naturally, in that case they would not have welcomed you in Valençay but thrown you into some dungeon."

"And what was I going to do in France, imbecile, in the hands of that bandit we all thought was invincible? Let myself die? This is man's greatest madness. Cervantes himself says so in *Don Quijote*, though I don't remember anything else from that book. You didn't die then either, not from hunger and not in the war. You had the indecency to survive because you were too much in your right mind to die or kill in my name. You and I are alike, cut from the same cloth, as I said. Let's allow the dead to bury the dead and look each other in the eye. I need you just as every man needs a mirror, so I won't go mad. You, and for that matter the entire country, are mine, because I didn't end up better or worse than my subjects. That's why you'll have to wait for my death, the death of a despot who doesn't want to die or abdicate now, in order to free yourselves from me!" His exaltation diminished somewhat after reaching the point where he was shrieking. Soon, smiling and pulling my ear as if I were a hunting dog, he said to me: "I don't think I'll allow you to return to Bordeaux. I can't do without you."

"If you want to arrest me, Señor, you should do it personally and right away. Here, in Madrid, I always sleep with a cocked pistol under my pillow. I've made my will, disposed of my possessions, and every night I think about Saturn so I won't forget who I am. In a few days I'll take the stage back to France. Before that, if they come at dawn one day to arrest me, I'll fire a bullet into my brain at the precise moment they break down the door."

I didn't hear my voice and he didn't seem to listen to me, though he took careful note of the hard conviction in my words. He lowered his eyes and with the hand that held the cigar he gestured as if he were driving away absurdity or tedium.

"Why would I look for your destruction when it pleased me so often to prevent it? You have very powerful enemies, but I'm not one of them."

"I humbly beg Your Majesty to allow me to continue. When the war was over, I painted the portrait of Juan Martín Díez, the Undaunted. He was a peasant from Castillo de Duero, almost as strong as your father in his youth. In May 1808 he took to the mountains and fought the French, at the head of a band of shepherds. When peace came, he commanded thousands of men, and the Central Junta had made him a general. He read with difficulty, but his eyes burned with intelligence, and he had a natural talent for describing this hell that tomorrow they'll call our history. He told me how, in your name and to defend your divine rights, they had put out the eyes and cut off the ears of a woman, then paraded her naked on the back of a donkey through Fuente de la Reina, with a sign on her chest that read: 'This is the end that whores to the French always come to,' and then they nailed her while she was still alive to the door of the church. Twice he was defeated and his forces decimated in the field and twice the villages of Guadalajara emptied out to follow him. In those lands people adored him almost as much as you because he had given them a reason to survive and to murder. The French governor himself learned to respect him almost as much as he feared him. The Undaunted sent him a letter, written in his own hand, inviting him to join his guerrillas 'because it was always more honorable for a soldier to serve liberty than a tyrant's ambition . . .'"

"What's the point of all this? He soon betrayed me and had to be executed, just as he had crucified that woman on the door of the church. That's all there is to it."

"He made the mistake of still believing in liberty after your return, and he was one of those who imposed the Constitution on you in 1820. Last year, your divine absolute power restored, with the help of other French troops he was arrested in Castillo de Duero. Locked in an iron cage and carried in a cart, he was displayed for weeks on end to his own neighbors, and in all the villages where they first set fire to the houses and the harvests to follow him, as if he were a god. The same men who fought in his bands spat on him, stoned him, jabbed him with their pitchforks, shouting 'Long live slavery! Long live the absolute King!' He struggled like a rabid dog behind the bars, perhaps more enraged by the irrationality of men than desperate over his own fate. Still on the scaffold, almost dead, he fought with the executioner before he was garroted. There, in the public square, they burned his remains to the cheers of the crowd. The stink of burned flesh must have reached all the way to the palace."

"It didn't, but when I learned he had been executed, I exclaimed: Long live the Undaunted!" He smiled. "It was my tribute to a dead enemy."

"It was what it was; but I'll never end up like that, not your victim and not sacrificed by this country, where you say you can look at yourself as you can in my eyes. That's why I sleep with a pistol, ready under my pillow."

"Sleep however you like and go back to Bordeaux whenever you feel like it." He yawned openly, his mouth filled with smoke. "I had hoped you'd die here, as an old man, so I could give you a funeral worthy of Apelles. I would have displayed your body in the Puerta de Alcalá, watched over by the royal halberdiers and mounted troops. In single file, all the way to the Ventas del Espíritu Santo, people would have waited nights on end to see you dead. The rabble comes to both executions and funerals. All ceremonies are part of the same circus."

Circus. Almost two years have passed since I last saw His Majesty the king, and now I'm dying in Bordeaux. One of my hands froze this dawn. I saw it lying rigid on the coverlet, as distant and immobile as if it belonged to someone else. I didn't try to wake Leocadia so as not to upset her with my dying, which I thought would be brief. Two or three hours later I unexpectedly recovered the use of my fingers, but I couldn't control their sudden tremors. At the same time my eyelids became heavy and I supposed that death was half-closing them. "It doesn't matter very much," I said to myself, "because this winter I was going blind. I drew with the help of a magnifying glass, though I kept my hand very steady until last night." Leocadia was frightened by my pallor and sudden fits of stammering. The doctor came and then returned later with a colleague. His grave, pensive air confirmed my belief that my case was hopeless. I turned my face away on the pillow in order not to read on their lips the foolish things they were saying to me. *Vous étes un grand homme, un peintre de la Chambre. On va vous soigner!* Then Moratín turned up here, Leocadia must have brought him up to date regarding my difficulties, because he hadn't visited me for days. For the first time I noticed that his hair, a blond between sandy and straw-colored, was graying and turning white. He seemed uneasy, but he could not hide his feminine curiosity about my dying. He sat near the bed, close to the pillow so that I could read his lips. "Leandro," I said, "this is ending. Take care of Leocadia and little Rosarito for me when I'm gone. I'd just like my son and grandson to come before I'm dead. Do you think I'll get to see them?" "Death is something that always happens to someone else," he said ironically. "You and I have the duty to outlive the despot so we can return to Spain." "Spain? Spain does not exist. It's one of my *Absurdities*, established long ago in the dark depths of time." He smiled, moving his graying head. "I'm not far from thinking the same thing."

"Spain does not exist. It's one of my *Absurdities*, established long ago in the depths of memory." Why am I assailed, now and then, by the conviction that these words are not mine? Another man is saying them, perhaps very different from me in appearance, in another century that hasn't existed yet. In this case my voice is his, although he doesn't exist yet. Spain does not exist; but perhaps Moratín is right. It is our duty to return there when the despot, Moratín, and I are ashes. It will truly be like returning to one of my *Absurdities*, to the "Ridiculous Absurdity" or the "Raging Absurdity." I'll be a different man on that tomorrow, although our witches' sabbath of a country is basically always the same. I'll be someone who before being incarnated appropriates my voice, perhaps to try it out. As I said to His Majesty the king, at our last meeting, it is strange that a man may last for eighty years and then realize that his earlier actions have ended very differently from what had been intended. Perhaps no one knows himself in this world because no one knows exactly who he might have been.

Circus. I'll never go back to the circus on the rue du Manège, where I would take Rosarito to forget about myself, watching the acrobats suspended for a moment between heaven and this hell we call earth. There animals turned into clowns and men played with beasts, as in the garden of earthly delights. Elephants, tigers, lions, crocodiles, serpents, and bears punctually recited their lessons. They seemed to know everything; but they had forgotten how to kill. There Claude-Ambroise Seurat, the Living Skeleton, told fortunes in any language and said to Rosarito that one day she would teach drawing to a queen. Then he shuffled the cards, took me aside, and predicted that the girl would live only to the age of twenty-seven. I became furious but the Living Skeleton shrugged. He only read the future. He didn't condemn or flatter anyone.

That day he insisted on telling my fortune. I told him it wasn't worth the effort, because an old man like me had his hours numbered. He refused to give me reasons, but he assured me that something in me disconcerted him very much, but he did not know precisely what it was. I yielded to the persistence of Leocadia and Rosarito, or at least I believed then that I was submitting to their pertinacity. Claude-Ambroise Seurat shuffled the cards, dealt them out on the table, and nervously picked them up again. Then, ignoring us, he spent an eternity contemplating the French deck, his head sunk between his long, bony palms. "It's all very strange, Maestro," he finally said to me. "At these points I don't see you but another man, whose name I don't know because perhaps he hasn't been born yet. I see him confusedly, accompanied by a woman, in a house beside a river that runs over a bed of very white stones. Neither the man nor the woman exists yet; but, in the cards, he is trying to write a book about your grace." He shook his insolent head, as if making an effort to frighten away the shade of an absurdity. "Give me ten *sous*, Maestro, so I can drink a thimbleful of burgundy."

THE MONSTERS

The Prince of Peace

Manuel Godoy Álvarez de Faria was born in Badajoz on May 12, 1767. According to his own statements, his family was of middling nobility and lesser wealth. The ancestral home of the Godoy family was in Castuera, populated by his paternal forebears. In his old age, Godoy said it had been ruined by time.

The Godoy sons were drawn to the military, riding, and weapons. They did not pass through university classrooms but were educated in mathematics, humane letters, and philosophy by private tutors, chosen by their father. Godoy described his teachers as illuminated by the light of the age, though "without blemishes or illusions." Luis, a brother of Manuel Godoy, joined the Corps of Guards to the Royal Person, in the days of Carlos III. He was rumored to be the lover of María Luisa, the princess of Asturias and wife of the future Carlos IV. He probably had been confused with another officer in the same corps, named Diego. In any event, and with the help of Luis Godoy, Manuel entered the Corps of Guards at the age of twenty-one. In September 1788, when riding in the military cortege of the prince and princess, between La Granja and Segovia, he fell from his horse but controlled the animal, remounted, and continued to ride. The prince and princess took a personal interest in his status, and he soon became María Luisa's lover. According to Cándido Pardo, Godoy was slightly taller than average, with gray eyes and excellent teeth. His most attractive features were his "thick, golden hair and splendid white and pink coloring."

A year later the Revolution erupted in France, and Carlos IV ascended the Spanish throne when his father died. A secret pact between the king and the prime minister, the ancient count of Floridablanca, stipulated that the queen would freely determine offices and distinctions. Godoy was promoted to lieutenant in the Flemish Guard. On February 28, 1792, Floridablanca was suspended and exiled by the king. At the time, the queen was pregnant with Prince Francisco de Paula, whose resemblance to Godoy would later be called "simply scandalous" by Lady Holland. The Ministry of State was passed to another aged aristocrat, the count of Aranda, who immediately visited Godoy to pay him public homage.

In April, when María Luisa went out to Mass for the first time since giving birth, Godoy received the titles of duke of Alcudia, making him a grandee, and marquis of Álvarez. On July 14, the anniversary of the Revolution in France, he joined the Council of State. That summer he was named lieutenant colonel in the Corps of Guards, admiral of Castilla, and captain general. On the day of Saint Louis he received the Order of Toisón. A dog appeared on the streets of Madrid wearing a sign that read: "I belong to Godoy. I fear nothing." The dog was sent to military prison. On November 16, Aranda was unexpectedly dismissed, as Floridablanca had been earlier, though he was allowed to remain on the Council. At the age of twenty-five, the duke of Alcudia was prime minister. Obliged by the people and the crown, Godoy declared war on revolutionary France to honor the Family Pact, signed with the old regime, and to avenge the execution of Louis XVI. The campaign began well for his army, and the Catalan soldiers robbed, raped, and burned in Roussillon in the name of Christian charity. They reached the gates of Perpignan, took Collioure, and in Banyuls they deported the residents, all suspected of republicanism. A year later the French took the offensive. They occupied Irún, San Marcial, San Sebastián, Bilbao, and Vitoria. They reached Figueras in Cataluña and took the Castle of San Fernando. Godoy found himself obliged to sign the Peace of Basel on

July 22, 1795. There it was agreed that France would return all the sites she occupied in Spain in exchange for the Island of Santo Domingo, and the delivery of cattle from Andalucía at no cost for six years. The king gave Godoy the title of Prince of Peace, with the privilege of having a herald to announce and precede him, holding aloft a head of Janus, symbol of prudence and wisdom.

In August 1796, Godoy signed the Treaty of San Ildefonso with the Directory and placed the Spanish navy at France's disposal in her war against England. Two months later, Nelson defeated the king's fleet at Cape Saint Vincent and lay siege to Cádiz and Santa Cruz de Tenerife. On many mornings Carlos IV appeared in the bedroom of the Prince of Peace to help him dress. Then they strolled together through the gardens of Aranjuez. At one o'clock Godoy returned to the palace to be present at the queen's luncheon, as a gentleman-in-waiting. Afterward María Luisa met with him in his own rooms by means of a secret staircase that communicated with the queen's chambers. There, according to the German ambassador, they decided on policy. At eight, after meeting with the king, Godoy held his audiences. Men came to these, for it was a well-known scandal that their daughters, wives, and sisters were more apt to obtain the favor of the Prince of Peace. If they were young and attractive, they tended to come out of his study weeping or laughing, many half-dressed, with their hair in disarray. Godoy pawed at all of them and enjoyed many on the rugs in the sitting room.

On September 16, 1797, Godoy married María Teresa de Borbón, countess of Chinchón, first cousin to the king and daughter of a former cardinal-prince. Yet it was well known that the Prince of Peace had an official mistress, much to the distress of the queen. Her name was Pepa Tudó, the orphaned daughter of an artilleryman. It was also said that Godoy had committed bigamy, for many believed he had already married the Tudó woman right in the palace chapel. After his marriage to María Teresa (Goya painted the countess of Chinchón wrapped in lengths of sheer tulle and with a strange expression of childish sadness on her face) Godoy took Pepita Tudó to live in her own house and even granted her the title of countess of Castillofiel. A year later, when María Luisa made the political power of the Prince of Peace conditional on his breaking with the artilleryman's daughter, Godoy refused to leave her and resigned the post of prime minister. The king's distress was infinite.

He replaced Godoy with Saavedra, a former minister of finance, and Saavedra with Urquijo. It was said that both had also been María Luisa's lovers. In any case, in December 1800, Pedro Cevallos, cousin-in-law and straw man to the Prince of Peace, succeeded Urquijo in the ministry. Godoy returned to power. Two months earlier he reconciled with the queen, without abandoning Pepita Tudó, when the Princess of Peace and countess of Chinchón gave birth to a girl. The joy of the sovereigns was so great it spread from El Escorial to Madrid, and they attended the baptism accompanied by the palace musicians, the first gentleman-in-waiting, the intendant superior, the queen's ladies, and His Majesty's hunting equipment. The grand inquisitor baptized the infant in the Royal Palace and in the king's own chamber, an unprecedented event, even for a prince or an infante.

A year earlier, in Paris, Bonaparte delivered the coup d'état of 18 Brumaire, proclaiming himself first consul. On December 2, 1804, he was crowned emperor of the French. "The name of King has lost its prestige and would make me an heir; I do not wish to descend from or depend on anyone." In the spring of 1801, the first consul obliged Carlos IV to invade Portugal, where his daughter Carlota was married to the prince regent. Godoy placed himself at the head of the troops, entered Portugal on May 16, and two days later the regent sent him his prime minister with full powers to negotiate the peace. Godoy's soldiers offered him branches from the orange groves of Ribatejo, which would give that piece of buffoonery its name: "the oranges." During the campaign he received anguished letters from María Luisa: "Here only sadness reigns, and inactivity, uncertainty, watching to see if the mail arrives and constantly thinking: this will be the hour of our glory. But oh! I tremble at the risk, Manuel, and do not live. This dryness and harshness will lodge in my throat with a feverish heat that consumes me."

On December 12, 1804, a few days after the crowning of Bonaparte, Carlos IV found himself obliged to declare war on Great Britain when the English attacked and captured Spanish frigates carrying gold near Cádiz. On October 12 of the following year, Nelson defeated the allied fleet at Trafalgar. Admiral Gravina, who had vainly opposed a battle lost before it was fought, died, as did Nelson, as a consequence of wounds received in the battle. The French admiral, Villeneuve, committed suicide. The Spanish fleet was sacrificed. Meanwhile Godoy received the Grand Cordon of the Legion of Honor. In his immense vanity, he was still sufficiently lucid to see that power had converted him, very unwillingly, into a mere puppet of the emperor.

On October 12, 1807, the Prince of Peace signed the Treaty of Fontainebleau with France for the invasion of Portugal. Half the country would be for Godoy, who had acquired the hereditary title of prince of the Algarve. Napoleon guaranteed to Carlos IV his European possessions and his American empire. A secret clause granted Marshal Junot the combined command of French and Spanish troops during the campaign. On the same day (which in another century would be called the Day of the Race), the prince of Asturias hatched a plot in El Escorial to overthrow Godoy. When he was discovered, he denounced all his co-conspirators and threw himself at the feet of Godoy and his parents.

On March 16, 1808, with the forces of Murat, grand duke of Berg and the emperor's brother-in-law, at the gates of Madrid, there was not the slightest doubt that Napoleon intended to annex the entire Peninsula. At a meeting of the Council of State, before the king and the prince of Asturias, Godoy proposed that the monarchs flee to America by way of Sevilla and leave their firstborn in Madrid as supreme commander of the troops. Fernando embraced him, kissed him, and said to him: "Manuel, I see clearly that you are my friend!" Later, behind Godoy's back, he confided to his loyal followers in the Corps of Guards: "The Prince of Peace is a traitor. He wants to take my father away. Stop him from leaving."

The next day a crowd inflamed by Fernando's agents filled the streets of Aranjuez. Godoy seemed unaware that his hours in power, and for that matter in history, were numbered. In the afternoon he visited the king and queen in the palace. María Luisa seemed uneasy, but Carlos IV joked and recounted a hunter's tall tales. At 10:30 the Prince of Peace withdrew to his country manor. He dined alone with his brother Diego and went to bed with one of his mistresses. Soon the shouting mob attacked the doors, while the Corps of Guards fraternized with the crowd. Diego Godoy was cudgeled by his own troops when he attempted to help his brother. The pavilion was opened and the servants arranged for a woman, covered in heavy veils, to flee. Then the looting began, while the multitude shouted for Godoy's head. In a bedroom they discovered the Princess of Peace, terrified and embracing her daughter. Protected by the rabble and the guards, they took her to the Royal Palace. Until her death she would live with her brother, the cardinal de Borbón, forbidden to see her daughter because she was also Godoy's child, or to pronounce her husband's name.

The Prince of Peace was not taken that night. Hidden in an attic, not wrapped in a straw mat as would subsequently be repeated so often, he eluded the eyes of the pack. Thirty-six hours later, consumed by thirst, he slipped downstairs while on the ground floor one could hear jugs, glasses, and card games. On a landing he ran into an artilleryman smoking his pipe alone, sitting on the stairs. "Listen, wait, I'll know how to be grateful . . ." The artilleryman betrayed him, shouting his name. Captured by the mob, he asked to be taken into the presence of the king and queen. In his own plundered house, the soldiers treated him correctly. At his urging they gave him a cape and a three-cornered hat and prepared to escort him to the palace. On the street the crowd recognized him immediately. To the shouts of "Death to the chorizo-maker!" they stoned him, beat him, and stabbed him. He fell among the horses' hooves and the animals trod on his legs. A knife cut open his cheek, another his thigh. At times clutching the forebow of a saddle, at times dragged along by his neck, always more dead than alive, he was taken to the Royal Palace. There they threw him into a stable. The crowd had invaded the rooms, calling for the prince of Asturias. In the presence of the rabble that pressed into the salons and crowded the staircases, Fernando looked at the fallen man, who refused to be humbled. "I grant you your life." "Your Highness, are you already king?" asked Godoy. "Not yet, but I shall be very soon."

The rest is the tale of a phantom. On March 19 Carlos IV abdicated the crown in favor of the prince of Asturias. On the anguished urging of María Luisa, Murat obtained the emperor's permission to transfer Godoy to Bayonne when Napoleon called together the entire royal family there. Soon afterward Pepita Tudó, accompanied by their two children, joined the Prince of Peace. In exile a strange and profound friendship would be born between María Luisa and the countess of Castillofiel. When one of her children died, the former queen wrote to the Tudó woman: "I have no consolation for you; you know that very well, and there are no words to express my sorrow." Godoy did not leave María Luisa. He followed the deposed monarchs from Bayonne to Compiègne, from Compiègne to Nice, from Nice to Rome, where they would hear the news about Waterloo. When María Luisa died there, it would be Godoy, not her husband, who happened to be in Naples, who watched over her until the last moment. In 1820 the Princess of Peace and countess of Chinchón died in Madrid. Then Godoy married Pepita Tudó and recognized her child. In 1833, Fernando VII died. In Paris the exiled man waited in vain for the restoration of his estate. Tired of waiting, Pepita left him and returned to Madrid with her child. Carlota, the daughter of the Prince and Princess of Peace, declared in Parliament that her father had died. Godoy barely survived on a pension of five thousand francs a year, granted him by Luis Felipe de Orleans, in a third-floor room at number 20, Rue Michaudière.

The young Mesonero Romanos visited him there in 1838. Godoy asked what opinion the younger generation had formed of him. Mesonero reminded him of the charitable, scientific, and cultural works undertaken during his government; the protection granted to the best talents of the period; the expedition to America to introduce vaccination there; the reform of teaching according to the Pestalozzian system. The old man seemed pleased and stated that his greatest desire was to return to Spain and take a stroll through the Salon del Prado. He spoke French and even Castilian badly, with Italianate turns of phrase and an Italian accent. In the Tuileries Garden he would take the sun and enjoy playing with the children. He would collect their hoops and toys, lend them his cane so they could ride it around the ponds, sit them on his knee. He also had a group of old retired performers there who took him for a Spanish actor. The deception pleased him and he never revealed his true identity to them. Two days before he died, he sent a letter, still unpublished, to his learned defenders in Madrid. "At times I believe I have lived someone else's dream," he told them. "The dream of reason." He died in Paris on October 8, 1851.

October 25, 1975

"Since 8:30 yesterday, His Excellency the chief of state has experienced the following crises in the evolution of his illness:

At 22:00 hours he suffered an episode of abdominal distention because of intestinal parexia, which was resolved with the usual medication. Consequently the advice of Professor Marina Fiol was requested, and the procedure was approved.

Likewise, Professor Obrador Alcalde was consulted regarding the possible influence of his anti-Parkinsonian medication on the digestive episode. During the night and early morning he was calm. At 8:30 on

the 25th the signs of cardiac failure increased and a pulmonary edema
developed that responded to the appropriate treatment.

At the time of this report, at 11:00 in the morning, the intensified
signs of congestive heart failure persist."

He turned off the television and swept away the books that covered
the table. *Library of Spanish Authors.* 202. *Works of Mesonero Ro-*
manos, Library of Spanish Authors. 203 *Works of Mesonero Romanos,*
Malraux. Saturn: An Essay on Goya, Hugh Thomas, Goya: The
Third of May 1808, Library of Spanish Authors. 88–99. *Memoirs of*
the Prince of Peace, J. Gudiol, Goya III, Editions Weber, Hans Roger
Madol, Godoy, Jean-François Chabrun, Goya, Saint-Paulien, Goya.
Son Temps, ses Personnages. Hanging from the carriage of the Royal
portable was a typed sheet of foolscap corrected in the margin: "We
must see ourselves with Goya's eyes in his goblins and his Monarchs,
in the two antechambers of our destiny. Goya's ethical precept opens
each day with the doors to the Museum. It is the first principle of an
indispensable, even incomprehensible dialectic in which he attempts
to anticipate the ultimate redemption of mankind: You shall love
your neighbor, the monster, as yourself." Surrounded by the Royal,
Gudiol's catalogue, and *The Third of May*, he poured himself a beer
and drank it down in one swallow. It was the fourth or fifth he'd
had that morning, before eleven, while Franco's intensified signs of
congestive heart failure persisted. He had tried to count them and
stopped immediately with a shake of his shoulders. When he poured
the beer he had spilled some on the table and the keyboard. His hands
were trembling.

"Yesterday at two in the afternoon, they said the signs of Franco's
heart failure were decreasing," he exclaimed. "The evolution of his illness was taking its course without incident. The Ministry of Tourism
declared that it would not withhold any truthful information from
the Spanish public, 'as an armor against rumors.' These were their

exact words. On Tuesday they declared that abroad they no longer knew what to invent to alarm us. That was, I suppose, the eternal Judeo-Masonic-Protestant conspiracy against our organic democracy." He paused, and in too loud a tone he concluded: "This isn't a country. Spain has never existed. It's one of Goya's *Absurdities*, created ages ago."

"I don't know why you're shouting like that," the woman replied in a whisper. "You're talking almost like a deaf man."

He didn't hear her, because he didn't listen to her either. "This isn't a country. Spain has never existed. It's one of Goya's *Absurdities*, created ages ago." Only when he repeated the words to himself did he know they were his. Before, in an abrupt shock to his consciousness, he'd had the incredible sensation that another man was saying them with his lips. "It was like knowing you were asleep and having a nightmare and at the same time being convinced that the dream belonged to a stranger." He shook his head to free himself from that error. *"Je suis un autre, sic.* To hell with Rimbaud and his arms-smuggling in Abyssinia! I don't want to end up in the hospital with an amputated leg while gangrene finishes me off! *I'd rather drink myself to death,* as conspirators and those on military bases say so elegantly, because that was always my thing. I'll drink down judgment as soon as I finish this book. You drink too much."

"More than an *Absurdity*, perhaps it's a *Caprice*, because in the *Caprices* there's a tone of grotesque frivolity that fits better with this chimera. Think of Goya's donkey that reviews its lineage in the family book. That's what our history is like."

"I also don't know why you, you of all people, are writing a book about Goya." The woman interrupted him harshly. "Goya had twenty children . . ."

"My dear Marina, the supposed twenty children of Goya belong to a fiction generally transmitted and immortalized by Don Eugenio d'Ors, the man who spoke every language with a foreign accent, according to Unamuno, and whose accurate biographical sketch was drawn by Professor Aranguren in prehistoric times, in a work filled with praise of Francoism, which for obvious reasons the aforementioned professor refuses to reprint. To God what is God's and to each specter its candle, in the burial of this *Absurdity*. In the baptismal records of the parish churches in Madrid, there are only five registered children of Don Francisco de Goya Lucientes, son of José y Gracia, and Doña Josefa Bayeu de Goya, the sister of his brother. Of the five one survived, the youngest, Francisco Xavier Pedro, *dont l'histoire est très banale*."

"I don't care how many children Goya and Josefa had, and I'm not interested in knowing how many of them died," she interrupted him again. "The one I could have had with you never managed to be born and I'll never have another."

This time he did hear her reply, though he didn't want to listen to it. He limited himself to hiding it in some corner in the labyrinths of his memory while he contemplated Marina, as if this were the first or last of their encounters. Very blonde and small, her straight hair hanging to her shoulders, in a heavy turtleneck sweater and tight velvet pants, she seemed the same girl he had met in the courtyards of the old university almost thirty years ago. "My God!" he thought, desperately invoking one in whom he had never believed. "Can she see me as I see her? Identical to the boy I was, or perhaps the one I never have been, both mummified, like everything, absolutely everything, in this country where one never grows old with dignity, because life repeats itself here in vain, as the hours would be struck in the farthest reaches of the universe."

"What's this all about, woman?" In the end he replied to her reply and did so to become involved in an argument, as unexpected as it was idle, which would free him from his brooding. "Franco is dying. An empire is sinking with its revolution still pending, and you talk to me about impossibilities."

"I'm talking to you about myself and the children I'll never have because that's the way you wanted it. I'll never know who I could have been, just as no woman knows who hasn't been a mother." She spoke in a measured tone and an even quieter voice. Cautiously, looking at her hands, she continued: "As a matter of fact, I also don't know what I'm doing here with you. It's all like a nightmare that lasts too long."

"You can leave whenever you want to. I'm not throwing you out but I warn you, I don't intend to go after you. I'll stay in this house until I've finished my biography of Goya, where I plan to say exactly the same thing that everybody has said before me as proof of my erudition. I have a grant to write this book from the foundation that bears the name of the last pirate of the Mediterranean, and I plan to meet my obligations as demanded by my respect for such high-ranking patrons."

"I'll go when it suits me. After all, it's all the same whether I leave or stay with you, because no relationship between us ever made any sense."

In the brick-paved pool in the courtyard of the School of Letters, the water lilies were withering in the lukewarm sun. "Miguel de Unamuno and the poet Villaespesa were walking in the Retiro," R. was telling him and Marina. "*How beautiful these flowers are! I wonder what they're called*, exclaimed Villaespesa. *Don't be an idiot, Villaespesa. These beautiful flowers are water lilies, which appear day after day in all your poems.*" It was the spring of 1947, and the monarchist students had nailed the manifesto of Don Juan de Borbón, dated in Estoril, on the bulletin board: "What the country desires is to emerge immediately from an increasingly dangerous interim period, not understanding that the hostility surrounding the Nation in the world is due for the most part to the presence of General Franco in the leadership of the State." In front of the board monarchists and Falangists were exchanging blows. With shouts and punches some were struggling to tear down the manifesto, others to protect it, while R. spoke to Marina and him about Unamuno, Villaespesa, and water lilies in the Retiro, the three of them disregarding the brawl. In the uproar, Manuel Sacristán and Antonio de Senillosa were shouting and hitting out with their fists. Sacristán would later become Provincial Head of the S.E.U., everything in capital letters, and eventually a Communist ideologue. He would meet Antonio de Senillosa again almost by accident, many years later, during that same autumn, *the autumn of our discontent,* when the five executions took place, the last political executions of Francoism. They were in a bar at midmorning. He was already very inebriated, and he vomited on the table. "You drink too much," Senillosa told him as he held his forehead. "It's the only rational thing you can do in this country," he replied, retching. Senillosa agreed softly: "Perhaps you're right."

In all the shouting he didn't hear Marina's last name when R. introduced her, because at that time all the students called one another by their last names. He remembered saying: "I'm Sandro Vasari, a descendant of Giorgio Vasari and three generations of émigrés *terroni.*" He smiled to himself, thinking that after almost thirty years, Marina still didn't know who Giorgio Vasari was. Twenty years after their meeting he would have said: "I'm Sandro Vasari, a descendant of Giorgio Vasari and three generations of Italian *xarnegos.*" Then R. intervened: "Not a single being on earth is capable of knowing who he is." Much later he would learn, without too much surprise, that the phrase was not R.'s but Léon Bloy's. "In this joke of a country, no human being is capable of knowing who he is, precisely because here everything's the same," he concluded to himself, during a pause in his memories.

No, even if he had known that the phrase was Bloy's, he wouldn't have criticized R. He looked at Marina and felt vaguely attracted by her air of withdrawn indifference: of a girl curled up in the center of herself in order to have nothing to do with anything or with herself. At the rear of the courtyard, next to the bottom of the old staircase, the disturbance was increasing. Memory moderated the noise in its waters but repeated the grotesqueness of the shouts until they were transformed into a kind of caricature of sheer nonsense. "Long live Franco! Up with Spain!" "Long live the king!" "We don't want imbecile kings!" He thought, or at least he believed he had thought, that in another century the forebears of all those boys had leaned over their balconies and out their windows to toss bouquets of roses and early broom as the Desired One, returned from Valençay, passed and they screamed: "Long live our chains! Long live absolutism!" Again he repeated to himself that Spain was not a country because it had never existed as one. It was only one of the *Absurdities*, illuminated by its own tragic light in the depths of time. Again he felt that those words belonged to someone else, though he pronounced them to himself and only half-heard them. Perhaps to avoid the uneasiness of their echoing deep inside him, he made an effort to stop recalling his first meeting with Marina. He believed then that R. was observing them both, sketching them in his memory as if preparing to portray them another day, with the tumult as his easel and withered water lilies at their feet.

Then, when he made Marina his lover with her cold, dispassionate consent, he did it in a little house surrounded by eucalyptus and almond trees, under the Vallcarca Bridge, its bedroom with its saints enclosed in chimney globes rented out by invisible panderers. It was R. who obtained the place for their meetings and took care of financing them with loans that Sandro would never repay. In a corner of the room, between the recently whitewashed wall and the bureau with the saints, the one that smelled of burning reeds through all the cracks in the wood, "which was how all of Guatemala smelled, as I discovered later when I passed through those regions," there was a sink with a pitcher and basin made of Manises ceramic. Above it hung an old mirror, with a carved frame, that time had darkened and where the light reverberated in long, purplish streaks. Without making too much of it, he always believed the looking glass was false and transparent: its quicksilver backing also a small window through which an unknown third person, implacable and impassive, observed him and Marina.

He told R. of his suspicions, in detailed summaries of their intimacy in the bedroom. Instinctively modest even when drunk, he still felt obliged to recount his affair to him for inexplicable reasons. He wasn't driven by vanity or moved by an eager exhibitionism. He was even sufficiently rational to reproach himself in vain for his confidences without knowing how to stop them. Once again he sensed that R. was making a note of these episodes, preparing to write them down the next day in his own words. "We're another man's rough draft," he said to himself one afternoon when he was naked, his arms around Marina, and not knowing what to think of that.

The following autumn he had to confess to R. that Marina was pregnant. Sandro urged her to have an abortion, to which she resigned herself with the same silent indifference she had shown earlier when she agreed to go to bed with him. At noon on a day filled with red and gold leaves, R. took them to a house on Calle Moncada, at the corner of Arco de San Vicente, and a stone's throw from the palace where for many years Picasso's *Las Meninas* would be housed. He left them there alone with an old woman who wore a capelet over her shoulders and a satin ribbon around her neck. All cajolery and smiles, the old woman told him not to worry and to come back in five or six hours. He spent them pacing interminably around the tiled courtyard; it led to the stream, and the tiles decorated the rim of an old well. To one side, where perhaps carriage houses and stables had once been located, was a large door leading to some wine cellars. Against a background of cobwebs, demijohns, kegs, and drip trays, workers walked past wearing long leather aprons, as if in the tapestry of a guild. Night had already fallen when he decided to go in the house, through the pinewood door beneath the overhang at the top of a staircase with a stone balustrade. Like someone entering his own nightmare, he found the door ajar and the rooms almost in darkness. Lying on a sofa beneath a shuttered, mullioned window, Marina was waiting for him. An unexpected drizzle was falling outside. Sandro put his topcoat over her head and then, when she was made small and trembling, he put his arm around her waist and they went out to the courtyard, where the smell of acid wine still lingered. At the corner of Calle Princesa they found a taxi that took them back to the park.

"If what we had was completely senseless, why have you met me here? Why did you leave your husband after so many years?"

"That's a question a woman would ask, precisely because it has no answer," Marina replied, shrugging her shoulders. "It's the equivalent of demanding why we sometimes wish we'd never been born and at other times want to be as immortal as stones. All I know is that I always did what you wanted, but now I'm prepared to do what I want. I'll leave when it suits me."

"If you'd rather wait until I finish alcoholizing myself, I make no guarantees. I immodestly postponed death or madness because I want to finish my life of Goya first. I'm sorry to disappoint you."

"You're free to kill yourself however you choose, even if I'll never have your children. As for the rest, you'll never finish the life of Goya. You know that as well as I do."

"Go to hell!"

Actually, he was the one who left, slamming the door. Stumbling from side to side and almost falling, he went down the stone staircase, slipping on the moss that appeared on the treads and backs of the steps. He crossed the garden, which had turned into grassland that autumn, and took the path to the oak groves. The day was gray and calm, the mountaintops enveloped in motionless fog. He stopped only when he reached the river, high after the recent rains. There he lost track of time, listening to the murmur of the water flowing around the polished, whitened rocks. He had forgotten about Marina, himself, Goya, and the house R. had lent them so he could write the painter's life. "By now," he said to himself aloud, "Franco must have died," and his indifference caught him by surprise. Only then was he fully aware of being alive, and he swore again to himself that he would finish that book, even if there was no one on earth capable of knowing who he was, and even though everything passed away, like tyrants, rivers, clouds, and shadows.

As the flow of the river continued among rushes and brambles, memories dammed up the invisible waters of the past. "In rivers the last water is identical to the first of the waters that will come. Like the present day," R. had said to him in September and in this same spot, paraphrasing Leonardo, while the current carried away the reflection of the heavens. "*Qu'est que tu as fait de ta jeunesse?*" He smiled to think of how poetry, the word in time, transformed into clichés as it passed from one century to the next. "Just a trifle and of course less than Rimbaud, who at least knew how to forget about his youth as a genius and a queer to delve into other hells significantly more sordid." A kingfisher, brilliant green, flew out of the branches to peck at the water.

He didn't see Marina very often at the university after the abortion. Without avoiding each other, they were growing more distant, perhaps because neither one had anything left to say. When Sandro and R. finished all their courses, she hadn't been in a classroom for a year or two. By then monarchists and Falangists had also stopped fighting in front of the bulletin board. The United Nations lifted its sanctions against Franco's Spain, and Eisenhower's America was preparing to form an alliance with her. From Estoril, Don Juan de Borbón wrote to the caudillo, who almost a quarter of a century later would be dying now in El Pardo: "If Your Excellency is moved by the same desires for concord for the good of Spain (which I certainly cannot doubt), I am completely certain that we shall easily find the practical formula that can overcome present difficulties and establish definitive solutions."

Four or five years later, Sandro had left for the United States. He arrived in time to read in the *Times* the statements of Agustín Muñoz Grandes, former commanding general of the Blue Division and current minister of the army, who had recently landed in New York. "Here you have a war criminal who has not lost his admiration for Hitler's Germany." The general wore the insignias of the Blue Division, the Iron Cross First Class, and other Nazi decorations. Sandro had a contract to teach Spanish language and literature in a secondary school near Newburg, Vermont, where twenty-four years earlier Lorca had written "Poems of Lake Eden Mills." He found all of Spanish literature, except for the *Quijote*, immeasurably boring. Compared to English or French literature, it seemed the work of metaphysicians of irrationality or realists terrified by their own senses. He completed a doctorate in art history at Columbia University "because, after all, the Catalan Romanesque, El Greco, Velázquez, Goya, and Picasso endorse the roots of someone named Sandro Vasari through three generations of immigrant *xarnegos* and justify the existence of a culture that could express itself in words only in Cervantes."

After earning his doctorate, he began his teaching career at the University of Colorado. In the summer of 1973, after two divorces and two children by his second wife, whom he would always refrain from seeing, he returned to Barcelona for the first time since 1955. By then his parents had died, and in their apartment of a middle class insistent on not forgetting its national origins, he spent almost two weeks shut in and alone. He entertained himself by contemplating the fake Murano red glassware behind the glass doors of the cabinet; the imitation porcelain naiads like those that adorned the Bucentauro, the sculpted ship from which every year the Dux officiated over the *sponzalizio di mare*, the marriage of Venice to the Adriatic, when the sea was still as green as the mountain pastures, according to D'Annunzio; the busts of Camillo di Cavour and Giuseppe Garibaldi, yellowed by time beneath the mirror; the large prints of androgynous slaves sculpted by Michelangelo, and of Michelangelo himself, flatnosed and pensive in the solitude of his workshop, contemplating his completed Moses; the old editions of *Goethe's Travels Through Italy*, the covers lined in red satin and the title on the spine, where Johann Wolfgang von Goethe listened in Malamocco and Pellestrina to the verses of Tasso and Ariosto sung by gondoliers, *In exitu Israel de Aegypto / Cantavan tutti insieme ad una voce, / Con cuanto di quell salmo e poscia scripto*; the reproductions of *The Birth of the Lord* by

Piero della Francesca, with its chorus of five shepherdesses also singing their hallelujahs and its magus king pointing at heaven with his index finger, and *La Calumnia* by Sandro Botticelli, with the naked truth also pointing her finger at the firmament.

He drank alone until all of it, Piero, Botticelli, the gondoliers, the slaves, Moses, Michelangelo, Garibaldi, Cavour, the Adriatic, the Bucentauro, the naiads, and the false Murano glass became confused, darkened, and eventually merged into the same closed shadow. But not even then did he manage to sleep. For the first time he was ambushed by a tenacious insomnia that Sandro could not overcome or explain. He lost track of the days and nights until he had a presentiment that the endless sleeplessness was not his but had been imposed by someone he did not know as an implacable punishment for faults he knew nothing about. Then he told himself that insomnia was the expectation of a dream or nightmare that in due course would free him from his punishment. One morning at daybreak (he would never know after how many) he finally was able to fall asleep. He did not wake until the middle of the afternoon, refreshed in body and spirit, as if he had come back from a swim in a very sunlit ocean. He would have sworn he'd had an incredible dream, which he had forgotten, perhaps forever. A telephone call woke him completely. R. had learned of his return from sources he refused to name. He invited him to supper that same night in the Pasaje de la Trinidad, a stone's throw from the old brothel whose residents had inspired Picasso's *Les Demoiselles d'Avignon*, thereby creating Cubism. He accepted immediately.

On that same night, R. spoke to him for the first time about the book on Goya. A publishing house was prepared to offer him excellent terms for a definitive biography of the painter from Fuendetodos, along with an exhaustive study of all his works. His book would be published in an elaborate edition that Goya himself would have been proud of. He did not pay too much attention to how ambitious the project was or to the clauses in the contract. They seemed like accidental means to an indispensable end. The next morning, with R. as a witness, he signed the contract. He felt the same panic that overwhelmed him when he tried to stop drinking. An absolute terror before the impossible, which had become cruelly imaginable, the fear of knowing himself condemned to immortality in a perishable world that, once it had disappeared, would leave him, alone and eternal, in the midst of a universe hostile to life. The horror of being dead and destined to disguise himself as himself in another existence, to attend a masked ball in a gallery of mirrors. When those afflictions had been overcome, he got drunk again to free his spirit from the tedium that terrified him after his anguish. He wondered whether boredom would lead him to abandon the book, and he rejected those doubts immediately. The life of Goya began to be his own life.

He spent that summer traveling through Spain to study works by Goya he had never seen. The portrait of the duke of San Carlos, in the collection of the marquis of Santa Cruz. The portrait of Moratín, in the Bilbao Museum, painted four years before Goya's death in exile. The *Appearance of the Virgen del Pilar to Saint James and his Disciples*, in the Zaragozan art gallery of Pascual Quinto. The *San Cayetano*, the property of José Olabarría, part of the dispersed paintings of the palace of Sobradiel. *The Three Dandies with a Bird*, in Juan Cué's house in Barcelona. The only full-length self-portrait of Goya standing, in the Madrid gallery of the count of Villagonzalo, and wearing a top hat whose band is in reality a candelabra to light up his canvases. ("The final touches, the ones that would bring his most personal effects to his paintings, were always done at night, and with artificial light," Xavier Goya wrote when his father died.) *Gaspar Melchor de Jovellanos*, also standing, and with the sea as a background, in the Valls i Taberner collection. On the walls of the duke and duchess of Sueca, *The Countess of Chinchón*, pregnant by her husband, the Prince of Peace, when Goya painted her. Previously he had portrayed her at the age of two and a half in the palace of Cardinal Infante, her father. Both of them, Goya and the princess, would die in the same year of our Lord, 1828.

In the autumn of 1973, Sandro was back in Colorado. He taught that semester at the university, but requested and was granted a leave of absence for the next two terms. With a fellowship from the Institute for Philosophical Studies, he traveled during the summer and fall of 1974 in search of other works by Goya. In the National Gallery, in Washington, he met up again with the countess of Chinchón as a little girl. "La S. D. María Teresa, hixa del S. R. Prince Don Luis, at the age of two years, nine months." In the Meadows Museum in Dallas, he contemplated the portrait of a *Man with a Fencing Sword*. Folke Nordstrom identified the unknown subject as Francesco Sabatini, Carlos III's architect. In the Fine Arts Gallery in San Diego, he spent a long time before *The Duke de la Roca*, and in the David-Weill collection in Paris, before *The Marquise de la Merced. Time, Truth, and History*, together with *The Allegory of Poetry*, brought him to the National Museum in Stockholm. *The Countess of Haro* kept him for long hours in the Burhles's collection, in Zurich, as did *Doña Isabel Cobos de Porcel* in the National Gallery in London. Early in 1975 he was back in Spain. By then he would have been able to start writing the book, having studied thoroughly the most pertinent bibliography about Goya and his period. But he spent his free time rereading index cards, notes, and citations, without deciding to give them their own flesh and voice. One afternoon he reviewed with pleasure the conclusion of his notes on Godoy: "He spoke French and even Castilian badly, with Italianate turns of phrase and an Italian accent. In the Tuileries Garden he would take the sun and enjoy playing with the children. He would collect their hoops and toys, lend them his cane so they could ride it around the ponds, sit them on his knee. He also had a group of old retired performers there who took him for a Spanish actor. The deception pleased him and he never revealed his true identity to them. Two days before he died, he sent a letter, still unpublished, to his learned defenders in Madrid. *At times I believe I have lived someone else's dream,* he told them. *The dream of reason.* He died in Paris on October 8, 1851." At the bottom of the page, in a drunk's trembling hand, he then had written: "The life will be divided into five parts: THE ABSURDITIES, THE DISASTERS OF WAR, TAUROMACHY, THE CAPRICES, and FURIOUS ABSURDITY." On one of the nights when R. invited him to his house for supper, the other guests included Andrés Bosch, with Isabel and Rafael Borrás and, unexpectedly, Marina and her husband. He was amazed to see how little she had changed physically, as it would leave him flustered from then on in almost all their encounters. Only Marina's silences seemed to have aged. Now they were much more prolonged and apparently emptier of reflections and hopes, perhaps populated only by mute words. Her husband, whose name he did not wish to remember, turned out to be younger than she was, a professor of philosophy at one of the Institutes of Secondary Education. He was short and paunchy, with rimless eyeglasses and the tiniest of feet; but he maneuvered like a spinning top. When he learned that Sandro had lived for years in the United States, he asked him whether he didn't share his belief in a media conspiracy to overthrow Nixon, "whom I would say was guilty only of using too free a language in the presence of tape recorders. The definitive proof of his innocence is evident in his handing over the tapes, which he could have destroyed quietly at any time." He supported freedom of the press because it was one of the rights of man, he continued orating without a pause and at length, while Sandro looked at him in astonishment, without deciding definitively whether to accept his reality; but he was roused at finding himself condemned to live in a world subjected to the most absolute and ominous of tyrannies: the power of its reporters. When Francoism fell ("which will end with the mortal life of the Caudillo"), a wave of pornographic publications devastated the country because here liberty was always confused with license. He was realistic enough to foresee the universal triumph of Communism, precisely because in the socialist countries there was a sense of history that would never permit another dictatorship even more absolute than theirs: that of supposedly objective information.

A few days later Sandro phoned Marina. They began to see each other in dingy bars behind the Municipal Slaughterhouse or at the foot of Montjuïc. Soon she was following him to his house, with the same silent meekness that in another life had accompanied her to the bedroom surrounded by eucalyptus and almond trees beneath the Vallarca Bridge. They were lovers again surrounded by androgynous slaves, the angels of Piero, and Botticelli's naked truth. There, with Garibaldi, Cavour, and Michelangelo as their only witnesses, Marina confessed that the abortion performed by the old woman with the capelet and the satin ribbon had left her unable to become pregnant. Then Sandro did not know what to think or say. That night, hours after Marina had left, he drank until he collapsed facedown on his desk. He awoke with a start, shaking, before dawn. He groped to turn on the light and wrote in a notebook in a trembling scrawl what he could not forget or read: "Saturn is my self-portrait and only tonight did I come to understand that."

That summer R. left Spain and lent him his house in the Pyrenees when Sandro asked him to, "so I can hide there to write the entire book once and for all." He did not see Marina in July or August, though they phoned each other several times a week. In *the autumn of our discontent*, after the executions of El Xiqui, Otaegui, García Sanz, Baena Alonso, and Sánchez Bravo, and the next-to-last appearance of Franco looking out over the Plaza de Oriente to thank hundreds of thousands of Spaniards for their cheers, Sandro thought seriously about forgetting Spain and Goya forever, returning to the United States, this time with Marina, and never coming back. That was when, on a two-day trip to Barcelona, he met Antonio de Senillosa almost by chance and vomited on the counter of that bar in the middle of the morning. ("You drink too much." "It's the only rational thing to do in this country." "Perhaps you're right.")

At home he bathed and changed his clothes. Then he phoned Marina, making a date to meet her there in the middle of the afternoon. "All this is sinister foolishness: our lives and this country of ours, because in the long run only we made it possible. If we can't escape our history, at least let's run off its stage. Leave your husband today and let's go together to R.'s house in the Pyrenees. Then we'll leave for the United States and there I'll finish the book on Goya." Marina agreed immediately and in silence, with a gesture. "Keep in mind that I, at least, won't return. I've finished with this country, with its people, and with myself, because you represent the only part of my past I don't want to renounce. If we go, we'll never come back." She concurred again, with an identical gesture.

A month later, when he recalled all that as he descended along the riverbank, he thought he'd had another man's nightmare: a dream as confused and murky as the pebbles glimpsed on the riverbed. He had not mentioned again their leaving for the United States, and Marina had not deigned to remind him of it. He continued to get drunk and talk constantly about Goya and his book, though he never decided to write it. Marina's husband, the philosopher who would never confuse liberty with license, showed himself willing to negotiate a separation if Marina persisted in her determination to leave him. He told Sandro on the phone that he forgave them although he did not understand them. Sandro deduced from his attitude that events had created a break they had secretly desired for a long time. They said goodbye to each other very politely.

The kingfisher pecked at the water again. The waves grew larger in the backwater, shattering the reflection of the branches and the slate-colored sky, and died out near the marsh and the dog roses, dispersing a school of dark fish. The river grew quiet again beneath the trees and the sky. "If I could remember that dream, at the end of all my insomnia, everything would make sense," he thought as he looked at himself in the water. At a bend in the river he came across a grove of bare poplars that sheltered an old mill. A ray of sun sharpened the darkness like a lance on some millstones, half buried among the grass and shrubs. Suddenly he recalled a strange story that R. had told him without Sandro's really believing it. The previous winter, in that mill, the Civil Guard had discovered a dead man wrapped in an old blanket made threadbare by rot. Upstream, on a bed of stones, they found the corpse of another, much younger man, disfigured by water and time, the bones of his face broken by blows, and a gold medal around his neck. Apparently the two bodies were never identified. When he asked R. who they could have been, he shrugged. "Every man," he said, "is capable of every crime."

The mill had seen centuries beneath that sky. Around the window the decaying stone was becoming porous. The stout walls, made of craggy rock gilded by the centuries, seemed to have been built by blind giants, or by men who went mad thinking they were Cyclops. Three stone steps led to the oaken door, damaged by a lightning bolt that had fused part of the latch and the bolt, previously fastened with two turns of a key, twisting the metal and blackening the wood with its burn. Two shoves with his shoulder opened the door for Sandro. The mill was empty of creatures and furnishings. Dampness from the stream saturated its abandonment, and its one room reeked of cattle surprised by the storm. In the fireplace he saw an empty cauldron on abandoned tripods. On the bare walls the outlines of a cot and some high shelves were turning black. Between the chimney and the vent of cracked red tiles, Sandro stopped to crouch down, hesitant and shuddering. A large stain, like dried blood, was spattered on the floor and then extended, lighter in color, to the doorway. On his knees, he ran his fingers along the trail, feeling the absorbed anguish with which a devout man, sick and perhaps on the verge of death, would caress a relic. Immediately he remembered the forgotten dream at the end of his long periods of insomnia, the one that had preceded by several hours the call from R. offering him the assignment of the book about Goya.

He had dreamed a slow, interminable nightmare that his memory brought back to him with implacable clarity. Lost in the depths of the Great Pyramid and ignorant of his own destiny, he searched tenaciously for the pharaoh's burial chamber. He lit his way with a lantern that had four glass sides, stepping in the yellowish light and feeling with his palm the walls of endless corridors. At times he tripped over the bones of other men who had also lost their way in the labyrinth. They crackled under his feet like kindling and forced him to walk faster. Then he became aware that he was carrying out the search while he was asleep. With absolute certainty he told himself that all he had to do was wake up to free himself from his agony. "If I put the lantern on the ground and lie down beside its light, covering my head with my arms, I can dream in my dream that I'm sleeping and wake up. Everything will disappear immediately, the Great Pyramid, the spiderweb of its passages, the stepped-on skeletons, the darkness that surrounds me, the stone spattered with saltpeter that I touch with my fingers. Everything but me, Sandro Vasari, a descendant of Giorgio Vasari and of three generations of Italian *xarnegos*, because asleep or awake I'm always the same man, and perhaps shall be the same when I'm dead, if death is interminable insomnia or a nightmare of corridors the dead don't wish to flee." He repeatedly renounced the freedom of avoidance because his destiny was supposed to lead him not to the exit from the Great Pyramid but to the pharaoh's catafalque. Abandoning that would be a betrayal of himself when he believed he was close to reaching his goal.

Not only pilgrims and thieves had perished in the pyramid, searching for the burial chamber. Hunting parties and entire armies had lost their lives in the same pursuit. Their motionless shadows, forever etched and made enormous on the walls, fled in disarray toward the hidden center of the labyrinth. Following them, he turned an infinite number of corners, climbed walled slopes, slid and slipped down stone declivities. Slowly the passageway narrowed as the ceilings lowered. He found himself obliged first to crouch down and then to drag himself through a winding tunnel with hardly enough room for his body as he pushed the lantern with one hand. With a certain bitter satisfaction he told himself then that the final dice were rolled, although he did not know yet how they would fall. It was impossible to go backward in that passage and retrace his steps. Crawling and pushing himself forward with elbows and knees, he had to keep moving ahead to proceed with the dream pilgrimage and go deep inside the pyramid. Suddenly he came into a more spacious environment: his arms spread wide did not reach the walls, and his head did not brush the ceiling when he stood. As he picked up the lantern from the ground, he wondered, trembling, whether he had reached the pharaoh's burial chamber. His own shout deafened him then as it was enlarged and repeated by echoes. He found himself in a square chamber that must have measured some ten feet by ten feet: a false crypt, perhaps constructed in the very heart of the pyramid to confuse intruders. In the back, built into the wall, he saw the livid, reverberating mirror from the house where he'd had his meetings with Marina, reflecting his exhausted image.

As soon as he tried to touch the glass with his fingers, the mirror disappeared. On the other side of the mirror he stopped at a crossing of several paths. Some would lead to the Pharaoh's tomb or to another false catafalque. Others would take him to the desert. At random he chose a gallery that soon began to break into multiple right angles. He had lost all hope of coming to the end of those confusions, when he thought he could see a faint reflection that illuminated the walls in the most distant angles. Having reached the end of the corridor, he was blinded for a moment by the light of some streetlamps. This time he bit his lips to silence his shout, fearful that his own howl would wake him. He had returned to the courtyard of the house on Calle Moncada, near the Arco de San Vicente, at what seemed to be soon after nightfall. He saw again the stone rim around the old well and walked on the large flagstones with small, hesitant steps. The large door to the storehouses was still open; perhaps carriage houses and stables had been there before. Against a background of casks, wineskins, basins, barrels, spigots, demijohns, and spiderwebs, workers walked back and forth in their long leather aprons. He did not dare speak to them or approach them, suspecting they would then disappear like the mirror in the false crypt.

He hesitated, wondering whether the burial chamber, hunted by so many dead men over the centuries, really existed. Did the pharaoh perhaps build the pyramid precisely in order not to be buried in its interior? Could that be the greatest and most inconceivable of ironies, the eternal search for a corpse that in reality did not exist? Why not wake up then and return to life, insisting with all its might on reclaiming him? Other opposing forces, the same ones that had grimly buried him in that nightmare, overcame his doubts and obliged him to continue the search. At the top of the stairs with the stone balustrade and beneath the tiled overhang, the half-open pine door waited for him. The house seemed abandoned now, the furniture draped in ghostly white covers. At the foot of the latticed mullioned window he made out the sofa where Marina had waited for him in the irrevocable past. "Everything, even this dream of mine, is another man's rough draft," he said to himself as he crossed deserted rooms. By the light of the lantern that he still held, almost forgotten, in his hand, he read an inscription in golden letters over a closed door: "Not a single man on earth is capable of knowing who he is." With cold indifference, which did not even manage to surprise him, he understood that he had reached the end of his odyssey. That was the hidden center of the pyramid. With ironic, exhausted slowness, he lifted the latch and pushed the lock.

In a vast salon, lit by large crystal chandeliers, His Catholic Majesty King Carlos IV was posing, accompanied by his august family. Behind him two large paintings covered a good part of the wall. On the right, an elusive landscape in the translucent light of dusk or dawn. On the left, the wantonness of three naked titans, a male and two females, frolicking as they embraced. At one end of the room, behind the royal models and in front of the giants' bacchanal, a tall

canvas mounted on two easels. Sandro told himself that the monarch must have been very strong before he had aged prematurely.
His chest, covered in medals and crossed by the blue and white sash
of the Order of Carlos III, was that of a burly old man made for Leonese wrestling. His younger brother, Infante Antonio Pascual, peered
over the shoulder of the sovereign. He was younger but looked older
than the prematurely aged king. Both of them contemplated Sandro
with identical, very light blue eyes, where torpor mixed with a weary
sadness. Three other infantes formed part of the group. The prince of
Asturias, Don Fernando, almost hid his brother, Don Carlos María
Isidro, behind his narrow shoulders and long arms. Sandro told himself that the anomaly of the precedent was repeated in their generation, because Infante Don Carlos seemed to be a kind of aged
elf, shorter and drier than the heir to the throne, as well as more
advanced in years. The youngest of the brothers, Don Francisco de
Paula, dressed in scarlet and adorned with the sash of Carlos III,
occupied the center of the group. He could have been anywhere between five and ten years old, with an ordinary kind of beauty and a
crafty glance disconcerting in so young a boy. The prince of Borbón
Parma, son-in-law of the monarchs and a nephew related by blood to
the queen, was young, blond, and very tall, though already paunchy
in his youth. He held an infant in his arms, almost a newborn, and
already decorated with the order of his great-grandfather Carlos III.

Queen María Luisa raised her head, her breasts, and her shoulders, as if she were attempting to overshadow her own daughters.
Her high hairdo, adorned with a diamond pin shaped like an arrow,
accentuated her prominent height. Sandro thought he remembered
having read somewhere that the coiffures of the queen, appropriate
to a much younger woman, both amused and scandalized Napoleon
in Bayonne. In the family group, the queen was the only one who
smiled vaguely at Sandro as she observed him fixedly. That toothless
smile upset him very much, just as Don Francisco de Paula's perverse glance did. María Luisa enclosed the shoulders of her youngest

daughter with one of her heavy arms, *di Contadina o di pescivèndola di grido.* The infanta was thin, pale, and rather ugly. In her hair, light brown with orange-tinged locks and highlights, was another pin like her mother's. Her older sister, Carlota, hid behind the prince de Borbón Parma. She showed only a birdlike profile and a cheek made rosy by cosmetics. Sandro also recalled that some writer of the time, Villa Urrutia or Lady Holland, said she was hunchbacked. Another girl, rather tall and with large breasts adorned with the order of María Luisa, which all the ladies displayed, stood erect at the side of the prince of Asturias. Sandro could not see her face, turned to the wall where she looked at the orgy of the giants. Between Fernando and the unknown girl he glimpsed a witch in a feathered wig, as brazen and old as death itself, with narrow, light blue eyes, a copy of the king's gaze. She was Infanta María Josefa, the older sister of the king and Don Antonio Pascual.

This was the family group. Someone, whom Sandro could not bring to mind, was missing. It must have been the man called to immortalize these august personages on the canvas resting on the easels. Whoever he was, Sandro could not recall his name. The lantern he was holding went out, and he kneeled to put it on the floor. The smiling glance of María Luisa followed him, resting on his shoulders and his hips as if he were a stable boy. Surprised, he turned his head to see that the panels on the closed door behind him were a double mirror in which all those present were reflected. At that moment he was stunned by the queen's voice. It was shrill but affable, lisping on account of her toothless gums and somewhat melodic in her Italian singsong.

"Let's go, let's go," the queen said to him. "We're ready and waiting for you, just as you ordered. You can begin the painting whenever you like."

Then he woke up.

THE DISASTERS OF WAR

THE DREAM OF REASON

May 3, 1808, in Madrid

The Executions on Príncipe Pío Hill

The canvas, housed today in the Prado, is one of the most important and largest of Goya's paintings. It measures six feet, six inches wide by nine feet, ten inches high. In the absence of Fernando VII, who would return to Madrid two months later, Goya offered his services to the regent of the kingdom, to honor his return and his victory over the French. Presiding over the regency was the cardinal Don Luis de Borbón, primate of all the Spains, brother of the countess of Chinchón, and Manuel Godoy's brother-in-law. Six years earlier, on May 22, 1808, he had written to Napoleon, assuming "the sweet obligation of spreading at the feet of the Emperor the homage of his respect and fidelity" and entreating His Imperial and Royal Majesty to put his obeisance to the test. Now, on March 14, 1814, the cardinal primate employed a very different language when he dictated the sanction approving Goya's project:

"Let it be known that on the twenty-fourth day of this past month D. Francisco Goya, H. M.'s Court Painter, directed to the Regency of the Kingdom a statement of his ardent desires to perpetuate by means of his brush the most notable and heroic actions or scenes of our glorious insurrection against the tyrant of Europe, and making manifest the state of absolute penury to which he finds himself reduced and as a consequence the impossibility of his defraying alone the expenses of so interesting a work, he requests that the public treasury provide him with some assistance to carry it out. With this in mind, and with

Your Highness taking into consideration the great importance of so praiseworthy an enterprise and the well-known ability of the aforesaid practitioner to carry it out, I have deemed his proposal a good one and have consequently ordered that while the aforesaid D. Francisco Goya is employed in this work, he be paid by the central Treasury, in addition to what his accounts indicate was invested in canvases, materials, and paints, the amount of fifteen hundred copper reales a month as compensation."

The order was issued that same day, and Goya signed the receipt. Two months later, on May 11, 1814, *May 3, 1808, in Madrid: The Executions at the Príncipe Pío Hill* and *May 2, 1808, in Madrid: The Battle Against the Mamelukes* adorned a triumphal arch erected next to the Alcalá Gate, to celebrate the return of Fernando VII, nicknamed The Desired One. In *La Gaceta* that morning a royal decree annulled the Constitution voted into effect in Cádiz two years earlier, as well as the Parliament, and all its resolutions. On the Calle de Alcalá, the crowd cheered the king, roaring "Long live the Inquisition!" "Long live Fernando VII!" "Long live our chains!" On the Plaza Mayor the mob invaded the Casa de la Panadería, destroyed the memorial to the Constitution of Cádiz, and dragged the pieces in a sack past the prisons and barracks crowded with imprisoned liberals. Goya, who had signed the effigy of the Intruder King, Joseph Bonaparte, in his *Allegory of the City of Madrid*, and then painted portraits of his generals Guye and Querault and his minister of police Manuel Romero, accepting the Order of Spain and Joseph I from the hands of the usurper, was not interfered with on that day of festivities and persecutions. No doubt he was sheltered by secret, personal orders from Fernando VII, the only one who could protect him under such circumstances.

It has been said that *May 3, 1808, in Madrid: The Executions at the Príncipe Pío Hill* was an unexpected act of contrition. Jean François Chabrun correctly pointed out that if this were the case, no greater repentance could be imagined. Further, Goya could not have painted that slaughter and *May 2, 1808, in Madrid* in two months' time. The drawings of *The Disasters of War*, whose date is unknown, are intentional or unintentional drafts for *The Executions*. Two sketches for *May 2, 1808, in Madrid* survive: an oil on paper, currently the property of the duke of Villahermosa, and another oil on wood, which had been in the Lázaro Galdiano Museum.

The Executions at the Príncipe Pío Hill take place at daybreak, probably just before dawn, the preferred time for executions in every civilized country, as Hugh Thomas so correctly says. Antonio de Trueba took the statement of an old servant of Goya's, who perhaps confused true lies with incredible truths when, more than half a century later, he recalled that night. The old man told Trueba that Goya had witnessed the slaughter through a window at his villa on the banks of the Manzanares, by the light of the moon and with a spyglass. The anecdote is baseless, since Goya did not acquire the Deaf Man's Villa, the Quinta del Sordo, until 1819. In 1808 Goya was living in a house he owned on Calle de Fuencarral at the corner of San Onofre. It may be true, however, that Goya insisted on going to the Príncipe Pío Hill, escorted by his servant, to sketch those who had been killed. Like someone conjuring all the monsters in the dream of reason, he would entitle one of the *Disasters of War* "I saw it." In another, at the foot of a pile of corpses, not very different from the pile of dead in the painting, he would write his denunciation to the impassive universe: "This Is Why You Were Born."

"We sat on a rise, with the dead at the bottom, and my master opened his portfolio, placed it on his knees, and waited for the moon to come out from behind the thick black cloud that hid it. At the foot of the rise something fluttered, growled, and panted. I . . . I confess I was shaking like a leaf; but my master remained perfectly calm, preparing his pencil and pasteboard almost by touch. Finally the moon shone as bright as day. Surrounded by pools of blood, we saw corpses, some facedown, others faceup, one in the posture of someone who kneels and kisses the ground, another with his hands raised to heaven pleading for vengeance or mercy, and some hungry dogs feeding on the dead, panting in their eagerness and growling at the birds of prey that flew in circles above them, wanting to compete for the prize!"

Isidro, the servant, recounted asking Goya why he insisted on painting the savagery of men. "To have the pleasure of telling them for eternity not to be barbarians," his master replied. Regardless of the invention of the servant or of Trueba himself, in this account based on fact, the victims, covered in their own blood, some facedown on the ground, others fallen, looking up at the firmament, and almost all of them with their arms spread, seem to agree with the old man's testimony. But Goya does not confine himself to depicting the dead he saw at the foot of the Príncipe Pío Hill; he also portrays the executions themselves, which he could not have seen from the Quinta del Sordo. The shooting and the shouting were over when he reached the place with Isidro; but Goya painted the killers he did not know from the back, and at the same time he painted the howls of death he would never hear.

Some have died. Others are going to die irremediably. The same men who killed the first were now preparing to kill the rest. No one can accuse them because neither the painter nor we will ever see their faces. And we do not know the names of many of the victims, although the features of some of these men about to be shot would be forever unforgettable. All of them, in fact, the executioners and the condemned, probably belonged to the same social class and to very similar worlds. But they spoke different languages and would never understand one another. The shouts of the condemned were as impenetrable to the firing squad as they were to Goya himself in his deafness, which in a sense we share with him before his painting.

In his book *Goya: The Third of May 1808*, Hugh Thomas describes the soldiers in detail. They are Frenchmen and belong to the Napoleonic armies, for they wear the drab trousers that sometimes replaced the troops' gaiters during the imperial period. This was when the shako was imposed, imitating the helmets worn by the Polish cavalry serving France. The sword with a rectangular hilt was typical of the period and of Napoleon's officers. The members of the firing squad were probably from the Legion de Réserve, which a short time before had guarded the Atlantic coast, or any of the twenty "provisional regiments" that the emperor sent to Spain, a total of thirty thousand men, when he still supposed that second-rate forces would be enough to take control of the country. It is also possible that these soldiers come from the Italian, Swiss, German, or Polish detachments of the French army. In any case, they would have been humble, perhaps illiterate creatures forced to wear a military uniform because of orders they did not understand or a poverty they knew all too well. Hugh Thomas rejects the possibility that the executioners in the painting formed part of the Garde Impériale, which at the time was protecting Murat, Napoleon's brother-in-law and the interim viceroy assigned to Madrid.

The day before, once the popular uprising in Madrid had been crushed, the first executions began at three in the afternoon against the walls of the convent of El Buen Suceso. The shootings continued until well into the following morning in the Prado, the Buen Retiro, before the walls of the Convent of Jesús, in the Casa de Campo, along the banks of the Manzanares, in Leganitos, in Santa Bárbara, and at the Puerta de Segovia. Between four and five in the morning (the preferred time for official massacres in the name of civilization) the last forty-three men were shot to death on the slopes of the Príncipe Pío Hill. One of the condemned, Juan Suárez, managed to escape at the last moment. Pursued by shots, he was lost from sight in the dark and finally took refuge in the Hermitage of San Antonio de la Florida, whose frescoes Goya had painted eighteen years earlier and where the artist's decapitated corpse now rests. The names of some of the *canaille* executed in the name of reason, law, and order in the clearings on Príncipe Pío have reached us. Rafael Canedo, occupation unknown. Juan Antonio Martínez, beggar. Julián Tejedor de la Torre, blacksmith. Manuel García, gardener. Manuel

Sánchez Navarro, an employee of the courts. Martín de Ruicarado, stonecutter. Juan Loret, shopkeeper. Antonio Macías de Gamazo, unskilled laborer, seventy years old. Domingo Braña, muleteer employed by the Tobacco Custom House. Fernando de Madrid, carpenter. Lorenzo Domínguez, saddler. Domingo Méndez, mason. José Amador and Antonio Méndez Villamil, hod carriers. Also on the list is a cleric, Francisco Gallego Dávila, chaplain at the Monastery de la Encarnación, who is probably the friar awaiting death, kneeling, with his hands tightly clenched, on Goya's canvas.

All or almost all of them were men who could have shared the hungers of the disinherited with those who were shooting them. (An exception was a boy of a more comfortable class who dies there: Antonio Alises, page to Prince Don Carlos María Isidro.) It is also very likely that not all the victims were innocent. When on March 23 Murat had entered Madrid at the head of his troops, the people gave him a welcome reserved for an ally. Somewhat disconcerted, the crowd courteously applauded that marshall of the empire with his long black curls, Siberian fox jacket, crimson shako with peacock feathers, and scarlet boots. The cuirassiers of the Garde impériale deserved great huzzahs. The infantry (the Legion de Réserve or the forces of the "Provisional Regiments") was welcomed with baffled pity. No one could have imagined imperial troops so exhausted and badly dressed, or in worse formation. The same men the public felt sorry for then formed the firing squads. The day before, Sunday, May 2, many of those soldiers, isolated in the labyrinth of streets surrounding the Plaza Mayor or the Palacio de Oriente, would be gutted with knives. In a French military hospital, Madrilenian attendants coldly slit the throats of the patients and the wounded.

If the victims in *The Executions on Príncipe Pío Hill* had survived that night, as Juan Suárez did, on the following day they would have turned into executioners. Goya could have entitled his painting *With Reason or Without It*, the name he would give to the second etching in his series *The Disasters of War*, in which other soldiers of the Legion de Réserve hack at guerrillas with their bayonets. In the next print, it is the guerrillas who cut up the French with axes and pikes. This etching has a two-word caption written in Goya's somewhat trembling hand: "Lo mismo," The Same Thing.

Undoubtedly forced by the firing squad, the stonecutter, the beggar, the mason, the court clerk, the manual laborers, and all the other prisoners die on their knees. This is why the dead lie with their arms spread wide, trying in vain to brush away the darkness of an impossible sky, the same sky that the friar perhaps persists in attempting to capture between his hands. Civilization will subsequently teach us to shoot people who are standing, which is much more dignified, modern, and honorable for the accused. Perhaps this reform began in our war for independence. Etchings 15 and 38 offer us two of the favored variants of the period. In the first, "and there's no solution," the prisoners are executed on their feet, tied to a post, and blindfolded. The contrary method, "Savages," consists in riddling with bullets the back of a man tied to another post, or perhaps the same one, in this way salvaging the handkerchief that would have been used to blindfold him.

In the human center of *The Executions on Príncipe Pío Hill*, placed a little to the left of the spectator and the geometric center, Goya's ragged pauper shouts eternally. Fired by rage, to judge by his expression, he is the only one who does not plead for clemency or mercy. He dies with his eyes open wide, challenging his executioners or proclaiming beliefs that for him are sacred. His right palm is clearly pierced and perhaps his left as well, as Folke Nordstrom indicates in *Goya, Saturn, and Melancholy*. The same writer interprets the vague, blurred figures to the left and behind the prisoners as a Pietà, in which the Virgin hides the face of her Son against her breast to spare him the Calvary of these men. It should be remembered that Goya always headed his letters with a cross, even though he was fervently anticlerical and perhaps no longer believed in the immortality of the soul.

Almost at the end of *The Disasters*, a skeleton returned from death identifies it in writing with nothingness. The epigraph emphasizes this: "Nothing. The event will tell."

Goya believed in "Divine Reason," as he called it in *The Caprices*. If he seemed to identify morally with the victims here, ideologically he was on the side of the executioners. André Malraux's often-cited phrase from his *Saturne. Essai sur Goya*, describing *The Disasters of War*, is still valid: "The notebook of a Communist at the moment his country has been invaded by the Soviet Union." *The Disasters, The Shootings*, and *May 2, 1808, in Madrid* were also the testimony of a deaf syphilitic who saw more deeply than any of his contemporaries into the dark labyrinth that occupies and, in the final analysis, summarizes human nature. There he also discovered the ironic monster that inhabits man and obliges him to kill in the name of the noblest social abstractions: Liberty, Faith, Progress, and Reason itself. As a man he believed himself to be as guilty as his fellow man, regardless of the language in which he expressed himself at the moment of the executions, which always preceded a dawn that was, perhaps, impossible. Perhaps even guiltier, because Goya knew himself to be both violent and cowardly in the chaos of war. *May 2, 1808, in Madrid, The Executions*, and *The Disasters* were much more than the testimony of a supporter of the French at the moment his country had been invaded by the Napoleonic Legion de Réserve. They were the terrible examination of conscience by a rationalist Christian in the name of all his brothers, the killers.

March 26, 1828

I'm recovering little by little and in no time I'll be like new, at the age of eighty-two. If my daughter-in-law and grandson would come right now, I'd be fine. This miracle is due to valerian, ground up fine in the mortar, which Leocadia gives me every noon. I even found the strength to go to Galos's house, all wrapped up and in a carriage, to sign receipts for the last remittances. The trip did not tire me as much as I feared, and I plan to repeat it in April on my own feet. With Leocadia's help I walk a little around the house every morning and then, comfortably stretched out in the armchair filled with pillows, I draw events that happened thirty years ago or even more, using a board as a table. It may be an illusion of mine, but I believe that even my sight improved this week. Sometimes I dispense with the magnifying glass to draw my sketches, using only eyeglasses with metal frames. A real painter should be able to reproduce the most distant memories with a pencil or a dry point needle. When I can't do that, I'll be blind or I'll have died.

> Dear Xavier: I'm dying of impatience as I wait for my dear travelers. You gave me the greatest pleasure when you said in your last letter that they wouldn't go to Paris in order to spend more time with me. They'll enjoy it here, and if you come in the summer, my happiness will be complete.
>
> On Saturday I was in Galos's house and received the two monthly stipends. I also have in my possession the other draft for 979 francs. As soon as you send the next pair of stipends, I plan to invest the income, some 12,000 reales annually, in a country house for Marianito and his descendants. What do you think of the idea?
>
> I'm feeling much better and hope to be as healthy as I was before the attack. My improvement is due to powdered valerian; but the best remedy for all my ailments will be the visit from my dear travelers. They will help me to recover completely. Goodbye for now, my son, from one who loves you very much . . .

I reread my own letter several times, now with the help of the magnifying glass. Though I'd give my eyes to have my daughter-in-law bring Marianito to me and not to live waiting for their arrival, I scrawled the note to Xavier, not really paying attention to what I had written. Lightning bolts of memory repeatedly returned me to that spring of 1796 or 1797 and to the house on the slope of Sanlúcar Hill. Months earlier, back when María Teresa began to go to bed with me, she had become a widow. She went to Sanlúcar to hide her mourning and I joined her there, on the pretext of painting her full-length portrait again, as we had agreed earlier in Madrid. In reality even our few precautions were excessive because in whispers and behind my back, the back of a deaf man, the entire court was saying we were lovers. Josefa must have known all about it, though she never reproached me for anything. She must have imagined in silence that the affair between a peasant and a woman of such high nobility, and twenty years his junior besides, would end like the rosary at matins: in a scandal destined to be forgotten as soon as María Teresa chose another lover. And in fact, that's what happened, although Josefa would never guess that I, the oldest of the three and a sick man, would outlive all the women in this purgatory.

I see María Teresa's house again, halfway up the slope that leads to the village, as I sketch it rapidly in the notebooks on the board. My hand does not tremble, even though ten days ago it was stiff, and now it transfers memories to paper at full speed. (Valerian will condemn me to live for a century, like Titian, and die painting! *Vous êtes un grand homme, un peintre de la Chambre. On va vous soigner!*) It was midafternoon, and beneath the bedroom window the Guadalquivir slipped out to sea past the inlets. On its way to setting, the sun turned an orange-red that set the water on fire beneath the shrieking gulls. Couples in boats crossed the gleaming river. The men rowed, shirtless, and the women protected themselves from the glare with flowered parasols and wide straw hats decorated with glass grapes. I made love to María Teresa, and she smothered me again, anticipating her cries when she climaxed, which the servants would listen to, smiling, behind the door. At times, and before I left the bedroom after dressing, she would call the maid with a bell and ask her to change the stained sheets. I asked her how she dared humiliate the girl in that way, and looking me in the eye, she replied:

"What I don't understand is why she lends herself to being humiliated. If these people are as despicable as we are, what sense do our lives make, or theirs?"

We fell asleep in each other's arms in the dazzling afternoon. I awoke after an interminable dream in which I had seen the Prince of Peace, surprisingly aged and badly dressed, playing with some children in gardens that a thunderstorm erased from memory. María Teresa was still lying naked, facedown on the bed, her jet-black hair spilling over her shoulders and the sheets. It must have poured while we were sleeping, because the sky was still cloudy on the other side of the wet glass. A fantastic rainbow crossed the sky and the inlets. It came to us through the window and illuminated María Teresa's back with all the lights of the prism. I woke her and said:

"I dreamed I saw Godoy in a park where I'd never been. He was very old, but I recognized his features because I never forgot a face. Sitting on a bench and dressed like someone unemployed, he was talking with other old men as poorly attired as he. At times the children would approach him and he lent them his walking stick so they could ride it around a pond. The dream washed away in a storm. I don't understand it, but I'm afraid it is a harbinger of misfortunes."

Curled on the bed, her hands crossed under her chin, María Teresa seemed to pierce me with her eyes. Her gaze was lost in the void, following a Godoy very different from the omnipotent favorite of an earlier time, in whom she scorned excessive power, satanic ambition, and the roguery that led him to satisfy them. The account of my dream must have evoked in her an abandoned and impoverished man submerged in a misfortune as incredible as his earlier fortune. At that moment I realized I had lost her forever. Not long afterward she became the concubine of the greatest of satyrs, the Prince of Peace, who, ironically, would always favor me with his affection. In one of my *Caprices* I portrayed María Teresa, in mourning and flying through the air, standing on three monstrous squatting figures. In another drawing that I did not have the courage to engrave, "Dream of the Lie and Unconsciousness," I portrayed her again with two faces, like Janus, embracing me but at the same time looking at a stranger who approached slithering along the ground. To begin with I drew a snake holding a turtle spellbound in order to devour it. *The Caprices* were published thanks to the authority of Godoy, who probably never understood them. Engraving them freed me from my jealousy, because for me, art was always my redemption from madness. By then, María Teresa had tired of the Prince of Peace and he did not pursue her body, only the plunder of her estate.

Leocadia arrived holding Rosarito by the hand and I immediately closed my sketchbook. I shared my jealousy with others, but my memories were as much mine as the silence of my deafness. She told me that Moratín had come to say goodbye, because tomorrow he was returning to Paris. (No doubt he had given up waiting for my death and was leaving now, at a calm, empty time, because only the burial of other exiles revives our hope of seeing Spain again.) We invited Moratín to have lunch with us: Madrid garbanzo stew and suckling pig. He accepted very courteously and enthusiastically praised Leocadia's cooking with the irritating discretion of an effeminate man. We had lunch right in the bedroom, and I ate with Rosarito on my lap, the drawing board serving as our table. Looking at Moratín, I suddenly asked him:

"Leandro, how old are you now?"

"I'll be sixty-eight."

"No one would ever guess. You look almost twenty years younger," Leocadia chimed in.

The hunger he would have suffered recently in Paris had made him thin and pale, although he had always had that whitish color touched with pink so typical of conch shells and girls. He had been the librarian and personal friend of the Intruder King, and had been obliged to follow him into exile. Joseph Bonaparte gave almost his entire personal fortune to create a pension fund for destitute supporters of the French. Now the Bourbons had confiscated those funds. One day he'll die in Paris and someone will have to give up part of his own grave for him. He will turn into ashes and his theater into silence. In this world of madmen, our personal fate is undoubtedly something that happens only once.

"I'd also take you for half a century if I hadn't known you since the days when we would get together in the Fonda de San Sebastián, where I heard you talk about the Encyclopedists for the first time. Half a century badly lived, in fact, because if that were your age you'd look older. I'd like to paint another portrait of you to know for certain who you are."

"Did you find that out about yourself?" He smiled, carving the meat with those thin, sensitive hands, as white as mushrooms very well hidden in the bush.

"No. The fact of the matter is I never could find out, and the older I get, the less I know about it."

Vous êtes un grand homme, un peintre de la Chambre. Everything was clear to the doctors: I was a former painter of kings to whom they gave powdered valerian in order to keep him alive. "We know each other too well," I said to His Majesty the last time I spoke with him. The fact is that nobody knows anybody, as the title of one of my caprices says: that masked ball where everything is false, the people, their words, and even their disguises. The king laughed like a parrot imitating men. And yet he thought he was Saturn, devouring our people. That's where he was wrong, because I too supposed I was Saturn, and we couldn't both become the same monster. In Sanlúcar, when I painted the portrait in which María Teresa wore two rings without our names, she said to me: "You immortalized me twice. I'll live forever in people's memory for having been your mistress and because you made this painting of me." At least, that's what I thought I read on her lips, because I could no longer hear her voice. In a few days she was Godoy's, as she had once been mine, with the same cries I never could hear, though she was in my arms, the same kisses, the same bites. Now she has been ashes for more than twenty years and I don't know what could have happened to her portrait with the two rings. The queen and the Prince of Peace stole it, along with everything that was hers, after her death.

"That's precisely why we grow old and die," said Moratín: "to forget who we are if we ever knew it."

"Grandfather, are you going to die soon?" Rosarito asked, sitting in my lap.

"Rosarito! How dare you say terrible things like that?" said a furious Leocadia. "What will Don Leandro think of you?"

"Don Leandro doesn't think, Señora," Moratín said with a smile, speaking very slowly, as he usually does. "Don Leandro is in exile, just like yourself, for having dared to think."

"That's enough, Leocadia," I intervened in order to cut short these fits of rage, so sudden and so exasperating. "The girl isn't to blame for thinking freely, in her innocence. Don't attempt to be more than the despot. Go on, pour me a little wine."

The wine was poured and I drank; but we didn't resolve anything. I am less and less sure of knowing who I am, more and more suspicious in the most tortured way that I'm beginning to be someone else. For thirty-six years I haven't heard a human voice, including my own, reading other people's lips to discover what they are saying to me. And yet, with a start that I can barely manage to control, at this very moment, I heard in my mind the words of an unknown woman: "I'll never know who I could have been, since no woman knows that who hasn't been a mother," she says to me. "For that matter, I also don't know what I'm doing here with you. It's all like a nightmare that goes on too long." I would have liked to smother this faceless voice; but she replied: "I'll go when I like. After all, it's all the same whether I go or stay with you, because any relationship between us never made any sense." Then she stopped speaking and I needed a few moments of quiet to get used to her silence. Moratín's gestures

got me out of the critical moment, for he was talking to me and trying to look me in the eye.

"To continue with our sad exegesis of old age, I ought to confess
an almost unimaginable I adventure had in Paris, shortly before my
trip to Bordeaux. One Sunday I was walking alone through the Tuileries gardens, and I ran into the Prince of Peace."

"Godoy? I thought he was dead," said Leocadia.

"Grandpa, who's the Prince of Peace?" Rosario asked, turning
her head so I could see her lips.

"The Prince of Peace is the devil," responded Leocadia.

"Don't be stupid," I interrupted her, "and don't talk about someone you don't believe in. I see no reason to teach the child to hate in
vain. When she's a woman, no one will remember Godoy. The Prince
of Peace, my little ladybird, is a man your grandfather knew in Spain.
He tried to have everything in this world, where almost nothing is
worth the effort; but now he suffers as we do, because he has to live
far from Madrid and his country."

"He didn't seem to be suffering too much when I ran into him,"
Moratín continued. "He was taking the sun on a bench, near the
pond, speaking very bad French with other old men. It turned out to
be a get-together of retired actors and trapeze artists who met there
every Sunday. With them, and with no touch of irony, because he
never had any, the Prince of Peace said he had been a Spanish clown.
Some of those old men would go to the Tuileries with their grandchil-
dren. The children showed an instinctive affection for Godoy, and
he more than reciprocated. They climbed on his knees and brought
him their toys and balls so that he would lend them his walking stick
of varnished cane. Although I had often seen him before the war, I
didn't recognize him then. There are people who age badly, whom
the winters not only blur but disfigure as well. He was one of those.
Time had bent his back and made him so thin that nothing remained
of his insolent bearing. Moreover, I never could have imagined him

so modestly dressed in badly pressed clothes shiny with wear, and a shirt darned on the front. It was he who approached, limping, after saying goodbye to his friends. Smiling, he extended a trembling hand, spotted by the years. 'You're Moratín, aren't you? I'm the Prince of Peace.'"

"What else happened, Leandro? What else happened? For God's sake, don't stop now!"

My heart pounded in my chest, the way fulling mills pounded cloth. Moratín had experienced and was recounting the dream I'd had in the distant spring of Sanlúcar. This Godoy, eaten away by old age and poverty, was the same man I had dreamed thirty years earlier. The man whom María Teresa could have loved now, as she had loved me when syphilis had deafened me, as she had loved beggars, lepers, blind men, orphans, the destitute, as she had left all her goods to the poor, before the queen and Godoy himself had stripped her bare after her death.

"Don't you feel well? Why are you so upset?" Leocadia and Moratín asked at the same time, astonished by my agitation and the impatience of my words.

"I'm perfectly fine. Go on, Leandro! Go on!"

"There isn't much to tell," he said with a shrug. "We walked for a time through the garden and Godoy spoke almost the whole time about himself. He had a singular Italian accent, which he had brought from Rome, where, as he told me, he kept a vigil over the death agony of Queen María Luisa. He added that the Princess of Peace had died in Madrid, in 1820, without ever answering his letters. Their daughter, Carlota, also refused to write to him. 'She doesn't want to know anything about me, alive or dead,' he repeated dispassionately, as if he were accustomed to thinking of that ingratitude. He lived on the fourth floor, near the Tuileries, thanks to a modest pension from the French government. When the Princess of Peace died, he married Pepita Tudó in order to recognize the son he'd had with her. 'On that fourth floor,' he said with a smile, 'we were all waiting for the death of the despot, also known as the Desired One. I think he's very sick again.' I told him that a people who called Fernando the Desired One had no forgiveness from God. He nodded his agreement in the twilight: 'No, no they don't, not even in hell.' I was going to reply that Spain was hell, when he muttered in a very quiet voice: 'I consider my current wretchedness well spent, because it is the guarantee of my conscience. I at least did not have the opportunity to experience that war in which Spaniards found themselves obliged to betray or defend the rights of a traitor, committing all kinds of atrocities.' I replied that I had been librarian to King José, precisely in order to serve my country. He smiled, shaking his head. 'That's your affair, Moratín. I congratulate myself because destiny forced me to withdraw.'"

"He probably was right," I interrupted. "On May 2, in '08, when the Mamelukes ran down women with their horses, when French soldiers shot men in clusters, those of us not born to be butchers should have abstained from collaborating with the invader. That was a war all of us would lose, hopelessly, regardless of how it turned out. Our obligation was reduced to maintaining the integrity of our personal dignity, but unfortunately we lost that along with the conflict. The day when Fernando VII, recently returned to Madrid, summoned me to the palace to tell me he absolved my past, I felt the same sorrow I had suffered when my children died. I would have preferred a thousand times over to be exhibited in a cage, like the Undaunted, and then executed."

"The king didn't have the right to absolve anybody, because nobody could pardon a wretch like him for his greatest sin: having been born," said Leocadia.

"You sound very Calderonian, Señora," said Moratín, with a caustic smile. "I don't know how this predestination can accommodate your liberalism."

"Grandpa, what's liberalism?" asked Rosarito.

I preferred to ignore her question, for if I responded I would have to tell her that Spanish liberalism had been reduced to waiting for the death of a man who would, perhaps, outlive us all except her. Perhaps she would understand it by herself one day, or maybe she would never understand it at all, which is what would happen to most of our compatriots. That's how it is today and how it will probably be the day after tomorrow, when we are ashes and the eternal despot had changed his name in order to be reincarnated with the same ambition and cruelty he'd always had.

"When I went to Zaragoza, after the first siege, I saw the naked corpses of guerrillas impaled on trees along the road by the soldiers of the same king for whom you were librarian and I an incidental painter," I said to Moratín. "They were in every field, amputated and castrated by saber blows, their eyes empty and eaten by birds. Undoubtedly Godoy was right. It was a lucky man who could withdraw when those horrors were occurring."

"Do you know what our people did? Do you know about their atrocities during the war?"

"Of course I know about them!" I protested in a rage. "I told you already that as far as I'm concerned, all those slaughters were the same crime. They murdered with reason or without it. Our side did the same."

"No, it wasn't the same," he replied with a passion not at all usual in him. "Our closest neighbor, the one we instinctively tend to identify with in this labyrinth, is from our country and speaks our language. It becomes as difficult to absolve him as to forget one's personal faults, because he too is the object of our individual conscience . . ."

"Who can talk about conscience nowadays? Who, really, when we all sold ourselves for a dish of lentils?"

"I can!" He interrupted me. "I could pardon the French for those naked, profaned corpses, just as I pardon the crows that devour their eyes. But I cannot forget the crimes of my own people, because in a certain sense they are my own crimes. In Santa Cruz de Mudela, between Valdepeñas and Desdeñaperros, in the small hours of June 5, 1808, horsemen from Castaños surprised two hundred sleeping Frenchmen. Before killing them with axes and pikes, the women cut off their ears and their private parts as they had done earlier in Lerma. Then they cut them all into pieces, one by one, and threw their remains to the pigs. In Cádiz, cradle of our Constitution and our useless freedoms, ten thousand French prisoners were piled into ten old hulks with barely enough room for a thousand. Dysentery, gangrene, scurvy, typhoid fever, and finally cholera reduced their number to six hundred. Many committed suicide and more lost their minds. When sea breezes blew, the stink from the ships infected the entire city."

"Forgive me, Leandro, but I'm taking the child away. I want to spare her this savagery," Leocadia intervened.

"But Grandma, I like it very much," Rosarito protested. "It's like a fairy tale."

"It is a fairy tale, my child," Moratín insisted, while Leocadia looked at him in a quandary. "All this happened in a very distant, very remote country: our country, which according to your grandpa never existed. One day all of us will have to invent it. In the meantime, we should limit ourselves to keeping in mind a past that never should have been. It is believed that sixteen thousand French soldiers and officers were deported to the island of Cabrera," he continued, staring at me so I wouldn't lose a single word from his lips. "A Mallorcan was supposed to supply them, but he made a fortune selling the provisions in Palma. On Cabrera, as on the old ships in Cádiz, the prisoners died of hunger, of cholera, of scurvy, of gangrene, and of typhoid fever. The commanders ordered the corpses burned because their companions would dig them up to eat them. Although at that time I was cataloguing the books of the intruder king, I feel responsible for these horrors because they were committed and tolerated by my compatriots. And all this, in whose name? Well, in the name of God and the Desired One."

"And meanwhile, the others impaled living peasants in order to

free them from the Holy Office, or shot them on Príncipe Pío Hill
to the greater glory of reason. Nations always justify their crimes in
the name of history. Then history transforms their crimes and sacri-
fices into sarcasm. When I became deaf and spent two years at death's
door, I discovered in the solitude of my silence that a monster lives
in each man. Much later I would see the beginning of the tragedy in
the Puerta del Sol, through the windows of my studio, as the Egyptian cavalry charged, shooting their guns and wielding their swords,
into a crowd armed with shouts and razors. Did you ever stop to
think, Leandro, about the spectacle of a war seen by a deaf man? I
couldn't hear the shouts, the shots, the neighing, and the artillery
fire that filled Madrid that day. In that sinister quiet, which seemed
to split my skull, the battle in the street took on a distant, unreal air,
as if life insisted on plagiarizing the nightmares of my dying. Those
who killed one another in silence, a silence as interminable as the
silence of insomnia, looked more like marionettes than people. Then
I understood that if a monster lived inside each man, the monster was
always a puppet."

"Is that when you conceived of the painting of the charge in the
Puerta del Sol, which you then painted for the Desired One?" he
asked, smiling.

"I conceived of absolutely nothing then. I limited myself to recognizing my true nature as vampire and clown. Almost twenty years
later I would buy the Quinta del Sordo and decorate the walls of the
house with my image and likeness: monsters that resembled puppets.
I believed I had painted my confession and contrition, but perhaps
I made a mistake."

"Why would you make a mistake?"

"Because perhaps I painted the entire history of my country
there without realizing it, as Leocadia once said."

"Perhaps you did."

"But I wanted to confront history in the early hours of May 3,
when I went to the clearings on Príncipe Pío with my servant to

sketch the carnage. In the moonlight, crushed to the ground or looking toward heaven with eyes wide open, all the puppets were dead.
The whole hill smelled of early rockrose in that dawn filled with hungry dogs and crows."

Moratín left, not consenting to my accompanying him to the
stairs. We said goodbye in the bedroom, and he embraced me and
kissed me on both cheeks as if we were Frenchmen. For a moment I
tried to ignore the presentiment that we would never see each other
again. Leocadia preceded him as she accompanied him to the staircase, and I fell back in the easy chair with Rosarito on my knees. The
child was silent and looked at me, expectantly, her large, dark eyes
fixed on mine.

"Grandpa," she said at last, "if men are puppets, who's playing
with them?"

"Time, my little ladybird, time that devours everything, just like
mice and wood borers. Only you will remain forever, like an eternal
flower, in the middle of the universe and beneath the stars."

"The Living Skeleton told me at the circus that one day I'd teach
a queen to draw."

"It must be true, ladybird, because he spoke all languages."

"The child will be the art teacher of a sovereign, Maestro,"
Claude Ambroise Lurat repeated to me in a corner of his tent on
the Rue du Manège. "She'll probably do that because your grace has
adopted her. One afternoon, on the way to the Royal Palace, she'll
run into an uprising or a riot. She'll race back home as fast as she can
and die of fright a few days later. She'll have just turned twenty-six.
Don't be angry with me, Maestro, *je vous en prie*. I read only the
back of the cards." Rosarito fell asleep on my lap. Leocadia looked
in the half-open door and I signaled to her impatiently not to wake
the child and to leave us alone. She left and closed the door slowly. I
made Rosarito a drawing of the Living Skeleton, leaning on a bamboo
cane and wearing a chef's hat on his smooth, hairless head. Naked,
except for an apron to hide his private parts, he resembled a boiled,

fleshless mummy. All his bones and cartilage were visible beneath his whitish skin. He was small and pigeon-chested, but his thinness sharpened him like a shadow. He told me he had been born in Narbonne and was the son of the count de Saint Germain, the man who never spends two days in the same city and is believed to be six hundred years old. The Skeleton never learned to write, and he read only cards, but he could speak all languages, as if the Pentecostal flame had descended over his kitchen cap.

"Pardon me, your grace, for what I said about the girl. I can't take it back, though I should have kept silent. To prove my good will, I'll deal the cards free of charge and your grace can read your good fortune on my lips." I laughed and asked him what future could await an old man of my age, and Claude Ambroise Lurat shrugged. "One never knows, because the only truth is in the cards. My presumed father, the charcoal seller Lurat, from Narbonne, had no faith in the cards and died not knowing that my mother had conceived me with the count de Saint Germain while he was shoveling burned charcoal. My mother told me all about it on the day of my first communion, when she taught me to lay the cards. She could specify the day and time of any future *évenèment* if it fell in a leap year. I'm not that good, but I get by in the circus. Let's sit down, Maestro, and I'll tell your good fortune right now, *bien entendu que pour rien, absolument pour rien*." That was when he said he saw in the cards a man and a woman who did not exist yet. The man was attempting to write a book about me, and the Living Skeleton seemed very disturbed by those messages. "Give me ten *sous*, Maestro, so I can drink a thimbleful of burgundy."

Ten days ago I told Moratín that Spain did not exist and was only one of my *Absurdities*, set up in the depths of the night of history. I sensed immediately that those words were not completely mine. At the back of my deafness and with the ears of the spirit, I thought I knew they had been said by a man at once very different from and very similar to me, perhaps in a century that did not yet exist. I wonder now whether that stranger could have been the same one the Living Skeleton saw in the cards, just as the Prince of Peace I dreamed of in Sanlúcar thirty-two or thirty-three years before turned out to be the same Godoy, old now, and with a darned shirt front, that Moratín ran into this winter, on a Sunday, in the Tuileries. ("You're Moratín, aren't you? I'm the Prince of Peace.") Perhaps in another time and in another world, because each era is a universe as dissimilar from the previous one as the moon can be from earth, a man waits for me and extends his hand to me in the emptiness in order to say: "I'm the one you have been."

To distract Rosarito, a few days ago I sketched a caricature of myself for her: an old hunchback, all wild hair and whiskers, emerging from the shadows and leaning on two canes. "What are you saying in the drawing?" inquired the ladybug, and at an angle I wrote: "I'm still learning." Then I began to wonder what I could be learning and concluded that my whole life as a painter was nothing but a search for myself, a clumsy attempt, which always failed, to recount my entire existence in my art. Then I thought of the man who, according to the cards, was struggling to write my biography. Was he perhaps pursuing himself while he believed he would gradually discover me in my paintings?

Ten years ago I painted the walls of the Quinta del Sordo. There, behind the Segovia Bridge, I supposed I would close myself away forever with my frescoes and my paintings. I was in the midst of that when I met Leocadia in I don't remember whose house. As it turned out, she was from the Aragonese family of the Monegros and a distant relative of mine. When very young she had married a certain Isidro Weiss, son of a Bavarian watchmaker and a Jew, who abandoned her and her two recently weaned children, who by now were a man and a woman. As well read as she was liberal, she was involved in the conspiracies of Mina, Porlier, Lacy, and finally of Riego to impose the Constitution of 1812 on Fernando VII. From politics and its plots she had inherited only debts, sorrows, and the subjects of long tirades about the intrigues plotted in the Café Lorencini or the Fontana de Oro. "Come live with me, in my house in the Manzanares lowlands," I said to her one day in the Cruz de Malta. "I'm old and lost among my paintings and my servants. I need a housekeeper and someone to talk to, although I can't hear your voice or mine." She followed me and I painted her at the entrance to the house, self-absorbed, an elbow on a rock, covered with a veil, among deaf, howling friars, decapitated kings, witches' sabbaths, crowds of monsters, Fates, buried dogs, drunkards, phantom horses, disputes with sticks, knives, illusions, skeletons, flying wizards, blind men, madmen, witches, phantoms, idiots, and masturbators. When I finished, I asked Leocadia what she thought of it. I was hoping she would tell me that the house was my self-portrait, but to my surprise she replied: "All of this, clearly, is our country seen from the inside: the burning heart of a volcano." I argued that I had been mistaken, then, since I had wanted to paint on the walls my own nightmares and the hell that lived inside me. Leocadia agreed with a gesture. "We've both said the same thing, isn't that so? Recounting the history of this Spain of ours is the same as confessing hidden transgressions."

The child fell asleep in my arms and I was surprised to find myself nodding. In the half-sleep of this nap, the lips of María Teresa and the Living Skeleton spoke to me. "If these people are as despicable as we are, what sense do our lives, and theirs, make?" And then: "In these points I don't see you but another man, whose name I don't know because perhaps he hasn't been born yet. I see him in a blur, accompanied by a woman, in a house next to a river that runs over a riverbed of very white stones. Neither the man nor the woman exist yet; but in the cards, he struggles to write a book about your grace" ... The dream is a river that carries me gradually to the center of the earth. I know I'm asleep and I feel like another man. I'm sitting on the last of three stone steps at the foot of a mill door. But I almost don't recognize myself, though deep in my soul I find my own being hidden in a different man. The house and landscape are new to my eyes, or at least I would swear I had never seen them. The walls of the mill, made of large stones faded by time, are gilded in the sun of a winter sky. Nearby a stream rambles by, the sound repeated in my ears as if the dream had freed me of deafness. The door is oak, cracked and blackened by a lightning bolt that had twisted the latch and the bolt. In front of me is a poplar grove, all the leaves gone, with large stones half buried among the bushes. Inside I again hear the words of that unknown woman. "I'll never know who I could have been, as no woman knows who has not been a mother. In fact, I also don't know what I'm doing here with you." Again I tried to silence her deep inside, as I had done before when I was talking to Leocadia and Moratín. "I'll go when I choose to. After all, it's all the same whether I leave or stay with you, because every relationship between us was always senseless." Then I become aware of her presence beside me and her voice sounds no longer in my consciousness but in my ears. She says in a different tone:

"If you really want to write the book, let's get away today. Let's go wherever you say and I'll follow you, if that's what you want. But let's leave here right away, before it's too late for all of us!"

THE MONSTERS

The Duchess of Alba

María del Pilar Teresa Cayetana Manuela Margarita Leonor Sebastiana Bárbara Ana Joaquina Josefa Francisca de Paula Xaviera Francisca de Asís Francisca de Borja Francisca de Sales Andrea Abelina Sinforosa Benita Bernarda Petronila de Alcántara Dominga Micaela Rafaela Gabriela Venancia Antonia Fernanda Bibiana Vicenta y Catalina, the legitimate daughter of the legitimate marriage of Don Fernando Francisco de Paula de Silva y Álvarez de Toledo y Portugal, duke of Huéscar, count of Oropesa, Alcaudete, Belbis, Deleitosa de Morente, y Fuentes, marquis of the city of Coria, the towns of Héliche, Tarazona, Jarandilla, Flechilla, and Villarramiel, to Doña María Ana de Silva Sarmiento y de Sotomayor, was born on June 10, 1762, the feast day of Corpus Christi, in her parents' mansion, located at the corner of the Madrilenian streets El Duque de Alba and Los Estudios: right in the heart of the flamboyant lower classes, the *manolería*, according to Joaquín Ezquerra del Bayo, future biographer of the newborn two centuries later.

It is well known that María Teresa (she never called herself Cayetana in the forty years of her stay on earth) came into the world with a great deal of very thick hair between bluish and deep black, the same color that would later highlight her white beauty. The truth is she was baptized in her parents' bedroom by special dispensation that does not appear in the record, since the archbishop of Toledo had ordered baptismal waters not to be used outside of churches except in emergencies, when the lives of the infants were at risk. Her godfather was the confessor to the duke and duchess of Huéscar, and acting as witnesses were Don Miguel de Bujanda, secretary to Don Fernando de Silva; Don Ignacio de Ahedo, deputy to the chief minister of the Indies; and Don Blas Carranza y Cornejo, archivist of her grandfather, the duke of Alba. On her father's side, María Teresa was the granddaughter of Don Manuel José de Silva, second son of the duke del Infantado and Doña María Teresa Álvarez de Toledo, eleventh duchess of Alba, who would share the title with her husband, according to the terms of their nuptial agreement. Her mother, Doña María Ana de Silva Sarmiento y de Sotomayor, was the daughter of Don Pedro Artal, eighth marquis de Santa Cruz and del Viso, and Doña María Cayetana, countess de Pie de Concha and marquise de Arcicóllar.

The Ursulines did not educate María Teresa and neither did the Royal Salesians. Her grandfather the duke of Alba had maintained a long correspondence with Rousseau. He admired *Émile* and debated by letter with the Genevan philosopher regarding botany. Doña María Ana de Silva painted, wrote plays and verses, translated, and spoke several languages. On the walls of the house one could see a prodigious private collection that included a Raphael, a Correggio, and Velázquez's *Venus with a Mirror*. Inevitably the popular street airs, between Lavapiés and the Rastro, would also enter this fiefdom of very cultivated nobles who were as free in their thinking as in their customs. In short, during this time the aristocracy began to imitate the common people, as Ortega rightly pointed out. The duke's parents banished their wigs and wore long pigtails like those of bullfighters, much to the despair of Jovellanos. Soon they would pepper Castilian with phrases from the slums, which couldn't catch up to the archaizing American Spanish language. In the next generation, when María Teresa was already a woman and the duchess of Alba, no one would know whether *The Naked Maja* was her portrait as an undressed slum dweller or the nude of an actual lower-class woman, disguised in the unclothed image of María Teresa de Silva, duchess of Alba and of Huéscar.

Don Fernando Francisco de Paula de Silva y Álvarez de Toledo died suddenly on Thursday, April 26, 1770, on the seventh day after being attacked by a "stabbing pain in his side in the house or palace of Barquillo, which his father had just purchased," according to the death certificate. María Teresa was eight years old at the time, and people were already talking about her beauty and daring wit. Her mother, Doña María Ana, consoled her widowhood by having an affair with the marquis de Mora, lover as well of Mademoiselle de Lespinasse, and the actress Mariquita Ladvenant, with whom he had four children. In spite of his lubricious youth, the young marquis had been recommended to Voltaire himself by D'Alambert, and three or four times a year he would make his pilgrimage to Château-Ferney to kiss the hands of the maestro. He died of consumption, spitting blood, in Bordeaux in the autumn of 1773. Doña María Ana then became engaged to the count de Fuentes, the widowed father of the marquis de Mora, a long, erect, silent figure described by Ossun, the French ambassador. María Teresa, in the meantime, had been promised to the eleventh marquis de Villafranca, Don José Álvarez de Toledo Ossorio Pérez de Guzmán el Bueno. And so the uncommon circumstance occurred that on the same day, January 15, 1775, mother and daughter were married in Madrid's Chapel of San José.

María Teresa was barely thirteen on her wedding day. The marquis de Villafranca was almost nineteen. Twenty years later Goya would leave us his portrait, leaning against the edge of a table and holding the score of four songs by Joseph Haydn. By now the marquis was the duke consort of Alba and looked ten autumns older than his thirty-nine years. His hair turned gray prematurely and receded high on his forehead. He had the sad gaze and circumspect expression of very resigned cuckolds. Beneath his dark eyes and long eyebrows, his nose and cheeks were thin. His lips, however, were small and sensual, though pale. Within a year he would be dead, and with no anxiety he probably had a presentiment of it now. Joined to a woman completely different from him, with whom he could not have children, this solitary man avoided other people and took refuge in music, his only passion. From Vienna Haydn sent him quartets for violin, cello, viola, and piano. By mutual agreement oboes, trumpets, and other wind instruments, which neither of them liked especially, were excluded.

In the year of the two weddings the count de Fuentes and the old duke of Alba, María Teresa's paternal grandfather, died. At the request of the deceased, his jester occupied a place of honor in the funeral rites and wore on his chest the most valuable of the dead man's decorations. Madrid was infuriated, but María Teresa would always admire the eccentric distinction of the old man. Very soon, barely an adolescent, she would create an even greater scandal. "In 1788," wrote Godoy in his memoir of exile, "the Duchesses de Alba and de Osuna fought over Joaquín Rodríguez (*Costillares*) and Pedro Romero, the leading bullfighters of the time. No one talked of anything but this ignoble licentiousness. The incidents, the acts of passion, and the generous gifts of each rival were recounted." In the end, with the hypocrisy or cynicism of a vindictive lover, the old satyr concluded with a shrug: "But that immorality did not scandalize anyone."

Costillares was the favorite of the gray-eyed duchess de Osuna. A Sevillan, he invented the *volapié* and the *veronica*. The flashy bullfighter had great success with the ladies, who dreamed of being lively chestnut sellers like those in the farces of Don Ramón de la Cruz. Jovellanos wanted in vain to prohibit the national fiesta, "that barbaric amusement." In 1805, after mature reflection in the Council of Castilla, Godoy would believe he had done away with "fights to the death with both mature and young bulls." When the war was over, Fernando VII reestablished them. "They were granted in exchange for the liberties and all the rights the heroic people of Spain had won with their blood," Godoy would write when he recalled the moment. "Bread was not given to anyone, but bullfights were . . . The wretched common people believed they had been well paid!" Almost half a century earlier, Tomás de Iriarte, the poet for hire of the duchess de Osuna, lamented in vexation: "We live now among Costillarists and

Romerists. Nothing else is talked about from the time we get up in the morning until we go to bed at night." María Teresa dispensed her favors to the Romero brothers, Pedro and José. Goya painted both of them before following them between the same sheets. Pedro Romero, creator of the Rondan school, killed more than five thousand bulls without being gored. In his portrait, which is certainly one of Goya's best, a man contemplates us with his graying sideburns and stylized features and the instinctive distinction that only the lowest class has at times. His eyes reveal an intelligent, indefinable sorrow: that of a mathematician facing the square root of darkness, or a surgeon searching for the soul.

María Teresa, that woman born in the heart of the flashy lower classes, did not confine herself to rivaling the duchess de Osuna. Circumstances led her to measure herself against the queen, who would always proclaim her fierce animosity. When María Luisa was still princess of Asturias, they shared the same lover: a handsome, harebrained soldier, Juan Pignatelli, son of the count de Fuentes, the stepfather of the duchess de Alba. Boastful and indiscreet, Pignatelli gave María Luisa a little gold box adorned with diamonds, a gift from María Teresa, in exchange for one of her stepsister's rings. The fool then showed the ring to the princess, who snatched it away in a rage. Soon afterward, in a hand-kissing ceremony, María Luisa extended her hand, adorned with that ring, to the duchess. Then María Teresa gave the gold box to her French hairdresser, who is also the princess's hairdresser, to take to the palace, filled to the brim with cosmetics when he went there to make up María Luisa.

Carlos III died after a long death agony, interminable hours when he sometimes could find no one to bring him a bowl of hot broth, in that court where efficiency was limited to the ceremonial, as it would later be reduced to intrigue. When the months of obligatory mourning were over, the new queen ordered the latest fashions from the Parisian *modistes*. María Teresa copied them and went out riding through the Prado in an open carriage with her maids, all of them in identical clothes, hats, and muffs. A short time later a sudden fire burned down the palace that the duke and duchess de Alba had built on Calle de Alcalá. María Teresa laughed when she was asked at a ball to comment on the incident. "Next time I'll burn down the house myself. I don't want to give others the pleasure of destroying it whenever they choose."

Posthumous diagnoses, a century and a half after her death, called her both sterile and frigid. Her high bosom, too opulent for her height, now suggested some endocrine disturbance. She gave herself to men as if she were blindly looking for herself in them. Another woman, Antonina Vallentin, stated that in María Teresa voluptuousness was inseparable from compassion. In her an anguished sense of justice combined with flesh and mercy. She protected defenseless animals, the old, the crippled, the mad, the mendicant, the wretched. All the rest, from the monarchs to her own servants and herself were, to María Teresa, the true rabble. At her table in Sanlúcar she sat Goya, her deaf lover, prematurely aged and dyspeptic, next to the sexton and the village idiot. She had taken into her house Brother Basilio, a very old and lame friar with a stammer, whose naïveté provoked the mockery of the footmen and lady's maids, to the immense pleasure of the guests. María Teresa was furious. "This riffraff will make me think that Brother Basilio and I are the only decent creatures!" Referring specifically to the domestics, she said to the duke, terrified by her rage: "This trash will make me think that even we are better than they are!" Goya painted her full-length portrait in 1795. Standing on sandy ground or on a beach, the duchess points with her index finger at the respectful signature of the painter, written on the ground with a twig: "To the Duchess de Alba, Fr. Goya." The year follows in highly visible figures. María Teresa wears white, with red bows on her chest and in her hair. Her two-strand necklace and wide sash are also red. If once she dressed her maids in the queen's fashions, now she dresses herself like her spaniel. At her feet and beside the painter's name, the little animal wears a twist of silk on its paw the color of her mistress's bows. In 1797, when the duke was already dead, Goya painted her again in Sanlúcar. They were lovers now and the entire painting proclaimed their love. On her right hand she wears a wedding band and a ring; the first says *Goya* and the second *Alba*. So that no one could allege fraud, another inscription in large inverted letters also says, on the ground crowding the little silver shoes of María Teresa: "Sólo Goya." As if time did not concern the lovers, the date appears in smaller figures, facing the viewer, almost going over the edge of the canvas. Again the duchess points at the name of the man she believes is her beloved. "Sólo Goya." One would say that María Teresa herself bears witness to this in the sand so that the deaf man cannot doubt it. Goya also makes some sketches of his stay at Sanlúcar. In a charcoal drawing his mistress tousles her hair in front of the mirror in an outburst of childish rage before the sardonic eyes of her lover. "She tears her hair and stamps her feet because the priest Picurris told her she looked pale." In another the duchess takes a siesta, fully dressed and on her back, while a maid removes a chamber pot from under the bed. Finally, with her arms spread and her back to a fierce bull, she nonchalantly incites the animal, which, motionless and sad, contemplates her as if it cannot believe she is real.

At times jealousy became apparent in the Sanlúcar sketchbook. The duchess had fainted or pretended to faint beside a low wall. Two maids take part in the game, opening her bodice and fanning her with their hands. An attractive young man holds her by the shoulders and looks at her chest while she embraces his slim banderillero's body. On an incline a masked figure in a three-cornered hat dozes and next to him sits María Teresa. Delicately she adjusts her mantilla at her waist and steals sideways glances at the man. A dandy pursues the duchess with his compliments. At the bottom Goya asks: "Who is more smitten?" and responds: "Neither one. He is merely a charlatan of love who says the same things to each woman, and as for her, she thinks only of the five appointments she has made between eight and nine o'clock and that it's already seven-thirty." The hours were also diminished for Goya in the duchess's inconstancy. When he returns to Madrid, withdrawn into his deaf man's silence and with the portfolio of sketches under his arm, his *affaire d'amour à la mode canaille* has had its stormy ending. María Teresa has become Godoy's mistress and Goya denounces her fickleness in sketches and caprices. "Birds of a Feather," "Not Even Now Can You See the Difference," "May God Forgive Her," "Good Advice," "Three bullfighters pick up the Broken Pieces of the Duchess of Alba, who finally loses her Mind because of Inconstancy," "Dream of Lies and Inconstancy." Then the former lovers arrange a truce and become good friends. On her way to a ball, the duchess appears one afternoon in Goya's studio and asks him to paint her a face she can wear as a disguise. Goya agrees to the game, and to judge by a letter to Zapater, his only confidence regarding that affair, they enjoy each other again in memory of the old days. In 1798, when he is working on the frescoes in San Antonio de la Florida, María Teresa drops in unexpectedly one morning. "Goya! Goya!" she calls to him, laughing, without his being able to hear her or see her lips from the high scaffold. "You painted all the whores of Madrid in this dome to celebrate a miracle of the saint!"

Another *affaire beaucoup plus canaille*, the one between María Teresa and Godoy, ends in blazing rancor. He will despise her as perhaps he had never hated anyone, not Fernando VII or the men who one day will drive him through the streets of Aranjuez with blows from their cudgels and slashes from their knives. In April 1800, the queen, always jealous, writes to Godoy: "The Alba woman left us this afternoon; she had lunch with General Cornel and left: she's a wreck; I don't think what happened to you before will happen now, and I also believe you're very sorry about all that." On September 5 of that year Godoy proclaimed his anger and rage very loudly in a letter to the queen. "Alba and all her supporters ought to be buried in a vast abyss. Cornel, who ever since his affair with Alba has taken her part, should not exist." Lieutenant General Antonio de Cornel y Ferraz would be María Teresa's last lover. An Aragonese like Goya, a knight of the Order of Santiago, fiftyish and very well read, he maintained an elegant appearance in spite of his age. His legend preceded him and dazzled women. It was said that he remained a bachelor to keep a vow of celibacy made twenty-two years earlier, when his fiancée burned to death in the fire at the Teatro de Zaragoza. He had been an aide to the count de Aranda, and in the Rosellón Campaign he rose to the rank of field marshal to celebrate the war of the French villages after the women had been violated by the pious soldiers of Cataluña. Godoy's circumstances fell in the stormy spring of 1798, and Saavedra replaced him as president of the Council of Castilla, and Urquijo, an intimate friend of Cornel, inherited from Saavedra himself his position in the Ministry of Finance. When Urquijo moved on to govern, he would make Cornel his minister of war. In December 1800, Pedro de Cevallos, Godoy's political messenger, took power. Urquijo and Cornel found themselves in prison. The Prince of Peace did not forget to take his revenge, although in the end, and in his memoirs, he pardoned all his enemies with the exception of the duchess de Alba.

A sudden and unexpected hidden death carried off María Teresa. When she was unconscious, she received the Holy Sacraments and died at two in the afternoon on July 23, 1802. By the expressed desire of the deceased, she was buried without pomp and at night in the Oratory of the Missionary Fathers of the Savior. On August 6 they opened her will in the presence of her brothers-in-law the marquis de Villafranca and the count de Miranda. She left her immense fortune to her servants and the poor, not forgetting her jester Benito, who received a pension for life with an executor to administer it for him. A separate bequest was made to the son of Don Francisco de Goya Lucientes.

The gossips of Madrid repeated the rumor that the duchess de Alba had been poisoned by Godoy and María Luisa. On July 25, the night before María Teresa's funeral, the public prosecutors of the Council of the Treasury would inventory her estate on the pretext of a claim brought against her because of a late payment of taxes on her estate in Oropesa. They took her jewels and had them appraised, and then the queen appeared wearing them. An order from the king to Godoy himself demanded the record and confiscation of María Teresa's documents, using base reasons as an excuse. "The magistrate, who heard the case against the suspects in the inheritance, has been able to determine that disloyal servants removed papers from the Duchess's strongbox at the moment she expired." Godoy took advantage of the process to acquire everything the queen rejected, including Velázquez's *Venus with a Mirror*, along with all of María Teresa's other paintings. The beggars, the servants, the son of Don Francisco de Goya Lucientes, and the jester Benito would never see any part of everything that legitimately belonged to them.

When the estate of the Prince of Peace had been sequestered in 1808 and then in the uprising of Aranjuez, his canvases were moved into the Cristales storehouse and his works of art inventoried. Entry 122, published in 1919 by Aureliano de Beruete, describes: "Two paintings five feet, four inches high by six feet, ten inches wide, one representing a nude Venus on a bed, the other a clothed maja, painted by Francisco de Goya."

October 25, 1975

Marina found Sandro sitting on the steps at the foot of the mill, his elbows leaning on his knees and his hands crossed under his chin.

"He's gotten worse," she said in an indifferent tone, not looking at him. "At noon he heard Mass and received extreme unction from the palace chaplain. Perhaps he's died."

Sandro was silent, absorbed, unmoving. His gaze lost among the hillocks of the woods, he did not seem aware of her presence. Marina thought of a man ironically turned into salt while he looked ahead, past the trees and brambles along the riverbank.

"Who received last rites?" he asked suddenly, looking at her in confusion. "What did you come out here to tell me?"

She did not reply. The only sunbeam that crossed the poplar grove disappeared, and the autumn light turned the air to a gray somewhere between quartz and slate. Observing Sandro, Marina told herself that they both must be the same age, but he looked twenty years older. Before another five had passed—ten at the most—she had a presentiment she would survive him. All her conscious life, "if a Spanish woman could ever have a conscious life," as Sandro himself would have commented, had been spent intertwined with that man's, even if at times, and in a Guadiana manner, other couples and an entire generation might come between them. However, the slightest retouching of the destiny of either one, or for that matter a circumstance distant from them both, such as the nonexistence of R., would be enough for their fates to disengage. Now, in spite of her own protests and the revulsion that Sandro's drunkenness inspired in her, she knew with certainty she would never leave him, just as he would never succeed in finishing the book on Goya. She would have sworn to any of those hypothetical realities with identical certainty. She repeated silently, as she had so many times before, that they were both equally sterile: two lost creatures numb with cold on the banks of the torrent of life that they would never even graze with their fingers. It was R. who had shaped their common destiny to resemble a design unknown to her and to Sandro. R. introduced them beside the tiny water lily pond. R. found them the bedroom where they had their first encounters and the place where Marina miscarried the only child she might have had. R. joined them again, almost thirty years later, and they were living in his house even though Sandro had promised her that by now they would be in the United States. It was through R. that Sandro got the contract for the life of Goya and even the grant from "that foundation that bore the name of the leading pirate of the Mediterranean."

"If you really want to write the book, let's get out of here today," she exclaimed aloud, to her own surprise. "We'll go wherever you say and I'll follow you if that's what you want. But let's get out of here right away, before it's too late for all of us!"

Sandro looked at her as if he couldn't hear her and barely recognized her. He stood slowly, stretching and shaking his head. Marina had the impression of a man who had wakened from a hypnotic trance in which he had been made to think he was a bull pierced by banderillas: that horned bull painted by Goya as soon as he had recovered from syphilis and accepted his deafness, whose reproduction in the Gudiol Catalogue, when Sandro showed it to her, disturbed her as no other painting had. "The original belonged to the duke and duchess de Veragua," he had told her then. "Wouldn't you like to see it?" "No, absolutely not," Marina replied immediately. "I'd be afraid of going blind afterward."

"What did you come to tell me? Who had extreme unction?" Sandro repeated, in a daze.

"I suppose it was Franco. I heard the news on the radio and came out to tell you."

"Do you think he's died?"

"Yes, I have the feeling he passed around noon. Tonight or tomorrow they'll have the courage to say so."

"If that's so, before you know it it'll seem as if he never existed," replied Sandro. "The past is never corrected here. It's simply forgotten and repeated later with slight variations. In any case, we'll soon witness the disintegration of the only Empire of God the world has ever seen. I wonder what became of the Imperial Order of the Yoke and Arrows, created in 1939 or 1940 to be offered to Hitler, Mussolini, and His Diminutive Majesty Vittorio Emanuele, the third of the *terza* Italia."

"In any event, you must be the only one who remembers it now," said Marina with a shrug. "They ought to give it to you before the empire breaks apart."

She was overcome by fatigue. "If you really want to write the

book, let's get out of here today. Let's go wherever you say and I'll follow you, if that's what you want. But let's get out of here right away,
before it's too late for all of us!" She wondered why Sandro would not
hear those words or why he would pretend to ignore them. She was
embarrassed at having shouted them, above the sound of the torrent
and beneath the skies of stone, when she always spoke in murmurs.
Only then did she understand that she had never uttered that plea.
Her scream had stopped between her temples or in the deepest part
of her throat, there, between esophagus and chest, where the mad
affirm instinctively that their identity is hidden. "It's better this way,"
she said to herself, "because we'll never be able to escape this house."

"I remember a good deal about those years: the years of our imperial infancy, with ration books," Sandro repeated. "The bimonthly
phrases with the words of the Caudillo who is dying now, and that
educational warning for girls at church doors: 'Woman, do not enter
the house of God without stockings or in short sleeves. Do not be a
tool of Judaism.' The world will say that here concludes the final military and clerical version of Fascism and Nazism. In the end, history
is summarized in simplifications in order to become comprehensible
or to amuse the mad gods who are dreaming us. It's also within the
realm of possibility that we're the ones who are mad and the gods
don't exist."

"Yes," Marina agreed quietly, "that's very possible."

" 'That was a collective madness,' a former Franquista soldier,
badly wounded at the university campus, said to me about the war.
Then I asked him, as I could ask him the day after tomorrow: 'And
this?'" He took Marina's arm and they began to descend the slope
of the oak grove behind the mill. "Perhaps your husband is the only
one who's right . . ."

"What does my husband have to do with anything?"

"In the end, history turns into poor reporting, and he believes
that all the ills of the West come from the despotism of the media. By

now, in the United States, they'll probably identify Franco with the recipients of the Order of the Yoke and the Arrows, ignoring poor Vittorio Emanuele, whom nobody remembers. Still, Germany and Italy provided fewer than four thousand trucks to Franquista Spain. The United States sent more than twelve thousand through General Motors, Ford, and Studebaker. And Texaco supplied approximately half a million tons of petroleum, with extensive credit, in each year of the conflict. Even in 1945, the Spanish deputy secretary of foreign affairs truthfully told a reporter: "Without American oil, without American trucks, without American credit, we never would have won the war."

"I didn't know all that."

"There's more. In April 1938, at a press conference, President Roosevelt stated that he had read that American-made bombs were dropped on Barcelona a few weeks earlier. This, according to what he said, was very possible and would be in compliance with perfectly legal operations. The bombs would have been sold to the German government or to German companies to be reexpedited later to the Franquista forces. The bombings of Barcelona were carried out by Italian planes, using gasoline that Mussolini imported from the USSR. Another operation that may seem paradoxical to you, although its legality is also clear. All of this, of course, is past history today, and could barely turn a windmill. In the American attack on Nagasaki, more people died than in Hiroshima. Nevertheless, no one remembers Nagasaki now, just as we all forgot about the tiny king of Italy, because great crimes absolve themselves when repeated. In another generation, more explosives would be launched in Vietnam than in the entire world during the Second World War. Historical memory in our time is nothing more or less than a 'scaling' of genocides."

"I suppose Goya would think the same thing about his time."

"Probably, although back then the art of killing was still innocent. It was limited to shooting men on a slope or stringing them up alive in a tree and quartering them afterward. No one, not even Goya, could have foreseen a century like this one." Doubtful, he tried to correct himself almost immediately. "Perhaps he did predict it after all, and we all have our place in the frescoes at the Quinta del Sordo."

In silence now, they walked down the path that climbed between groves of oaks and cork oaks. The last rains were drying in the livid earth, but the woods still smelled of wet juniper and rockrose. Down the hill, where hawthorn and giant ferns narrowed the path, another aroma of recently emerged but hidden patches of mushrooms, honey, and very old wood awaited them. In the hollow, at once distant and very near, Marina thought she could see a dark, wild grove of chestnut trees.

"Where are you taking me, Sandro?"

"We're almost there now," he replied, obliquely. "It's a very quiet backwater of forgotten history."

A dry stream ran among the chestnuts, and farther on, at regular intervals, there were abandoned gardens with grapevines and dead almond trees. At the bottom of the slope and the final incline of the path, Marina saw three stone crosses, a base of carved marble, and two gravestones. Time had begun to devour everything and the moss to turn it green; but clearly visible on the marble was the eagle, imperial before it became organically democratic, the swastika, and the emblem of the Fascio. Marina read very slowly the inscription that was being devoured by the winds: "Passerby: here the red fury rushed past, leaving as an imprint of its Satanic passage forty martyrs . . . Remember them with a prayer. 7-2-1939." It took more than a year and a half to carve the other stone: ". . . They are present in our zeal. Long live Spain! Up with Spain! 22-11-1940." Above that lost verse from *Cara al Sol* appeared the names of Colonel Domingo Rey d'Harcourt; Don José Pérez del Hoyo, lieutenant colonel of artillery; Commander Don José Pereda; Second Lieutenant in the Civil Guard Don Joaquín Rodrigo Ginés, "and thirty other martyrs." The other tablet remembered Fra Anselmo Polanco y Fontecha, bishop of Teruel; Don Felipe Ripoll Morata, vicar general; Don José Coello de Portugal, commissioner of police; Don Antonio Galea, Italian captain; Bolgioni, Italian soldier; and Gerardo Imping, German soldier.

"I can't believe it," murmured Marina.

"R. showed me the place this summer," Sandro continued. "Farther up, near the highway, there's another stele as tragic and grotesque as this one, that remembers the same crimes. The forty prisoners were killed here on February 7, 1939, in full Republican retreat, and two days before the victors reached these places. Facing the hollow you'll see that house, Molí d'en Calvet, I think it's called, where they heard the shots and saw the light of the bonfire where they tried and failed to burn the corpses. Eleven days later a shepherd happened to find the bodies, although by that time the entire village was probably concealing the tragedy. No doubt about it, this must have been the last slaughter in Cataluña before the Franquistas began their own executions. In 1941 an Augustinian published a book, written in illiterate prose, recounting the atrocity. He said there was no sign of a bullet in the bishop's remains and suggested the possibility that he had been burned alive. He affirmed that during the autopsy the body bled fresh blood, to the astonishment of the forensic scientists, and erroneously predicted the forthcoming canonization of Monsignor Polanco. He did not know or said nothing about the fact that the prelate could have saved himself."

"Let's go," Marina interrupted. "You shouldn't have brought me here without warning me."

Sandro shrugged. In the half-light of the ravine, she looked pale. And yet now she climbed the slope along ruined paths with agility. In a window of the Molí d'en Calvet, behind olive trees and yews, a light flared that seemed to be of cinnabar. From time to time a stone rebounded down the precipice. Dead leaves and broken heather rustled under their feet. A young eagle came out of nowhere and flew over them, flapping its wings, toward the foliage. Marina did not even look up to follow it. When they reached the old town highway, they were panting and slowed their pace. A laborer was digging at the side of the road, and his dog lapped three times with its pink tongue at the edge of a pond. Only then, not looking him in the eye, did Marina ask:

"How could the bishop have saved himself?"

"The day before the slaughter, Azaña had fled to France. A year and a half earlier, when his brother-in-law was consul in Geneva, the notebooks containing the diaries of the president of the Republic were stolen there. A member of the consulate had taken them to the other side as a kind of safe-conduct. Azaña wanted to recover them at any price. Part of the manuscript, with derogatory judgments and observations of Prieto, Largo Caballero, and other Republican politicians, had been published in the *ABC* of Sevilla. He was prepared to trade the papers for the prelate, but Franco did not agree to the deal. Azaña himself wrote about it in another entry, shortly before the offensive against Cataluña."

"We'll never know the price of a man."

"Or of children and women for that matter," Sandro continued. "As you read, along with Monsignor Polanco they killed Colonel Rey d'Harcourt there. They had captured them both at the fall of Teruel, which Rey d'Harcourt defended to the end and in the most desperate circumstances. When he yielded, with the written agreement of his entire general staff, Queipo de Llano accused him on Radio Sevilla of being a traitor. Apparently the Generalissimo's general headquarters could not forgive his surrendering the stronghold while still alive. If he had shot himself, the church probably would have pardoned him and the army decorated him. One never knows the correct way to die in our unhinged history."

"What do women and children have to do with it?"

"Ah!" Sandro exclaimed. "I'd almost forgotten about them. Before surrendering the fortress, when the entire city was frozen during the hardest winter of the century, without provisions, without weapons, and without a network of hospitals, Rey d'Harcourt arranged a truce with the Republicans in order to evacuate women and sick children who were freezing to death in those bombed-out ruins. A Franciscan friar, who managed to flee and reach Franco's lines across snow-covered fields, wrote later that the children and their mothers screamed their pleas for death rather than salvation by the Reds. According to our monk, everyone knew the truce was prologue to the surrender, arranged by the cowardly rabble of Rey d'Harcourt. In the opinion of that raving mad determinist, the death of innocents at the hands of the enemy was preferable to mercy from the adversary."

"Probably the friar never had any children and had desired every woman in vain," murmured Marina.

"It's possible, but it doesn't matter. If we don't know the price of a man, we can also disregard his conscience, which turns out to be totally superfluous. It seems evident that Franco's was never troubled by the death of the bishop or the sacrifice of Rey d'Harcourt when he atoned for the errors of general headquarters. He even permitted his men to thoroughly insult him before the others killed him in that ravine. In fact, sometimes the greatest solidarity exists between the victims and their executioners."

"What are you referring to?"

"I was thinking about another collective shooting, the one by Commander López Amor and Captains Lizcano de la Rosa, López Varela, and López Belda. They were the real leaders of the military uprising in Barcelona on July 19, 1936. When the insurgency failed there, a summary and hurried judgment condemned them all to the maximum penalty. I know the terrible details of their execution through the writing of two witnesses: an anarchist who took part in carrying it out and Jaume Miravitlles, who published two accounts of the incident. On the eve of his death, Lizcano de la Rosa sent a pathetic message to Miravitlles: 'You're the only friend I have left in the world. Please, be with me in the last moments.' The next morning, Miravitlles went up to the Castle de Montjuïc, where the condemned men would be shot. He did this in accordance with Lizcano's desires and probably as an official witness for the Generalitat, though this is irrelevant. At about six in the morning soldiers arrived, in uniform but lacking stripes and insignias: the firing squad and an unexpected truck filled with anarchist civilians. Among these, all armed to the teeth, was the witness I spoke to you about and whose name we'll omit. He also happened to be a friend of another prisoner, Commander López Amor, though he didn't go to Montjuïc to comfort him in his dying, but to kill him.

"In the depths of the castle, while they were preparing for the shooting, the two men shook hands. 'You came to execute me, as I suppose you people will call this tragic farce?' asked López Amor. 'I came to do my duty as a Spanish citizen in response to your Fascist rebellion.' López Amor nodded. 'Do it then, as I did mine when I rebelled. Do it quickly because you'll lose the war and then all of you will be executed.' They spoke calmly, with no rancor of any kind. Perhaps with the same serenity that the anarchist brought to his account almost forty years later. In another century, as R. once pointed out to me, Bernal Díaz del Castillo had passed judgment on the destiny of our country: you will kill and they will kill you and whoever killed you. Before they took López Amor away to stand him with his back against the wall, the two men embraced.

"Miravitlles said he would never forget Lizcano de la Rosa's eyes, fixed on his, in those eternal moments when a line in time separated his life from the death of the other man. Four black coffins awaited the remains of the men facing the rifles. López Varela, badly wounded in the battles of July 19, sat on a chair and nervously pressed a rosary in his hands. López Belda smoked with terrifying serenity and smiled carelessly. At the command to fire, Lizcano de la Rosa shouted '¡Viva España!' with all his strength. The shot was delayed a few seconds. López Belda continued smoking and smiling. '¡Viva!' shouted the militiamen in unison. The squad and all the anarchists fired at the same time, while Bernal Díaz del Castillo must have been laughing in hell. It was almost impossible to identify the mangled victims when they tried to carry them to their coffins. No, there's no doubt at all that in the black paintings at the Quinta del Sordo, we all have our place."

"I'm not very far from thinking the same way," Martina agreed. "If Goya had been born blind, we wouldn't be talking about these deaths today."

"Soon you and I will be the only ones to remember them. Most history is made up of forgetting. Those sacrificed in its name should wait for their turn in posterity. For close to forty years the legal victims of Franquismo were prohibited. I'm referring to those shot during the war and those executed in the peace, when the volleys from that ravine with the chestnut trees were barely silenced. As soon as Franco dies, we'll begin to revere many of his specters, and the other dead will be forbidden. This is the memory of justice in this country of butchers and clowns."

"Still, some dead always fiercely resist disappearing," Marina disagreed. "They also survive entire generations conceived after their time on earth."

"I suppose you're referring to Federico García Lorca."

"I was thinking of Lorca," she agreed in a quiet voice, looking down at her feet. "But I wasn't alluding to his work but to his death. They never could deny it or make it be forgotten."

"They tried in many different ways," replied Sandro. "In September 1936, a few weeks after the crime, a paper in Huelva declared, unabashedly and with no embarrassment, that Lorca had been murdered in Madrid by Marxist elements and his body tossed in the gutter. Another daily from the same province said he had been arrested and killed in Barcelona, where he had been hiding in the home of a shopkeeper. The Burgos press again situated the event in Madrid in order to round it off with the supposed upset of French literary circles at the news. The little marquis de Merry del Val declared that Lorca, whose literary merits were, in his opinion, inferior to his political zeal, had been a dangerous agitator, condemned to death by a military tribunal. Later, a journalist of the Falange from San Sebastián paid homage to the dead man, calling him a coreligionist and denouncing 'the 100,000 violins of envy' that had taken his life forever. Franco himself eventually declared to a Mexican correspondent that the loss of Lorca was regrettable, but in Granada no poets had been shot. Even in 1956 *La Estafeta Literaria* echoed the article by Schonberg—'*Enfin, la verité sur la mort de Lorca! Un assassinat, certes, mais dont la politique n'a pas été le mobile*'—that appeared in *Le Figaro Littéraire*, to change the political crime and its systematic concealment into vengeance taken by homosexuals. It was necessary for the regime to enter into its death throes so that a book like the one by José Luis Vila-San Juan could be published and we could find out the names of the real guilty parties. One of the killers boasted in the bars of Granada: 'We came to kill Federico García Lorca. I put a bullet up his ass for being a faggot.'"

"The dead bury the dead and Lorca has buried his killers," murmured Marina. "We wouldn't refer to any of them if they hadn't murdered him."

"Yes, I imagine this must be their certificate of glory, although there are some who still encourage it. If each man is capable of every crime, each people has its leprosy and its weeping, as León Felipe would say. Victims and their killers pass away, but countries survive them. More than the death of Lorca himself in that immense crime of our civil war, I am astonished and repelled by the reaction of so many right-thinking souls, who tell you even today that when they killed him they did him a favor, because he had already written his best work. This is our people, and this is the leprosy that has always consumed it."

In silence they entered the town, its streets, with their boundary stones, paved in pebbles. At Marina's suggestion they stopped in a tavern to eat. Behind the wooden bar covered with zinc, a man in a stained apron was arranging some glasses. He greeted them with a nod while they found seats along the whitewashed wall. In the fireplace kindling flared under some logs. In the rear and through a half-open door, the sound of pots and pans grew louder. On recently painted wooden shelves, bottles and cans of food were lined up. Next to the fireplace and almost at the feet of Sandro and Marina, they saw two large baskets filled with apples and dried mushrooms. From the ceiling hams hung on hooks. A gilded cage with a stuffed green bird inside, two bullfight posters from Figueras, and a couple of calendars with pictures of naked women decorated the walls. Old laborers or peasants were sitting at the round tables, watching television and waiting for the news. It smelled of vinegar, scorched meat, quicklime, and old straw.

On the screen a message from the pope was being read. "With our trust placed in God, we follow reports of the ill health of Your Excellency, to whom we renew assurance of our fervent prayers invoking divine help, and reiterate from the heart the consolation of our apostolic blessing. Paulus PP. VI." The reply was read immediately: "I have received with emotion the loving message from Your Holiness and am deeply grateful for the prayers raised to the Lord for my sake, and for your blessing, which is a great consolation. The most devoted son of Your Beatitude, Francisco Franco, Head of the Spanish State." Other news followed, all of it fairly significant. Monsignor Cantero Cuadrado, archbishop of Zaragoza and member of the Council of the Realm, had left for Madrid in a car at one in the afternoon. In Palma de Mallorca, another bishop, Monsignor Úbeda Gramaje, asked for prayers for the Caudillo. "Given the recent news regarding the illness suffered by His Excellency the Head of State, I ask all the faithful in the Diocese of Mallorca to join my prayers for the health of the illustrious patient. Priests should include this intention in their liturgical celebrations." Ministers were gathering in the presidency of the government. At two-thirty the ministers of industry and the army arrived.

Sandro drank a couple of whiskeys in three swallows, while Marina ordered roast lamb, onion soup, and chicory salad for the two of them. He barely tasted the meat and escarole but consumed an entire bottle of red wine, and had three cognacs with his coffee. Marina ate slowly and silently, not looking at him. The farmers watched them out of the corners of their eyes, amid slow whispers. A shepherd who had seen them earlier in the fields greeted them with his toothless smile. His gums were black, like those of a purebred dog. "This is the memory of justice in this country of butchers and clowns," Sandro said to himself again. Suddenly, behind his forehead, from the darkest springs of his consciousness, he heard his hidden voice again: "Those killed in silence, a silence as interminable as the silence of insomnia, looked more like marionettes than people. Then I understood that if a monster inhabited man, this monster was always a puppet." He closed his eyes, pressing his hands against his temples. He thought he had returned to the labyrinth of the Great Pyramid, where he became lost in that dream he had remembered in the mill. All the sounds in the tavern, including the commentaries on Franco's slow death, had been silenced, and the voice of another man interrogated him behind his eyelids. "Do you know for certain what our side did? Do you know their atrocities in that war?" it asked. "Of course I know them!" he replied. "I told you before that in my opinion all those slaughters were the same crime. They murdered with reason or without it. Our side did the same." "No, it isn't the same," the voice argued. "Our closest neighbor, the one with whom we instinctively tend to identify in this labyrinth, is from our country and speaks our language. It becomes as difficult to absolve him as to forget our personal guilt, because he is also the object of our individual conscience . . ." "Who can talk about conscience in our time?" it interrupted. "Who, really, when we all sold ourselves for a dish of lentils?"

He stumbled and staggered to the lavatory. The man in the stained apron followed him slowly with his eyes as he dried some glasses. Marina did not look up from the stone table. The bells in the town rang sonorous, spaced hours. Gradually the tavern emptied out. Only the old shepherd with the black gums remained in a corner, beneath the bullfight posters, to offer her his toothless smile. He saw Marina get up to whisper to the man in the stained apron. He didn't hear her words, but he could hear the clink of a ring on the zinc when she placed her palm on the bar. The tavern keeper nodded his agreement with everything the woman was telling him. He dried his hands on his apron, and they disappeared together toward the courtyard and the kitchens. Then the shepherd left some coins next to his empty glass and went out to the street, where the wind from the mountains was beginning to blow.

Sandro had passed out on the floor of the W.C., his back against the wall and his head fallen on his chest. He had vomited on himself, and his clothes stank. From time to time his hands trembled on the tiles. The tavern keeper put his apron over his shoulder and carried Sandro as if he were a butchered cow. On the street, the shepherd saw them arrange him, more or less laying him out on the back seat of the tavern keeper's old car, with Marina's lap as a pillow. Then the man in the apron got behind the wheel and the car disappeared upstream, clattering and clanking.

The tavern keeper put Sandro to bed in R.'s house and refused to accept the money Marina offered him. The hand she shook when they said goodbye was as hard as stone, but he barely dared to touch her. When she was alone, Marina undressed and cleaned Sandro with a sponge, telling herself that it resembled the washing of a corpse. Then she wrapped him in the red blanket from Momostenango that served as a bedspread; she lit the fire in the hearth in the study, and left the door to the bedroom ajar. In the Royal typewriter was a sheet of paper that seemed to conclude a biographical sketch. "An order from the King to Godoy himself demanded the registration and confiscation of María Teresa's documents, justifying this with mean-spirited reasons. *The magistrate who heard the case against the suspects in the inheritance has been able to determine that by using disloyal servants, papers had been taken from the Duchess's chest at the moment she expired.* Godoy took advantage of the lawsuit to acquire everything the Queen had cast aside, including Velázquez's *Venus with a Mirror,* along with all the other paintings that had belonged to María Teresa. Beggars, servants, the son of Don Francisco de Goya Lucientes, and the jester Benito would never see any part of all that legitimately belonged to them." She picked up the sheet at a corner with her fingertips and turned the roller in order to continue reading the last paragraph. "The belongings of the Prince of Peace were sequestrated in 1808 following the revolt of Aranjuez, and his canvases were moved into the Cristales storehouse and an inventory made of the works of art on his estate. Entry 122, published in 1919 by Aureliano de Beruete, described: *Two paintings five feet, four inches high by six feet, ten inches wide, one representing a naked Venus on the bed, the other a clothed woman of the lower classes, by Francisco de Goya.*' She poked the fire, which tended to go out, making an effort to think of nothing but the burning heather. Through the window she looked at the woods, where they had carried logs to the tripods. In the vast gray landscape of the valley, naked branches would gleam at times. Before dusk the first snows would arrive. Helplessly she evoked "The Dead," the last story in *Dubliners,* which R. had lent to her in translation when she dropped out of the university after the miscarriage. At a winter dance, a melody awakens in a woman the memory of a dead man whom she had loved. When she returns from the party, while she is falling asleep, her husband begins to share his memories. Then he notices in the sleeping face of his wife that beauty is beginning to give way to age. He feels deeply and strangely joined to the dead boy who used to sing that distant song. Through the window a heavy, silent snow is falling on Dublin. Intangible time melts into interminable serenity, while the snow crosses the sky as if the final hour of all the living and all the dead had arrived in order to conclude silently in nothingness.

She heard coughs and groans from the bedroom. Sandro was sitting on the bed. He was shaking and holding his head, pressing his palms against his ears. Marina saw him again as she had found him that morning, at the bottom of the mill: absorbed in a world unknown to her where her words lost all meaning and her very presence was an intrusion.

"What did you say? Were you calling me?"

"No, no, I must have been talking in my sleep."

"You called me." Her tone vacillated ambiguously between affirmation and question.

"I didn't call anyone, Marina, I assure you." He shook his head again, then looked at her with squinting eyes, as if he couldn't quite place her image. "Leave now, I beg you. Go and leave me alone in this house with my damn book."

"Go? Where would I go?"

"Wherever you like!" He began to be exasperated. "Go back to your husband, if he'll take you back, or go to the devil! Choose for yourself, because it makes absolutely no difference to me! Before you said you'd leave whenever you pleased, because our affair was always senseless. Well then, leave right now, whether you want to or not!"

"No, I won't leave." All hesitation had disappeared from her voice. Her tone was firm but polite, as if she had given herself an unbreakable order, ripened in long reflection.

"What's this about? Why do you contradict yourself this way? You were prepared to leave when you felt like it!"

"I can also disagree with myself, because at bottom I know very well I ought to leave you. Still, I have other reasons for not doing it."

"What reasons are those? Death and damnation! Get out once and for all and leave me alone! I don't need you to work! I don't need you to get drunk or to go crazy!"

"No," replied Marina deliberately, "you need me only to survive."

"This is my business. I'm my only master."

"I'm also mistress of my staying. I won't leave you. That's my final word."

"If necessary, I'll throw you out bodily!"

"No, Sandro, you won't. Can it be you don't understand that I can't leave you as I left my husband?" Perplexed, she seemed to waver for a moment. Then she said: "As you abandoned your children."

Enraged, he hit her on the mouth with the back of his hand. Marina fell back on the red bedspread and seemed more astonished than hurt as she looked at him with wide-open eyes. In a lethargic gesture she raised her thin blond eyebrows without actually frowning. A thread of blood crossed her half-open mouth. In vain she tried to resist when Sandro, naked and howling like a savage, threw himself on her. He hit her again, this time with his closed fist, on her forehead and ears. Then he took her though she was dressed, immobile and enervated, like a grotesque mannequin. With open eyes she looked at the white ceiling. Through her tears, it was changing into a slow snowfall that silently moved across space and time in the empty firmament of stars and men.

Panting, Sandro collapsed beside her. In the fireplace in the study, a log split by the fire fell with a dry, muffled sound. Marina wiped the blood from her lips with a hand that did not tremble. Suddenly she bit her knuckles to stifle an unexpected scream that was burning her throat. She did not hate Sandro. She thought that perhaps she had loved him once, though she had forgotten when. All her rancor, a cold, distant rancor that one would feel toward a mythological monster, was for R. He could foresee their destiny, hers and Sandro's, in some inexplicable way, but he had no right to determine it, even when Marina knew he was hidden nearby, watching them dispassionately like an old voyeur. One could say that even the story by Joyce, with the snowfall into which the ceiling was gradually transformed through her tears (the story lent by R. almost thirty years earlier) was another piece of that puzzle, summarized in a hell made to her measure and Sandro's.

Sandro moaned again between gasps, his head wrapped in the pillow. Under his brows he heard that voice, identical to his, in stray pieces like those in a dream. "Grandpa," a little girl was saying to him, "if men are puppets, who's playing with them?" Immediately he heard himself respond: "Time, my little magpie, time that devours everything, like mice and wood borers. Only you will remain forever, like an eternal flower, in the middle of the universe and beneath the stars." "The Living Skeleton told me at the circus that one day I'd teach drawing to a queen." "It must be true, little magpie, because he spoke every language." Trembling, he dozed off without silencing the whispers inside his ears. Quietly, and knowing he didn't hear her, Marina murmured:

"No, I'll never leave you in this state."

At midnight they found themselves sitting in the study, eating bread and foie gras. Marina washed it down with wine and Sandro avidly drank glasses of mineral water. They spoke of trifles, avoiding each other's eyes. The snow that had threatened in the afternoon didn't appear this time. The wind blew the storm out to sea and then quieted down on a cold, clear autumn night. The last report stated that at 23:10 hours the clinical situation of His Excellency the Head of State was stable. He was resting quietly and his vital signs were constant. They said his level of consciousness was normal.

TAUROMACHY

THE DREAM OF REASON

Wild Bull

The painting had been in the former collection of the duke and duchess de Veragua, and an old copy, executed perhaps by Esteve or Vicente López, was the property of the marquis and marquise de Casa Torres. It is oil on canvas, seventy-five centimeters wide by eighty centimeters high, shown for the first time in the exposition *Art in Tauromachy*, which opened in Madrid in 1918.

It represents a life-size head of a fighting bull, which fills almost the entire canvas, against a mottled sky. It is an enormous, bluish-black animal, with a white muzzle and wide-spread horns. Blood drips from the end of one of the pikes and spills onto his left flank. Different blood, a more fiery red, fills his inordinately staring eyes around the glittering pupils. Also covered in blood, though dimmed and resembling cinnabar, is the tongue of the wounded, panting animal. A salmon pink cape, its other side silvery, spills over the thick neck. One would say the animal carried it off in the same charge that gored or killed a banderillero, because two broken barbed darts still dangle from the bull's side.

The subject is a live bull in the middle of a bullfight, Gudiol states unnecessarily. Even more incredible, José María de Cossío refrains from citing the painting in *Bulls*. In this case it would have been better to omit the world, because for the painter the entire universe was reduced to the head of this animal. The tiers of seats and men disappeared. Even the firmament disappeared, because the background of jasper or feldspar has nothing to do with the heavens.

Perhaps it is a glimpse of hell, or it might be that hell itself has turned into nothingness in this moment of truth. Our point of view, outside the painting, is the same as the painter's, a step away from the beast. If he or we were to extend a hand, we would touch the horns or the panting maw. ("His eyes did not shut/when he saw the horns close by." And the executioner in his joy at fulfilling his duty: "We just came from killing Federico García Lorca. I put a bullet up his ass for being a faggot.") Although he paints from memory, Goya looks closely into the eyes of the bull. Perhaps in them he sees us, as in the eyes of the beast we can sense him.

Even if I didn't know the original, I would swear that in the world there is no representation of a wild bull more powerful. Possibly there never will be. Picasso's minotaur and the horned bull in *Guernica* are effeminate versions of this incomparable beast. (When I showed it to Marina in the catalogue, to ask her whether she would like to see the painting, she shook her head of a doll that had forgotten to age. "No, absolutely not," she told me. "I'd be afraid of going blind afterward." I was right then not to doubt it, because this head of a bull is at the same time the head of the Gorgon, who even when decapitated blinds men with her dead eyes.)

The painting is not dated. Josep Gudiol believes Goya probably painted it during his slow convalescence, following the illness that deafened him and kept him for an entire year, between 1792 and 1793, on the brink of death. Toward the end of that agony, and permanently deaf, he wrote his most quoted letter to Zapater: "I'm the same as far as my health is concerned, sometimes raging with a temper that not even I can stand, at other times more moderate, like this moment when I have taken up the pen to write to you, although I'm already tired. I'll tell you only that on Monday, God willing, I'll go to see the bulls and I would like you to accompany me next Monday, even if I said foolish things about your having gone crazy. Your Paco."

The greatest artist of the two centuries that his life spanned never learned syntax or orthography. To become Goya he would have to forget the drawing he learned in his youth, first from José Luján, and then from his brother-in-law Bayeu. In this way he broke and eliminated contours and outlines. In the only reality, he affirms, triumphant and in anticipation of Cubism: "I do not distinguish more than luminous bodies and dark bodies; planes that advance and planes that retreat; reverses and concavities." After the illness that enclosed him in the silence of deafness, Goyaesque harmony was not reduced to the limits of "divine" reason but became centered in the total truth of creatures. To be is to know you are other. To know you are, for example, this black, wounded bull, blood flaring in the whites of his eyes.

Human reason, the reason in which Goya had believed with the faith of the convert two years earlier ("I have gotten it into my head that I should maintain a specific idea and maintain a certain dignity which man ought to possess, and this, believe me, does not make me very happy"), human reason, I repeat in order not to lose my train of thought, was found outside the painting and was identified with the painter, and with us when we shared his point of view face to face with the animal. By way of contrast, the bull would be nature, fierce, brutal, and dark, with the blood of another on the tip of his horn, though paradoxically vulnerable in his monstrous power. ("Oh white wall of Spain! / Oh black bull of grief!" "Have you shot world-famous Spanish writers?" they asked Franco. "The truth is that in the first moments of the revolution in Granada, that writer died mixed in with the agitators; these are the natural accidents of war. Granada was under siege for many days and the madness of the Republican authorities in distributing weapons to the people gave rise to flare-ups in the interior, and in one of them the Granadan poet lost his life.... As we have said, we did not shoot any poet.") The confrontation of nature and reason would be enough to catalogue the painting if the eyes of the animal were not so obsessive. Goya would have painted this head with a very different, less intriguing gaze before his illness, when according to Cardadera he would go to the bullfights wearing a soft broad-brimmed hat, frock coat, a cape draped across his shoulder, and a dress sword, to talk at length with the bullfighters beside the barrier. Now, with the labyrinth of his ear sealed off, and lost in the delirium of his mortal illness, he learned to believe in the specters of his nightmares as he did in himself. Long before Freud denounced his fellow men for parricide and incest, Goya discovered Saturn inside himself, devouring his children at a witches' sabbath. The eyes of this fighting bull belonged to the choir of monsters that populated his soul and inhabited the man. He had seen them in the absurdities of his hallucinations as he approached death. If Gudiol dated the painting correctly, as soon as Goya knew he would survive he rushed to paint them from memory, beneath the horns of the beast.

The eyes of the minotaur that Picasso sketched among his notes for *Guernica* were those of Picasso himself, which were not too large or too dark, according to Brassäi. They seemed enormous due to his singular ability to open them very wide, even above the iris, where the light glitters and is reflected on the sclera. ("Screams of children, screams of women, screams of birds, screams of flowers, screams of pieces of wood and of stones, screams of bricks, screams of furniture, of beds, of chairs, of curtains, of casseroles, of cats, and of papers, screams of odors that scratch one another. . . . In Granada they murdered Federico García Lorca, in Salamanca they shouted 'Death to intelligence!' *'Enfin la verité sur la mort de Lorca! Un assassinat, certes, mais dont la politique n'a pas été le mobile.'*")

The eyes of this bull of death came from deeper abysses. They were the eyes of Saturn, which Goya saw in fits of fever, and which he would paint a quarter of a century later in the dining room of the Quinta del Sordo. They were equally large and savage, although those of the animal filled with blood and those of the monster glinted with bestial hunger. (Marina feared going blind in the presence of that painting. A few days ago I took her when I was drunk, howling for my children. Then we fell asleep in each other's arms. She woke me hours later, because my shouts frightened her. I lied when I told her

I remembered nothing of my nightmare. I had forgotten the images but not the voices of that dream. One, that seemed to be mine when I recalled it, was exclaiming: "There's no need to scream like that. I already told you I read lips!" Someone, I don't know who, replied: "I'll scream all I want. You outlived your wife, who was good only for bearing you the children you destroyed with your syphilis, but I don't know how you could outlive your own duplicity and indecency. I mean to say, I do know, since with your cowardice, they made you in the image and likeness of our people.")

If this fighting bull had been Saturn before, it would soon be transformed into the ragged man murdered in *The Third of May, 1808, in Madrid: The Shootings on Príncipe Pío Hill.* The eyes of the horned beast became the eyes of the man who was told he would be executed at dawn. The bloody gaze of the animal, who had charged and gored there, is brightened here and illuminated by the beam of a gigantic lantern. We pass from the monster to the bull; from the bull to the man sacrificed by his fellow men. The monster was Saturn or Time, father of the gods and devourer of his own children. They called the animal the bull of death and it was prepared and raised for goring and sacrifice. The man was unemployed, a beggar, a muleteer or a mason. He died proclaiming the injustice of that crime and paradoxically shouting: "Death to liberty! Long live our chains!" To the greater glory of the faith of his people, perhaps he also shouted: "Long live the Inquisition!"

("It's finished; what happened? Look at his figure: / death has covered him with pallid sulfur, / has placed on him the head of a dark minotaur." *La Estafeta Literaria*, October 13, 1956: "At last, we must say, the rock of scandal has been broken. For twenty years using the death of García Lorca as a political tool! Of course this is an international action, neither unique nor original. But after all, the fact of the death of the Granadan poet had to be exploited without scruples or honor, even at the cost of committing the most painstaking, vile, and systematic deception of people of good faith. Those public acts, those solemn recitals of his works, that constant waving of his name as a victim, those crocodile tears. Who does not remember?" Along the path of the same first-rate prose, so typical of this beautiful nation of sun and lies, as my friend Carlos del Valle Inclán would have written, the anonymous commentator continued: "At last, the French writer J. L. Schonberg, author of the most comprehensive and documented biography of the poet, has come to Spain several times between 1953 and 1956, has traveled through Andalucía, visiting towns close to Granada, has spoken with those he has deemed appropriate or necessary. He has done research in archives, inspected locations. And, at last, he has reached this conclusion: *De politique, pas question. La politique, s'etait alors la purge que vous évacuait sans preámbule.*")

If the bull of death was transformed into the prisoner in *The Third of May, 1808, in Madrid*, twenty years later *The Shootings on Príncipe Pío Hill* became, in turn, the palimpsest of the most savage bullfight. On various occasions Goya had declared that his great teachers were nature and Velázquez. The plane of lowered bayonets, held by the firing squad in *The Third of May, 1808, in Madrid*, could be a horizontal version of the Velazquean lances in *The Surrender at Breda*. It could also be seen as the repeated metaphor of the long straight horns of the bull painted by Goya twenty years earlier. In fact, in the *Fierce Bullfight of the People in the Plaza Partida*, an oil executed around 1810 and today in the collection of the Metropolitan Museum in New York, another black bull, with horns almost as slender and parallel as the bayonets of the firing squad, charges a picador mounted on a white horse.

The myth of the minotaur is almost as ancient as the myth of Saturn. The monster, for the Greeks, child of a bull and the queen of Crete, had a human body and a horned head. Ovid calls him *semibovenque virum, semivirumque bovem*. Dante believed he was a bull with the head of a man. In the seventh circle of hell, where the violent suffer, the poet encountered the beast wearing the mask of a person: *"en su la punta della rotta laca / l'infamia di Creti era distesa / che fu concetta nella falsa vaca.*" Borges supposed the legend was the expurgated result of other older, more terrible ones that were then mysteriously forgotten. In reality everything must have happened in reverse, because the myth of that monster was the augury of greater horrors.

The firing squad in Goya's painting lacks faces and almost lacks forms. Seen from the back and in the light of the lantern, it is almost impossible to decide how many soldiers are in it. In this way the squad becomes a compact ensemble of greatcoats, knapsacks, and straps, almost completely dehumanized. The rifles, lengthened by the bayonets, appear beneath the dark shakos and outline the image of a herd of long-horned bulls, wounding the air in their charge. The knapsacks of this troop, hunched to better assure the shot, heighten the illusion of the humps of bulls crammed together as they charge. Only their arms, legs, and feet in ordinary shoes belong to men, while torsos and heads are transformed into the loins and necks of fierce bulls. A herd of furious minotaurs springs up simultaneously in the dark to consummate a sacrifice.

("The cow of the old world / passed its sad tongue / over a muzzle of bloods / spilled in the sand, / and the bulls of Guisando, / almost death and almost stone, / bellowed like two centuries / weary of walking the earth." On March 11, 1937, a certain Luis Hurtado or Urbano Álvarez, who at one time boasted of an old friendship with Federico García Lorca, and of "blood shed in the most intense exposure of a battlefield," wrote in the Falangist paper *Unidad*, of San Sebastián: "Your body fell, forever, and your laughter was erased from the maps; and the earth trembled through your agonizing hands when it felt the arrival of your spirit. And yet I cannot resign myself to believing that you have died; you cannot die. The Falange awaits you; its welcome is biblical. Comrade, your faith has saved you. No one like you to harmonize the poetic and religious doctrine of the Falange, to gloss its points, its aspirations. They have murdered the best poet of Imperial Spain. Spanish Falange, with its arm on high, pays homage to your memory by hurling to the four winds its most powerful HERE

PRESENT. Your body now is silence, silence nonexistent and dark: but you continue living, intensely alive in the forms that throb and the life that sings. Apostle of light and of laughter. Andalucía and Greece remember you. UP WITH SPAIN!!").

"We have seen," writes Moratín, "a man sitting in a chair or on a table, with shackles on his feet, place the banderillas and kill a bull." *Martincho*, or Martín de Barcáiztegui, a native of Oyarzun immortalized four times by Goya in his *Tauromachy*, set the banderillas in the manner of Melchor Calderón, that is, divided in two and driven in like daggers or blows, on occasion going down on his knees as he incited the bull. The prisoners in *The Third of May, 1808, in Madrid* also die on their knees. Their executioners made them kneel to humiliate them before shooting them point-blank. In the muleteers, beggars, unemployed, farmhands, and laborers, the men of the Legion de Réserve, also from the depths of society, found even humbler victims whom they obliged to abase themselves when it was time to sacrifice them. This murder in an open space does not maintain the appearance of executions in Christian, civilized countries. Here there is no surrendering of weapons or coups de grace. Prisoners are sentenced in clusters and allowed to sauté in their own blood, while others are herded together at bayonet point to be destroyed with more shots, three steps from their eyes. Only the time of the crime is the correct one for *real* shootings, as Hugh Thomas so carefully reminds us. Which is to say, before dawn, at the hour of the minotaur.

In a lecture delivered in 1926, Don Ventura Bagüés commented on another etching from the *Tauromachy*, in which the aforementioned *Martincho*, inciting the bull with movements of his body, places the banderillas. According to this critic, that kind of placement belongs to an old kind of banderillero called *topa-carnero*, which soon fell into disuse. In this primitive, fearsome variant, the body movements were not indicated until the bull entered the bullfighter's territory and lowered its head to charge. It is very well known that *Martincho* set pairs in this way, kneeling, without ever being gored. On his knees before the minotaur, the human monster with several shako heads and bayonets for horns, Goya's ragged man raises his arms and opens his palms, as if he were inciting the monster in order to pierce him with invisible bandilleras. In the unreason of despair, this supposedly rational martyr, who perhaps dies cheering the Holy Office, refuses to surrender to the monstrosity that is half bull and half man, which is the final and most sarcastic dream of reason. *The Third of May, 1808, in Madrid*, must therefore be the great bullfight painted by Goya to celebrate the return of the most undesirable of kings, Fernando VII. That bull of 1793, the one with the blood on its horn and the salmon pink cape on its hump, has been transformed into this squad of executioners. If the ragged man they are going to execute or murder, supposing that the terms are not synonymous ("How awful with the final / banderillas of darkness!") were to extend his hands instead of raising them, open, in the night, he would brush against the bayonets of the firing squad, as we could have touched the horns of that fighting bull.

("But now he sleeps without end. / Now the mosses and the grass / open with unerring fingers / the flower of his skull. / And now his blood comes singing: / singing through marshes and meadows, / slipping along horns numb with cold, / slipping soulless through the fog / finding thousands of hooves / like a long, dark, sad tongue." They killed him at daybreak on August 20, 1936, along with two banderilleros, a lame teacher, and his son. The crime took place on the road from Viznar to Fuente Grande, Ainadamar in Arabic, Fountain of Tears. José Luis Vila-San Juan cites the authorized view of the commander of military interventions and the civil governor of Granada at that time, José Valdés Guzmán: "All teachers are reds." The teacher for the Paulines was missing a leg. He had been detained by a police officer with whom he had quarreled. When his son tried to protest, they took him away too. Neither one could have foreseen then that a few days later, both would be killed along with Federico García Lorca. Nobody knows with certainty where their bones lie, among the olive trees or in a ravine that served as a grave for hundreds of victims. An old gravedigger believes he recognized the teacher's corpse because of his one leg, and remembers Lorca's very well because of his ascot. Many years later he told Ian Gibson: "You know, those things artists wear." The death certificate for the poet attributes his death to "wounds produced by an act of war." There could not be a better title, or a more sinister euphemism, for one of the crimes that Goya etches in his *Disasters*.)

Hugh Thomas writes that Goya's ragged man, the anonymous martyr who incites the minotaur with invisible banderillas, is going to die immediately. Nothing or no one can save him. In an instant a volley will sink him into eternity, as the dry thrust of the horns of a wounded bull might have done.

Yet the volley has been delayed for more than 200 years. For more than 160 years that man has defied it on his knees and with his arms open wide. His moment of truth, perhaps at the brink of hell, is eternalized in the longest of agonies. In 1939 the prisoner, the dead, their killers, and the night that envelops all of them, almost disappeared when another war was about to devour the painting. Evacuated with the entire museum to save it from the bombing raids on Madrid, *The Third of May, 1808* was taken to Las Torres de los Serranos, in Valencia. From there it was sent to Cataluña, where it and the Prado followed the withdrawal of the Republicans, first to France and then to Geneva. In an open truck the canvas crossed a bombarded Mataró. The metal railing of a balcony, broken and twisted by shrapnel, tore the canvas behind the squad's lantern. In the Castillo de Peralada and in the so-called Museo del Vidrio, Mateu's collection of crystal, the steward's grandmother's nightgown was sewn onto the back to restore the painting.

In one of Borges's tales, "The Secret Miracle," a Jewish scholar is condemned to death in Prague by the Nazis. The night before his execution he is overcome by the terror of being shot to death. Hanging or beheading would not have frightened him in the same way; but the circumstances of his death seem more terrible to him than his own irrevocable destiny. The scholar prays to God that if in some way He exists, if He isn't an erratum or a repetition of Divinity, he be allowed to conclude his play *The Enemies* before he is killed. He begs for only a year to finish it. Facing the firing squad he hears the command, sees the officer raise his arm (Borges has a somewhat operatic sense of Hitlerian executions, which tended to be less ceremonial), hears the order to fire, and sees the arm suspended in air in a truncated gesture.

(In R.'s library a few nights ago, I consulted the passage while Marina was sleeping and the tramontane howled as if it wanted to pull out our souls by the roots. Until that point, the account proceeded essentially as I remembered it. Having reached the secret wonder, the shooting and the earth halted in time, I read, shuddering in astonishment: "*The wind had ceased as in a painting.*" Only much later, when the other wind had also ceased, the one that crashed against the walls and windows of the house, did I notice that R. had underlined that phrase in red, to remind me of it. There could be no doubt, and before I could anticipate it, he had focused on the hidden origin of *The Secret Miracle*, the painting that a blind writer would silently transform into one of his fables.) Time is suspended and the prisoner concludes the play. Then a volley erases him from the face of the earth. In *One Hundred Years of Solitude*, when, before another firing squad preparing to shoot him, Colonel Aureliano Buendía recalls his life and the history of a paradise founded and lost by his people, Gabriel García Márquez also breaks with Borges and *The Secret Miracle*, although afterward no one executes him. These literary versions are marginal and contingent. They would not have existed if Goya had not painted *The Third of May, 1808, in Madrid*. In contrast to what happened in *Las Meninas*, in which Velázquez captures only a fleeting instant between instants, Goya paralyzes time when the ragged man on his knees spreads his arms before the muzzles of the rifles. That is what one of those birds from another age, immobilized forever in amber in midflight, would say.

Naturally, the time that is arrested is not only historical; if it were, *The Third of May, 1808, in Madrid* would be a simple act of propaganda. The painting transcends the circumstances of its commission, as Goya survives Fernando VII. At the same time, the amber of its time attracts other beings and destinies and identifies them with those who remain immobilized there. A bull, painted twenty years earlier (which in another evolution of its species will become Saturn) is transformed into the man who rebukes the firing squad with his arms spread wide. Two lines by Lorca, "His eyes did not close / when he saw the horns approach" combine this prisoner sentenced to death with a poet murdered 123 years later. Another pair of Lorquian lines from the same poem ("How awful with the final / banderillas of darkness!") move the crime from the canvas to a bullfight. That ragged man, who was a bull, who was Lorca, is transformed now into *Martincho* inciting the bull with banderillas at topa-carnero. Two banderilleros fall with Lorca on the Ainadamar road without anyone drawing up a document regarding their "death caused by an act of war," because all the dead are pugnacious rabble and all the teachers are reds. By means of another of Goya's bulls that three years earlier charged a white horse, the firing squad in *The Shootings on Príncipe Pío Hill* is transfigured into a repeated minotaur, with bayonets for horns.

"There's not a single being on earth capable of knowing who he is," R. said on the morning I met Marina, before I knew that the phrase wasn't his but Léon Bloy's. The entire theory of evolution, the unanimous metamorphosis that goes from fishes to men like Fernando VII and Franco, passing through all monsters, and from *The Third of May, 1808, in Madrid* to *One Hundred Years of Solitude*, through *The Secret Miracle*, seems to confirm that certainty, in art and in life.

Silently, with restrained shock, I wonder who I might be and who Don Francisco Goya Lucientes might have been.

March 27, 1828

The bullring burned in the sun and the tiers of seats were deserted. Up above, an oceanic midday blue, without clouds and without birds. A blue so uniform and radiant I thought it opened over the exact center of the firmament.

On the king's balcony, facing the bullpens, His Majesty Don Carlos IV smiled distractedly and, like a *majo*, a lower-class dandy, leaned his elbows on the railing, adorned with a tapestry that had the standard of Castilla embroidered on it. Queen María Luisa, in black and enveloped in tulle, fanned herself and looked at the sky. Among the very Catholic sovereigns, I saw the deceased monarch Don Carlos III, may God bless him and keep him in His glory. He was yellowed and seemed to have as bad a cold as in the first audience he granted me in my youth. I thought I hadn't known until then that ghosts were subject to ailments and caught cold in the middle of the summer. From time to time the dead king extended a translucent hand and Doña María Luisa would hand him a lace handkerchief that she took from her bosom. Then His Majesty would blow his nose very delicately, with only two fingers, and spit into the bullring. Then he would return the handkerchief to his august daughter-in-law, as if he were giving her his hand to kiss, and she kept it, crumpled into a ball, between her breasts. When he blew his nose, Don Carlos would show me his profile of an exhausted phantom. Death had made him thinner, raising his cheekbones and brows beneath his pale skin. A long blue vein, like the sky itself, crossed his neck from ear to jabot. "As a young man they took me for a hungry greyhound, and now I resemble a poorly grazed sheep," he said to me with a smile as I prepared to paint him in a hunting outfit. "How are you going to portray me so I finally know who I am?"

My Josefa sat next to the queen. Her lips were pursed, like two withered petals, and her eyes were fixed on the empty stands. I looked at the deep, sharp eyes of the entire Bayeu family: the stare of people descended from ancient shepherds on dry, barren land, accustomed to brooding a great deal and jealously guarding their thoughts. A shout choked back in the middle of my gullet burned my mouth and jaws as I watched her. Now Josefa held our dead children on her lap. There was Vicente Anastasio, as white as he was that dawn when we found him stiff in his cradle, a thread of blood between his lips. There were my two unfortunate little girls, María del Pilar Dionisia, with her gargoyle's head and flattened forehead, and poor Hermenegilda, the one they baptized in a great rush because Josefa brought her into the world asphyxiated. There was my Francisco de Paula, the one who died laughing in my arms, as if an unseen bolt of lightning had snatched him away. From time to time the queen turned to the shades of the children to smile or caress their heads with the edge of her fan. Then the backing of her fan would open and close, close and open to the clicking sound of the ribs.

They had smoothed and cleaned the sand as if preparing it for a bullfight. But the barriers and projections called out for a good coat of paint, and the enclosures were split by horn thrusts. Alone in the center of the arena, under the eyes of the living and the dead, I felt naked and diminished among the empty rows of seats. Avoiding the eyes of my children, I lowered my head and saw my shadow grow pointed on the ground, like a tongue or a pike. In my right hand I held my watch, attached to a long gold chain. It was the one my father had given me when I came back from Italy in my youth. It never gained or lost a second, and it had never stopped. I always carried it attached to my cummerbund, my shirt, or my frock coat. Every night when I went to bed I wound it completely and put it under my pillow. Then I fell asleep listening to its sound of a tiny stream forever returning to its own sources. With that tick-tock beneath our pillows, Josefa and I conceived our dead children; we dreamed about them as adults before they were engendered and wept for their deaths, licking away each other's tears. With that tick-tock under my ears, my eyes open in the dark, my neck resting on my crossed hands, one insomniac night I imagined my paintings of time through the passing of the seasons, *The Flower Girls, The Threshing Floor, The Grape Harvest,* and *The Snowfall,* to illuminate the nuptial chambers of Prince Gabriel, in El Escorial, when he was betrothed to Doña María Ana. In the meantime, and in the brilliant stillness of the empty bullring, the queen's fan opened and closed, closed and opened, bringing together and separating the ribbing of her fan there on the royal balcony.

I didn't notice another sound then because the watch had stopped at twelve sharp, just at noon. I carried the mute disk to my ear, then held it in my palm and looked at it, baffled. My astonishment was no greater when I realized I was standing and that my heart had stopped in my chest. I tried to beg for the assistance of the living and of the specters in the box, as they had begun to call the balconies at bullfights then, but they seemed to disregard my mute pleas. The old dead king looked at his nails and smiled to himself. (*Allora, appena il crepuscolo, il giorno comincia a scolorire e nel traspasso de colori tutto rimane calmo,* he had told me about twilights in Madrid at my first audience). In the arena, however, it was midday, and at precisely twelve, exactly twelve, my watch stopped. At that bewildered point I remember saying to myself that perhaps everything was happening in reverse, and the watch hadn't stopped, but time. It was held back this way in each of those pictures of mine, painted for the prince's wedding, in which the hours stood still in four moments of four seasons.

His Majesty Don Carlos IV, fortunately reigning, still leaned on the railing like a picador on the planks. (*Saper fare e condursi a aquel modo.* "No one can resist my blows, the hardest grooms fall like ninepins. When you return we'll fight with the bar in the stables, and then I'll play the violin for you, if you like.") Suddenly he raised his hand and the queen closed her fan. Josefa held our dead children even closer, and the specter of the old king shook his cold-ridden head with tiresome fatigue. The doors of the bullpen had just opened by themselves, and out came a black bull with wide-spread horns; he would carry away the barrier on half of his forehead. He charged straight ahead, bellowing, his tongue visible at the side of his muzzle. He came toward me, staring at me, as a man would whose brother had just castrated him. His eyes were enormous and shining, the whites filled with blood and the pupils jet-black with fury. I realized that this bull was my executioner and that my own children had condemned me to this death for having sired them dead, and the sovereigns for daring to judge them while they were alive. I wasn't afraid and I didn't try to flee during those hurried, interminable moments. It satisfied me to feel that the hand holding the watch by the chain was firm, and to know that the beating of blood in my chest was regular and calm.

The dream must have cut off my shout and transformed it into panting, because the first gleam of consciousness was to realize I hadn't heard it. I sat up in my nightshirt among the tangled sheets and blankets on the bed, while Dr. Arrieta had his arms around my shoulders, making an effort to hold me down. Josefa, upset and thinner than ever, was trying to wipe the sweat from my hands and forehead with a towel that had long fringes. Gradually, with the labored confusion of a half-sleeping animal, I recognized my own bedroom, as if I were returning to the room after a very long absence. There was the marble-topped bureau in whose drawers my wife scented the clothes with quince, and the image of the Virgin del Pilar, which Josefa brought to the marriage with her dowry, and my parents' crucifix. Also on the wall was the cartoon of *El Parasol*, in a copy I had made for Josefa when I was working in the Royal Tapestry Factory of Santa Bárbara. Two adolescents looked at me from the picture. The boy protected the girl with a green sunshade, its cap round and pink, while a little black dog, curved like a whiting, slept in the girl's skirts. Behind the couple, the breeze made a willow tree sway.

Slowly I was remembering what had happened: the Calvary of my illness, at the end of which I had just regained consciousness. It all began with sudden, terrible headaches that seemed to set my brains on fire inside my skull. There was no chamomile, no vinegars, heat, or medicines that could relieve the pain. Then it got worse as it passed from my forehead and temples to my ears, as if two scorpions had taken shelter in the wax of one ear only to make their way very slowly to the other. Then I lost consciousness and sank into an interminable nightmare, though I retained the memory only of some fragments of that delirium. I saw part of what I would etch in *The Caprices* and *The Absurdities*. Two old bawds and a pair of seductive girls sweeping away three plucked chickens with shaved human heads. The same old hags and flashy girls impaling another live chicken with a human face beneath a shrub where birds with known features were perched. One, fan-tailed and with large open wings, was me, wearing a ruff, a rapier hanging around my neck, and a low-crowned hat with a rolled brim. Another, a pigeon with a woman's breasts, hair tied back with white ribbons, seemed the living image of María Teresa. Skeletons with parchment-like skin, followed by ancient harpies, persisted in raising the tombstones of their graves beneath a setting sun as red as an egg. A girl dressed in white rode a bay with an extremely long mane, standing in the saddle and secured by glossy reins. The horse, in turn, stood on a slender rope that bent under the hooves of that mount with a robust gait. Some Turks were teaching a chestnut elephant how to read in a book as big as the tablets of the law. Aged, open-mouthed friars crowded in ecstasy at the foot of a pulpit where a parrot preached from the railing. The bird, pompous and full of himself, raised a claw in the shadows to emphasize the profundity of his sermons. In a landscape of processions and spires, two naked devils were in animated conversation. Half the head and chin of one were human, but the face resembled a bird's, with an eye and a brow in the middle of the beak. The other had very long, fine-drawn lines; his ears drooped like those of a Dalmatian dog. With closed eyes and hands piously crossed, he at once resembled a mastiff, a pig, and a friar. Both monsters were mounted on donkeys with the torsos and hooves of hairy gorillas. Dawn was breaking behind the hill of the witches' sabbath, while distance made a town on the plain smaller. In the air a cretin sat astride an owl, while a pair of sorcerers settled an obese naked woman on their shoulders. A cat, grasping a tiny open umbrella, ascended with them toward the orgy. A flashy girl, half her face covered by her shawl and her eyes looking to the side, stretched on tiptoe on an adobe wall to pull out the teeth of a hanged man, while a monkey intoned madrigals for a donkey, accompanied by a large guitar and the men's applause.

Monsters, executed criminals, penitents in *sanbenitos*, witches, devils, whores, fops, duennas, chimeras, lovers, goblins, monks, maidens, streetwalkers, hunchbacks, bailiffs, prisoners, bandits, misers, bullfighters, painters, muffled men, men in mourning, notaries, executioners, barbers, beggars, street vendors, men with huge heads, giants, Arabs, clowns, blood-letters, masqueraders, men sentenced to hard labor, tailors, fetuses, overly pious women, decrepit old men, lions, owls, cats, sheep, bats, cockatoos, sparrows, hedgehogs, male goats, donkeys, turkeys, spiders, leopards, chimpanzees, dogs, chicks, bears, foxes, rats, worms, fireflies, elephants, tigers, fish, eagles, horses, moles, rabbits, turtles, salamanders, wolves, falcons, lizards. In a moment of darkness, that rout suddenly melted into the empty bullring, except for the monarchs' box, where I awaited the defeat of the young, high-horned bull, my watch hanging from its chain. Awake, I recalled with complete clarity that final dream at the end of my delirium, and reliving it I noticed that the pain in my temples and ears had disappeared, leaving my skull feeling empty. Yet I believed I was witnessing another nightmare with my eyes wide open. Josefa and Dr. Arrieta were talking to me and smiling without my being able to hear their laughter or their words. My voice was also denied me when I tried to answer them. Opening and closing my mouth like a fish, I felt submerged in silence. One might say I was swimming under invisible waters, lit by the sun through the bedroom window, where everything had been unalterable quietude since the dawn of the world. With more astonishment than despair, I realized then that I had been left as deaf as a post.

The first thing I painted during my convalescence was the forehead of that huge black bull. I made it life-size and as close as I had seen it at the end of my nightmare: some three feet from my chest and within reach of my hand. If a painter cannot repeat his dreams perfectly in a painting, he won't be able to paint from memory either. If he can't paint from memory, he isn't a painter but a dauber with badly painted pictures. I also confirmed that the silence of my deafness, to which I never could and never can become accustomed, had not diminished my faculties though it did change my manner with the brushes. Now it was much more sparing and expressive with colors, more succinct in the design. Lines and outlines had disappeared from my art because they had never found enough space in my consciousness. I noticed, too, that I had known everything about light but learned then about darkness. With the shadows in my own spirit scraping at my dreams and my memory like a man digging a trench in the center of his being, I created that bull as bestially human as Velázquez's buffoons.

I put blood on one horn without knowing whose it was. I added bandilleras, placed and twisted beneath the withers, and a cape caught on the back of his neck, along its dark nakedness. When I finished, when the last brushstrokes were still fresh, I said to the beast: "Now charge, you bastard." I repeated it without anger or boasting, emphasizing a duty of his that seemed obvious if he was really as alive as I felt him to be. Then I shook my head in discouragement when I realized I had painted him deaf, in my own image and likeness. When I showed the head to María Teresa, in my studio, asking her if she thought I was crazy, she replied, terrified in part and in part scandalized:

"Of course you are. Absolutely mad. How did you risk inciting him to leave the painting and really gore you, you fool?"

Since I didn't understand her, because I wasn't yet used to reading lips and she always spoke very quickly, she scribbled everything nervously on a piece of paper. Then she added: "This bull makes me feel naked down to my bones. He looks at me as if I were a rag doll." I burst into laughter, I pulled her to me, and we made love on the floor, beneath the skylight, since in my studio there was no other place for it. After seeing her call out with pleasure, without hearing her, I told her that in my silence her cries seemed to be of incredible pain, as if she had been crucified.

"I always lived crucified," she replied very slowly so that I could see the words on her face. "I didn't want to be born."

The absurdity astonished me, for I always thought María Teresa was more full of life than any other creature on earth. Then I realized how far apart two lovers can be, even when they roll around on the floor, as far apart, in fact, as María Teresa seemed to have lived from herself. At the same time, and in a separate light, I realized I would always be much closer to my art than to any person, including my dearly loved son Francisco Xavier Pedro. In the meantime, María Teresa dressed before the mirror of my self-portraits. She wore a widow's veils and clothes because the mourning period for her husband, the duke, had not yet ended. With the complicity of a coachman and a maid, that afternoon had been her first secretive excursion since the funeral. On that day we also arranged my visit to Sanlúcar and her anticipated trip to the salt marshes, where we would meet in secret.

In May of 1801, María Teresa had only a year to live, though neither of us could have believed it then. We had not been lovers for some time, but we became good friends. I advised her regarding the purchase of paintings, and she came sometimes to cry in my studio, during the time when Godoy imprisoned her last lover, Lieutenant General Cornel. María Teresa was not at the bullring on the second Monday of that month, when *Pepe-Hillo*, José Romero, and Antonio de los Santos were to fight in a great corrida. I was there and kneeled like everybody else as soon as the king and queen entered their balcony. Then, when they were settled, we stood to applaud them. Looking at them I remembered them in my dream and in the portrait of the August Family I had painted the previous summer. As in my distant dream, His Majesty the king leaned sideways against the railing of the box and smiled, just as he had done in the empty arena of my delirium. Yet now he was a distracted old man with blue eyes, his former robustness turned into rounded fat. He aged as ghosts must age: gradually losing their appearance and their memory until they definitively disappear. Beside him the queen also made an effort to greet us with her toothless mouth that seemed to sink her jaw into her skull. She despised bullfighting and came to the bullring because of royal duty.

Pepe-Hillo wore a blue costume with silver braid. He saw me and approached the barrier to talk to me. He too had aged prematurely over the winter. He was never very tall, but the proximity of half a century made him even smaller. His face had bloated, and his swollen belly protruded over the top of his breeches, while a dewlap, sister to his goiter, crowned the lace trim of his shirt. Between drooping lids his eyes still shone like two heads of a pin, but large, sickly circles under his eyes turned his skin purplish down to his cheekbones. Beside him, José Romero seemed like a giant resplendent with youth and titanic strength, like all the men of his lineage.

"Pepe," I said to *El Hillo*," why don't you leave the circus? Is it so hard for you to follow the example of *Costillares* and Pedro Romero and retire in time?"

We were connected by a certain friendship, the one I always had with all the bullfighters, and it wasn't my purpose to irritate him. Indefinite presentiments had begun to trouble my spirit since the start of the parade around the ring. Although deaf, I couldn't silence those confused voices inside me. They became real webs of muffled howls, whispers, and whistles, woven together by the apprehension in my chest and throat.

"Where would I retire, da cemetery?" *Pepe-Hillo* asked, smiling. "I don' fight ta die but ta earn my living."

Then he told me the bulls would be good even though they were Castilian, from Peñaranda de Bracamonte. Sunday morning, after Mass, he had gone to Arroyo Abroñigal to take a look at them. He liked them all for their high, well-proportioned horns, but especially one called Barbudo, which he told them to put aside for him. They would run him in the afternoon, and *El Hillo* added that the beast and he had been born for each other, "like lovers in da theater."

"When I've controlled 'im, I'll toss away da cape and fight him wit' my watch, so he'll see it's his hour dat's come, not mine."

The bugles sounded immediately afterward and the fiesta began. In the morning the bullfighting went on without major incident, although a gray bull with greenish horns, wearing Briceño's colors, knocked *Pepe-Hillo* down and must have scratched his leg, because in the afternoon he came out limping slightly, his calf bandaged under his stocking. ("Maestro, that bull and I are born for each other, like lovers in da theater.") A corrida seen by a deaf man resembled theater more than bullfighting because of the silence in which the spectacle took place. A tragedy where you died for real, as *Costillares* once said, but a tragedy after all, and therefore the representation of a secret drama whose meaning and outcome none of us knew. Barbudo came out, the sixth or seventh of the afternoon. I realized right away that *El Hillo* had made an incomprehensible mistake when he chose him. The bull was large and very black, with good horns, but dangerous and inelegant because he was skittish and dim. He took three lances, slipping away from all of them, and three pairs of banderillas. I remember an excellent one, the charge of Antonio de los Santos, always superb at that part of the fight. The death call sounded, and *Pepe-Hillo* made a couple of passes in their natural order. Barbudo became agitated at the second one with the excessive speed that made him wound because he was nervous, and trapped *El Hillo* at the barrier. *El Hillo* got out of the difficulty in part with a chest pass but was to the right of the bullpen, his head tilted slightly toward the barrier, prepared for the kill. He hadn't tossed away the muleta to fight with his watch, as he used to do in the days of his spats and rivalries with Pedro Romero. Later his banderillero, Manolo Jaramillo, told me *El Hillo* was in a great deal of pain at noon from the fall he had taken that morning. His cuadrilla told him not to fight in the afternoon under these circumstances, but *Pepe-Hillo* refused to listen to them; he had a contract with the Puerta de Alcalá bullring, and for him those commitments were as sacred as if he had sworn to them before the Virgin del Baratillo.

With Barbudo trapped in the worst place, beside the right-hand door to the bullpen, *Pepe-Hillo* rushed forward to give him a running sword thrust in the old style of *Costillares*. The thrust did not go all the way through and was on the wrong side, and at the same time the bull's horns caught on his breeches. With one butt of his head, the animal turned him around and threw him into the ring on his back, dazing him with the blow. Everyone in the bullring stood and shouted in horror, waiting for the goring that would draw blood, their shouts of terror as soundless to me as the cries of María Teresa in my arms. Barbudo buried his entire left horn in the belly of *Pepe-Hillo*, as if looking for his watch by way of the watch chain. Having threaded him in this way, he rocked him back and forth and swung him around for interminable seconds, while *Pepe-Hillo* was dying, conscious now and crazed with pain, clutching at the other horn with tormented hands. Juan López was the first to hurry to attract the bull and save *El Hillo*, and while a bullfighter made passes with the cape and the muleta, he came at him with a lance and thrust it into the bull from a rearing horse. Antonio de los Santos and Manolo Jaramillo carried *El Hillo* in their arms, the three of them as red with blood as firebrands as they tried to hold his intestines inside his ripped belly. In the royal balcony, His Majesty the king remained motionless, leaning on the railing where a tapestry with the banner of Castilla was hanging, just as in my dream, but open-mouthed with astonishment now. The queen was turned to one side, hiding her face in her hands. In the ring the cuadrilla were using capes to change the position of the bull. They were so confused that one left his cape caught on Barbudo's banderillas. Only José Romero, with the vigorous, almost inhuman dignity of the bullfighters in his family, kept a cool head in misfortune. As soon as he had cornered the animal, with the tip of his own sword he pulled out *El Hillo*'s and Barbudo didn't budge. While Romero prepared for the thrust at the boards, I looked at the bull looking right at me across the passageway between the barrier and the first row of seats, and over the barrier.

With no astonishment I recognized him then. He was the living image of the bull I painted when I had come out of my delirium and entered into my deafness. The bull of death in my nightmare, which I waited for, holding my watch, placed in the center of the ring by those I had imagined or judged. Barbudo's blazing, jet-black eyes looked into mine, as if he was also making an effort to recognize me. The fresh blood of *Pepe-Hillo* ran down his horn and dripped along his left shoulder. In the pauses in his panting, he licked his snout with the tip of his tongue, as red as vermilion. "Who are you?" I asked without moving my lips, but also without moving my eyes away from his. "The dead king asked me to paint his portrait so he could learn who he was. You can't fool me because we're too much alike. You're not only a bull. *Pepe-Hillo* himself knew that when he chose you in the Arroyo Abroñigal so you could kill him." There was nothing else because José Romero came between us and stabbed him from the inside out, plunging in the sword up to the hilt. He repeated the maneuver, burying the entire blade from the tip to the cross-guard. Barbudo fell, his legs already stiffened by death, with no need for the final dagger.

Throughout the night of the Second of May, 1808, we heard in my house the volleys of the executions. In the small hours the next day, before dawn, I took my servant to the Príncipe Pío Hill, where, according to the whispering neighbors, the French were still firing. Josefa tried to stop me with weeping and words that, fortunately, I could not hear. In the doorway she was still embracing me, more agitated than I had ever seen her before. Controlling her despair, with all the force of her slimness resembling that of a playing card, she spaced the words on her lips so I could read them without difficulty. She told me that we had achieved a comfortable, respectable position, almost in our old age. We had a barouche, a coach for horses and another for mules, when many nobles had nothing but a calash. We had a grown son after having buried four others. Now it would all be lost if I had myself killed in the street like a dog. What would become of her as a widow? How would she manage to take care of her son, the carriages, and the mule team? Ironically, she was the one who would starve to death in the war that was just beginning, not me. She looked as narrow as a thorn in the child's coffin, beside which Xavier and I would hold a vigil on another, not too distant night.

It was close to dawn and the moon was almost full. We didn't see anyone on the street, although near the Palacio de Oriente, as Isidro told me, you could hear the sound of mounted patrols. The lantern trembled so much in his hand that I finally snatched it away from him in a rage. From then on I held it, leading the way, while I kept the portfolio and papers tightly under my other arm. My servant followed me like a beaten dog, the two of us moving forward as if in a dream toward San Antonio de la Florida and the Príncipe Pío Hill, step by step past the Convento de los Padres Agonizantes, the Escuelas Pías, la Casa Real de las Recogidas, the Convento de Mercedarios Descalzos de Santa Bárbara, the Huerta de la Beata María de Jesús, and the Saladero de Carnes. As I told Moratín yesterday, as we approached the slope of the executions, I began to smell the fragrance of early-blooming rockrose. We also saw flocks of crows flapping their wings over the corpses and a pack of street dogs, lapping the blood and dew around the victims. We drove the dogs away with blasphemies and stones. We could only shout at the crows and rebuke them with our fists. Isidro told me they responded with an uproar of cawing and that the dogs barked at us from the darkness. I wondered whether those animals thought we were two ghosts gone mad. Some fifty men were lying on one side of the hill. Curled up on the ground, fallen on their stomachs or their backs with their arms opened wide, as if they had been shot one on top of the other. My servant, who at the time was little more than a boy, vomited and wept at the feet of the dead. I slapped him like a madman and he huddled next to the lantern, holding his head with both hands, still shaken by trembling and sobs.

Long afterward, in the second or third year of the war, I looked for and met José Suárez, a transporter at the Tobacco Custom House, about whom it was said that he fled in the middle of those killings. He was a small thin man who seemed as agile as a monkey. Kneading his cap with the tips of his fingers and smiling constantly, he told me the details of the terrible night. He spoke with mocking indifference about those atrocities, as if the delight of knowing he was alive diminished the horrors he had experienced. Among the victims was a friar, whom I recognized because of his tonsure though he wore no habit. José Suárez told me he was the chaplain at the Monasterio de la Encarnación. He was the one who told them when they were going to be shot. "Father," the mule driver pleaded, "absolve me before they kill us." "My son, if God isn't blind He'll see that we're innocent." "Father, and if He's deaf to our voices like these executioners who kill us and can't understand us?" Then he remembered my own deafness, which obliged me to look at his lips and not his eyes when he spoke to me. "I beg your grace to forgive me, I meant no offense. I wasn't referring to your impediment but to God's. At that moment I would have sworn He didn't hear or understand our language. Then it turned out that I was the one who would be spared." He recounted how the squad crowded them all together, sticking them with their bayonets and forcing them down on their knees. "That's how they controlled us, and insulted us too, because they didn't have ropes to tie us." In the end they were divided into groups of five or six men, shot point blank, then they pushed the next ones forward with bayonets and killed them on their knees as well, among the dead bodies. When José Suárez saw that it was his turn, he jumped up not to escape but in order to die on his feet, as he himself indicated in his account. In the face of that unexpected gesture there was a moment of uncertainty on the part of the firing squad, and impelled by his instinct to survive, he began to run. They shot at him several times but couldn't wound him, and the monks took him in and hid him in San Antonio de la Florida.

In fact he wasn't telling me anything new; but he helped me to be exact about my memories and to understand my own painting years before creating it. The fallen on Príncipe Pío Hill were piled up, mangled as if gored by a gigantic bull. The soldiers in the firing squad were a monstrous, repeated beast, their bayonets the horns on its forehead. The morning itself, when it was darkest and clouds hid the almost full moon before dawn, took on the color of the bull I painted while convalescing from my death agony. I planned then to name the canvas *For This You Were Born*, which is what I would later call one of the etchings in *The Disasters of War*. In a corner, among the shadows, behind the men who were going to die, I imagined Josefa almost hidden, with Vicente Anastasio in her arms, both of them turned into the *sfumato* sketch of how I would see them in the bullring of my dream. The same bull that had emerged from my encounter with death and was completed in two sessions, when I could barely manage to stand, reappeared in the arena of the Puerta de Alcalá to disembowel *Pepe-Hillo* and fix his eyes on me, from the ring to my seat, before José Romero stabbed him with a sword. Born in the delirium of an invalid, the beast passed from my nightmare to my painting and from my painting to the bullring like a salamander through fire: without destroying or denying himself. On Príncipe Pío Hill and in his final incarnation, he sprang up multiplied into a minotaur with eight heads armed with horns as long as bayonets. As he passed, men, cut to ribbons, fell into a lethargic heap beside a slope.

María Teresa confessed to me that this bull made her feel like a rag doll, and naked to the marrow of her bones. The dead men in a heap that Isidro and I saw in the small hours twenty years earlier looked like rag dolls too. Only the crows flapping their wings as they waited to peck out their eyes, and the stray dogs lapping up their blood, knew instinctively that those dolls had been born of woman.

"Señor," my servant, still sobbing, asked me, "why do you want to draw the terrible things that men do to other men?"

"To tell them once and for all not to behave like brutes," I replied, sitting in the light of the lantern as I sketched the men who had been shot.

Five years later, when I painted *The Third of May, in Madrid,* I knew that a rag doll lived in other people and in me. I also knew that the same puppet could become someone resembling *El Hillo,* his entrails spilled out in the bullring, or the prisoners fallen at the bottom of that slope, or other marionettes dressed in full regalia, like the royal family itself, may God bless them and keep them in His glory, when I painted their portrait in Aranjuez. The truth is I began to think that our country, now so distant because of my exile, was alternatively the land of the monster or the moron. Their moments followed one after the other, ravaging or retarding our history. At times the bull attacked the puppets brutally and destroyed them, as if they hadn't also been men. On other occasions, when it was the time of the simpletons, he meekly licked their hands when they offered them to be kissed. A long time ago now, Moratín pointed out that the celebration of the coronation of His Majesty Don Carlos IV coincided with the French Revolution, the one that would enthrone reason on an altar in the name of liberty. I had believed in liberty and above all in divine reason with as much faith as Moratín. When they finally reached our country, the land of the bull and the puppet, they had been transformed into the minotaur, disguised in the cloaks of the Napoleonic army, which gored mule drivers with thrusts of their bayonets. The day I finished *The Shootings on Príncipe Pío Hill,* on the eve of the return of the Desired One, Isidro asked me if it was the picture I had decided to paint in 1808 to tell men for all time not to be savages.

"No," I replied, shaking my head filled with evil presentiments. "This is the painting I made for the king so he doesn't hang me for having collaborated with the invaders."

In reality *The Third of May, in Madrid* was very different from how I had conceived of it at first. Then I saw and sketched the firing squad, the bayonets, and the dark gloomy sky as a kind of savage nocturnal bullfight in which a minotaur with more heads than the hydra sacrificed men instead of having them fight bulls. The victims fell one after the other, and, in fact, the painting lacked an end, just as the crimes committed in the name of history had none. Something told me, however, in the only voice my deafness could not silence, that this was not the entire truth. Then I imagined a living specter who rose from his knees among the dead to denounce the atrocity in the name of all the dead. I conceived of him with his hands pierced by bullets, as I had seen many men who had been shot, their palms punctured when they had irrationally attempted to protect their faces from the bullets. The man, that ragged one in the yellow trousers, grew then into the center of the painting to confer a brand-new meaning upon it. With his arms opened wide, as if nailed to the cross of Saint Andrew or ready to place a couple of invisible banderillas, he stopped not only the firing but also time in the center of the canvas. For eyes I gave him those of the bull, just as I had painted them in the first days of my convalescence.

Fifteen years have passed since then, and the world of yesterday, of María Teresa, *Pepe-Hillo*, and the Prince of Peace, has disappeared forever. As Moratín would say, the coronation of a king like His Majesty Don Carlos IV and the French Revolution do not coincide with impunity. And we, men like Moratín and like me, have passed with our world and now waste away in exile. Yet somewhere in Madrid, my beggar with the yellow trousers continues to stop time and the firing, his arms spread wide as he insists on shouting something to his executioners that I shall never hear. I would like to believe that in a century and a half he will still be there, making that brutal moment eternal in order to denounce all the torments committed on earth to the greater glory of faith or reason. I would also like to believe that by then another man, who perhaps is myself, as the Living Skeleton would say, will live obsessed by that painting of mine and eventually come to realize its hidden meaning and its manifest truth. Perhaps at this very moment in another very distant time, that double of mine whose words I would swear I hear sometimes, sits down at a table and writes: "Silently, with restrained astonishment, I wonder who I am and who Don Francisco de Goya Lucientes was."

THE MONSTERS

Pepe-Hillo

José Delgado Guerra was born in Sevilla, in the Baratillo district, on March 14, 1754. He was baptized three days later in the Colegiata de San Salvador; his godfather was José de Misas, first cousin to a renowned picador. His father, Juan Antonio Delgado, was a dealer in wine and oil from Aljarafe, or the Morisco Strip, as the county of Niebla was still called then, according to Cossío. He was established in Sevilla not long before the birth of *Pepe-Hillo* to look after the shipping of those spirits, but was soon ruined. When he had barely learned his first letters, the only ones that *Pepe-Hillo* ever knew, his father placed him as a cobbler's apprentice. The only thing known about his mother is her name, Agustina Guerra. By a strange coincidence of fate, she gave birth to the future bullfighter in the same year that his most outstanding rival, Pedro Romero, was born in Ronda.

His father was infuriated when he heard about *Pepe-Hillo*'s escapades at the slaughterhouse in Sevilla, fighting with yearlings, young bulls, and even full-grown bulls in the pens, almost never spending time at the cobbler's workshop. The slaughterhouse was the leading school of bullfighting in the kingdom, according to the historian José Daza, and it undoubtedly was for *Pepe-Hillo*. He was discovered there by Joaquín Rodríguez, *Costillares*, when the boy used his own shirt for lack of a cape. At that time *Costillares* was competing for primacy among bullfighters with Juan Romero, as he would later be the rival of his son, Pedro. *Costillares* had also trained with yearlings at the slaughterhouse and moved on to be the inventor of the *volapié* and the *verónica* in their modern versions. He was a rational bullfighter, consistent and original, who, booed once at an advanced age by the actor Isidro Máiquez, would shout at him with cold logic from the barrier: "Señor Máiquez, Señor Máiquez, this isn't the theater because here you die for real."

Costillares was pleased by *Pepe-Hillo*'s disposition: his tenacious, joyful courage, his ambitious audacity, his imaginative and haughty postures. Perhaps he was somewhat frightened by his stunning pride — blind to danger, bending at the waist, filled with grace — precisely because in the bullring you die only once and always for real. In any case, and in spite of the protests of the wine dealer, he took on *Pepe-Hillo* as a matador's assistant. In the bullfights in Córdoba, in 1770, he was already second sword. *Pepe-Hillo* had just turned sixteen at the time. Four years later he was married in the Colegiata de San Salvador to María Salado. Soon his fame had spread throughout Andalucía, where they already preferred him to Pedro Romero. In Madrid, on the other hand, everyone still swore by the Romero name. When the Junta de Hospitales de la Villa y Corte could not arrange for the Romeros to fight in that bullring, they turned unwillingly to *Costillares* and *Pepe-Hillo*.

In 1778, *Pepe-Hillo* and Pedro Romero were both at the bullring in Cádiz. Pedro Romero, a Herculean man, serene and immune to envy, told him during an interval: "Friend, what God took from you in strength He made up for with grace." *Pepe-Hillo* was challenging a bull with his beaver hat before killing him with a volapié like those of *Costillares*. Pedro Romero fought his with the comb he kept in his hair net. That same year they competed again at the Real Maestranza in Sevilla, where *Pepe-Hillo* suffered one of his twenty-five serious gorings. Pedro Romero, who had never been wounded by a bull, risked his life in a parry to save him. That was the beginning of the deep friendship between the rivals, attested to by Romero himself.

In 1784, *Pepe-Hillo* appeared as sole matador in Burgos, in one of the bullfights celebrated in honor of the Count de Artois. According to a manuscript in the collection of Ortiz Cañavate and cited by José María Cossío, *Pepe-Hillo* was so outstanding in courage and skill that "several times he even killed a bull while holding a watch in his left hand instead of the killing cape." In Madrid in 1789, in the celebrations of the coronation of Carlos IV, Pedro Romero and *Pepe-Hillo* again appeared in the same bullfight. Armona, the director of the Villa y Corte bullring, drew lots to determine first place in the ceremony that acknowledges a bullfighter as a full-fledged matador; it fell to Pedro Romero. Then, hesitating, he asked: "Well, Señor Romero, since it has been determined that you will fight first, do you pledge to fight bulls from Castilla?" That imperturbable creature replied: "If they're bulls that graze in a field, I pledge to; but Your Grace must tell me why you have asked me this question." The director shrugged, while *Pepe-Hillo* listened to them, silent and livid, and then read a letter from José Delgado Guerra, in which he had first stipulated in his contract to fight only bulls from Andalucía and Extremadura, because the ones from Castilla were thought to be difficult and dull-witted killers.

The bullfighters presented a complete contest in the morning and in the afternoon. Pedro Romero dispatched the bulls from Castilla and *Pepe-Hillo* the ones from Andalucía, as had been agreed. The last one of the afternoon, which was José Delgado's, was from a Castilian herd, the result of a joke or a mistake on the part of *El Tío Gallón*, who separated them in the bullpens and despised *Pepe-Hillo*. According to Pedro Romero, José Delgado became furious when he saw its colors and then made a series of lackluster, shaky passes that astonished and irritated the audience. The kill was sounded and the surly beast, which until then had demonstrated a fondness for the haven under the royal balcony, pressed its haunches against those boards and *Pepe-Hillo* could not shift or square him for the kill. "Friend, leave it, we'll get him out of there," Pedro Romero said. *Pepe-Hillo* stared at him without replying, and went straight to the bull. His rival moved away but observed his attempts to attract the bull because he had a presentiment about the goring. That happened immediately, when the bull seized and turned over the uneasy *Pepe-Hillo*. In the gesture of a cynical great lord, or in anticipation of a character out of Valle-Inclán, Pedro Romero picked up *Pepe-Hillo*, bleeding and stunned, carried him to the box of the duchess of Osuna, and left him at her feet. Then he squared the bull and dispatched him with a single sword thrust.

Néstor Luján has understood better than anyone else the socio-logical significance of *Pepe-Hillo*'s bullfighting. For the first time, and as a result of his rivalry with Pedro Romero, enthusiasts were divided significantly in their preferences. The indiscretions of *Pepe-Hillo* and the somewhat superficial showiness of his bullfighting would turn him into an idol of the masses, a term that included the aris-tocracy. A man obsessed with renown became the first bullfighter of great multitudes. His bullfights on working days interrupted projects. If he fought on Sunday, the fiesta lasted until Tuesday in order to comment adequately on his passes. In the bullring, commoners and nobility rubbed elbows in order to kneel and remove their hats when the king entered and then to cheer enthusiastically for *Pepe-Hillo*. "The Spaniards are good, peaceful, and enthusiastic," the Prussian minister concluded in the language of an explorer when he informed his court about those customs. If the people seemed remiss in be-coming civilized, the most cultured part of the nobility became de-based with dedicated passion. To the greater glory of *Pepe-Hillo*, they copied the speech of the slums and disseminated it in their salons. In the meantime, Pedro Romero, indifferent to prestige and applause, would persist in the purity of his art, followed always by a minority of true connoisseurs. When he finally retired from the bullring, weary of the crowds and his conflict with *Pepe-Hillo*, he had given to bullfight-ing a precise mental esthetic, which was the meaning and reason-for-being of the most elaborated of spectacles.

The absence of *Costillares* and Pedro Romero meant that *Pepe-Hillo* was sole master of the arena. Year after year, as he approached half a century, his faculties diminished and the gorings increased. He created the Aragonese pass or behind-the-back cape work, and perfected dodges, parries, and evasions with the cape folded several times and draped over the forearm. Thirteen times he was thought dead when he was removed, wounded, from the bullring. Yet when asked whether he planned to retire, he replied, smiling: "I'll only leave here with my guts in my hand." In 1796, five years before he fulfilled that promise, he published in Cádiz *Tauromaquia, or the Art of Bullfighting*. The book was written for him by a friend, José de la Tixera, since *Pepe-Hillo* had difficulty signing his name. But many pages of the book seemed dictated by him and written down word for word. His essential advice for young bullfighters is the triple repetition of an imperative: courage, courage, courage.

Because of so many indescribable reckless acts, the people had a presentiment of an obscure panic, which perhaps *Pepe-Hillo* himself was not aware of. When he fought in Sevilla, he always went down on his knees and asked for the blessing of his father, the former wine dealer from the Morisca Strip. Then, covered in scapulars, he prayed for a long time at the altar of his favorite superstitions. A sad seguidilla seemed to anticipate his tragic destiny. "What pity I feel / when I see *El Hillo* / praying in the chapel of Baratillo!" *Pepe-Hillo* did not believe too much in that commiseration. He knew how savage spectators could become; their applause was the primary purpose of his life. He had seen them go after old bullfighters with prods and sticks when they sought refuge in the safety enclosure, or took cover, so they would return to the center of the ring. In the blink of an eye, at a time and in an arena he refused to imagine, that could be his humiliating end. Yet he refused to desert his destiny, as Pedro Romero had done. He had already said it many times. He would abandon his profession only with his guts in his hand.

In the meantime he squandered wealth and women, which always returned to him renewed. Cockfights, Gypsy dances, too much drinking, too much eating, brothels. Uncouth and ugly, he had the masculinity of an arrogant suicide, and it charmed lower-class women as well as ladies with the bluest blood. From the time of the celebrations of the coronation, when Pedro Romero carried him, wounded, to the duchess of Osuna, people wagered on which of the nobility's boxes he would be taken to after each goring. He dedicated part of his wealth to buying rustic and urban properties in Sevilla. He attended two regular get-togethers there, one on Calle Gallegos and the other at the Tomares water kiosk, across from the king's warehouses. For some time he was thought to be almost tempted to abandon the bullring and retire to his properties, where everyone treated him like a monarch. Yet his legend preceded him and obliged him to live cheered on by the public, if only by chance. When he was watching a bullfight in Calatayud, a bull jumped into a row of seats filled with people. The authorities, as terrified as the crowd, hesitated. *Pepe-Hillo* took a sword, mounted a picador's horse, and galloped to where the incident had occurred. He faced the bull, waited for his charge, and killed him with a single lance thrust.

On Monday, May 11, 1801, a complete bullfight was announced for the Puerta de Alcalá bullring. In the morning eight animals from Gijón and Briceño, and in the afternoon another eight from the herd of José Gabriel Rodríguez, in Peñaranda de Bracamonte, for *Pepe-Hillo*, José Romero, and Antonio de Santos. Some time earlier *Pepe-Hillo* had renounced his prejudices against Castilian bulls. Now, like Pedro Romero before him, he was obliged to measure himself against every animal that grazed in a meadow. The night before the bullfight, *Pepe-Hillo* rode out to Arroyo Abroñigal to see the bulls that had been purchased. He liked the look of a black bull with wide horns from Peñaranda de Bracamonte, one they called Barbudo. He demanded it for himself and no one dared argue with him.

The king and queen attended, as did Goya, who in his deafness sketched passes in the new, grotesque silence that now surrounded bullfights. In the morning, *Pepe-Hillo* was knocked down and suffered scrapes and contusions. In the afternoon, still in pain from the fall, he faced the beast that he himself had chosen for his own glory. Barbudo was the seventh to leave the bullpen and *Pepe-Hillo* must have realized when he saw him that he had been totally mistaken when he thought he had detected his spirit. The bull took three lances, always running from his fate, and three pairs of banderillas; he was cowardly wounded, and dangerous in the way he came out. The time came to kill the animal and *Pepe-Hillo* delivered two naturals and a chest pass, while Barbudo swung around and threatened to trap him against the barrier. *Pepe-Hillo* stabbed him while the bull stood still and thrust half the sword into his left side. Barbudo in turn caught him by a fold in his trousers and threw him flat on his back in the ring. The blow dazed the bullfighter, and the bull plunged his left horn into the pit of his stomach. That is the tragic instant that Goya captured in Etching 33 of his *Tauromaquia:* the tragic moment when the pain returned *Pepe-Hillo* to consciousness so that he would die aware of his suffering and clutching the shaft of the other horn. Then Barbudo held him in midair, swinging him back and forth for a whole minute, according to José de la Tixera. The autopsy report spoke of a terrible wound that cut in two the colon, stomach, liver, and right lung. The entire large lobe of the liver passed into the thoracic cavity, and several vertebrae and ribs were broken. The autopsy pronounced his instant death, although other less realistic and more pious versions conceded him a terrified quarter of an hour to receive the sacraments. The picador Juan López came late to the efforts to distract the bull, but he speared the bull from his rearing horse. José Romero finished off Barbudo with a couple of sword thrusts. Don Manuel Godoy was in Portugal at the time, winning the inglorious War of the Oranges. His mistress, the queen, wrote to him from Aranjuez, recounting the goring of *Pepe-Hillo.* "He was killed by a single thrust of the horns, on the spot, without the Unction arriving in time. At the moment of aiming the sword, the bull caught him, picked him up by the sternum, which is in the chest, cut open his stomach, went as high as his liver, cut the intestine in half, broke four ribs on one side and six on the other; he left all his blood in the ring and was on the horns for a time. Many people left the bullring, Manuel, my friend, and I, who don't like the bullfights, what will happen now?"

November 7–8, 1975

—*At 15:30 hours, faced with the considerable increase in gastric hemorrhage alluded to in the previous report, and his lack of response to medical treatment, a new surgical intervention was decided upon. To this end, His Excellency the Head of State was moved to "La Paz" Hospital Complex, where he was immediately placed in the care of Professor Hidalgo Huerta, with the collaboration of Doctors Serrano Martínez Cabrero and Artero Gurao and the surgeons Paula Seminario and Sagrario Parrilla. The team for anesthesia and recovery comprised Doctors Llauradó, María Paz Sánchez, and Francisco Fernández. Supervision of the cardiorespiratory constants during that tragedy was the responsibility of Doctors Vital Aza, Señor, Mínguez, and Palma. The operation revealed the existence of multiple new ulcerations of the stomach, which were bleeding profusely. For this reason they proceeded with a partial gastric surgery. The intervention, which lasted four hours, required the administration of five liters and six hundred milliliters of blood. All of this was well tolerated. At the time of the writing of this report, at 21:00 hours, vital signs are within normal range. The prognosis is very grave. Tomorrow, at 9:00, a new medical report will be issued.*

"If the road to Berlin were open, it would not be a division of Spanish volunteers on their way there but a million Spaniards offering their services," Sandro quoted Franco in the winter of 1942. Two years earlier it was two million fighters that the Generalissimo had offered to fulfill the "mandate of Gibraltar and the African vision." Then Sandro referred to a character of Huxley's, unknown to Marina, who asserted that death was the only absolute value not yet corrupted by men in spite of their efforts to degrade it. He wondered aloud whether those million bayonets stationed at the entrance to "La Paz" would impede his passage to a secret death, after asking him for identification. After all, you can do anything with bayonets except sit on them. Charles Maurice Talleyrand-Périgod, master of the art of political survival, pointed this out very well. Immediately afterward he began to speak of other bayonets, the ones in *The Third of May, 1808, in Madrid: The Shootings on Príncipe Pío Hill*. He compared and identified them with the horns of the bull of death painted by Goya ("the one you didn't want to see in the original for fear you'd be left blind"), and with the horns of another of Goya's bulls goring a picador's white horse. He ended by describing the slaughter in the Prado as a bullfight in which a minotaur with multiple heads sacrificed herds of men. Marina half-listened to him, not understanding his words very well and almost not crediting his existence. For more than ten days Sandro had not tasted alcohol and had drunk ice water with his meals. Yet he expressed himself now with the reckless urgency of intoxication, hastily summarizing *à bout de souffle* some incomprehensible hypotheses for her that he had been working on obsessively. From the huge bullfight that *The Shootings* had been, he went on to refer to time halted by art in the midst of history's atrocities.

"What does this have to do with Franco's dying?"

"Everything," Sandro replied immediately. "In spite of the eroticization of our consumer society, death made into a spectacle is still at the center of the Iberian arena. We know that Franco is slowly wasting away in a totally aseptic room. We also know that they keep him dozing with sedatives and artificially assist his respiratory and urinary insufficiencies. One of his doctors told a reporter that he had palpated his open intestines and swore that the dying man was not suffering from cancer and showed no symptoms of metastasis. That last sentence is one I certainly don't follow since metastasis is the reproduction of a very real disease in a place different from where it appeared initially. They've sutured a ruptured artery and several stomach ulcers. His heart stopped, but they stimulated it and regulated its rhythm electrically. There's not a single drop of his own blood in his body, since it all bled out intermittently and had to be replaced by transfusion."

"I still don't understand," Marina repeated, shrugging. Profiled against the opening of the window and leaning against the side of the bay, her gaze seemed to be lost in the dark night where another snowstorm threatened.

"Let's witness again the death of Felipe II. We know almost as much about that as we do about his life and, of course, about his person, for history does not know who that man really was. Consumption, gout, tertian fevers, and a cancer of the knee finished him off in El Escorial in a death agony that lasted two and a half months. Hydropic tumors swelled his belly and legs horribly. He burned with thirst, and only his fortitude or his pride allowed him to die slowly, without a single complaint. His tortured body could not tolerate the touch of hands or cloth. It was impossible to change or clean the bed, and the bedchamber reeked like a sewer. Lying in his own filth, a bedsore opened along the length of his back, from the nape of his neck to his buttocks, and the ulcers became worm-ridden. In these conditions they operated on his leg, and pus poured out of the swelling. They brought his father's coffin and opened it next to his bed. Felipe II ordered them to wrap him in a shroud just like Carlos V's, and he died, lucid, in the forty-second year of his reign, with the crucifix of the emperor in his hands. His death was an obvious parable of the corruption of absolute power."

"Absolute power is the most transitory," murmured Marina. "In two years, no one will remember Franco. It will simply be as if he had never existed."

"But the country will be the same: the land of the tragic sense of death and the picaresque or murderous sense of life. In fact the picaresque is our Renaissance, and if we freed ourselves here from the wars of religion, it wasn't because we had burned the heretics but because we believed in death on the one hand and in the ragged beggar boy on the other. Our future was reduced to waiting for the one man's end. Our past was the chronicle of other death agonies. Even the history of bullfighting, before it became a spectacle for foreign tourists, became a backwater and was reduced to a few fatal gorings, beginning with *Pepe-Hillo*'s.

Sandro was quiet for a few moments, recalling his notes on the tragedy, taken the night before from Cossío, Luján, and de la Tixera. As he wrote them he believed he was describing a bloody event he had witnessed personally in a mirror or in a world similar to the one in the paintings. Almost like the flash of a hallucination, he was struck suddenly by the memory of the fighting bull painted by Goya right after he had survived his grave crisis of 1792 and 1793. He felt certain that another very similar bull, or perhaps the same bull in a kind of brutal reincarnation of the painting in the bullring, killed *Pepe-Hillo* in Madrid eight or nine years later. Goya had attended the bullfight and witnessed the death of the bullfighter between the horns of Barbudo. But then Sandro imagined Goya in the vertigo of an absolute certainty as true as it was inexplicable, asking himself who he was, who Don Francisco Goya y Lucientes really was.

After *Pepe-Hillo*, Sandro spoke of Joselito, Granero, and *Varelito*. Three more bullfighters killed in the bullrings of another century, where symmetrical and concentric destinies all converged in a kind of determinism that anticipated the goring itself. On May 15, 1920, almost on the anniversary of the death of *Pepe-Hillo*, Joselito was fighting in Madrid. The next day he was supposed to fight in Talavera on an equal footing with his brother-in-law, Ignacio Sánchez Mejías. As they had done earlier with *El Hillo*, the audience demanded greater and greater risks and marvels of him, perhaps in anticipation of the sacrifice about which Lorca's "terrible mothers" had a presentiment with a certainty unknown to the bullfighters themselves in their ambiguous solitude. In Madrid the crowd booed him, threw seat pads into the ring, and howled: "Get him out! Get him out!" In a moment of silence, a girl shouted at him from the seats: "I hope to God a bull

kills you tomorrow in Talavera!" In Talavera the fifth bull of the afternoon was named Bailador and was as black as Barbudo. He seemed
surly and confused, and in the end turned out to be half-blind, seeing well enough from a distance but not up close. Joselito observed
the defect and challenged him more with his voice than by working
the cape, which was almost invisible to the bull. Having concluded
a series of passes to attract the animal, the bullfighter moved away
from Bailador, thinking he had dominated him and forgetting for a
moment about his far-sightedness. As he walked away from the bull,
the sword entered the animal's field of vision and Bailador quickly
charged. Joselito attempted to guide his route with the muleta, but
the bull, too close now to the cloth to see it, continued to attack the
man. He gored Joselito in the left leg, as Barbudo had gored *El Hillo*,
tossed him in the air, and as he fell the bull received him with another
goring, sinking an entire horn into his belly, as the bull had done to
Pepe-Hillo. He died on the horns. Later, looking at his opened body
in the infirmary, one of Joselito's banderilleros would say: "If a bull
killed this man, I tell you that here no one escapes dying in the ring."

Manuel Granero quickly attracted attention after the death of
Joselito, and fans believed him the indisputable heir to that incomparable genius. Dead soon after his twentieth birthday, the boy was
Valencian, tall, chubby-cheeked, his appearance somewhere between dim-witted and effeminate, who in some old photographs
looks like an altar boy and in others a gelding. He was also a man
of exceptional valor and very thoughtful intelligence. He spent no
more than three years in the ring, and at first he doubted his gifts for
bullfighting. People said he was ready to leave it with no misgivings
after his first fights with young bulls, because he did not want to be
mediocre, much less make a fool of himself. He had studied music
and played the violin wonderfully. If he left bullfighting, he would
become a professional violinist. Yet in his first year as a matador, he
engaged in ninety-one bullfights, a number not matched even by
Joselito soon after the ceremony making him a matador. On May 7,

1922, four days from the anniversary of the death of *Pepe-Hillo* and almost two years from Joselito's last goring, he fought in Madrid with Juan Luis de la Rosa and Marcial Lalanda. The fifth bull of the afternoon, Pocapena, was Granero's, farsighted like Bailador and skittish like Barbudo. He leaned a great deal to the right and tended to charge near the barrier. When it was time for the kill he withdrew to the bullpen and backed onto the base of the barrier, just like Barbudo. A man in the cuadrilla who had formerly been with Joselito attempted to bring the bull to the center of the ring. Granero immediately stopped him: "Leave it, I can take care of him." Pocapena began to charge, closing in on Granero, who waited for him, not moving a muscle. The bull gored Granero in his right thigh, suspended him in midair as Bailador and Barbudo had suspended Joselito and *Pepe-Hillo*, and tossed him to the base of the barrier. There he horned him over and over again, destroying his sash and breeches. In one of those thrusts, he sank a horn into his right eye, tearing it out by the roots and splitting his brain and frontal bone. He was alive when they carried him into the infirmary but died a few moments later.

Six days after the death of Granero, Manuel Varé, *Varelito*, perished in Sevilla after three weeks of agony, the result of another goring. He was Sevillan, like *Pepe-Hillo*, and carried to unmatched perfection the running sword thrust up to the hilt, which *Pepe-Hillo* had learned from *Costillares*. Although correct, he was less brilliant with the cape and small killing cape, but at the moment of truth, he entered in close and very slowly, his left leg slightly bent, thrust the sword with a skill identical to the courage that makes it possible. He lacked the physical gifts of Joselito and suffered many mishaps in handling the cape, yet the wounds did not diminish his stubborn courage. On April 21, 1922, he was in Sevilla, appearing in the fourth bullfight of the fair. Joselito was dead, and Belmonte, a Sevillan like Manuel Varé, had retired, and with increasing imperiousness the public demanded everything from bullfighters. As they had done to Joselito in Madrid in his next-to-last kill ("I hope to God a bull kills you tomorrow in Talavera!"), the crowd in the stands booed *Varelito*, exasperating him with their hissing and insults. The fifth bull of the afternoon, Bombito, fell to the bullfighter from Sevilla, just as Bailador and Pocapena, also in fifth place, had fallen to Joselito and Granero. The animal was black, like Barbudo and Bailador, but with shorter horns. Always hounded by the shouting of the crowd, *Varelito* thrust the sword into the bull's neck, not killing him at the first jab. Then Bombito gored him as he turned away, destroying his sphincter and rectum. As he was carried to the infirmary, in the shocked silence in the bullring, he shouted at the crowd before he disappeared: "Now he's got me! Now you have what you wanted!" In the ring he left a stream of blood and a bull that was dead after he had wounded him.

"Let's leave this country," Marina said slowly. "Let's leave together, tomorrow, if you like. After all, neither one of us belongs here. At heart you're Italian, and I never knew who I was."

"Nobody does. R. told us that on the day we met. But it isn't true. Goya knew that perfectly well, even though he spent almost his whole life finding it out. Perhaps the rest of us move through the world without distinguishing ourselves from shadows, or understanding with any certainty why we pretend we were born. In any case, I can't leave the bullring without finishing my book, and I can't finish the book without understanding the meaning of the bull in this arena."

"The bull? Which one are you referring to, to Goya's, to Barbudo, to Bailador, to the one that hollowed out Granero's head?"

"Possibly they're all the same. The bull is the symbol of death, with his thrusts and charges. It's well known too that *Pepe-Hillo* himself chose Barbudo the day before he was gored. On the other hand, the beast is transformed into the victim of a bloody sacrifice to an unknown or forgotten god, with the public as witness. Only reason is able to propitiate the animal when it is time for the sacrifice, and bring into play human dignity and existence. Do you know *Espartero*'s response to his assistant?"

"How would I know it if I never went to a bullfight?"

"A nervous banderillero was having difficulties placing the darts. In two impatient sentences, *Espartero* indicated how to drive them in. 'If I do what you tell me to, this bull will gore me.' *Espartero* looked at him in stupefaction and shrugged. 'And what does that matter?' His logic seems appropriate to a ritual, about whose mysteries we know absolutely nothing. The bull can be both the victim and the one that offers up the sacrifice. Besides, the bull is one of the animals with which men tend to identify magically. From the Middle Ages until the eighteenth century, a bull was at Mass and in the procession on Saint Mark's day. When Fernando the Catholic married Germaine de Foix, he had bull's testicles served at the wedding banquet to increase his virility. On the other hand, our only contribution to the natural sciences was *proving* the bull's dominion over all the wild animals."

Then Sandro spoke of the public encounters between fighting bulls and other animals, to the greater glory of the crowds of the Bourbon Restoration. In 1894 in Madrid, the bull Caminero faced the lion Recadé in a cage fifty meters in diameter. The king of the jungle became frightened at the first attack and Caminero pursued him, tossing and goring him as he chose. The lion died of his wounds the next day. Three or four years later, and again in the Madrid bullring, a black spotted bull was locked in with a Bengal tiger. When the tiger saw his enemy with his back turned, he leaped onto his shoulders and took the back of his neck into his jaws. Regatero, which is what they called that bull, shook off his adversary and gored him repeatedly. The tiger turned around and bit his dewlap, but Regatero cornered him against the bars and gored the tiger to death. The public protested, believing that so unusual and attractive a spectacle had ended. The bullring attendants poked the tiger with sticks through the bars to rouse him. He moved again and Regatero attacked him one more time. The tiger, whose name has, unjustly, not passed into the chronicles, sank his fangs into the bull's snout, and the bull finished off the tiger by attacking frenetically with his head. The crowd roared then and patriotically cheered the Spanish bull to the sound of the chords of the *Marcha de Cádiz*. They took away the tiger, emptied of blood.

The following year, and again in the capital, another duel was presented between the bull Sombrerito and the elephant Nerón. They chained the pachyderm to a post driven into the center of the arena, but he broke the chains and panic invaded the stands. They chained him again and Sombrerito charged him several times, but the giant paid him no attention. The bull ceased his efforts and the crowd booed the two animals, throwing oranges at them, which the elephant calmly devoured. They took away Sombrerito and sent out another deadly bull from the same herd. This one immediately attacked Nerón, put him to shameful flight, knocked him down and gored him in the belly and the head. The public became impassioned and applauded the bull and the Fatherland. The brass band again played the opening measures of the *Marcha de Cádiz*.

Other public festivities no less notable and always employing wild animals took place during the years of the Restoration. Times that still open in the waters of antepenultimate history, like Japanese flowers in the bidet, while a king died telling the queen: "Cristinita, hide your cunt and protect Cánovas from Sagasta and Sagasta from Cánovas"; while Cánovas himself outlined the first article of the Constitution: "Those who cannot be anything else are Spaniards"; while the French were Spaniards with money and kissing a man without a mustache was like drinking down an egg without salt; while "The bourgeoisie, egotists all, / who despise the rest of humankind, / will be swept away by the socialists / to the sacred cry of liberty . . ."; while Guerra declared he would fight no more bulls in Madrid, not even for the benefit of Most Holy Mary; while *Espartero* affirmed that "hunger gives more gorings than bulls," until a final goring by the bull Perdigón, the "traitorous little bull" that Fernando Villalón wanted to conjure up twenty-five years later after a spiritualist session, killed him off in Madrid. Then, also in Madrid and in the bullring where the blood of that esteemed matador had been spilled, a supposed son of Perdigón himself, with wide-spread horns and a dull yellow-ish color, fought with the lionesses Sabina and Nemea. He chased and constrained them so much that not even flaming arrows could force them to risk resisting him. The competitions between animals become baroque and churrigueresque, like Jesuit architecture in its dazzling decline. They enclosed the bull Carasucia with a she-bear, a she-panther, and a she-lion. Only the bear fought with any honor, while the lion and the panther, gored multiple times, fled in terror. The excited crowd, emotional and enthusiastic, gave the conqueror a standing ovation.

The final competition was held in San Sebastián, shortly after the turn of the century. The bull Hurón was measured against a tiger whose ferocity the posters guaranteed and predicted. Yet the feline became as timid as a mouse at the first charges and fled the thrust-ing horns, offering no resistance. Hurón knocked down the tiger, gored him, and tossed him against the grillwork with so much power that the crash bent several bars. Improvised blacksmiths straightened them immediately with hammers, but the president ordered the fight suspended, sick of the spectacle or having a presentiment of immi-nent disaster. The honorable public became enraged, stamping their feet and roaring their demand that the battle continue until the death of the tiger. The president gave in and ordered the animal harassed with goads, clubs, and flaming banderillas, but the singed and beaten animal did not cease its panting or its trembling as it cringed on one side of the cage. The fireworks maddened Hurón, a circumstance unforeseen by those strategists, and the bull threw himself against his terrified adversary, breaking the bars, and both animals walked out into the ring. Overcome by panic, the screaming public crowded together and became violent in waves, looking for the exits from the bullring. While people trampled on people, the Civil Guard shot the two animals in the ring. Whoever it was who gave the order to fire, which no one ever found out, spectators armed with pistols followed his example from the stands. The bullets rebounded on the cement stairs, increasing the terror of the noble masses. The day yielded one dead and almost a hundred injured by bullets, falls, or trampling. The memory of the bull and the tiger was lost after the incident.

"Let's leave here right away," Marina repeated, her arms folded over her chest as if she were making an effort to contain a shudder. "Let's go and never come back to this country."

Sandro shook his head and then repeated promises to get away as soon as he turned in his book, which was almost finished. Then they would go to Colorado and spend the summer with his children. Marina would be delighted to live a few months with them. In reality he spoke without hearing himself, vaguely aware that she wasn't listening to him either. Looking at her in the dark night of the window, where small snowflakes were beginning to fall, he thought of a Piero della Francesca. One of those cold, serene female profiles in the frescoes of the Church of San Francesco, in Arezzo, or the *Diptych of Federigo da Montefeltro and Battista Sforza*, in the Uffizi in Florence. The same decided will appeared to have traced their common features, beneath which the passions veiled a hidden fire or a resplendent light whose moderated brilliance barely showed through. Five hundred years earlier, Piero had loved a woman almost identical to Marina, although his art was then characterized by a supposed emotional coldness. Loving her, he immortalized her obsessively in almost all his works, perhaps because he also knew she was very similar to him. Then Sandro thought of another Piero: *The Birth of Our Lord*, in the National Gallery. Beneath its reproduction and on the sofa in his house, he had made love to Marina, before *the autumn of our discontent*, when they began to meet in those dissolute bars behind the old Municipal Slaughterhouse. He had never noticed then Marina's resemblance to the Virgin, the one kneeling in prayer next to the choir of shepherdesses. If he identified her now with Piero's beloved, he did not feel certain that he, and only he, was the one who remembered the frescoes in Arezzo and in the Uffizi. Perhaps another man saw them in a century closer to the Florentine painter and silently was helping him to evoke them. Sandro refused to say his name.

That night they went to bed naked, not touching beneath R.'s sheets and blankets. Sandro dreamed about the recently painted *Wild Bull*. On an easel of wood smoothed with a plane, the wet oil painting gleamed. A woman who was still young, whom Sandro recognized in his dream without recalling her name, talked to him beside the canvas. She was dressed all in black, her clothing and lace trimming from another time, as if she were going to a masquerade ball. Sandro asked her whether she thought he was mad, convinced all the while that he had lost his mind since he could not hear his own voice. And he could not understand what she replied, her words vanquished by the same silence. Facedown on the table at the foot of a transom, the mask looked for paper, pen, and an inkwell and nervously scratched some sentences in a small, very clear hand: "Of course you are. Raving mad. How did you dare to incite him so that he would leave the painting and really gore you, you fool. This bull makes me feel naked down to my bones. He looks at me as if I were a rag doll." Sandro burst into laughter, and laughing, he awoke.

The sun shone on the whitewashed walls in the house. Dressed in jeans and a sweater, Marina was sitting beside the window in the studio. She was motionless, as if she had spent part of the night waiting for the snow to cover the earth and the heavens to shine. The television was on and from the auditorium of La Paz hospital complex, the minister of information and tourism read the latest medical bulletin about Franco: *At 8:30 a.m. on November 8, the clinical evolution of His Excellency the Head of State is the following: he has spent the night sleeping. He awoke from anesthesia at 3:00 a.m. and has been sedated to avoid pain. His vital signs remain normal. The cardiocirculatory situation has shown no change. From the beginning of yesterday's surgical intervention and up to the moment of this current report he has received seven liters and two hundred milliliters of blood by transfusion. At the end of the surgical intervention an arteriovenous*

circuit breaker was implanted in his right forearm for hemodialysis.
The thrombophlebitic process in his left thigh continues unchanged.
The prognosis continues to be the same.

Immediately afterward there was a report on the true nature of the "arteriovenous circuit breaker." It consisted of placing a tube in an artery and another in a vein, so that the artery brought enough blood to the hemodialysis, or artificial kidney, and then returned to the organism through the other tube. The dialysis purified the patient's blood, placed in contact with the artificial plasma through a semipermeable membrane. In peritoneal dialysis, used then on the dying man, the peritoneal membrane functioned as a semipermeable membrane, cleaning the toxins accumulated in the organism.

Then Sandro thought of *Morocco: Diary of a Flag*, the chronicle and memoir of the campaign written by Franco at the age of thirty. The official cornetist had a Moor's ear to show to the other legionnaires. "I killed him!" he boasted. He had found the Moor at the bottom of a gully, hiding among some rocks. Aiming his carbine at him, he had him walk up to the road together with the other troops. "Fren, fren, no kill!" the prisoner pleaded. "No kill! Now you'll see. March over to that rock and sit down." The prisoner obeyed, trembling, and the cornetist fired at him. Then he cut off his ear, as a kind of trophy, as if the Moor were a recently killed fighting bull. That was not, Franco stressed, the first exploit of the young legionnaire. In a new edition that appeared after the Civil War, the paragraph had been censored.

Outside, the snow sparkled in the silent woods. Looking at it, he recalled the naked whiteness of the woman he had dreamed about. Laughing, Sandro had pulled off her mourning clothes with the black lace trim, like a mask ready for a costume ball. They made love at the foot of the easel where the fresh paint still gleamed on that head of a vicious bull, on a floor badly made of creaking wooden boards. Sandro didn't hear her laughter or her shouts because a silence of eternal ice had filled his head. Then he told the woman that in his deafness her shrieks of pleasure felt like those of a woman crucified.

"I always lived crucified," he thought he read on her lips. "I didn't want to be born."

Du Sang, de la Mort et de la Volupté. He passed his eyes over the thickness of trees in order not to think about the dream whose final and perhaps only meaning he did not want to admit to himself. Up the slopes and beneath the blazing blue sky, the snow seemed to turn pink in the late-morning light. Behind the first hilltops, in a hollow covered with ferns, lay a pond as round as a medal. Sandro and Marina had discovered it that autumn, when they had come across the spot, almost by accident. On the final slopes the trees disappeared, and the foliage was reduced to hawthorn, lost yews, and fields of carline thistle. The images of a man and a woman lengthened in the water, turned golden by midday, but far from the shore the pond grew dark and deep, like a trap. For Sandro, the clearest memory was of silence. Perfect quiet in a world still without cicadas or serpents, without wind and birds. He thought that deafness would illuminate his memories and evoked what he had written one dawn, totally drunk, in his notebook: "Saturn is my self-portrait and only tonight did I finally realize it." Then he had weighed a coin in the palm of one hand ("Francisco Franco Caudillo of Spain by the Grace of God"). On an impulse he threw it into the water. It must have fallen in the exact center of the pond, because the waves that began to ripple across the surface were perfectly concentric with the contour of the banks. It was Marina who noticed that they traced the outline of a bullring, with high rows of seats. An arena and its stands ironically disappeared as it grew.

Only then, as he recalled that morning before the snows a few weeks later, and told himself that the pond would freeze in the gully, he thought he could detect the meaning of everything he had been writing recently about Goya, in the chapter he would call TAURO-MAQUIA. Marina refused to see the original of *Wild Bull* for fear she would go blind. According to Néstor Luján, after centuries we know almost nothing about bulls. We don't know why all the bullfighters named *Pepete* died in the ring, or why it was always May, not April, that was *the cruelest month*, the one that left the most blood and the most dead in the arena. Rudolf Arnheim observed that the bombing of Guernica, on April 26, 1937, and the sketches for Picasso's mural came under the sign of Taurus, the celestial bull. Now Sandro amplified the coincidences of the constellation, through time and to limits that were incomprehensible for calculating probabilities. Between April 20 and May 21, two events took place: the massacre of May 3, 1808, and Goya's display of his painting, *The Shootings on Príncipe Pío Hill*, on a triumphal arch celebrating the return of the Desired One, May 11, 1814. The most savage of bullfights, the one in which the minotaur multiplied in order to charge men with bayonets, denounced history forever as the masses shouted: "Long live our chains!"

If the wide-horned black bull painted by Goya during his convalescence seemed to transform into the firing squad in *The Third of May in Madrid*, another wide-horned black bull killed *Pepe-Hillo*, in Goya's presence, on May 11, 1801. Still under the sign of Taurus, though in another century, a bull as dark as night fatally gored Joselito on May 15, 1920, in a horning identical to *El Hillo*'s. If the 1801 bull was named Barbudo, the one in 1920 was called Bailador and was the fifth bull of the afternoon. Another bull that also appeared in fifth place killed Granero on May 7, two years later. He was a skittish beast like Barbudo and short-sighted like Bailador. He caught Granero next to the barrier, as Barbudo had caught *Pepe-Hillo*, also by the leg, and finished him off on the ground with horn thrusts to the head. Again in fifth place, the bull Bombito appeared in the ring and gored *Varelito* on April 21, 1922. As a consequence of the wound, the matador died on May 13. The four bullfighters were gored when it was time for them to kill the bull.

The snow was beginning to freeze and turn golden among the trees. On May 2, 1808, always under the same constellation and in the Puerta del Sol, kilometer zero in all Spanish territories, the contemporary history of a reckless people began, which since that time has charged savagely in search of itself without success. He thought of a Christmas Eve, in a year he did not care to remember, when the car in which Sandro was driving his wife (his second wife) and two children skidded on an icy highway from Boulder to Denver and turned over an embankment of snow frosted like all the snow in those woods. At Boulder Hospital his wife (his second wife) was declared technically dead. Even so, the doctors struggled bravely to revive her, perhaps by means of a desperate logic that reduces realism to achieving the impossible. An hour later they succeeded, and two weeks later they discharged her and she returned home, where Sandro was a tangle of guilt-ridden contradictions for having escaped the accident unharmed.

His wife (his second wife) was a rationalist and an agnostic. Even so, she never concealed what she had experienced when she was dead. She said she suddenly felt deprived of substance and transformed into serene consciousness, undertaking a journey through not time and space but brilliant peace and light. Her pilgrimage was suddenly interrupted when she became conscious of physical pain in the hospital bed. She was in distress and was perfectly lucid, because suffering isolates and defines. She remembered everything: her name, her address, and even her final scream before the car overturned. Sandro said to himself then that perhaps there was a special, nontransferable hell for Spaniards, a people responsible for their slow suicide over the centuries, where each citizen would awake in an empty bullring that would be eternity for him. There, and although his name was Sandro Vasari, a descendant of Giorgio Vasari and three generations of Italian *xarnegos*, he too would find himself one day perpetually imprisoned in the center of the arena and the infinity of concentric circles of bleachers, facing the bullpen and with an ironic, useless watch in his hand (a watch attached to a long silver chain, like *Pepe-Hillo's*), under the same pitiless sun of May 2, 1808.

"Early this morning, while you were sleeping, R. telephoned

from the United States," Marina whispered suddenly, returning him to the other reality. "He insisted that I not wake you. He wanted to talk to me alone and ask me how the book on Goya was going. I said you were constantly working on it and said it was almost finished."

"That's the truth, more or less."

"He seemed to believe me." She hesitated for a moment, and then added: "R. was in Boulder, Colorado, and was calling from your wife's house, your second wife, according to what he said."

"He's very free to do that," Sandro interrupted drily. "He can telephone from another life of mine, if he wants to."

She wasn't listening to him. Reverberating on the frozen snow, the sun lit her profile again as if she were one of Piero della Francesca's figures. Looking at her hands crossed on a knee, and without raising her head, Marina asked:

"Sandro, do you think I'm going crazy? Tell me the truth."

"You must be if you really came to me after all these years and if in reality you're here now with me. In other words, if we truly are who we think we are."

He rested his palm on Marina's shoulder and observed his own hand as if it belonged to someone else, while the sun turned the veins stretching from his wrist to his knuckles blue, and reflected on his wristwatch. It was exactly 10:00 in the morning.

"I know very well who you are, but every day I know myself less and less," Marina repeated. "If we left here, then perhaps I could find myself."

"We'll go, Marina, very soon, and maybe earlier than you suppose. The book will be finished before you know it."

"I hope it's not too late. I hope I don't really go crazy then, if I haven't already lost my mind." She paused, and Sandro felt her shoulder beneath his palm harden, as if it had turned into stone. "Before dawn and R.'s call, I got up and dressed because I couldn't sleep. It was still snowing, but soon the wind would rise and sweep away all the clouds. I turned on the porch light and sat in this same chair, next to the window. That was when I saw it, as soon as the light went on . . ."

"What did you see, for God's sake?"

"It was Goya's bull and he still had that cape caught on the banderillas still piercing his back. He stood motionless in a clearing in the wood, under the oak trees. He must have seen me at the same time, because he approached the window slowly, shaking the snow off his forehead, tossing his head. He came up to the edge of the windowsill and began to stare at me so fixedly I thought I would sink while still alive into his eyes. They were bloodshot and wide open, like they are in the painting; but his gaze wasn't an animal's, it was a man's, a man chained in hell. I don't know how long we looked at each other; perhaps eternities. Suddenly, very slowly, he made a half turn and was lost among the trees. I sat contemplating his hoof prints on the snowy ground. More flakes, the last ones, finally erased them at daybreak."

THE CAPRICES

THE DREAM OF REASON

Blind Man's Bluff

In 1788 Goya created his last four works for the Royal Tapestry Factory of Santa Bárbara: three sketches and a cartoon, that is to say, a large painting on linen to be embroidered. According to Gudiol, the drawings were *The Meadow of San Isidro, The Hermitage of San Isidro,* and *The Country Meal.* As for *Blind Man's Bluff,* one of the artist's most reproduced creations, the Prado has the sketch and the painting. *The Meadow of San Isidro* and *The Hermitage of San Isidro* both belong to the same museum. *The Meal* is the property of the National Gallery in London. All the oil paintings had belonged to the duchess of Osuna and were acquired by the museums in 1896, at the public auction of her family possessions.

The three sketches are of different sizes. *The Meadow of San Isidro* is a canvas 44 centimeters by 94 centimeters. *The Hermitage* is much smaller and almost square; it measures 42 centimeters wide by 44 centimeters high. *The Meal* is the smallest of those sketches: 41 centimeters by 26. The sketch of *Blind Man's Bluff,* another oil on linen, has dimensions similar to those of *The Hermitage of San Isidro:* 41 centimeters by 44. The corresponding painting or cartoon, which today is on the ground floor of the museum, appears horizontal in memory; but its width is 2.69 meters and its height measures 3.5 meters.

After *Blind Man's Bluff, The Meadow of San Isidro* is the best known of these paintings. In May 1788, Goya wrote to Martín Zapater to tell him he had proposed doing a cartoon of the celebration at the San Isidro fountain during the festival dedicated to the saint. The painting is singular in the work of the artist. The man who in his youth broke the contour of his figures and in his old age would say he could not perceive more than shadows and lights, forms and volumes advancing and retreating, had recourse here to the fine points of a miniaturist and individualized all the figures with the detailed rigor of a Breughel. An angled slope, where wild mallow and vines grow, extends in the foreground. At the top of the hill a row of figures, dressed in light or gaudy colors and visible in the distance, enjoy the leisure of the festival. Two girls chat or gossip under a parasol. A lower-class girl in a red bolero jacket and neck scarf pours wine for a couple. Many gentlemen wear feathered two-cornered hats and silvery jackets, but there are a good number of the short jackets and tight sashes of Lavapiés. A young woman all in white points at the meadow at the bottom of the slope. There the crowd swarms, made small by distance. Barouches, carriages, and tents stand there. A light-colored greyhound runs among the people. The multitude rides horseback, plays circle games, flirts, and converses in groups. Even farther away, the Manzanares flows by, silvered by the metallic light of an indecisive spring. Across the river is the view of Madrid, with the walls of the Royal Palace and the rounded dome of San Francisco el Grande.

The Hermitage of San Isidro would not be transferred to a cartoon or to embroidered silk. It remained a sketch, like *The Meadow*, and both are approaches to a common theme, each with a different focus. The light is the same beneath a sky covered with gray and bluish clouds. Finally, in the background, as Goya would have said, one sees the temple with the double dome, the watchtower, the spire topped by the cross, and the three belfries of the campanile. In front of that are the *majos* and *majas*, the lower-class men and women grouped together and enjoying the miraculous water of the fountain. More men and women crowd together at the portico of the church. The young men are muffled in their capes, because this May is still uncertain, as we used to say. Still, in the foreground, an adolescent girl wrapped in a white shawl uses her fan as she talks with a friend. For Antonio de Onieva, the blues, grays, oranges, yellows, and greens of this sketch anticipate and recall Camille Corot in his best moments. At the Osuna auction it sold for three thousand pesetas. *The Meadow of San Isidro*, on the other hand, was purchased for fifteen thousand.

Ironically, the penultimate sketch for a cartoon that Goya made in the service of the Royal Tapestry Factory had the same theme as the first: *The Country Meal*. In 1776, through the intercession of Bayeu, they commissioned Goya to create the model for a tapestry that would depict a meal beside the Manzanares. The children of Van Goten, first director of that industry, directed the Santa Bárbara workshop, but the man who really controlled it was Antonio Rafael Mengs, first painter of the King's Royal Chamber and president of the Academy of San Fernando. Mengs ordered Goya to be paid eight thousand reales "for the moment," as if the commission were still in doubt. The result, however, pleased him very much and Goya would continue working for the factory until, twelve years later, he grew tired of serving it. This was the close of a period in his life and work that would produce the most finished example of eighteenth-century art. Characteristically, he called the last work of this phase *Blind Man's Bluff*. Soon, according to André Malraux, modern painting would begin, also with him, while Goya became Goya after having brushed the doors of death.

The first Bourbon, Felipe V, founded the Santa Bárbara Royal Tapestry Factory. An English traveler, whose opinion was collected by Antonina Vallentin, visited the twenty looms and wrote with complete justification: "These workshops have been organized in a puerile manner, as a pretentious copy of the Gobelins workshops. The generosity of the King supports them at great cost, and their poor results are attainable only by the most affluent." Jacob Van Goten and his sons used paintings by Teniers and Wourwerman as models for their tapestries for two generations, until their taste for the French mythological and allegorical baroque began to weary their landed clientele. As for the rest, the industry experienced technical difficulties in a period of enforced transition, in which it could not reconcile its many contradictions.

Another workshop, directed by the Frenchman Antoine Langer, where Goya's cartoons would be woven, was united with the Van Gotens' workshop. The Van Gotens maintained the traditional technique of a low-warp thread, with the chain threads extended horizontally and the chain over the cartoon, which the loom repeated inverted, like a mirror. The eighteenth century brought high-warp thread, among other innovations, and Langer introduced it in the Royal Factory in 1730. The threads of the chain now extended vertically, and the operator traced the contours of the model to be woven onto transparent paper. Nevertheless, he kept the cartoon at his side and turned to it constantly to confirm the fidelity of his work. In this way, as Chabrun observed, the weaving of tapestries lost all substantiality and became mere copying of the painting.

At the same time, tapestry abandoned its functional value as a screen or portable door and became a decorative element. Jean-François Chabrun pointed out certain engravings of Abraham Bose, printed in the seventeenth century, in which paintings and mirrors appeared hanging on tapestries, which served as walls. One hundred years later the Gobelins would be shown among paintings in the Paris salons, as if they were somewhat shameful imitations of the oils. The industry suffered a crisis in France and in Spain, even though the Spaniards always maintained it artificially. The Gobelins attained technical perfection but were limited to copying known paintings until the Revolution closed down the plant.

In Spain Mengs attempted to renew the genre with a return to its popular sources. He thought then of a second-rank painter, Miguel Angel Houasse, whom Felipe V had brought to Madrid in 1720 to decorate La Granja with paintings called *Men and Women Playing Blind Man's Bluff, Country Meal, Meal on the Grass, Game of Ninepins, The Swing, Washerwomen*. Among the painters contracted at the time by the Royal Factory of Santa Bárbara, Goya very soon proved himself the most gifted and prolific. Between 1776 and 1779 Ramón Bayeu, Francisco's brother, delivered twenty cartoons; José del Castillo painted seventeen; Antonio Velázquez completed twenty-three; Goya signed thirty in the same period of time. He also gradually reformed the technique of the craft until he transformed it into the first manifestation, brilliant though somewhat hesitant, of his most successful and inalienable work. At first the workers protested because he included an excessive number of nuances and ornamentations in his cartoons, difficult to repeat in silk embroidery. Goya was furious, but then he learned to synthesize the horizon and summarize nature, giving an almost transparent air to the Velazquean light of Madrid in order to accentuate the human dimension of his figures.

"I have no more than twelve or thirteen thousand reales annually, and even so I am as contented as the happiest man," Goya wrote to Zapater at that time. In 1785 he would earn another twelve thousand reales for a single painting, his first portrait of the duchess of Osuna. A year later he would be named court painter, along with Mallea and Ramón Bayeu. "My dear Martín, I am now painter to the King with fifteen thousand reales." In 1780 he became a member of the Academy of San Fernando, with its corresponding compensation. He bought shares in the Bank of San Carlos, forerunner of the Bank of Spain, and at times he complained to Martín Zapater for no real reason while he gradually became wealthier. "My only steady income are the securities from the Bank and my compensation from the Academy."

The contradictions that characterized his entire existence were also revealed in the management of his wealth. For a long time frugality was the norm of his household, when a pound of beef cost only two reales and a pound of oat bread the same. He bought a two-wheeled barouche, it overturned, and he hurt a knee that would give him pain for months. Unwillingly he acquired another with four wheels, along with its corresponding mules. Yet he always refused to give up his personal pleasures among *la canaille*, as he learned to call them in French and in some letters to Zapater. He never missed a bullfight at the Puerta de Alcalá, and was always the welcomed guest of bullfighters and their cuadrillas, with a reserved seat at the barrier. The world of fights, brothels, and taverns in the Rastro and Lavapiés was as familiar to him as the world of bullfighting.

In part, and as a witness to his time, he must have felt himself an observer of those environments. In part he also must have identified with the city of Madrid, for if he had not been court painter, he would almost certainly have remained there because of his origins. Lustful, a drinker, and antagonistic as a young man, according to his servant, he burned up the last of his youth in quarreling, fighting, and whoring as he approached the age of fifty. In Madrid, which at that time was a village near the rural palaces, his sudden fame must have reached even that nether world behind the Plaza Mayor. If people reminded him of it, he would brush aside any mention of his celebrity. He was just Francho, their familiar companion who would have liked to have been a torero. He was one among many in that hell, which he had known as well as his own house for many years. That's all, by God. Soon, very soon, he would realize, stunned, how uselessly he had deceived himself.

He was not ignorant about himself. He was ignorant about his incomprehensible country, the one whose endless disaster was in fact beginning in Goya's time. El Capricho, the palace of the Osunas that he frequented after painting highly praised but not very accomplished portraits of the duke and duchess, celebrated Mardi Gras for the entire year. Before Goya's astonished eyes, the slums of Madrid invaded the gardens and salons, not like a windstorm but like a masquerade party. The wide, tight sashes of the majas, the short jackets of the slum dandies, and the dissolute talk of the lower classes replaced overnight the modes, manners, and language of Versailles. Goya, who had learned some French in order not to be out of place among the powerful, and to write pretentious letters to Zapater with almost as

many mistakes as the ones he wrote in Spanish, realized in stupefaction that the language of El Capricho had suddenly become the
thieves' slang of Lavapiés.

Almost immediately, as soon as these people without employ-
ment began to open the muffling parts of their capes and mantillas,
the true faces of many acquaintances appeared. Not only were the
models for Goya's cartoons and the real personages of Ramón de
la Cruz's one-act farces present, but the actors and bullfighters as
well. In other words, the same people to whom, in another time, holy
ground would have been denied after they were dead. Pepa Figueras,
Costillares, and *Pepe-Hillo* were suddenly praised and talked about
more than Goya, Iriarte, and Jovellanos. If once the quartets and sym-
phonies of Haydn were commented on, now the *volapié* and banderillas *a topa-carnero* were discussed with greater passion. Goya met *El
Hillo*, *Costillares*, and Figureras in the gardens of El Capricho. Between two pruned trees, not yet greened by spring, a swing had been
hung. The duchess of Osuna, that haughty, sarcastic woman, laughed
wildly now as she swung above a background of sunlit meadows and
woods. With open hands *Pepe-Hillo* received her and pushed her by
the hips. *Costillares* returned her to *El Hillo*, caressing her knees as
he pushed her back. Pepa Figueras chatted with another actress in
farces, the two of them sitting on stools hidden under their wide skirts.
A picador whose name Goya perhaps did not remember lay stretched
on the ground, his cheek resting on his hand and his Cordoban hat
pulled low as he contemplated with a smile the duchess's ankles at
each swing of the rope.

("I have got it into my head that I should maintain a resolute idea
and affirm a certain dignity that a man ought to possess, with which,
believe me, I am not very content.") In Ortega's opinion, Goya understood the opposition between *the idea* and the plebeian and would
never again live completely in either of those worlds. In fact, just the
opposite occurred, because Goya was a man of moral syntheses. The
public festivities at El Capricho revealed to him both the complexity

of the real world in its human dimension, and the invalidity of any effort to apprehend it directly in art. Only by means of an increasingly deep and deceptive labyrinth would he be able to approach his fellow humans after this carnival, which was the last fiesta of a doomed era.

The commissions for cartoons for tapestries wearied him, precisely because the reality that needed to be expressed in those models was completely spurious in its pretended simplicity. He delayed work on the requests or tried to avoid it altogether. When he presented a preliminary sketch as detailed as the one for *The Meadow of San Isidro*, he knew very well that if it were transferred to a large cloth, they would never be able to weave the copy. An infuriated director of the Royal Factory wrote a long letter of condemnation to the minister of finance. Ramón Bayeu avoided working on his obligations to Santa Bárbara with the excuse of some portraits of the Infantes. "Goya, on the other hand, is entirely free and his attitude is as strange as it is irregular." He claimed that his appointment as court painter exempted him from all involvement in the manufacture of tapestries, because the salary of fifteen thousand reales did not include payment for the cartoons he made for the Factory. In the meantime, the weavers had no work because of those reckless artists. Many had to be discharged and found themselves living in dire poverty.

Goya's arrogance angered the minister, and the dispute became rancorous. The older Bayeu intervened in favor of his brother-in-law, and probably the duchess of Osuna herself was not removed from the search for a settlement, which the painter's obstinacy made increasingly difficult. Finally, a kind of tacit agreement was reached, under which Goya presented a final cartoon, *Blind Man's Bluff*, which the duchess would buy from the Royal Factory once it was woven. After giving in, Goya humbled himself and wrote a contrite letter to Francisco Bayeu. "The truth is, I very much regret that our relationship has changed and I ask God to free me from this pride that always overpowers me on such occasions. If I can remain moderate, if I learn to not let myself be carried away by my impulses, my actions will be less deserving of censure from now on."

Blind Man's Bluff, said Antonina Vallentin, was like a music box in which the hours of a dead century were struck. José López-Rey noted influences of Antonio Palomino in Goya's final cartoon. A century and a half before Oscar Wilde, López-Rey underscores Palomino's *Museo Pictórico:* "Just as Art is carefully diligent in imitating Nature, Nature too, rollicking in its works, endeavors to imitate Art." This same López-Rey gleaned a distinction Palomino made with regard to painting landscapes: those in which the story is subject to the nation and those in which the nation is subject to the story. In all his cartoons, and especially in *Blind Man's Bluff*, Goya decidedly favored the second. At the same time, and with notable fidelity, he followed the advice of the theoretician in his treatment of nature. "It is better to observe moderation in breezes (which are streaks) so that they do not offend the story and not to allow horizons to be too shrill and to keep them at the height of the perspective point you have or are considering in the story, figure, or floor you have; and the same moderation in the ground, mountains, and groves, endeavoring to have them help and not offend the principal part." Finally, and coinciding with a practice expounded in the epilogue of *Museo Pictórico*, Goya covered his painting with a light coat of varnish before applying the last brushstrokes in order to make them more brilliant.

Next to a pond an acacia is growing, as if the light of the Castilian spring were almost always Goya's favorite for his cartoons. Behind the water the slopes of some hills undulate, purple and gray with an occasional green shrub. More distant, on the same horizon, the mountains turn blue in the afternoon. Whitish streaks run down the long mountainsides, confusing the distance. It is probably May, as in *The Meadow of San Isidro*, but all the snow has not yet melted on the crags. The sky is high and very clear above the clouds that the wind flashes at intervals over the profile of the mountains. In the foreground appear some broken rocks and a triangle of grass is sprouting, bordered by plants and resembling a carpet.

At the edge of the pond four women and five men play at blind man's bluff. Their youth, almost their adolescence, is evident, although one of the gentlemen wears a wig powdered gray. He is also the only one wearing a long jacket with epaulets and a buttoned vest. His companions are dressed in the festive attire of majos: very tight breeches embroidered on the legs, short bolero jackets with tassels, and glossy blue stockings. They wear slippers secured with large silver buckles and gather their hair into nets adorned with combs and loops. Two of the ladies at opposite sides of the circle are wrapped in the white tulle of fashions popularized by Señora de Osuna and resembling the dress of the duchess herself in the family's painting signed by Goya. Another, wearing a satin doublet, perhaps part of a hunting costume, has on a wide-brimmed black hat adorned with pheasant feathers. Across from her, her back to us and facing the pond, is a maja, very young to judge by her figure and height, who seems to occupy the exact center of the picture, although in reality she is to the left. The deception comes from the color of her bolero jacket, as red as recently spilled blood, in contrast to the restrained hues of the rest of the group.

A young man, his tight clothing spangled with green sequins and his eyes covered, occupies the center of the circle and brandishes a long wooden spoon. The painting stops at the precise moment the man leans forward and tests the air with his spoon, while one of the ladies in white and another gentleman with his knee on the ground attempt to avoid it. An instant before, or for that matter a few instants later (one of those moments of the gallant Rococo in its long days of festivities) the figures will dance, holding hands, from right to left in the direction of the hands of a clock where the final hours of an era are tinkling.

It seems evident that all the protagonists in *Blind Man's Bluff* are wearing brand-new, made-to-measure costumes. They are golden scoundrels, as we would say now, dressed like the authentic *canaille* on pilgrimage mornings at the miraculous fountain. They wear masks for their own pleasure or to serve as models for the artist. In any case they play at being actors in a farce they haven't learned very well, which perhaps neither they nor Goya understand clearly yet. Their real condition as actors in the theater of a century reveals the artificiality of the landscape. Don Quijote had transformed Castilian horizons and places into the lands of his fantasy. In the background of some of his equestrian portraits, Velázquez painted not the panorama of the Casa de Campo but a tapestry that copies its skies and forests. The acacia, the pond, the mountains, the grass, and the clouds are a frame for the game and the dance with the spoon: a cartoon inside the cartoon, arranged like a trompe l'oeil, because at first glance one would say that the landscape represented there, not its painting on a background canvas, resembled the sets of one-act farces.

"Goya Far from his Subjects" is the title Ortega gives to one of the chapters in his unfinished book on the artist. August Mayer, in turn, notes that the cartoons, including *Blind Man's Bluff*, lack a protagonist. A goldsmith has no reason to be impassioned, declares Ortega. There is no doubt that at this time Goya was much more interested in the meaning of the period than in many of his models. Later, in his deafness, he approached his figures instinctively, as if he had begun to lose his sight instead of his hearing. Meanwhile, in this final commission for the Royal Factory, Goya removed himself from the nine dancers until he saw them as very similar to dolls or puppets. Without judging them he stripped them in his own way, and in his own way he also participated as a spectator in their frivolous game. After all, as Goya himself wrote to Zapater during this time, for the few days we have to live, we should live as well as we can.

In *Blind Man's Bluff* it never grows dark because the artist has stopped time and the sky is made of paper. But in the gardens of El Capricho, where *Pepe-Hillo* and *Costillares* push the duchess of Osuna in a swing, night begins to fall slowly on the pools and acacias.

Very soon, when it is dark, all the personages in this long masquerade ball will be as blind as the false majo who probes the air with his wooden spoon. Then, in the endless shadows that still envelop the country now, the eyes of Goya's monsters will begin to light up in his own *Caprices*: that labyrinth made to the measure of our recent, eternal history, where everything will always be the same, with reason or without it, because men don't know the way.

April 1, 1828

"Dear Xavier: It is impossible for me to tell you anything except that I'm a little shaken with so much joy and had to go to bed. God willing, I'll see you and welcome you when you arrive, and with that my happiness would be complete." I signed my name at the bottom and Marianito added a note of his own: "Dear papa: My grandfather sends you these lines and some other letters too so you can see that he's still alive." The truth is that life, what we call life, I'm not living with much pleasure these days. The day before yesterday my daughter-in-law and Marianito arrived to tell me right away that Xavier would come for them in a couple of weeks. So happy a hope, knowing they would all be together and with me made me crazy with happiness and then made me sick. I spent hours talking to them endlessly like an old parrot, and they didn't seem to grow tired of my chatter. My daughter-in-law, who's a good woman but reticent, like all the Goicoecheas, who are more Basque than Madrilenian, only smiled at me from time to time, shaking her head with an affectionate gesture. Marianito, on the other hand, turned out identical to me. He hasn't inherited anything of the Goicoecheas, or the Bayeus, from his grandmother, my dead Josefa. He's the way I was at his age, which now must be seventeen or eighteen years old. He turned out good-looking and strong, with a courage that suits his nature like a ring suits a finger. Passionate and disorderly, he's as violent as he is affectionate. At times he interrupted my talkativeness, hugging me and kissing my cheeks to celebrate some witticism or amusing recollection of mine. Women will fight over him, if they haven't started to already. And I'm afraid he'll keep men in their place with a sword or a knife, in too many duels and fights, as I had to do. It seems as inevitable as it is significant that he uses the formal *Usted* with his father, but *tú* with me. All these things and so many others I'd like to talk over with Xavier when he arrives in Bordeaux. God willing this trip of his that they tell me will be in two weeks isn't delayed again, and that I don't go out like a candle first. Moratín once told me that he had always tried to avoid happiness, because joy is more treacherous than sorrow. I'd prefer not to believe it, but I thought of Moratín this afternoon when I felt out of sorts and sick after lunch. Until then, and since the arrival of my dear travelers, my good fortune was as great as my good spirits. Now, under these blankets, I've remembered again that I'm eighty-two years old, and that at my age, my greatest joy, as I once told His Majesty the king, would be to die before Xavier and naturally before Marianito. Yes, I would like to speak to my son about these and so many other things when he comes to Bordeaux. In Xavier, unlike Marianito, my blood and the blood of the Bayeus are mixed in equal parts. Occasionally, like me, he flies into a rage and then, like a gale, he blows away everything in front of him. Yet most of the time he knows how to be prudent and astute, like his mother. In this particular we are very different, because when I attempt to act with prudence, I fall into cowardice and unworthiness. (The same thing will happen to Marianito if God doesn't protect him.) With his tact and moderation, Xavier would now smooth over Leocadia's asperities, which I do not even wish to think about. As soon as Marianito and my daughter-in-law arrived, she hid Rosarito I don't know where, as if she feared the contagion of leprosy. Then she, Leocadia, began to behave like a respectful servant, but distant and gruff. "At the señora's orders. Whatever the señora prefers will be cooked," I read on her lips when she addressed my daughter-in-law, who made an effort to overcome her own coldness in her dealing with that basilisk. At other times her irony cut like a knife at a carving table. "Does the young gentleman want his chocolate and *croissants* served in bed or does he prefer to have breakfast with the others?" she would say to Mariano. The night before last when we went to bed, I begged her to moderate her manner so she would not lessen my joy with her behavior. As if I had rubbed salt into her wounds, she transformed into a fury and beside herself with rage, began to berate me. She leaned on the pillows with one arm and in the other she held a lit lamp up to her face so I wouldn't miss a word on her lips. "You're so blind you can't even see your own stupidity! You old goat! Don't you understand that they came only to make certain you hadn't changed your will? They don't give a damn about your blood, your name, your life, if they're certain they'll inherit your money, your house, and your paintings. If they could count on all that now, they'd leave you to rot in exile without even a sideways glance. They don't care whether you're devoured by solitude or worms, because all they want from you is the inheritance. I can't reproach them for that either, because if they lived a thousand years they'd never understand you. They may be people with your name and of your flesh; but they'll never, never really know who you were in the world." In her fury she stumbled over her words, and I thought she was going to smash the lamp into my temple. "They aren't bastards because they're egoists, they're egoists because they're bastards!" she went on as soon as she had caught her breath. "Your son Xavier is even worse than your daughter-in-law the vixen or your grandson the ne'er-do-well! Even worse because he's more of a hypocrite and less of a simpleton than that pair of clowns. Now he waits in the shadows for news from his spies. If they wrote to him that you had died, he'd race here at breakneck speed to take over everything down to the last handkerchief. Then he'd sell your paintings one by one to buy feed for his mules or bonds in the Bank of San Francisco!" I closed my eyes so I wouldn't hear her and soon, her head fallen back on the pillow, she entered my sleep. ("It's almost seven years now that my mother passed in Rome and ten days later my father followed her to hell from Naples. Only then and for the first time in my life did I feel free. Then I told myself no, to really be free it would have been necessary for them not to have engendered me. Only those who never were are free, because even the dead serve their sentence. All the rest, including the crown, is a line in the water, the intrigues of pastry chefs.") In a dining room even vaster than the one in Venta del Aire, with almost all its tables empty, a man and woman were eating lunch. I thought I could imagine his voice, which was the same as mine in other dreams; but the couple was enclosed in silence. My last portrait of His Majesty the king, wrapped in his ermine and holding the scepter, was hanging on the wall. ("On the day my mother died, my sister María Luisa wrote to me from Rome. My mother had died almost in Godoy's arms, so to speak. For an entire week he sat with her in her agony at all hours of the day or night, the two of them alone in that room. The night before her passing, my mother called for María Luisa and said to her: *I'm going to die. I recommend Manuel to you. You can be sure that you and your brother Fernando will not find a more affectionate person.* When my sister saw that the thing was going badly she moved the sausage-maker away from her side—he was crying like a penitent Magdalene—and called for the priests.") The woman was sitting now on a fallen trunk at the edge of some pastures. She wore a knitted garment similar to the sheepskin jackets of shepherds from León, and long, narrow breeches, like the ones toreros wear when testing the bulls. That man whose voice was identical to mine, or to the memory I had of my voice in my disability, remained standing at her side. She had taken his hand between hers and spoke to him in words I could not make out in the dream, her expression absorbed and intense, lit by a wintry sun. On the snow in the meadow the figures from my last tapestry cartoon were playing blind man's bluff. They played, danced, and laughed in outbursts that were silent in my deafness. Looking at the couple, I read two questions on the woman's lips: "Do you know who you are? Do you really know who we are?" "*Blind Man's Bluff* tells you who we will be," her companion replied. I conceived of that cartoon in El Capricho, after a hateful dispute with the Royal Factory. I did not want to paint others but agreed to give them a final painting that recapitulated four of my sketches of the San Isidro fiestas. The games in the forests of the dukes of Osuna gave me the theme. I left out the hermitage and the miraculous fountain, which seemed too obvious to me then. I also rejected any reference to the view of Madrid in the distance. To replace it I invented a landscape, between the tapestry and the dream, as Velázquez would do. I dressed an aristocratic dandy as a flashy majo, put a blindfold over his eyes, a long wooden spoon in his hand, and left him in the center of the canvas. Then around him I painted four pairs of foppish men and overdressed women, like him in costume, holding hands and dancing in a circle. The cartoon was a success and at the Royal Factory they flattered me and begged me to provide them with others at my convenience. In secret they offered me fees for future canvases that Francisco Bayeu, the oldest of my brothers-in-law, would never charge. I absolutely refused. That period in my life, when I painted tapestries for Santa Bárbara, had ended. Artificially prolonging it would have been as absurd as insisting on delaying dawn until midday, or holding back the wake of a ship at sea. What I could only sense then and did not understand until many years later was that an entire century, the one in which it was our fate to be born, gain the use of our reason, and conceive our children, was ending along with that part of my career. I remember very well the festival of San Isidro in the year I painted *Blind Man's Bluff*, sometime in 1787 or 1788. It was the duchess of Osuna's idea that we should all go on an excursion to the hermitage that March. "Only by associating in this way with the common people, even if only once a year, shall we understand the meaning of our time on earth," said the duchess. I wondered whether she had forgotten where people like *Costillares*, *Pepe-Hillo*, and I myself came from, the first two brought up among the tripe sellers and swindlers in the slaughterhouse in Sevilla, and the other the son of an Aragonese metal worker and gilder. The truth is I had forgotten that, and not because people thought we were her lovers but because both she and the duke called us their friends. In the eyes of the Osunas, that name was worth more than the blood of the king. In various carriages and barouches we went from El Capricho to San Isidro, crossing Madrid. "The morning is so clear it looks as if it had come from one of your paintings," the duchess said to me. "Perhaps it did," I replied, and the two of us began to laugh. My deafness would not come for another few years, and hearing my own laughter and the laughter of women wasn't limited to dreams, as it is now. Through the arch erected by His Majesty King Don Carlos III, who would die that same year, we came into Calle de Alcalá. We passed in front of the Convents of the Bernardas, the Calatravas, and the Baronesses. In the early morning the bells of San José rang for Mass, as did the bells of the Chapel of Santa Teresa, where, the duke told me, the body of Don Rodrigo Calderón lay in state after climbing to the gallows with his proverbial arrogance. "One day a monarch's favorite, the next day condemned as an embezzler. They say that when Felipe III died, Don Rodrigo Calderón, marquis de Siete Iglesias, exclaimed: 'The king has died, I am a dead man too!'" remarked the duke of Osuna. "He climbed to the scaffold in mourning, a gentleman on a mule with a large escort of constables, town criers, bailiffs, and other persons of the law. Along the streets and roads to the Plaza Mayor, where they were going to hang him, he flirted with the girls as if it were all a carnival. At that time, thieves didn't live as well as they do now, but they died with great dignity." Near the orchard of the Convent of San José and within the boundaries of the Plazuela del Almirante, lived a still unknown soldier from Extremadura named Manuel Godoy. At the corner of the Prado de San Jerónimo and Calle de Alcalá, María Teresa, still very young, was building the Palacio de Buenavista. Neither she nor her husband, the marquis de Villafranca, would ever live in it or even see it finished. At the death of María Teresa and with the looting of its contents, they would give that building to the same Extremaduran officer, now called the duke of Alcudia and the Prince of Peace. A mocking justice, I don't know whether from heaven or hell, would also have the entire fortune of the prince plundered after his fall into disgrace. ("I'm going to tell you something that nobody else knows. My mother left her entire personal fortune to her lover, the sausage-maker. Naturally I never allowed Godoy to see a penny of it. He'll end his days in Paris, rotting away in poverty, I assure you.") Beside the hermitage we drank the water of the miraculous spring. I still remember very well that it tasted of hoarfrost and sierra winds. The duchess made some almost blasphemous jokes about the wonders of the fountain. *Pepe-Hillo* and *Costillares*, however, drank in a very reserved way, their eyes closed as if they were praying in silence, begging the saint for a respite in the bullfights. "Each period had its Golden Age, which was the age of wonders," remarked the duchess of Osuna. "In pagan times it was the age when animals spoke and propounded riddles. In Christianity it was the age of miracles. Even the demon had recourse to his magic and witches' sabbaths, when incubuses fathered children on the virgins of the very Catholic Biscay. Now reason is the only ambit of the extraordinary." "Don't forget liberty, my dear," the duke said with a smile. "We believe in it as we do in all-powerful reason, although I don't know if for exactly the same motives." The poet Iriarte inhaled a pinch of snuff and stretched out beside the tablecloths in the meadow. "Perhaps miracles are still happening even though we are too blind to notice them. This disregard of portentous omens seems typical of empires in their death agony. Think of Julius Caesar ignoring the omens of his death before he went to the Senate." "The analogy is invalid, my good Iriarte, because we can hardly compare our new monarch to Caesar, much less the Roman Senate to the Council of Castilla," replied the duke. "Exactly, Iriarte, don't be sacrilegious," the duchess interjected. "I never believed in the divine right of kings, only of emperors, and of course, dukes. Nonetheless, it must be admitted that Julius Caesar, although the emperor, was a fairy." Everyone laughed, including the toreros who barely understood everything they were attempting to discuss. "I wasn't referring to His Majesty or to the Council of Castilla," Iriarte said with a smile, "but to serious, decent people, like us. Miracles are everywhere, and we don't know how to see them. Changing water into wine is no small wonder; but our survival in the painting of this man"—he pointed at me with a lazy gesture—"perhaps centuries after our death, seems equally marvelous to me. The greatest portent does not consist of transforming the present but anticipating its future changes. In this way our ashes will become our portraits, just as paint from a palette turns a canvas into a mirror." "Ah, Iriarte, what you're telling us is so beautiful!" applauded the duchess. "You ought to put it in a farce and call it *The Fountain of San Isidro*. We would put it on in the little theater at El Capricho and we would play ourselves, just as we're living it now. In the end it could turn out that we were all part of a tapestry or the memory of our painter in his old age." Iriarte smiled, shaking his head. "The project surpasses my skill, Señora. One would need a biographer of great artists, like Vasari, to write it." Someone asked who Vasari was and Iriarte spoke of *Le Vite de'più Eccelenti Pittori, Scultori e Architetti*. I was pleased that the subject had changed, because I didn't know whether Iriarte was mocking me or being sincere in his extravagant praise. Possibly both at the same time. The light was leaving like a breath of wind. Like the day. Like our lives. Thirty or thirty-five years later, on my first excursion following the war, I went back to the fountain of San Isidro. By then everyone present at the outing had died except the duchess of Osuna and me, although the two of us would not see each other again either. The night before, I had been called to the palace, where His Majesty, who had returned from Valençay a few days earlier, was asking for me. He had liked *The Second of May, 1808, in Madrid: The Battle with the Mamelukes*, and *The Third of May, 1808, in Madrid: The Shootings on Príncipe Pío Hill*, displayed on the triumphal arch at the Puerta de Alcalá. Like all of his family, he had an instinctive sense of justice toward painting that he could never apply to other people or to himself. He was absolutely right when he praised the painting of the executions more than the other canvas. According to what I was told afterward, he had ordered his carriage stopped in front of those canvases and then stepped out, to the amazement of the crowd, to look at them carefully. "The old bastard saved his skin! There was never another like him!" those who were closest heard him murmur. Then, shaking his head and smiling his hyena's smile, he returned to the carriage. In the palace that morning he did not mention my dealings with the invaders and the French king. I knew him too well and knew his attitude was due not to deference but to his plan to keep me in doubt regarding possible legal proceedings for acts of treason against the crown. The truth was I didn't care very much what he did to me, because after painting *The Shootings on Príncipe Pío Hill*, I had lost my fear of death. In fact, I could have fled with the other Frenchified Spaniards and did not, although I did not want to remind him of it then. The audience was brief, reduced to a monologue by the king. He made various references to my painting and to art in general, all of them certainly very sensible; he spoke of creating a museum for the nation with the royal collections, and finally he said that the following day, San Isidro, I was to accompany him to the hermitage and the miraculous fountain, where the crowd was going to pay homage to him. "It will be a fiesta unlike any other: a celebration of the peace of the Desired One," he specified with his pale smile. "I should like you to make notes for a possible future painting." The next morning I was obliged to share the royal carriage with him. He greeted me with a wink and an elbow in my ribs. His breath smelled of boiled eggs and tobacco. "It's necessary to recognize that in a certain sense, we are indebted to your friends the French. I confess that to you with no misgivings, if you promise to keep my secret." For the first time he was making a reference, however oblique, to my dealings with King José and his people. I deciphered the words on his lips perfectly but did not reply and did not want to understand. On the other hand, he did not seem to expect my excuses or protests, for he continued speaking: "The Intruder abolished the gallows and introduced the base garrote, which indicates irrevocable progress in our juridical customs. Anybody can learn to hang in an instant, and I myself hanged one of my mother's poodles when I was a boy as a kind of revenge for some punishment or other. As you'll recall, I was extremely clever as a boy. It was a shame I didn't follow my natural bent and hang the sausage-maker from the same tree. Don't you agree?" I think I said to him then that I had seen too many crimes during the war to desire that kind of death for anyone. He burst into cackling laughter. "Don't be a hypocrite, old man! The talent the devil gave you excuses all your faults except duplicity. You are the first hangman in the kingdom because in days gone by you tightened the noose around our necks when you painted me together with my family. In each painting you executed us in the most offhand way. I don't reproach you for it, for you were stronger and subjected us to your law." I said I hadn't dominated anyone but only painted what I saw. He nodded with a shrug. "We've both said the same thing, because you saw us as we were, inside and out. And you obliged us to assume our total truth. It was too bad that with time you too weakened, because since then I no longer believe in anyone except myself. The problem is that in reality I don't exist. I'm only a madman who imagines he's the Desired One. Tell me, old man, do you believe in God as you do in your king?" I pretended to ignore the question and he continued, now without looking at me; legs spread, slumped in his seat, eyes fixed on the roof of the carriage. "I believe in the garrote. It is the inevitable result of the natural harmony of the past century. If we are discreetly prodigal with it in these early days of peace, it can turn this madhouse into an arcadia. I'm counting on a people who owe me everything after five years of killing in my name. Now they will offer me their submission in exchange for order." As we approached the hermitage, the crowds outside increased. His Majesty the king personally opened the carriage's tasseled curtains, which had been closed until then. On the slopes of San Isidro, the troops struggled to contain the mob that cheered the monarch as it tried to invade his carriage. The sovereign smiled and waved to the right and left, bending in obsequious bows. I thought I had descended to the final chasm of hell, a hell achieved with peace, whose accurate measure not even war itself could give us. A human tide of beggars, lepers, the blind, the mutilated, the starving came with their hunger, their nakedness, and their families from lands burned by the conflict to go on an excursion to the miraculous fountain to taste the water and offer their vassalage to the king. By express order of the palace, as I learned later, the soldiers had managed the crowd with brandy made of grape skins, and the bellowing of the besotted multitudes deafened the heavens. They shouted their hurrahs for the Desired One, the Holy Inquisition, for prisons and chains. The monarch took care to tell me about it so that not even in my deafness could I be free of their roars. A stink of gangrene, sweat, and wine penetrated the carriage, to the delight of Don Fernando. "It reeks of our noble people, old man! Enjoy the trail of their flesh, since you can't manage to hear their voices. They smell like us, since they were created in our image or in God's! In any of the apparently civilized countries, like the France of your friends, this mob would have a revolution and decapitate you and me. Perhaps you first, because you came out of the same soil and the same street where they still suffer. In Valençay the Corsican once repeated to me a phrase by some Jacobin or other. With complete reason that man said that no king is born unpardonable. It must be even more unpardonable to be born an artist like you. For beings of your stripe, the ones we count on one hand in history, there is no mercy and no place on earth, although we kings sometimes allow you to paint us as we are. When death makes you inoffensive, you will be remembered as a witness to our scandals and locked in the invisible cages that the future reserves for monsters." He opened the windows, and that sea of stinking, clamoring flesh threw itself at the openings to kiss the hands of the Desired One. He, laughing, offered them to the throng with its bulging eyes and open maws; the horror multiplied my silence. He guffawed and allowed them to lick his palms, suck his fingers, bite his knuckles, and fight over who would repeatedly kiss his nails. Suddenly, in one of his unpredictable tempers, he grew bored and knocked on the roof of the carriage with the handle of his walking stick. As if it were an agreed-upon signal, the coachmen attacked the mob with their whips while the guards in the escort dispersed them by firing into the air. His Majesty the king wiped his hands with a handkerchief scented with two commingled perfumes, eucalyptus and patchouli. Then he tossed it out the window with a gesture of disgust and lit a cigar. "With a nation like this, the keys of the kingdom are well protected. Neither you nor I have anything to fear. Any authentic revolution will always be impossible in a land like ours. With the help of the garrote we shall live in peace, and the executioner will be our guardian angel. It is a consolation to know that this court of miracles adores me, because when they are primed to kill, they are more savage than anyone, as our invaders could confirm. They are equally good as killers and as lackeys. If they were to take over our cities and our weapons, we would have to shoot them for years on end to get them back on the path. In the meantime, I shall establish the art museum where they'll show the family portrait you made of us. The day will come when people won't recognize us standing there in a group because they've forgotten my name and the names of my family. Yours, on the other hand, they'll remember forever, or, at least, that is what I expect." Halfway down the slope, that starving mob, drunk on dregs, was left behind. I stared at them, absorbed, while the carriage drove away from the crowd on the road to the hermitage. After the whip lashes and the blows from rifle butts, they huddled together like a flock recently corralled by dogs. Slowly, dragging their feet, which were bare or wrapped in rags, they continued their pilgrimage to the temple and the spring. They were led by a blind man with large blank eyes and a head twisted like that of a partially decapitated puppet. Playing the guitar, he must have been singing at the top of his lungs to judge by how wide he opened his mouth. The others seemed to be singing with him. Suddenly a May storm threatened and the sky grew dark in the middle of the morning. Now it was like old blackened silver that reverberated intermittently. Soon the first lightning flashes would cross the sky near San Antonio de la Florida. I won't say that for a long time I had carried with me the memory of excursions. Expressing it this way would not reflect reality. Memory stores in its attics too many lost images that we evoke only now and then. I would sooner believe that the horde of beggars, blind men, lepers, and cripples, blown about by the disasters of war and gathered together on that San Isidro Day by their faith in the fountain and in the Desired One, followed me beyond the hermitage, going deep inside me, as if at the center of my being, where deafness muffled their bellowing, they would find the end of their exodus. Five or six years later, when I bought the Quinta del Sordo, I painted them on a wall, determined to exorcize them, as I had done earlier when I painted Saturn devouring his child. ("Recounting the story of this Spain of ours is equivalent to confessing one's secret crimes.") Perhaps it is true, because this country has been devouring itself for so long now that it has the cruelty of the deformed. In any case, the farm and its paintings will soon be Xavier's, in spite of Leocadia. (". . . They couldn't care less about your blood, your name, even your life, if they're sure of inheriting your money, your house, and your paintings. If they could count on all of it now, they'd leave you to rot in exile without ever seeing you again. They don't care at all if you're devoured by solitude or worms, because all they want from you is the inheritance . . .") I had told His Majesty the king that my ideal of happiness was to die before my son. Now this doesn't seem completely true. My concept of happiness is increasingly ambitious. To fulfill it I would need Xavier to come to Bordeaux before my death. To see him again, even if it were only for an instant, perhaps as recompense for the torture of not having heard his voice since he was a very little boy. In fact, I'm deceiving myself again, because if Xavier were to come right away, as the daughter-in-law and Marianito say he will, then the greatest blessing would be not to die. Better to forget about

living or, for that matter, about death! Better to resign myself to waiting for the arrival of my son tomorrow morning, at the latest. ("... Now
he's waiting in the shadows for news from his spies. If they wrote to
him that you had died, he would race here to take possession of everything, down to the last handkerchief. Then he would sell your paintings one by one to buy feed for his mules or bonds from the Bank of
San Francisco!") Why would I care how much money Xavier makes
with my paintings when I'm dead? I didn't paint them for my family
to hide away, as if they were the relics of a saint. What do I care what
Xavier or Marianito think of their name, which is my name? I have
been friend to four kings and the last one, the Desired One, told me
with absolute accuracy that neither he nor I was anybody. At best, we
weren't worth more or less than the beggars on their excursion, because in the bloody farce of our country, we all share the same sentence. No, I didn't paint my paintings so my family would venerate
them, and I didn't choose my name so they would revere it. My name
and my painting were imposed on me by unknown forces much
greater than my will. I always painted to know I was alive, and I
wanted to believe that in eternity I would go on painting, because
otherwise, it wouldn't have been worth living. ("I had the hope that
you would die here, of old age, in order to give you funeral rites
worthy of Apelles. I would have displayed your body at the Puerta de
Alcalá, watched over by the Royal Halberdiers and a troop of cavalry.
In single file and all the way to the Ventas del Espíritu Santo, the
people would have waited nights on end to see you dead. The mob
comes to executions as well as funerals. It's all part of the same circus.") Thank God they will never show my remains to public curiosity. Very soon they'll be in the cemetery of the Grande Chartreuse,
here in Bordeaux. Still, I have the hope that this French earth will
not be their final resting place. I'd be very happy if they were taken
the next day to Madrid. Not to display them to the people but to bury
them in San Antonio de la Florida. The truth is I don't know the
reason for this desire of mine; perhaps it is due to reasons of perspec-

tive and symmetry. In San Antonio de la Florida, and for the first time in my life, I painted as I pleased without anyone daring to reproach me for it. In other words, there I began to be who I am, although until then I wouldn't have dared to pay attention to myself. And so it would be just that when those frescoes survive me, it will be their task to watch over my bones at the Greek Cross intersect in the floor plan of the hermitage, at the foot of the main altar, beneath the lamp. I said frescoes, and the truth is they aren't frescoes and never were but rather an invention of mine inspired by old Palomino's book and carried out with a mixture of fresco and tempera. With a pound and three-quarters of fine washed sponges, soaked in color, I smoothed the tonalities of the background. Then I prepared the fresco and let it set with the plaster. Afterward I put in the dark masses and waited until everything dried. Finally, and after so much preparation, I began to design the details around the edges of the masses. In this way I achieved a double purpose: to keep the blue, green, and gray backgrounds that an authentic fresco would have given me, and to free myself from the pressures imposed by this kind of painting, when the muralist applies the colors before the plaster dries. I liked the proposed subject, because it almost resembled one of my *Caprices* in the divine mode, and I was working then on that series of engravings. A young Portuguese monk heard the news in Italy that his father, Martín Bulloes, had been falsely accused of murder in Lisbon. Flying through the air, he appeared in Portugal and resuscitated the victim of the crime for a moment so that he could reveal the name of his killer. The young monk was Saint Anthony of Padua, and this was the most celebrated of his miracles. *The first saint's festival / that God ever sent us / is the feast of San Antonio / de la Florida.* I was over fifty then, already deaf forever, and had broken with the only woman I ever really loved in this world. And yet I received the royal commission to decorate the hermitage with the eagerness of a boy selling his first painting. Around the dome I painted a circular balcony and behind its railing more than one hundred figures, witnesses to the miracle.

San Antonio performed his resurrection in medieval Lisbon, but I transferred it to the streets of the Madrid of my day. Iriarte had said that marvels abounded all around us but we did not know how to read them. After so many years, that reflection inspired me to paint a crowd, pressed together in the dome and watching the miracle with the cold curiosity they would bring to the abilities of an acrobat. As the dead man rose uncertainly from his coffin, a trio of young girls chattered, their backs to him. A boy looked at them and smiled. A blonde, somewhere between a prostitute and a know-it-all, tried to tempt him with her bared bosom. Two half-naked sick men prayed piously at the feet of the saint. A pair of small, mischievous boys climbed up to the railing so as not to miss the smallest detail of the performance. The men crowded together in groups, commenting on other matters or flirting with the women. Wet nurses, midwives, and gossips whispered among the women or flirted with the young men. The radiant symbol of divinity appeared escorted by celestial choirs in lunettes, intrados, and pendentives. The angels were very young women, carnal and exciting in their very simplicity. Naked amoretti played the part of cherubs. I painted the world I saw in the market, at bullfights, at fairs, on excursions. A country of workers' mothers and wives, of maidens and duennas, of servant girls, bawds, actresses, dressmakers, market women, nursemaids, procuresses, chamber-maids, fishwives, barmaids, amusing women. A country of soldiers, students, winter bullfighters, constables, notaries, servants at inns, porters, sacristans, bricklayers, farm laborers, the jobless, swindlers, pimps, carnival workers. At the top of the scaffold, my assistant Asensio Juliá shook his head sadly. "When all this is made public, the Holy Inquisition will take us out of here in irons," he would say to me every so often. One afternoon, María Teresa appeared at San Antonio de la Florida. By then we had reestablished our relationship, former lovers turned into more or less indecent friends. Asensio Juliá and I were on the highest planks, and from that distance I saw her laugh without being able to make out the words on her lips. And my assistant dropped his rag, as if María Teresa's exclamations from the floor were the most indecent things he had ever heard. In a fury I climbed down from the framework and confronted her, kicking away the cloths that covered the floor tiles. "If you don't mind, what the hell are you doing here? I've told you a thousand times not to come and interrupt the work. If you wanted to talk to me, you could have sent a note with one of your servants." She, in turn, asked me, still laughing, what the hell all the whores in Madrid were doing divided between heavenly glory and the balcony of a church. I replied angrily that I hadn't painted any brothel but common humanity, just as we saw it on the street and in the theater. "Don't try to explain it to me! The frescoes are beautiful! If the Escorial is our Saint Peter's, it would be fair for San Antonio de la Florida to be our Sistine Chapel." "These aren't frescoes, strictly speaking." "Whatever they are, they'll bring you a lot of headaches. Don't say afterward I didn't warn you!" "Asensio's afraid we'll leave here in the chains of the Holy Office when they open the hermitage for worship. I don't think so." "I don't either, because after all, we're on the verge of the nineteenth century. But they may force you to scrape away the entire work. The king and queen will be the first to become indignant." That year, on the Day of the Virgin, my murals were shown to the royal family. Everyone, the people from the church and the court, praised their originality. On saints' days people would fill the hermitage each morning to see themselves in the dome. María Teresa sent me a message with a servant: "My congratulations! I'm beginning to wonder whether we don't really live in your paintings and the entire country isn't a ruse and a fantasy of yours." ("Spain? Spain doesn't exist. It's one of my *Absurdities* set up ages ago.") In any case, I have the firm though irrational conviction that San Antonio de la Florida will be my final resting place. At times, almost with the same clarity as if I had painted it, I imagine the burial of my bones in that chapel. Gentlemen in frock coats, holding their top hats, listen to an old man with a flowing beard who reads three pages where my name is mentioned very frequently. No one applauds when he finishes reading, but they all nod their agreement. Then some workmen covered in long smocks, like rustics in the Toledan countryside, lower a lead coffin into an open grave directly beneath the eye of the lantern. Then they cover the opening with a large gravestone that has my last name between two dates. On top of that they place a wreath of autumn roses with a gold ribbon twisting through it: a pious tribute, as they call it, from the Royal Academy of Fine Arts, of which I had been a regular member and even the president. When night falls they all leave, and the winter stars begin to burn above the lantern. Only the moon and the chancel lamp light the chapel, where a play of mirrors in the corners multiplies my paintings and the shadows. Suddenly, with no lifting of latches or pushing of doors on their hinges, the four couples of *Blind Man's Bluff* cross the walls and, holding hands, close a circle around my grave. In the half-light the measured blows of a spoon against the wall begin to sound. Outside, the flute of some shepherd picks up and maintains the rhythm. Then they share and speed up the rhythm, as if the two of them were joining the only sounds in a universe plunged into the silence of deafness or the quietude of chasms in a sea not yet discovered. To the rhythm of the flute and the spoon, the figures in *Blind Man's Bluff* are now dancing around my grave. They skip, laugh, and become filled with longing as they dance, while echoes of voices and laughter in the mirrors and corners of the naves become animated. Up above, in the dome, the pendentives, intrados, and lunettes, the people of the miracle peer over the railing to look at them, between the female gathering of angels and the flight, suddenly halted, of a swarm of naked amoretti.

THE MONSTERS

The Duchess of Osuna

María Josefa de la Soledad Alonso Pimentel Téllez-Girón Borja y Cenellas, countess-duchess of Benavente and duchess of Béjar, Arcos, Gandía, Plasencia, Monteagudo, Mandas, and Villanueva, princess of Anglona and Squilache, marquise of Javalquinto, Gibraleón, Zahara, Lombay, Terranova, and Marquini, countess of Mayorga, Bañares, Belalcázar, Bailén, Mayalde, Casares, Oliva, Osilo, and Coguinas, viscountess of Puebla de Alcocer, was born in Madrid in 1752. At the age of nineteen she married Don Pedro Téllez Girón, marquis of Peñafiel and ninth duke of Osuna, who was three years younger. The newlyweds were first cousins, and with their marriage the Osunas took in the countship of Benavente, the duchy of Béjar, the arms of Gandía, and the blood of the Borjas (known in Italy as the Borgias), which carried them to the papal throne in the midst of crimes and acts of incest that made even the Renaissance blush. On the other hand, and perhaps because in the house of the Pimentels there were almost as many mansions as in the house of God Himself, they also counted in their lineage the saintly marquis of Lombay and grand duke of Gandía, who swore never to serve masters who turned into worms.

Antonio Marichalar, who two centuries later would be the biographer of Mariano Girón, another duke of Osuna and the grandson of María Josefa, called the Osunas purebred, dissolute and prodigal, and the Pimentels foppish, insolent, and pretentious, very given in each generation to erudition and reading. In the eighteenth century in Spain there were only ten families and one hundred individuals with privileges as ancient as theirs, warranted by both branches since the days of the emperor Carlos V. They used the familiar *tú* among themselves and kept their heads covered before the king, who must call them cousins. Antonina Vallentin cited a French historian of the period, who spoke of the anxieties of another aristocrat of lesser distinction. "A recently created Grandee begged his whole life for a *tú* that he would have paid for with his blood, and from his peers he received only a Most Excellent Señor." The Osuna Pimentels have the right to four teams of mules for their carriage and an escort of four servants with torches. It was probably through Cardinal Prince Don Luis, the king's brother who was archbishop of Toledo at the age of eight, and at ten wore a cardinal's purple, that Goya met the Osuna family. By then Don Luis had left the church and its vanities and transmitted his rights to the throne, which he legally possessed, in order to marry María Teresa de Vallabriga, who thought she was a descendant of the kings of Navarre but was actually the daughter of a captain in the cavalry. Goya did an oil painting of the duchess of Osuna in 1785, and another portrait of her with the duke and their three children in 1790. The duchess and the cardinal prince had the talent to pay attention to Goya before he was even aware of his genius. In the rumor mills of the court they began to call her Goya's mistress, as earlier they had called her the lover of *Costillares* and especially of *Pepe-Hillo*. In any case, after his illness, between 1792 and 1793, Goya would abandon the world of the duchess for that of her despised rival: María del Pilar Teresa Cayetana Manuela Margarita de Alba.

In Goya's paintings, the duchess of Osuna, the Peñafiel, or Loyal Rock, as the painter called her in his letters to Martín Zapater, was a woman with gray eyes, tight lips, and a face like a razor, who reminded Antonina Vallentin of Egyptian queens in their hieratic statues. ("I'm feeling well and drinking well and enjoying myself as much as I can. But my ankle is still swollen, and even more so at night. It doesn't worry me too much, since I've been hunting twice. Once with the Peñafiel, and the other time with other enthusiasts, and on both hunts I've been outstanding in killing game.") Lady Holland called the duchess the most distinguished lady in Madrid, for her virtues and her *bon goût*. Since she was a very intelligent woman, perhaps the most cultivated in the Spain of her time, one doubts her mental health because of her unpredictable and extravagant acts. She was disappointed with her portrait by Esteve and slashed it with a knife in the presence of the painter. One night the card game at her table was suspended when someone dropped a coin that rolled and jingled on the floor. The duchess lit new candles with a roll of bills and handed the burning candles to the servants. The legate of the Most Christian King invited the Osunas to dine in the French embassy, where they skimped on champagne. When the duke and duchess returned the invitation, María Josefa ordered the ambassador's horses to be watered with champagne upon their arrival. General Córdoba, who had been present at the burning of the bills, was overwhelmed and called her the haughtiest lady in Spain and the most elegant and highest-ranking one in Europe.

Her thinness, both ambiguous and fragile, contradicted the vitality of the duchess. She would die at the age of eighty-one, many years after surviving the starvation and anguish of the war. As a young woman she would exhaust the strongest horses, riding at a full gallop across her lands. At times, and anticipating the teaching of Giner at the Free Institution of Teaching, she also went to the Guaderrama Mountains alone, climbing the cliffs by day and resting at night beneath the trees. In more daring adventures, and always without an escort, she walked the roads for weeks on end, "not fearing harsh weather or thieves," sleeping outdoors or in haystacks. On these spirited outings, she must have encountered the farmers of La Mancha as Cabarrús saw them on the road to Madrid, fleeing their homes because of poor harvests and epidemics of fever, begging, half naked. In Cádiz, where she also had properties and spent part of the summer, the duchess de Osuna y de Béjar would encounter the even greater wretchedness of the peasants of Lower Andalucía, which horrified Campomanes. The immense majority of them slept outdoors, lived on boiled bread soup when they were working while their wives prostituted themselves and their children became beggars. María Josefa de la Soledad Alonso Pimentel knew that her family and the other nine, who shared the privilege of using familiar address with one another, controlled all the farming and livestock wealth of Spain through the system of primogeniture. She also knew that the duke's rents, even reduced by the backwardness of agriculture, were among the highest in Europe, exceeding three million francs a year. María Josefa de la Soledad Alonso Pimentel, countess-duchess de Benavente and duchess de Osuna, would oppose primogeniture with the curious, prudent mental reservations of her teacher in economics, Gaspar Melchor de Jovellanos, who asked that those already established be respected but that the acquisition and bequest of other large estates be prohibited. And yet, above all, María Josefa de la Soledad Alonso Pimentel must have imagined in her deepest skepticism that all of it, the country, the king, her properties, the hunger of the peasantry, and she herself, were merely an almost transparent retable, painted in the air by her favorite artist, Don Francisco Goya Lucientes.

The first Pimentel was a Portuguese knight who died fighting for Alfonso the Wise in the battle of Campo de la Verdad. A descendant of his received the first countship in the family in recognition of his military deeds. As payment for other exploits, the Catholic Kings awarded the Duchy of Benavente to Rodrigo Pimentel. His family would continue calling themselves counts for entire generations, as if the new title were the coat of arms of upstarts. María Josefa Pimentel, duchess de Osuna, also took part in a military action to prove herself. In 1781, by order of the French admiral, the duke of Crillon, she embarked with her husband on the conquest of Menorca. Disguised as a cabin boy, in a scheme devised only by her and her husband, she endured without complaint all the difficulties of her feigned condition and experienced the triumphant naval battle on the first line of fire.

Essentially, however, this woman, full of contrasts as singular as they were inexplicable, was an intellectual. The Economic Society of Friends of the Nation, its Madrid branch presided over by Jovellanos, elected her director of its Council of Ladies, when they were admitted to the organization by royal decree on August 27, 1787. Although he recognized María Josefa's talents and the invaluable help she had given to the duke de Osuna when he occupied the presidency, Jovellanos himself accepted the king's decision with ironic caution. "Ladies will never frequent our Councils. Modesty will perpetually distance them. How will their delicate virtue permit them to appear at a meeting of men of such diverse conditions and states, to take part in our discussions and readings, to mingle their refined voices in the tumult of our disputes and arguments?"

Nonetheless, the duchess gave various lectures on economics and professed the science in the Alameda, according to the principles maintained by Jovellanos in his *Report on the Agrarian Law.* She denounced ecclesiastical amortization, augmented by trusts, benefices, and bequests of the dying. "If in this there is any abuse or any wrongdoing, application of the remedy is the responsibility of the Church. ... But in the meantime, can the proposal of a means to reconcile the considerations due to so pious and authorized a custom with those demanded by the welfare and preservation of the State seem foreign to our devotion?" In the final analysis, the progress of a country was reduced to the regeneration of all its estates, especially those that sacrificed material privileges to the common good. In economics, the word *primogeniture* was the one that presented the greatest difficulties, because there was hardly another more detestable in wise, just legislation. The right to transmit private property at death was foreign to the laws and designs of nature. Nonetheless, the Economic Society of Friends of the Nation would always view primogeniture among the nobility with great respect and greater indulgence, and if it could temporize in so delicate a matter, it would gladly do so to avoid the courts and violence. "It seems just to me, ladies and gentlemen, that if the nobility cannot gain estates and riches in a war, it sustains itself with those received by its eldest sons. Let it retain its primogenitures in good health; but if these are a necessary evil, let them be treated as such and reduced as much as possible."

In 1783 the Osunas bought from Count de Priego his rural properties to the south of Aranjuez, a league and a half from Madrid, close to the Aragón road. The lands, called the Alameda, consisted of a country house and several farms. Two years later, Goya painted his first portrait of the duchess, dressed like Queen María Luisa, who imposed in turn the fashions of the Trianón and Marie Antoinette of France. On the other hand, María Josefa changed the name of her new properties and called them El Capricho. From that time on, as Ortega carefully noted in his incomplete *Papers on Goya*, that name tended to be repeated in the artist's correspondence and in documents that referred to him. On January 4, 1794, having recently survived his very serious illness and just completed his *Wild Bull,* which would soon be copied by Esteve or Vicente López, Goya wrote to Iriarte, the duchess of Osuna's public poet: "To occupy an imagination mortified by considerations of my ills, and to compensate in part for the great expenditures they have occasioned, I began to make a series of boudoir paintings. In these I've succeeded in making observations which commissioned works regularly don't have room for, and in which caprice and invention have no place."

The other Caprice, the one belonging to the Osunas, was the convergence of two different worlds under the skies of Goya's tapestries. On one hand, the somewhat provincial copy of Versailles, with the vast granite staircase, the marble balustrade, the portholes, the tall columns, the wide mirrors, the busts of Trajan and Caracalla, the nude statues, the Chinese tapestries, the golden candelabra, the crystal chandeliers, the concert rooms, the theaters, the conservatories, the colored fountains, the gardens set out in straight lines, the avenues of polished pebbles, the boxwood trees pruned according to the Cartesian *Discours de la méthode.* On the other, a labyrinth of pleasant paths among poplars and acacias, aviaries, pools, swings, artificial meadows whose green resembled that of Paris, gazebos, Cupids, drawbridges, artificial waterfalls, rose gardens, weeping willows, parasols, fountains, oleander, Alexandrian laurels, midget horses, peacocks, kites, flamingos, and flocks of sheep whiter than snow ever was. At times the two worlds mingled in the theater at the Caprice. Iriarte wrote short artificial plays for that stage, in which the duchess of Osuna always played the principal role, dressed as a shepherdess or a maiden of another time. Her performances inspired pleasure that no doubt had a strong whiff of adulation. She had assurance, a well-modulated voice, and the naturalness of one who perhaps believed that the entire world was just another stage for a farce called history.

The Alameda was the theater, the image and likeness of its owner. As in the palace of those other dukes, the ones in *Don Quijote*, all was mask and costume in the Caprice, to the greater glory and gratification of madness. The one hundred cousins of the king, those who used informal address with one another, disguised themselves and their wives as lower-class dandies, fops, and blades. In another century, Eugenio d'Ors stressed the distinctions among these categories. The dandies, or *chisperos*, came originally from the district of Maravillas, where there was an abundance of forges and men of bronze. The fops, or *manolos*, came from Lavapiés and tended to be workers, though unmannerly and quarrelsome. The blades, or *majos*, were thugs, but very devout. They lived by gambling, smuggling tobacco, and pimping, but did not shun knife fights in defense of their honor. A blade would sell for one night his wife, his lover, or his sister if the deal were closed with the proper respect, in deference to the idea that from the king on down, no one is more than anyone else in the two Castillas. When times became difficult for procurers, the blade went down on his knees before God and prayed in San Francisco or in the Almudena, pleading for the assistance of heaven in his trade.

For those at the Caprice, blades, fops, and dandies could all be reduced to the people, recently discovered and glorified by the boredom and eroticism of the aristocracy. The ladies of the Alameda wore, like the majas, long black skirts, tight sashes, high bodices, and bolero jackets with tassels. On their heads they wore lace mantillas, among whose folds their breasts peeked out like doves. The gentlemen gathered their hair in nets like those of bullfighters and Gypsies peddling their goods at fairs. They wore a white shirt, a short jacket, breeches tight across the thigh, silk stockings, and shoes adorned with good large buckles. Reality penetrated behind the masks in the parks and the house of the Osunas. Toreros from the slaughterhouse of Sevilla, like *Costillares* and *Pepe-Hillo*, were transformed into María Josefa's preferred guests. They were men who could barely sign their names, but their pride, consisting of conceit and dignity, their heels coming down hard on all marble, and their contempt for death set fire to the ladies like hot embers. The Year of Our Lord 1789 would be, for some, the year of the French Revolution, and for others the year of the ascent to the throne of His Catholic Majesty Don Carlos IV. For devotees of the fiesta brava, it would also be the year when Pedro Romero lifted the gored, unconscious body of *Pepe-Hillo* up to the box of the Señora Duchess de Osuna and left it at her feet during the great bullfight of the coronation celebrations.

The war would end that Carnival ("Señor Máiquez, Señor Máiquez, this isn't the theater because here you die for real"). A year before the catastrophe, the duke de Osuna died. The duchess, about whom Jean-François Chabrun would say that she belonged to a species more subtle and perhaps more perverse than that of the blades and coxcombs, opened a public library in her house in Leganitos. The Austrian ambassador brought her forbidden books from Paris in the diplomatic pouch, such as Helen Williams's *English Letters* and Rousseau's *Confessions*. A French academic, Marius Charles Joseph de Pougens, took charge of buying other, less dangerous works for her, as well as tea from China, Jouy fabric, iris perfumes, and seeds for her gardens. In 1802, when Chateaubriand's *Le Génie du Christianisme* appeared, María Josefa was in a fury because Pougens removed it from the list and did not send it to her, believing it excessively dangerous. The academic offered ample excuses, and the tempest remained in a teapot.

She spent the war in her house in Cádiz, not collaborating with the invader, unlike many other nobles, in spite of her Voltairean and reformist disposition. She survived not only the reigning monarchs but also their son, the Desired One. She was too intelligent not to realize that, although she could save her properties, her time, about which Goya would leave the most complete artistic testimony in the cartoons he made for tapestries, had disappeared in the conflict. In her old age, the duchess de Osuna perhaps would say the era came to an end with the French Revolution of 1789, even though a country as mentally and materially backward as Spain would need another twenty years and the catastrophe of a war to understand that. Wearied and exhausted by so much failure, she died in her palace at La Cuesta de la Vega on October 5, 1833.

November 15, 1975

In "Blind Man's Bluff" it never grows dark, because the artist has stopped time and the sky is made of paper. But in the gardens of El Capricho, where "Pepe-Hillo" and "Costillares" push the duchess of Osuna back and forth in a swing, night begins to fall slowly on the pools and acacias. Very soon, when it is totally dark, all the figures in this long costume party will be as blind as the false majo *who probes the air with his wooden spoon. Then, in the endless shadows that still encircle the country, the eyes of Goya's monsters will begin to blaze in his own "Caprices"; that labyrinth made to the measure of our recent and eternal history, where everything will always be the same, with reason or without it, because men don't know the way.*

He reread the conclusion of his notes on the cartoons for tapestries on which he had worked all night, and put out the table lamp. Outside, morning turned the icy needles of a pine tree pink. A short while before, when dawn was just breaking, he heard Marina get up. Without exchanging a single word with Sandro, wrapped in an old gray coat, she crossed in front of the misted window after closing the door with a single dry bang. Then he heard her trying to start the cold, recalcitrant engine of the Simca in order to drive away, shifting gears, along the broad snow-covered path that disappeared into the woods.

He turned on the gas stove and poured a cup of boiling coffee. Only then, as he thought about the *Fight with Cudgels* and the other black paintings at the Quinta del Sordo, did he notice the radio lost among the books. The medical reports of the night before were summarized and confirmed that morning with no major changes. *At 15: 30 hours yesterday, His Excellency the Generalissimo presented an acute situation with arterial hypotension, an increase in venous pressure, and abdominal distension, agreeing with a critical abdominal diagnosis caused by a probable deficiency in suturing, in virtue of the local and general circumstances present in the disease. Having decided on an immediate intervention, it was carried out in the operating theater of "La Paz" Hospital Complex by Professor Manuel Hidalgo Huerta, with the collaboration of Doctors Artero, Alonso Castrillo, and Cabrero. The anesthesiology and recovery team was composed of Doctors Llauradó and Francisco Fernández Juste. Cardiological control was carried out by Doctors Vital Aza, Señor de Uría, Minguez y Palma, in the presence of the usual medical team. The surgical intervention confirmed a crescent dehiscence related to the aspect of shock described previously, at the level of gastro-jejunal anastomosis of reduced diameter, with the emergence of the intestinal contents into the peritoneal cavity. With the dehiscent zone newly sutured, drains were placed in the abdominal cavity and jejunal loop. The intervention lasted two hours and was satisfactorily tolerated. When it was over the prognosis was extremely grave.*

José Luis Pérez Olmedo, Madrilenian, married with three children, a technical specialist in the installation of air conditioning, twenty-six years old, an Apostolic Catholic and probably a fan of the

Rayo Vallecano soccer team, appeared at the door of "La Paz" to donate one of his kidneys to Franco. "My wife's a little frightened, but she understands. We Spaniards owe everything to this man who's suffering so much inside." They took down his information and the nature of the offer, while the media saved his image for posterity. Then the man went to work. A woman from Cuatro Caminos came to the clinic "to offer something that perhaps will help the miracle." Wrapped in a perfumed handkerchief she had a gold medal of the Virgin del Carmen; another of Our Lady of Lourdes; a ring with a ruby mounted in small diamonds; and a paper Spanish flag. She said that over the years and generations, these articles, kept in a reliquary, had worked many wonders in her house. Gerardo González Serrano, a gardener at the Pardo for three decades and now eighty-six years old and an invalid, was driven each morning to the doors of "La Paz" to follow the latest news up close. Anselmo Paulino Álvarez, ambassador of the Dominican Republic in Madrid, declared to the press that "the Generalissimo is the greatest chief of state left in Europe. After the last operation they are telling us that Franco has improved. The impressions are favorable and we are very pleased. I have been a personal friend of his for twenty years." Salvador Tébar Jiménez, a stevedore from Cartagena, traversed eight kilometers, the distance between "La Paz" and the Puerta del Sol, with fifty kilos of cement on his back. "I wanted to keep this promise, in gratitude to Franco," he said.

At 23:30 hours on the previous day *the evolution of the illness of His Excellency the Head of State, hospitalized in the Social Welfare Hospital Complex of "La Paz," was the following: the Generalissimo's condition of endotoxic shock could be surmounted during the surgical intervention. The postoperative evolution in the first five hours was satisfactory, with arterial and venous tensions, and cardiac rhythm and frequency within acceptable limits. The pulmonary situation did not deteriorate either. The prognosis continued being extremely grave.* The hospital was watched over by Franco's own bodyguards and a reserve company of the armed police composed of fifty-six members, two sergeants, and a lieutenant. Three companies relieved one another every eight hours, protecting the dying man from sunup to sundown. A group of Cuban exiles sent the Caudillo a bouquet of roses. Through the Subsecretariat of the Ministry of the Interior, the private residence of the Generalissimo received a letter, signed by Lorenzo Valverde Ruiz, where in the name of the wounded veterans of the Republic (who were always denied pensions) he expressed best wishes for a rapid recovery. The government was also congratulated in that note for its efficiency and calm. The child María Ángeles Lazcano López, hospitalized in the "Francisco Franco" clinic in July of the previous year at the same time as the Caudillo, in his penultimate illness, now brought him a bouquet of flowers with a note written in India ink and in colors, expressing her desires for an immediate recovery. Another little girl, Paloma Trujillano, sent a rose to the patient each day, accompanied by a card that said: "I keep praying." A priest from Alcalá de Henares sent a medal of the Virgin of Alcalá, and an old woman from Jaén offered another medal, along with an image of the Virgin de Tiscar, "because they are from lands often honored by the presence of the Generalissimo."

Today, November 15, at 9:00 a.m., postoperative progress continues with arterial and venous pressure constant, and rhythm and frequency of the pulse within acceptable limits. The pulmonary situation remains stable, with respiration assisted according to the usual techniques of postoperative recovery. The session of hemodialysis was well tolerated and efficacious. The prognosis continues to be extremely grave. The man dying in Madrid had promised to carry Spain to the heights or leave the country feet first. Now he was dying irremediably beneath the cloak of the Virgin del Pilar and guarded by the chaste arm of Saint Teresa, as well as by the medals of the Virgins of Tiscar, Alcalá de Henares, Carmen, and Lourdes. The economic, intellectual, and moral greatness of his country was rather less evident and much more arguable. As Raymond Carr once told Sandro, the victor in the civil war proclaimed that he had destroyed the Spanish nine-teenth century. In other words, the liberal tradition that filled almost a century and a half of history, in spite of so many armed interruptions and its own errors, falsehoods, political bosses, and limitations of every kind. "As the earlier prophets of the iron surgeon saw it," Carr continued, "the marginal cost of authoritarianism is, however, very high and it isn't as easy to cross the Rubicon a second time as it was before the first."

Sandro had shown himself to be partially in agreement with the English historian. From his own point of view, Francoism was not the final and most prolonged response of the iron surgeons to the liberal tradition, but the inevitable result of its own disaster. "In Spain, so far," he had replied, "everything has failed, the monarchy, the Republic, autonomous regimes, parties, institutions, and men. When Francoism ends, with the death of Franco, all that will remain will be the failure of the regime and once again we'll begin all over again from absolute zero." Raymond Carr burst into laughter, shaking his head, in the face of a nihilism that reminded him of Baroja's and seemed as ironic as it was absolute in someone named Sandro Vasari. "You're even worse than the Spaniards," he said, "you have the fanatical disbelief characteristic of all converts."

He didn't reply because the discussion had become useless. Then he said to himself that the country was still on the uncertain eve of the eighteenth century. Three fundamental and irreplaceable freedoms—of expression, representation, and association—would soon be *l'illusion mystique* of the Iberian arena, as André Malraux, in another time, would call the libertarian communism of the anarchists. Two and a half centuries after Diderot, Spain believed in the voice of democracy with the same fervent ingenuousness as Diderot had believed in the voice of nature. On a file card Sandro kept a citation as a possible epigraph for a chapter in his book. *Que nous dit cette voix (de la nature et des passions) de nous rendre heureux? Doit-on et peut-on en resister? Non, l'homme le plus vertueux et le plus corrompu lui*

obeissent également. Il est vrai qu'elle leur parle un langage bien dif-
ferent; mais que tous les hommes soient eclairés, et elle leur parlera à
tous le langage de la vertu. Slowly he tore up the card. He felt the fear,
familiar and therefore not too bitter, that the country would come
late to its appointment with the past. "From Socrates to ourselves we
have retreated centuries along the paths of the soul," R. had once said
to him, and then added: "The atrophy of science in our time is called
Hiroshima. The crisis of reason has no name." Sandro wondered what
name would fit the crisis of Spain, a nation condemned to look for
itself in a mirror lost behind its back. Immediately he shrugged. The
question was too evident and the answers far too obvious. Any of
Goya's titles would be the right answer to the question. For example,
Furious Absurdity.

Goya. In reality who was Francisco Goya Lucientes, and above
all who would he, Sandro Vasari, be in the eyes of Francisco Goya Lucientes? Until he learned how to establish his purpose as biographer
in those terms, he would not know with any certainty what kind of
book he intended to write about the owner of the Quinta del Sordo.
The interior of every biography, as Ortega had discovered and predi-
cated in vain with regard to that unparalleled genre, was, in the final
analysis, an ideal sketch of the chronicler as seen by the subject. "If
this land and its history are an *Absurdity* of Goya's, each and every one
of us is somewhere in his work, including, naturally, Franco himself
in his death agony." *Goya, cauchemar plein de choses inconnues, / De*
foetus qu'on fait cuire au milieu des sabbats, / De vieilles au miroir
et d'enfants toutes nues, / Pour tenter les démons ajustant bien leurs
bas. Baudelaire was mistaken. The nightmare seemed filled not with
the unknown but with the most visible contemporary history. In the
transition from the eighteenth to the nineteenth century, Goya had
predicted the destiny of the twentieth, as Bosch in the Middle Ages
had anticipated the surrealists. If Goya had not existed, the country
would have had to invent him in order to recognize itself, uselessly,
in his work. "In his paintings and prints, our time and our destiny are

arranged and ordered, just as, according to Cortázar, *Don Quijote* is hidden in the ink of an inkwell, and one of Garcilaso's hendecasyllables is wandering, dispersed, in the pages of a dictionary."

When thinking about the Spanish eighteenth century, it would be better to forget about the Rights of Man and turn to Goya's last four cartoons for the Royal Tapestry Factory. In Gudiol's catalogue, Sandro contemplated *The Meadow of San Isidro, The Hermitage of San Isidro, The Picnic,* and *Blind Man's Bluff.* Then he noticed for the first time that the four canvases, including the last one, comprised variations on a single theme: the fiesta and excursion on the saint's day. Suddenly he also recalled that it was May 15, again under the sign of the bull, like the shootings, the return of the Desired One, the coronation of his father, and the fatal gorings of *Pepe-Hillo,* Joselito, Granero, and *Varelito.* A stone's throw from the hermitage and its miraculous fountain was the Príncipe Pío Hill, the site of the Quinta del Sordo, and, naturally, Goya's tomb in San Antonio de la Florida. A trail of blood in the sand seemed to lead him to the exact center of that arena, presided over by the second sign of the Zodiac, at the top of the Ecliptic of a country always identical to itself, from Goya to Picasso, from *The Disasters of War* to *Guernica,* through *La Tauromaquia.* Then he evoked Godoy's final letter, still unpublished, whose photocopy R. had given him. "At times I think I've lived someone else's dream: the dream of reason."

The bells in the town repeated ten in the morning. Sandro began to feel uneasy about Marina's delay. As if he were waking from sleep, he also began to hear the radio still playing among the books. A popular Madrilenian figure, the *Pirulo,* displayed a poster of the princes of Spain, edged with the national flag, to the crowd gathered in front of the hospital complex. At the bottom of the profiles of Their Highnesses (Juan Carlos had not been acclaimed king, not yet) the caption said: *The people love their Princes. Everything is tied up and tied up tight.* The little girl María Mercedes del Mar Manzanares left a bouquet of flowers at the entrance to the hospital, along with an envelope she had written herself, which said: *For Franco.* Sandro turned off the radio and left the house.

The snow was beginning to melt. Puddles were forming along the larger path, the one that went deep in the woods along wide turns, in the soil that had been divided by the Simca. The morning was almost springlike, and a sun of polished gold shone past slow-moving clouds. Through the brittle ice on the branches, at intervals made iridescent by the light, the entire forest seemed made of malachite. High in the sierra and with its back to France, the centuries were crumbling a watchtower. Sandro stopped for an instant, stamping on the snow, when he heard a crow cawing. The bird had survived the first cold spells and stridently proclaimed its presence in the thicket. Then he shouted for Marina and waited in vain for her response, straining to hear her in the distance. For a moment as interminable as the time we imagine asleep at the bottom of a well, he felt completely deaf in the silence that enfolded him. Then he thought he detected in some fold of consciousness a remote presentiment of all the sounds asleep now in winter. Everything that slithers, buzzes, gnaws, or flaps, hibernating or larval beneath the snow, pierced his spirit in a language so quiet that Sandro himself could not understand it.

He followed the trail of the car on the road. With distant remorse, he blamed himself for having neglected Marina in recent days. ("Sandro, do you think I'm going crazy?") While he stopped drinking in order to lose himself in his work, Marina behaved in increasingly inexplicable ways. First she said she had seen Goya's bull in the forest, alive, with banderillas and the cape secure at the back of his neck, looking at her through the window with those eyes at once monstrously human and inconceivable. ("They were bloodshot and wide open, like in the painting, though his wasn't an animal's gaze but a man's, a man chained in hell.") Then she began to sink into long periods of remote silence that she savored, smiling and lying on the floor in any corner of the house. At times she burst into fits of completely unexpected and inappropriately shrill laughter. She would flee then to the countryside, regardless of whether it was day or night, and would not return until hours later, her hysteria apparently forgotten. At first Sandro tried to quiet her and reason with her. He became convinced almost immediately of the uselessness of his efforts, and isolated himself once again in his book. Now and then they would take a walk along that same path or have lunch at the inn in town, which smelled of vinegar, scorched meat, whitewash, and very old straw. One night they also had dinner at the hotel in town, under a large map of those lands and a reproduction of the last portrait of Fernando VII, painted by Goya, whose presence in the dining room Sandro could not explain to himself. On these occasions, and when they made laborious love at daybreak, they hardly spoke.

He saw the car and heard the laughter almost at the same time. The Simca was parked and empty beside a slope protected by a grove of dark mimosa. Marina must have left it impetuously, in a rush, because the key was still in the ignition and a door was half-open. Sandro closed it before he put the key in his pocket. He proceeded as if unaware of what he was doing, listening to the laughter coming from some level fields at the foot of the incline and behind the mimosas. He crossed the thicket by a small trail that Marina had undoubtedly used. When he was barely past the foliage, at the end of a bend in the trail, he saw her sitting on a fallen trunk, profiled against the sky, her hands crossed on her knees. He shouted her name and she did not respond, though she seemed to call to him with a gesture somewhere between uncertain and absorbed. She was listening in a daze to the laughter rising from the deepest grass, and she beckoned to him. Having left the grove, and now next to Marina, he saw the four couples of *Blind Man's Bluff* closing their circle in the scythed meadow around the young blindfolded man who tried to touch their chests with his spoon. He failed, perhaps confused by the shrieks of the girls and the guffaws of the men. Staggering around, he waved the spoon in the air, while the others evaded his attempts and went on with the dance, consumed with joy in the midst of their affectations.

"Sandro, do you see what I see?"

"Yes," he said in a voice as quiet as hers, "yes, I think I see it."

"Which is the hallucination here? Them or us?"

He took a long time to answer. He felt his heart pounding and smelled the vague scent of smoke from the snow-covered woods. ("The water we touch in the rivers is the last of what has passed and the first of what is to come; just like the present day," Leonardo had said so that R. could paraphrase it in that place.) The game of blind man's bluff continued in the snow, accompanied by laughter. He closed his eyes for a few moments, but the laughter did not stop as he touched Marina's back with a hand that seemed to belong to another man. The circle turned to the right, like the hands of a clock where the hours were living creatures. He recalled what he had written the night before ("It seems evident that all the protagonists in *Blind Man's Bluff* are wearing costumes recently made to measure. They are members of a gilded rabble, as they would be called today, dressed like the authentic *canaille* on morning excursions to the miraculous fountain.") Suddenly he also recalled the controversial adventure of Anne Moberly and Eleanor Jourdain. Seventy or seventy-five years ago (*Où sont-ils passes, les becs de gaz?* / *Que sont-elles devenues, les vendeuses d'amour?*) two elderly English schoolteachers, virtuous, corseted, and pale, took their first trip to France one summer. They went to Versailles and suddenly, as they passed in front of the Trianon, they crossed paths with ladies, gentlemen, and *petit-maîtres*, coiffured, dressed, and shod in the rococo fashion. They even saw Marie Antoinette's dairy and the queen herself, with her wide hoop skirt and triangular tulle shawl, sitting on a marble seat and leaning on a staff adorned with wild roses as she chatted with her ladies-in-waiting in a French the teachers did not understand. The next year Anne Moberly and Eleanor Jourdain returned to Versailles, and the scene was repeated. The ecstasy of Sandro and Marina, however, was different. They weren't conjuring up those who had lived in another century but figures in a painting, embodied as fops and dandies in

short jackets and buckle shoes, in order to make them dance in the
snow.

"Which is the hallucination here? Them or us?" Marina repeated.

"We're as true as they are," he finally replied. "They're playing
blind man's bluff for us."

"No, they're playing blind man's bluff for you. They don't even
notice my presence. This is a fiesta in your honor, a masked ball in
the woods. Sandro, do you know who you are?"

"This isn't a country. Spain has never existed. It's one of Goya's
Absurdities, established ages ago," he had said to Marina a short while
before. That day he'd had a premonition, confused and inexplicable,
that another man inside him was saying those words. "I'm Sandro
Vasari, a descendant of Giorgio Vasari and three generations of émigrés *terroni*," he confessed to Marina when he met her again. Almost
thirty years later, when Franco began his dying, he found himself
obliged to admit a very different reality. "In this joke of a country,
human beings aren't capable of knowing who they are precisely because everything's the same here." Last spring, also in another life, he
awoke at dawn, intoxicated, and scrawled in a notebook: "Saturn is
my self-portrait and only tonight did I understand that." Three weeks
before, when he got drunk for the last time in the tavern in town,
he heard again deep inside the hidden voice that, still sounding like
someone else's, seemed inexorably fused with his own. "Then I understood that if a monster inhabited man, this monster was always a puppet." He thought he had returned to the most diaphanous of dreams,
the one he ironically would forget for months on end only to recall
it in the abandoned mill. He had lost his way in the labyrinth of the
Great Pyramid, looking for its center, the point that would coincide
with the death chamber of the pharaoh. On that groping pilgrimage
through false mirrors, he began to wonder whether he was pursuing
a dead man who did not exist: whether the pharaoh, in the most foolish kind of sarcasm, had built the pyramid with the sole intention of

not being buried in its interior. When he finally found the crypt behind a door closed with a simple latch, he encountered the family of Carlos IV posing there, crowded together and waiting for a painter. Queen María Luisa smiled at him with her toothless mouth, and a moment before he awoke, she said to him: "Let's go, let's go. We're waiting for you, arranged just as you said. You can begin the painting whenever you like." That, however, was only a dream. ("The dream we see is the last of those that have passed and the first of those that will come; just like the present day.") On the other hand, now they confronted living creatures, although they had come from a painting, and their laughter stunned the woods.

"We are witnessing an illusion in reverse, in time and not in space; toward the past and not toward the future."

"I know very well what we are witnessing," replied Marina. "It's a painting but it's alive. I also know that we have gone crazy, though not even this madness is ours."

"We're not seeing a painting but its models." He had to raise his voice, drowned out by laughter. "This isn't *Blind Man's Bluff.* It's the final dance of the excursions to San Isidro, before those on the outing turn into monsters like the ones in the Quinta del Sordo."

"It's *Blind Man's Bluff* and they're calling to us to enter the dance. At least they're calling to you."

"It's the last festivity before the catastrophe; but it falls to us only to observe it. We're watching a May 15 of another century, and this is its dance of death."

"Its dance of death?"

"There's no other in this carnival. Everybody dresses as what they never were. They are the dandies and debutantes of the finest nobility. You can see that in their ease, their hands, even hear it in their laughter."

"It's true," Marina agreed softly. "More than figures by Goya they seem to be by Watteau."

"Still, they're dressed like Goya's dandies and flashy girls in order to dance in the snow as they do in the painting. Each era has its own dance of death, just as it has its own way of conceiving children." He could feel Marina's shoulder contract and straighten beneath his palm. "*Blind Man's Bluff* is the eighteenth century's. Ours, naturally, is *Guernica*."

This my dance now brings forward/these two beautiful maidens,/who came, very unwilling/to listen to my sad songs;/roses, blooms will not help them/nor their lovely adornments./If they could they would leave but/they cannot, they are my wives. From the *Dance of Death* to *Guernica*, passing through *Blind Man's Bluff*, the dead danced in living history, apparently condemned, with death as the only evidence. As the *Dance of Death* foretold from the agony of the Middle Ages, the fops and ridiculous beauties of *Blind Man's Bluff*, dressed in the clothes of lower-class followers of bullfights, would soon reach for other masks as mortal as they were. Waiting for them were the holy father, the emperor, the cardinal, the king, the patriarch, the duke, the archbishop, the lord high constable, the bishop, the knight, in the common certainty of their destiny. Then dancers not yet conceived would join the circle in the turning of blood and of time. Dancing along with the flashy lower classes would be José Luis Pérez Olmedo, who wanted to offer one of his kidneys to Franco; the woman from Cuatro Caminos, with her medals, her ring, and her little paper Spanish flag; Gerardo González Serrano, the invalid gardener at El Pardo; Anselmo Paulino Álvarez, ambassador of the Dominican Republic and a personal friend of the Generalissimo; Salvador Tébar Jiménez with his bag of cement on his back; the Cuban exiles with their bouquets of roses; Lorenzo Valverde Ruiz, the disabled soldier of the Republic; the little girl María Ángeles Lazcano López, with her vase of flowers and her note in India ink; the little girl Paloma Trujillano, who wrote on her cards: "I keep praying"; the priest presented a medal of the Virgin of Alcalá; and the old woman from Jaén, who offered another medal of Our Lady of Tiscar, because Franco would honor her lands with his presence. In the same dance, the fiesta of the end of the world, Pirulo would come in then with his sign and María Mercedes del Mar Manzanares with her envelope for the Caudillo. "We'll all go there and that's the end of it."

"Each century is a circle of dancers and together they seem concentric, until forgetting begins to confuse them. Today *Guernica* and *Blind Man's Bluff* seem like two completely different dances of death. Tomorrow they'll be thought of as the same picture. Then the flashy girls and the dandies will be identical to the mangled monsters."

"Sandro, do you know who you are? Do you really know who we are?"

"*Blind Man's Bluff* tells you who we will be."

"No, Sandro, this isn't an illusion in time and we are not who we are." She spoke in a very low voice that the laughter of the dancers still muffled, but her nails dug into Sandro's palm, and her hands were as cold as the blue wind that had just started to blow.

"Who are we then?"

"Neither we nor they really exist."

The circle quickened the turns, as if the wind were gently pushing the dancers. The laughter went from pealing to jingling and from jingling to chirping. The fop with the blindfolded eyes and wooden spoon hurried through his feints and charges. He also accelerated the turns, like a top when you let go of the whip.

"Aren't we anybody?

"No, not us, not them."

"We see the same thing, therefore we exist, Marina, and what we see is as true as we are ourselves."

"Everything's a lie, what's seen and the eyes that see it! If R. hadn't thought of *Blind Man's Bluff*, these people in costume wouldn't appear in the meadow. He's the one who dresses them like the figures in the cartoon, the one who makes them laugh and dance in the snow. When he decides to forget them, they'll disappear into thin air, as if they never had existed!"

"How would they vanish? What does R. have to do with all this?"

("Sandro, do you think I'm going crazy?") Filled with anxiety, he thought again of Marina's strange behavior in recent days: the long silences, the abrupt fits of hilarity, interminable and unexpected. The vision of that bull with the eyes of a man condemned to hell, preceding the fata morgana of *Blind Man's Bluff* that appeared to them both, as if a shared madness had united them in so unexpected and unbreakable a way after so many years. If Marina was crazy, there was a strange consistency in her madness, and above all a terrible accent of veracity in how it was expressed. "There is no certainty more convincing than that of madness," he said to himself in terror. "The other realities, of the senses or of reason, are always debatable."

"Yes," he repeated, hearing the uncertainty in his voice, "what does R. have to do with all this?"

"Didn't you ever stop to think that he determined almost every moment in our lives? It was R. who had to introduce us that day, in the courtyard of Letters. 'There's not a single creature on earth capable of knowing who he is,' he said then, and I still seem to hear his voice, after thirty years, as clearly as I hear mine today. In reality he already knew, or sensed at least, that you and I weren't anybody, because beginning that morning he was going to govern our future as if it were a farce perfectly suited to his whim."

"Let's not undermine reality, Marina. Calm down."

"Here there's no reality because we never had any. Our decisions and even our desires weren't ours but his. I won't say hopes, because he probably decided we didn't deserve them. It was R. who found that room for you, under the Vallcarca Bridge, where we unwittingly made love at his command. You didn't tell me but he did, so many years later when he decided we would meet again at supper in his house. He also told me then that he had given you the address of that woman, on Calle Moncada, where I lost your child and all the children I might have had. Do you remember the mirror in the room under the Vallcarca Bridge, blackened by time, with long purple cracks? Once in bed you told me that that someone, unchangeable and invisible, seemed to be watching us from the other side of the glass. Then I sensed the only truth, which is self-evident now. Nobody was looking at us because we really didn't exist, even though we thought we were naked and embracing, just as the mirror didn't exist, or the room, or the house. All of it, with us inside, was no more than a fiction woven by R. out of our supposed lives. We are only shades, like these phantoms dancing in the meadow, the shades of another man who never took pity on our fate after he had decided it!"

The specters of *Blind Man's Bluff* now seemed to become translucent, as if the fluid morning light were beginning to smooth and soften their profiles. And they slowed the turns of the circle, previously so hurried, as their tired laughter diminished. ("Sandro, do you think I'm going crazy?") He looked at the dancers to avoid Marina's eyes. Suddenly apprehensive, he asked himself what right he had to judge anyone, even Marina, at moments like those. One afternoon in the bedroom under Vallcarca Bridge, hadn't he said that the two of them, Sandro and Marina, were another man's rough draft, not knowing then either how to judge himself and her?

"Let's go home, Marina. We'll continue talking about it there."

"The house isn't ours. It belongs to R., like the lives we don't have."

"Let's go anyway. We can't stay here."

"The house is R.'s," she repeated, shaking her head. "The book you think you're writing is his too, since he thought of it and then entrusted it to you. You'll finish it when he decides to or you'll abandon it when he feels like it. If you suddenly stopped drinking, so incredibly and so improbably, it was only because R. wanted you to, even though you don't know it. He also decided that I should marry my husband and then leave him to follow you. He took control not only of our actions but of our words and our thoughts, too. If I lost my reason it was because he decreed my madness. I lost my mind but not even this insanity is mine! It belongs to him, just like our lives since that day in the courtyard of Letters!" She paused and let go of Sandro's hand, pressing her elbows now against her body, her palms open.

Blind Man's Bluff had almost disappeared above the horizon of sky and woods. The laughter ceased, and the rushing steps and skips. In the air, as if traced on glass, a few white, green, red, violet, and saffron brushstrokes lingered. Gradually they became transparent.

"We'll go now, Marina, and then you'll tell me everything again: who we are and who we never were. Not even the illusion keeps us here, because it's finished. There's nobody in the meadow."

"You don't understand anything!" she shouted now, infuriated, shaking that profile of a woman painted and possessed by Piero della Francesca. "We're the mirage! Since we really don't exist, we can't even hide our lies! Where are those two children of yours, by your second wife, who we were going to see in Colorado as soon as you finished the book?" Sandro's eyes and lips hardened, as if the expression on his face had turned to metal. "You can hit me again! You can punch me until you break your fists, but I won't be quiet now! You didn't abandon your children, because R. didn't want that to happen. Your children died! Do you hear me, Sandro, or do you want me to shout even louder? Your children are dead and no matter how you insist on forgetting it, you'll never be able to deceive yourself! They died, just as mine will never be born, by the sovereign and incomprehensible decree of the man who is dreaming us. R. himself told me so last Saturday, when he called while you were sleeping! First he asked me how the book was going and I lied, telling him it was almost finished. Then I added something that I sincerely believed was true then: 'As soon as Sandro turns in the manuscript, we'll go to the United States. He wants me to meet his children.' His silence surprised me, and the tone of his voice after that parenthesis. 'His two children died in an accident when they were very young. Sandro never wanted to accept or believe it. He finally convinced himself that they were alive and he had abandoned them. I learned the truth from his second wife, whom he divorced a year later.'"

Marina was crying now, her face hidden in her hands. An astonished Sandro said to himself that he had never seen her cry before. It was a distress without words and almost without sobs. A long sound of buried springs, and a tremor.

"They both died in a car accident on Christmas Eve, in a year I don't want to remember," Sandro said then. "My wife, who was with us, was thought dead when they brought her to the hospital; but in a few weeks she recovered. Then I had to confess the truth to her about our children. We never forgave ourselves for having survived them. We skidded on the icy highway and drove over an embankment. I was driving and survived the crash without a scratch. That's all. This is the first time I've had the courage to talk about it. My wife has despised me ever since because I didn't kill her too. We divorced the following year."

For the first time, although he still couldn't confess it to Marina, he told himself that on that Christmas Eve he hadn't killed anybody, even though his two children died then. He had been drinking, as his second wife would tell him repeatedly; but he was driving with the judgment and prudence of someone very accustomed to the wheel. The car skidded on an unexpected patch of ice, and then he couldn't straighten it out or stop it when it began its somersault down the embankment. If Marina was right and they were only a nightmare or a diversion of R.'s, then she would also have to say that their master and executioner also dreamed the ice in order to send him, Sandro Vasari, to the center of a hell different from the measure of his punishment. "What is your idea of happiness on earth?" a voice asked or asked again, deep inside, a strange voice but not unknown, at the thought of hell. He was going to answer it, or answer himself: "My return to that Christmas Eve, before the car turned over, to see my children alive, if only for an instant." And yet, without too much surprise, he heard himself murmur hastily: "To die before my son Xavier. My wife and I already buried four others before I had to bury her too in the famine during the war. I don't want to lose this one." The other voice, the strange but not unknown voice, burst into laughter at the bottom and in the middle of his chest.

Marina was sobbing. As he did on that distant late afternoon, at the corner of Calle Moncada and the Arco de San Vicente, Sandro picked her up to lead her away, his arms around her waist, not saying anything. He wanted to cross the plantings with her and give her time to calm down before starting the walk back to the car. "We're another man's draft." At times, in that other, distant life, and when he detailed for R. his erotic moments before the darkened mirror, he thought he had a premonition that he would divulge them on another day in his own words. Could Marina be right when she stated that they weren't part of a story, but the story itself? In other words, R. wouldn't write secretly about their lives. He would live them vicariously when he imagined them, and he and Marina would have no other existence except that of creatures in a book in the mind of its creator.

He stopped in the center of the meadow, Marina still pressed to his chest. The dancers had trampled and disturbed the snow, dividing it with their steps. At the bottom of their footprints the grass was green, as if it were made of the same malachite as the entire forest, though smoother and more polished. Incredibly, chance had in this way traced two words on the ground from the tracks of the figures in *Blind Man's Bluff*. Sandro read them letter by letter while the sun erased them as it melted the snow. Written in large, uneven type, they read: FURIOUS ABSURDITY.

FURIOUS ABSURDITY

THE DREAM OF REASON

A *Quarrel with Cudgels*

Xavière Desparmet Fitz-Gerald included a catalogue of Goya's works, edited by Antonio Brugada at the time of the painter's death, in his book, *L'Oeuvre de Goya. Catalogue Raisonné*. Brugada called the painting *Two Foreigners*, a title that the catalogue of the Prado changes to one much more precise and expressive: *A Quarrel with Cudgels*. The scene was painted in oils directly onto the wall on the second floor of the so-called Quinta del Sordo, the house bought by Goya in February 1819, behind the del Rey and Segovia Bridges. Between 1821 and 1822, Goya decorated the walls of both floors with eleven paintings, all of them in oils, in addition to the *Quarrel: Leocadia, Judith and Holofernes, Saturn, The San Isidro Excursion, Two Friars, The Witches' Sabbath, Two Old Women Eating Soup, The Great Goat, The Reading, Two Women and a Man*, and *Destiny or the Fates*. As André Malraux described them, the dark roads that lead from Carnival Tuesday to the Day of the Dead, or in this case, to July 18, 1936, passing through May 2, 1808, all cross one another in the labyrinth of these paintings, which the nation calls black.

The Quinta del Sordo no longer exists. When Eugenio d'Ors, still very young, looked for it early in the century in the environs of San Isidro Hill, no one could tell him anything about the house. Sixty years later, Saint-Paulien visited the tiny railroad depot erected on the property. *La station fut baptisée Goya. De Goya on peut aller à Móstoles, Navalcarnero, Alberche, Almorox: 148 kilomètres aller et retour*. Up the Manzanares one finds the reconstructed hermitage of the Virgin del Puerto, the fountain in honor of Juan de Villanueva,

and the tea gardens that once belonged to La Bombilla, where Joselito sometimes went to dance. Even farther away the guidebook of
Juan Antonio Cabezas indicates a fenced grove, with six cypresses
and an iron cross on a granite pillar. Here lie those shot on the slopes
of Príncipe Pío Hill at daybreak on May 3, 1808.

The Quinta del Sordo no longer exists. In 1912, when Hugh
Stokes tried to find Goya's house, he couldn't locate it. No one visits
the cemetery of the executed either. Rafael Canedo, occupation unknown; Juan Antonio Martínez, beggar; Julián Tejedor de la Torre,
blacksmith; Manuel García, gardener; Manuel Sánchez Navarro,
court employee; Martín de Ruicarado, stonecutter, and all their companions can rot in peace. Charles Yriarte did get to see the villa in its
final years. In his book *Goya, sa biographie, les Fresques, les Toiles, les
Tapisseries, les Eaux-Fortes, et le Catalogue de l'Oeuvre*, Paris, 1967,
he stated erroneously that Goya bought the house when he was working on the frescoes in San Antonio de la Florida. On the same page,
which is the ninth in his work, Yriarte presented a drawing of that residence behind a rather overgrown garden. At Goya's death it passed
to his son Xavier, who would bequeath it to the painter's grandson,
Mariano Goya Goicoechea. Along with the property, Mariano inherited everything that had belonged to his grandfather except his
talent. Unlike his father, who was prudent and circumspect, like the
Bayeus, Mariano was reckless, a womanizer, and profligate in the
extreme. He survived several duels, was sewn together with scars,
amassed and lost fortunes, and gradually sold off Goya's paintings. In
1860 he sold the property on the Manzanares plain to Robert Cour-
mont, a Frenchman. Seven years later the house, long uninhabited,
was in a state of disrepair, and a new owner, Segundo Colmenares, acquired it at a good price. By then Mariano Goya, indifferent to his last
name, invested the last of his fortune in buying his title from a penni-
less noble, the marquis de Espinar. A short time later he faded away
in obscurity, like smoke at night, recounting lies and memories of his
celebrated ancestor, who had immortalized him in three portraits.

Segundo Colmenares directed Eduardo Gimeno to restore the oil paintings in the Quinta del Sordo. Nevertheless, in 1873 the country house was sold, passing to another Frenchman, Baron Émile d'Erlanger, a banker. The new owner, obsessed with Goya's paintings, wanted to send slabs of the wall to Paris. A Madrilenian architect dissuaded him and put him in touch with the Martínez Cubells brothers, conservators from Valencia. They transformed the paintings, transferred them to canvas, and rescued them from the slabs of two walls. D'Erlanger's patriotic aim was to give his private, Goyaesque hell to the Louvre. First he exhibited them in Paris and at the Universal Exposition of 1878. The reaction of the general public and the critics was absolutely negative. Both the devotees of impressionism and those who saw painting as a luminous adornment conforming to the esthetic standards of the bourgeoisie rejected the *mauvais goût* of that descent to the depths of man. In that same year, the reaction of an English scholar, P. G. Hamerton, expressed the feeling of the French:

> The mind of Goya is debased in his own odious hell, a horrendous, repulsive swamp, devoid of sublimity, conceived in the form of chaos, bestial in its coloring and its denial of light, where the vilest monsters ever imagined by a sinner reside. Goya surrounds himself with these abominations, pursuing in them I can't imagine what diabolical pleasures while he revels in the audacities of an art entirely devoted to his repulsive subjects, in a manner that is, for me, completely incomprehensible. The most reprehensible of these monsters is his Saturn. He devours one of his children with the voracity of a starving wolf, and the painter does not omit a single detail of this horrific banquet. What has already been said suffices to demonstrate that Goya has retreated to a wild beast's lair, as the hyena hides with his carrion.

Infuriated by such a degree of incomprehension, Émile d'Erlanger gave the black paintings to the Prado.

In I can't remember which story by Borges, a man attempted

to sketch the entire universe in the sand on a beach. When he completed his work, in which all the rivers, mountains, and forests of the earth were diagrammed, he discovered in terror that the immense labyrinth was actually his self-portrait. With Goya in the Quinta del Sordo, I suppose that just the opposite occurred. Alone in his silence, the artist prepared to paint his innermost depths on the walls of his house, to take refuge in the bare center of his being. The result, however, was totally unforeseen, because it reproduced not his secret identity but rather the most brutal and truthful image of the land where it was his fate to be born. I imagine his last lover, Leocadia Weiss, walking with him through the rooms in the house and then telling him: "All of this, clearly, is our country seen from the inside: the burning heart of a volcano." Goya would protest then; he would even swear that the black paintings were his own nightmares, dreams as inalienable as the sleeping eyes that saw them. She would agree with a gesture. "We're both saying the same thing, aren't we? To recount the senseless history of this Spain of ours is equivalent to confessing all one's secret sins." Then I also imagine (not knowing why I'm obliged to imagine it) a still older Goya speaking alone with Fernando VII, perhaps in their final meeting. "I can pardon your actions but not your sins of thought," the king said to him with a smile. "I am your Saturn, devouring my people."

Whoever Saturn was — time, Satan, the Desired One, or a syphilitic Goya fathering children for death — its horror in the Quinta del Sordo was comparable only to the *Quarrel with Cudgels*, a rectangle measuring 1.12 centimeters high by 2.66 centimeters wide. Xavier de Salas stated that duels with cudgels between two immobilized men were frequent in Aragón. The painting, however, is as far from the anecdotal as it is from the estheticizing. I recall a quote by Jean Grenier, cited by Edith Helman in her book on *The Caprices*. "Every intellectual of necessity has the idea of a Paradise Lost." In the Quinta del Sordo, Goya tacitly renounced all paradises in order to come face to face with his own hell, in the name of the truth that, according to another visionary, ought to have made us free. In the end, and three centuries before Goya, Eustache Deschamps had written the sentence that R. showed me one day: "You have the rights that God Himself gave you, you have castles and keys, you have executioners and swords; but truth still exists on earth." Like the Quinta del Sordo, Eustache Deschamps would be renowned in his time not because of that sentence but because of his ugliness. With the passage of time, and south of the Pyrenees, in the country where *The Shootings on May 3* and *Guernica*, the coronation of Carlos IV and the return of Fernando VII, the fatal gorings of *Pepe-Hillo* and of Joselito, all coincided under the sign of Taurus, Goya would ask himself in anguish, perhaps without knowing it, whether our ultimate truth could not be reduced, plainly and simply, to being a country of murderers.

Two peasants, sunk into the mud to their knees, fight with cudgels. More than trapped in that swamp, one might say their legs were amputated and they stood erect on the stumps. The land, however, clamored for them and held them, demanding that the duel be to the death. The dispute, with no witnesses but us, has already begun when we stop in front of the painting. The rustic judges, in other words their fellows, buried them and left them to their fate. Cudgels raised, both were prepared to beat each other again and at the same time, to our fascinated horror. One of the combatants is bleeding from his forehead and chest. One of his eyes, resembling that of a dying Cyclops, looks at us wildly. His mouth, deformed by blows, is a dark stain reduced to silence. His adversary, younger, almost a boy, is practically unscathed. With his left arm and elbow in front of him, he covers his nostrils and jaw, conscious of the setback. The inhuman battle had a beginning but lacks an ending, like life sentences. While just one final man contemplates this painting on canvas that once had been part of a wall, the two peasants will continue to break each other's head with their cudgels, just as a tuna ends up in the net or despicable people in the pillory. Just as, certainly, the execution of May 3 will continue to be suspended in the face of the ragged man with his arms spread wide.

To us the world seems more ferocious than the fight. I made bloodthirsty, thinking trees of the antagonists, condemned to destroy each other. Unique trees, naturally, in this landscape. The plain turns in on itself toward the horizon, curving into hills where at times the sand turns green, with flashes of enamel. Dry, more desolate sierras rise in the distance. A reddish hill, perhaps an old, exhausted quarry, precedes mountains, sienna, blue, and purple, rising skyward on the right. The sky is as pitiless as the land itself. Great livid, ashen clouds, apparent brothers to the mountains, cover it almost completely. In apparent sarcasm, the high clouds break apart twice, and twice a candid, translucent blue appears in those clear spaces. Finally, at the far end of the valley, one can see a herd of black bulls. They graze in front of the low rise of red clay, and distance diminishes them until it transforms them into black pinpoints. The cattle and the two peasants, bestialized by a hatred that even animals do not know, are the only living creatures in these barren lands.

The fight and its landscape are not true and do not attempt to repeat a theatrical curtain, as was the case in *Blind Man's Bluff*. Duels with cudgels between two men buried in a swamp may have been frequent in Aragón, and it is even possible that the Goya family had witnessed them. But this painting represents not an incident but a nightmare. It also does not matter very much whether Goya dreamed it or not before painting it. A nightmare belongs to the one who sees it, and this one becomes ours as soon as we stop in front of the canvas. It seems undeniable, although so far it has not been written down, that the scene, its sky, its landscape, and the herd of bulls are part of a bad dream that is ours because we are looking at it. Incidentally, the same interpretation could be applied to the rest of the black paintings. The twelve oil paintings in that first-floor room in the Prado, therefore, would not be Goya's madness (the madness of the hyena delighting in his carrion, as an ass has said) but ours as we look at them.

In this way Goya would present his *Quarrel with Cudgels* from a perspective analogous to the one Velázquez obliges us to adopt before

Las Meninas or Picasso in front of *Guernica*. In the first, we make the monarchs' point of view ours in the artist's studio. In the second, we are obliged to share the vision of those who destroy the supposed monsters. In the *Quarrel with Cudgels*, or *Two Strangers*, as Brugada or the Prado wanted to call it, Goya obliges us to take possession of the nightmare of the Quinta del Sordo. Nonetheless, every nightmare is also the most intimate mirror of our consciousness. In other words, which are the words of Goya, the sleep of reason produces monsters. The bulls, land, sky, men, and clubs of this canvas are the reflection in synthesis of our interior world. They silently denounce the fanatical, ferocious battle that in a lucid or inadvertent way we bring with us to the Iberian arena. A constant, uncivil struggle, increasingly tragic and absurd, that has nothing to do with justice, as Antonio de Onieva so correctly pointed out.

Another justice, this one certain although oblique and hidden, presided over the incredible destiny of the *Quarrel with Cudgels* and all the black paintings. Goya did not conceive of them as paintings but as a bequest on the walls of his house to those of his blood. An instinctive caution, which at times contradicted his rashness, made him reserve this mirror of his entire nation for his intimates and descendants. The house, however, changed owners several times after his death, while the oil paintings deteriorated on the walls. Its last owner, a Frenchman, acquired it with the sole purpose of taking the paintings to Paris, without the Spanish authorities doing anything at all to stop him. The Baron d'Erlanger could hardly imagine the uselessness of his undertaking. Circumstances completely unforeseen by him, like the unthinking rejection by French critics and the brutal mockery of the Parisian public, obliged him to give the black paintings to the Prado instead of the Louvre. Now on canvas, they returned to the museum founded by Fernando VII. ("I am your Saturn, devouring my people.")

More than half a century later, when the last civil war transformed the *Quarrel with Cudgels* into an ironic redundancy, the oil would return to France on its way to Switzerland, along with the entire Prado. With the imperial peace, that of the National and Proletarian Empire and God, as we are assured that Álvaro Cunqueiro said, the empire in which Franco affirmed that he would take Spain to the heights or leave with his feet toward God, facing forward, the black paintings were reduced to returning silently to the Prado. There, not too far from where the Quinta del Sordo once stood, the *Quarrel with Cudgels* now hangs in vain. Perhaps no more accurate X-ray of another nation exists. Perhaps none more useless exists either. Over and over again, during so many years that were all alike, we passed in front of the painting without recognizing ourselves, because in Spain, as Goya himself stated with certainty in his handwriting of an old rustic, no one knows himself. No one ever knew himself, and hence our history.

April 16, 1828

His Majesty the king poured a little cognac into our empty glasses.

"Señor, you do me honor."

"Always at your service, old man." He pinched my cheek, smiling, as if I were a kitchen scullion or an apprentice groom. "*Servus servorum Dei.* That's what I am, and this Latin, along with the Latin of the Mass, is all I remember of the teachings of the bishop of Orihuela. It could have been less and it might have been worse, don't you agree?"

I didn't reply because he wasn't listening to me then either. He sank into the armchair as if it were a bathtub, and scratched his private parts again. Then he rinsed his gums with a mouthful of the spirit, seemed to belch, and spat on the floor, wiping away the saliva with his foot. I never could decide whether that kind of shameless behavior was authentic or the actions of a clown whose part he liked to play precisely as a caricature. Sprawling in his cushioned chair, he looked at the portrait I had just painted of him, half closing those dark, intelligent eyes, where the bright trail of a mocking secret always seemed to be losing its way.

"Naturally you must have noticed that the ermine cloak, embroidered in gold, the scepter, and even the fleece are from the theater," he said suddenly, pointing at the portrait on the easel, next to the cold fireplace. "Very good imitations, no doubt, but it's all from the theater."

"No," I said in surprise. "I didn't notice that when I was painting Your Majesty. Perhaps I didn't want to see it either. Everything I paint is pure truth for me. If it weren't, it wouldn't be worth perpetuating."

"That's why you painted me the way you did." He smiled as he lit a cigar, which he moved away from his face so I could read his lips. "I should have had you garroted, or better yet, garrote you myself, as if it were a jest. At least you would die at the hands of a friend. I can swear that to you."

"Yes, that's why I painted you as I did, Señor. I wouldn't know how to do it any other way, since this is how you are."

"It's very possible that this is how I am; but I'm not sure I know who I am. On the day of the opening of the Constitutional Parliament, imposed by the Riego revolution, they demanded that I inaugurate it wearing the royal mantle and crown. You revolutionaries are sometimes ridiculously conservative regarding protocol. I remember that I understood then why in France they decapitated a king in order to crown an emperor." He shook his head and shrugged his narrow shoulders. "In any case, I laughed in their faces; in their hearts they wanted to cut off my head too, and I comforted myself by telling them the most ironic of truths . . ."

"The most ironic of truths, Majesty . . . ?"

"I told them there was no mantle, no crown, and no scepter, because the French had stolen them when they withdrew. Your friend the Intruder King would share his bread with you in the war, but he took even the chandeliers from this palace. They decided then that I should attend Parliament in the uniform of a captain general. On a large chair beside the throne, they placed a mantle, a scepter, and a crown, taken from the statue of San Fernando in the Plaza de la Armería."

He burst into wholehearted laughter, his eyes closed and his long, thick, black brows wrinkled. He looked like a different man when he laughed — much taller, with a broader chest and shoulders. He unexpectedly recalled his dead father, whom he did not resemble in his physique or his features. (*Allora, appena il crepuscolo, il giorno comincia a scolrire e nel traspasso dei colori tutto rimane calmo.* "No one can resist my punches, the hardest grooms fall like ninepins. When you come back we'll fight with rods in the stables and then I'll play the violin for you, if you like.") How many years had gone by since the day when Josefa and I were presented to his parents and his widowed grandfather, long before he was born? Fifty? Perhaps more? Time grew thin in the distance, like rivers in their beds in the late afternoon. More often than not, one could say that the past had never existed. It was like one of those fairy tales that we anticipate, knowing we'll never get to live them.

"The whole country is made of shadows and theater," I said when he stopped laughing, because before that he wouldn't have heard me. "Here there never was and never will be anything real. Not even grief, because in the long run, that's forgotten too."

"Oh no, old man! You're wrong!" he replied, sitting up quickly. "When you paint, you must see what no one else can; in other words, what you call the truth. But sometimes, when you speak, you don't seem deaf but blind. In the final analysis, the country will have three undeniable realities: the people, you, and I."

"Why we three, Señor?" Even without hearing my shouts, I knew that I was shouting. "What moral right can accompany us when we deny everyone in times of trial? If God sits in judgment, you will be condemned just like the people and just like me."

"From this I ought to deduce that if you were God, you wouldn't absolve any one of the three."

"Your Majesty can deduce whatever you like best. Besides, in this case, you are absolutely right. I am nobody, but I know very well that you share in our condemnation."

"We're very different, old man, and naturally you're more heartless." He shrugged again. "With no remorse to speak of, I thought I was a tiger because I never pardoned any of my enemies. Not my mother, who's dead; or Godoy, in exile now; or Riego, after executing him; or Napoleon, in hell for having dispossessed me and insulted me when I was defenseless. All of them humiliated me as if I were a beaten dog, and to them I shall always be a rabid dog, in this life or any other. If the ghost of my first wife were to appear, the human being I loved most, and begged on her knees that I pardon any of them, including my mother, I'd turn my head so I wouldn't hear her." He made an effort to smile, as if trying to soften the severity of his tone. "You never thought I was so obstinate, did you? Rancor is another virtue I share with my people."

Rancorous, of course I knew that. But I also wondered who he thought the people were. Perhaps individuals like the Gypsy, his mistress Pepa de Málaga, or her charming former pimp, *Chamorro*, or like Ugarte, the odd-job man; the rabble who, as they said, would use *tú* with him when he was alone and call him master? I was convinced he would feel much closer to that scum than to all the kings of Europe. At the same time I was certain this was not my idea. It belonged to that man, who perhaps without knowing it was me in a time that had not happened yet: the man foretold in the circus on the Rue du Manège by the Living Skeleton.

"Even more than those dead and Godoy himself, who is dying in Paris, the people taunted and abused you when they assaulted the palace six years ago. You seem to have forgotten that."

"It was much worse afterward, when I withdrew my confidence from the government and precipitated the crisis, hoping that the hundred thousand Sons of Saint Louis would reach Madrid in time and rescue me from the claws of the liberals. The mob entered howling like demons, while the Royal Guard looked up to heaven or fraternized with them. With their sticks they smashed the cut-glass drops on the lamps because the clinking amused them, and they ripped open the sofas with their knives. We had to hide in a garret filled with brooms and old straw mats, and from there we heard them shouting for my neck and shrieking at the queen that they would send her back to a brothel in Germany. Imagine my poor wife, the third one, the pious one! The one who wrote verses to the Vespers Service on the Day of the Conception! Even greater humiliations were waiting for us that summer, when Parliament removed me from the throne, saying I was mad. They sent us to Cádiz from Sevilla in a closed carriage because the hundred thousand Sons of Saint Louis had already entered Andalucía. On the road, and as we passed through the towns, droves of peasants assaulted the carriage and forced us to push up against the windows in order to spit at us. Inside the heat was infernal, a heat I can't even describe to you when I remember it. The queen fainted several times. I even thought she had died . . ."

"And still you forgave them everything."

"That same people returned us in triumph to Madrid, after freeing us from the troops of the duke de Angoulême. By then I could have strolled alone and unarmed through the streets and the people would have argued over my feet in order to kiss them. In the churches they worshiped my plaster image, wrapped in a theatrical cloak. I pardoned the people for the same reasons that, long before, I had pardoned you for your treason when you collaborated with the Intruder King. For precisely the same reasons that I always absolved my own felonies. You and I and the people are identical. In this world of dreams we are all that's certain. To save our life we would pardon everything, our honor and our soul, because we are deeply convinced that no reality, at least on earth, exists beyond ourselves . . . I don't know whether you understood everything I said."

"I understood very well, Señor. But I also remember your taking revenge."

"The people celebrated the tortures, which were public and very much applauded. I showed no mercy to the truly seditious, those who hadn't committed treason in order to survive but to impose delusions like liberty and the rights of man. Along with Torrijos and his people, they arrested a boy of twelve who acted as messenger for the conspiracy. I remember that when they invaded the palace in order to impose the Constitution on me, they showed me another boy and roared that he was the son of General Lacy, whom I'd had shot earlier. Then I wrote in my own hand the order to execute Torrijos and his band. I put a note at the bottom: 'Have them kill the boy too.' Are you shocked, old man?"

"You don't shock me, Señor; but I prefer knowing I'm the one responsible for the death of my children and not of that boy."

"There are no disputes in questions of taste, my friend." He smiled and stretched out in the chair again. With his moistened fingertip he caressed the rim of the glass over and over again, absorbed in delight, until the glass shrieked like a rusty knife blade against the whetstone.

"Señor, I beseech you!"

"Ah, forgive me! I thought you heard absolutely nothing."

"Those shrieks I can hear. And claps of thunder sometimes, when they're very far away."

"In dreams I hear the voices of the emperor and my mother in the castle of Maracq, when they forced me to renounce the crown. I don't see them, I only hear them and always as close as if I had returned to that Dantesque day. *Vous êtes très bête et très, très mechant!* that bandit roared, and my mother shrieked at me in Spanish: 'Bastard! Bastard!'" He smiled, shaking his head, as if he wanted to drive away all the nightmares of the memory. "I was more afraid for my life at that moment than at any other time, including the journey from Sevilla to Cádiz. Yet even in my panic, I thought that my mother and Napoleon were as awful as they were grotesque. They were speaking languages that weren't theirs and anger made their Italian accent seem coarse."

"Your Majesty should have resisted that pillage by every means possible. Blood had already been spilled in Madrid and you, Señor, were not unaware of the uprising. You renounced the throne while men killed or were shot dead invoking your name."

"In Maracq they would have murdered me if I had refused to abdicate. History is nothing but forgetting all the blood spilled in vain. In the end, the result was almost the same, although now my brother would be king instead of me. In that case the Holy Inquisition would have been reestablished, and you would be living not in exile but in its dungeons, because he would have brought back autos-da-fé in the Plaza Mayor and burned people at the stake. My brother is a fanatic. I'm only a frightened man."

"What inheritance can your fear leave us?"

"The museum I'll open in the Prado," he exclaimed, suddenly becoming animated and slapping me on the knees. "The museum I'll create to your glory with the paintings from the Real Casa!"

"Tomorrow people will forget that you founded the museum, but they'll remember your betrayals and the gallows in the Plaza de la Cebada. In France Moratín once read to me a quotation from Shakespeare that you have no right not to know. The evil that men do lives after them; the good is oft interred with their bones. This is the fate of power, but yours could have been different . . ."

"Why would it have been?"

"When you returned from Valençay you were the Desired One, the Only One. I doubt that any other man on earth has been awaited with more fervor in his own country. Do you remember the mob that kissed your hands and sobbed on the way to the San Isidro fountain? Then you could have started from nothing and truly been the king of all of us. This is a nation of beasts and imbeciles that will never begin to find itself until it recognizes its ferocity and stupidity and overcomes them. It was up to you to help them, Señor, because an opportunity like yours will not be repeated. Your grandfather, who never had it, would have grasped it immediately. The illusion of an entire people is the most powerful force in the world, and you were ours. An uncommon destiny allowed you to bring us peace, harmony, work, and above all hope. But you left us hatred, fanaticism, poverty, and despair. If God doesn't prevent it, you'll leave behind a century of civil wars. This is your legacy: the law of the garrote, which was going to transform this madhouse into an arcadia, as you told me on the way to San Isidro. Now you can't even guarantee dynastic succession. Once again we're living between terror and uncertainty, because your days are almost as numbered as mine. You're not yet fifty and you look like a man almost my age."

"Did you stop to think that perhaps I couldn't redeem the people, as you say, precisely because I spoke their language and came from them?" he asked without warning, looking at me intently. "Despots like me do not improvise and are not fully responsible for their governmental actions. They are the inevitable consequence of the scars and leprosy of all of you. I come out of this people, like heat from a fire, and together we have touched bottom. About this, at least, we agree."

"Yes, Majesty," I nodded. "About this, at least, we agree."

He stopped speaking and sank back into the armchair and his reflections, biting his lips above his equine jaw, where the shadow of his beard was beginning to turn his chin blue. He drank the cognac in his glass in a sudden mouthful, grimacing as if it repelled him. Then he began again to rub the lip of the glass with distracted persistence. He finally produced that shriek of a swift that penetrated my deafness like a needle.

"Possibly we won't see each other again," he said with a sigh, facing me again. "The truth is that in spite of everything I said, I believe I feel closer to you than to the people." He burst into laughter when he noticed my confusion. "Yes, yes, closer to you, and not because I appreciate your painting even more than you can value it, but because at one time we both loved the same woman."

"The same woman, Majesty . . . ?"

"Someone who died a long time ago. It seems incredible to think that if she had lived, she'd be a very old woman."

"Yes," I nodded again, as my memory wove shadows in time. "It seems incredible."

"I was referring to María Teresa," he explained unnecessarily, laughing now like a madman. "Do you remember her, old man?"

"I think about her often, Majesty."

"My mother thought she was the very devil. I haven't thought about her for some time. Years, perhaps. I don't know why you obliged me to remember her tonight, without realizing it. When she was your mistress, I was a little boy, but I adored her in silence. That is, I was mad for her. Good God, you rogue, you didn't deny yourself anything in those days! You were a satyr in my parents' court! I would have liked to become you, down to the marrow of your bones, just to know I was hers! I began to desire her then as I would desire only my own life when they tried to snatch it away from me. And what a beautiful filly she must have been in bed! Isn't that right? If I close my eyes I see her again as clearly as I see you now, chipped by age. Women like her don't exist nowadays, do they? They broke the mold!"

Before I died I had to lose my speech as well. My entire right side, from my cheek to my foot, must be dead because I can't feel it. I look at my right hand on the sheets and again it seems to belong to someone else. Perhaps it belongs to that man whose voice sometimes sounds inside me from a time that hasn't happened yet. I return now definitively and forever to the "Frenzied Absurdity," which is life itself. Mine in this bed or in a book that he'll write in another century. In any case, I won't survive the Desired One, who at times had that look of a wounded fawn that my María del Pilar Dionisia had in the cradle. And I won't return to Spain alive, where he told me that letting himself die is man's greatest madness.

Xavier arrived and I still had time to embrace him before the final stroke. Then, when I was mute and crippled, he went to an inn with my daughter-in-law and Marianito, because his wife could not tolerate the sight of my agony. Leocadia told me everything when I asked for my son and my grandson. What she didn't tell me is that she herself is hiding Rosarito to spare him the interminable death of an old man. Leocadia herself, very thin and aged by her vigils, sits with me at all hours without mentioning my family or my inheritance. ("You're so blind you don't even see your own stupidity! You dumb bastard! Don't you understand that they came only to be sure you hadn't changed your will? They don't give a damn about your blood, your name, even your life, if they're certain they'll inherit your money, your house, and your paintings. If they could count on all that now, they'd let you rot in exile without seeing the whites of your eyes . . .") Leocadia went to bed tonight too, exhausted. Only people who are almost strangers sit with me. The two French doctors (*Vous êtes un grand homme, un peintre de la Chambre. On va vous soigner!*); the owner of this house, José Pío de Molina, the former mayor of Madrid after the victory of Riego, and a student of mine at the Academia de San Fernando who followed me into exile: Antoñito Brugada. I'd like to tell them that I'll soon be in the presence of Velázquez.

After my voice I lost my sight. In a sense, now the silence around me has become absolute, because I can no longer read lips. Yet I can still distinguish their shapes and, in a confused way, their faces. The doctors wear black frock coats. They have Van Dyke beards. They milk them, caress them, and comb them, according to their mood. They gave me valerian again, but valerian no longer cures anything. They applied leeches and the leeches didn't take hold. They rubbed me down, auscultated me, painted me with iodine, burned me with mustard plasters. I think they didn't sprinkle me with holy water and exorcize me because it didn't occur to them. Antoñito Brugada, who bustles all around the room, is a boy (to me he's still a boy even though he must be getting on in years by now) who paints very good seascapes. When I could still make out his features, I saw his eyes and nose reddened from crying so much. He leans over the bed and looks at me straight on, in profile, and from God's point of view. Whatever his sorrow, which I believe is very sincere, art has greater sway over him than grief, and he is preparing to sketch me when I'm dead, though perhaps he isn't aware of his own intention.

José Pío de Molina is tall, sad, and as thin as an official of the Holy Office. He is also the freest and most generous man I have ever known, though I came to know him well only in exile. I'm going to leave unfinished the portrait of him I was doing when I fell ill. As he was sitting for me, I recounted part of my last conversation with the Desired One. ("When you returned from Valençay you were the Desired One, the Only One. I doubt any man on earth has been awaited in his own country with greater fervor. Do you remember the mob that kissed your hands, sobbing, on the way to the fountain of San Isidro? Then you could have begun from nothing and truly been the king of all of us. This is a nation of beasts and imbeciles who will never begin to find their future until they recognize their ferocity and stupidity in order to overcome them. It was your responsibility to help, Señor, because an opportunity like yours will not be repeated.") "It is sad for a people to await the death of a man in order to find its future," said Pío de Molina, "because the dead only bury the dead. Christ himself said they aren't useful for anything else." I asked him whether he had not considered the possibility that we had no future at all and that in a century or a century and a half, two Spaniards like us, also exiled in Bordeaux, would repeat our doubts and our words. "It is possible," he replied, half-closing his narrow inquisitor's eyes, "because one would not call our destiny true; it is written instead in a madman's novel where everything is repeated in different centuries."

Yes, I would like to tell them that I'll soon be in the presence of Velázquez. When I was very young, long before His Majesty Don Carlos III and the prince and princess of Asturias granted me their first audience in response to his petition, my oldest brother-in-law took me to the palace to show me the paintings by Velázquez in the royal collection. Francisco Bayeu was the court painter then, and his contemptuous pride did not permit him to praise anyone in my presence. Which was why I was very surprised when he said to me: "Today you'll see the paintings of someone I could never envy, just as I don't envy God for having created light and air." It wasn't air or light that Velázquez created but man. This was the undeniable center of his universe, where the heavens were sometimes transformed into tapestries and sometimes into mirrors. Before his paintings and in spite of his intrinsic and almost distracted serenity, I felt a blow in the middle of my heart. If I had been alone, I would have burst into tears, and only the presence of Francisco Bayeu could stop me from doing that. "This man was a jester and a clerk in the court of Felipe IV. His name was something like Diego de Acedo y Velázquez, but they called him *The Cousin*, mocking his supposed family connection to the painter," my brother-in-law told me in front of the portrait of a seated dwarf, with a large book on his knees and a still life of notebooks, papers, pens, and inkwells all around him. "Notice the insistent disproportion between the smallness of his diminutive hands and the enormous size of the book, a quarto edition on fine paper, that he's holding on his tiny legs. And also his head, very large in comparison to his body, grows even bigger thanks to the black broad-brimmed hat he wears pulled far down on one side of his head." On the same wall and next to the portrait of that clown hung one of another buffoon, sitting on the floor and facing us. In the foreground, the soles of his tiny shoes were as clean as if he were wearing them for the first time. "About this one we don't know much more than his name," my brother-in-law continued. "He was Sebastián de Morra, the jester of Prince Don Baltasar Carlos. They say that once, when the queen sent a lady-in-waiting to buy sweets, the shopkeeper refused to give them to her because the palace owed too large a bill. The lady, in tears, happened to meet the buffoon on her way back from the shop, and he gave her a *cuarto* so that the sovereign would not be deprived of her dessert. Notice the disparity of his limbs in relation to his head, with its large forehead, and his tall man's torso." I was enraptured before the eyes of the jesters. One would say that Velázquez had begun by painting them in the middle of the empty canvas, as if it were the obligatory center of those unlikely creatures. Their eyes, streaming deep inside in long, moist glances, humanized the monsters born and trained to make others laugh, like the jugglers' dogs or tamed monkeys at court. When many, very many years later, the Desired One spoke to me about our people, deformed and grotesque like those unfortunates, I thought of the eyes of Velázquez's dwarfs and asked myself whether, in his long road to his own center, he would ever find his true reason for being and his authentic freedom.

From the jesters, Francisco Bayeu led me to *Las Meninas*. At that time it was in a room only slightly higher than the painting, covered by long draperies. When they were pulled back, the light came in from a railed balcony where starlings wandered. Not even in Italy, in the Sistine Chapel, had I felt greater emotion before the work of a man. I wanted to shout, fall on my knees, bite at my hands until I ripped them to pieces. Velázquez, who had died more than one hundred years earlier, crushed me with his merciless superiority; but it made me proud to think that a creature born of woman, like me, had been able to conceive of such perfect beauty. Velázquez had suspended an ordinary moment in the heart of the court, the moment when a lady-in-waiting offers a cup to the princess. I told myself convincingly that any moment, even the most apparently insignificant, deserves the greatest of paintings to celebrate it. In *May 3, 1808, in Madrid*, I suspended all of time in the shout and gesture of the man they are going to execute. ("Father, what if God was deaf to our voices, like these executioners who kill us without being able to understand us?") Not until I had finished the painting did I understand that I had painted the reverse of *Las Meninas*, and that *May 3, 1808*, was my response to Velázquez's serenity at the time of the greatest of tragedies. Or perhaps I didn't understand it, properly speaking, but rather the one who even now lives inside me as I'm dying.

After losing my voice, I lost my sight. I no longer see Brugada, or

Pío de Molina, or the doctors. I never had supposed that death was this peace, this improbable lucidity that seems to have come from a book rather than from the authentic agony of a flesh-and-blood Christian. ("It's possible that this is so, because one wouldn't call our destiny true but written in a madman's novel where everything is repeated in different centuries.") Moratín once quoted to me a phrase of Casanova's from his memoirs: It isn't bold to imagine a judicious pen describing a true fact when the writer thinks he is inventing it. Perhaps the other man, the one I think I am sometimes, believes he is describing an improbable death, which is at the same time my real agony now, in the small hours.

Now, before daybreak, when I distinguish only light and shadow, the phantoms come out and scheme in the penumbra that envelops me. My paintings, starting to move, are only the fleeting passage of the history of my time. The flashy boys and girls of *Blind Man's Bluff* dance, as they will prance around my tomb in San Antonio de la Florida. The fop with the long spoon and blindfolded eyes is transformed into my *Wild Bull*. Blindly and in vain he turns around and charges the dancers with long thrusts. They withdraw their bodies from his horn thrusts, ducking or sidestepping them with bends of the waist, laughing constantly. Nearby *Martincho* places banderillas *a topa-carnero* (his waist bending, his feet unmoving) in another black animal with wide horns that comes like a gale from the boards. In the ring Barbudo gores *Pepe-Hillo* in the pit of his stomach, while Juan López is late in luring the bull away and José Romero jumps the barrier to go to the aid of his rival. ("When I got him under control, I'll t'row away the muleta and fight 'im wit' my watch, so he sees it's his hour that's come, not mine.") A very Madrilenian crowd, all classes pressed together and getting along, celebrates the fiesta of their patron saint in the San Isidro meadow. They play circle games and cards, converse, stroll, and flirt among unmoving barouches and berlins. On white cloths spread on the grass, the wine from Valdemorillo flows at lunch, among white parasols, silvered jackets, red boleros, flannel jackets, and plumed two-cornered hats. ("The greatest of portents does not consist in transforming the present but in anticipating its future changes. In this way our ashes will become our portraits, just as paint on a palette becomes a cloth in a mirror.") In a room in the palace, Carlos IV and his family group together, smiling, and prepare to pose for my painting. In the center, the king takes a step forward and the rest step back. The Infanta María Luisa, princess of Bourbon Parma, holds her firstborn son, almost a newborn. Princess María Antonia turns her head and looks away at another painting, hanging on the wall behind them, where three giants, a man and two women, are taking their pleasure naked. I am the man. The queen raises her chest and smiles at me with her toothless mouth. ("We'll have to find a bodice for this boy. He's almost growing breasts like a girl.") Dressed in mourning and with her face doubled, like Janus, María Teresa embraces me at the same time that she contemplates a stranger, who sneaks closer, creeping along the floor. María Teresa herself, still in mourning, flies through the air on three squatting monsters. ("If these people are as base as we are, what sense do our lives make, and theirs?") In the Puerta del Sol the Mameluke cavalry charges the crowd. The entire square is a whirlpool of men, horses, spilled blood, torn flags, swords, knives, neighs, blasphemies, silent screams and shouts. ("That was a war we were all going to lose irremediably.") Another mob, this one composed of the crippled, the drunk, the eyeless, the hungry, the leprous, the deformed, comes up a slope preceded by a blind man strumming a large guitar. Although I don't hear their voices, I know they are hailing the Desired One and slavery. Gradually the crowds at that excursion, María Teresa, the flying monsters, the family of Carlos IV, the groups on the meadow, Barbudo, *Pepe-Hillo*, *Martincho*, all of them crowd and cluster around the circle in *Blind Man's Bluff* to watch them dance. In the midst of the dancers, constantly charging with eyes identical to those of Saturn and now blindfolded, my *Wild Bull* pursues the air with useless thrusts of his horns.

("My paintings, put in motion, are nothing but the fleeting passage of the history of my time.") When all my characters, including my own self-portraits, where I repeat myself and grow old, as well as preliminary sketches and drawings, have gathered around *Blind Man's Bluff,* the darkness unexpectedly sweeps them away as the shadows abruptly change direction. Now in a glass fishbowl that probably measures no more than three spans on each side, a black painting, initially unknown, comes to life. Slowly I begin to make out a Madrid very different from the one I knew and treasured in my memory. In the night, because it's late at night, perhaps fairly close to dawn, I recognize the palace and the Plaza de Oriente in the glass background. The plaza is the esplanade with gardens that the Intruder King flattened during the war, knocking down houses and clearing away alleys so that the cannon could shoot down any revolt like the one in May. The city, however, grew more than the trees. Extremely tall buildings that resemble the dream of a crazed master builder rise in a crowded noisy palisade against the sky. Large, many-armed streetlamps whiten the darkness between their bare branches.

An interminable procession of three and even four people abreast crosses the plaza and seems to lengthen by entire leagues. Improvised metal railings keep to one side that endless serpent that slowly penetrates the Palacio de Oriente. Men and women are dressed in a manner never seen before, as if all of Madrid (this Madrid of gigantic apiaries) had put on identical unknown masks. Enveloped in strange overcoats they tremble with the cold, press against one another, rub their hands, numb with cold, slap their arms with their palms, and spew out frozen breath with their voices. Suddenly, and with no surprise on my part, I heard their words, as clear and distinct as if I had never been afflicted with deafness. "He was like a father to the country," says an old man. "I've spent all night here, I haven't slept; but I won't leave without seeing him lying in state in the palace." "They say some priests are blessing the body as they pass. Some people cross themselves. Others fall to their knees." "We're the Gypsies from Pozo del Tío Raimundo. For us too he was a good man." "Do you think they'll let me give him a kiss when I get there?" an old woman keeps repeating.

The people around her are not unknown to me. In all of them I see the same crowds that hailed Godoy, the Desired One, the Intruder King, Riego, the Obstinate One. They are also the ones who dragged down Godoy in Aranjuez, knifing his legs; the ones who led Riego to the scaffold in a charcoal seller's basket and then stoned the quarters of his body, cut up by axes and displayed on the spires of twenty cities in a future Chile; the ones who disemboweled the Obstinate One with goads and razors while he was handcuffed in a cage and danced with joy while the executioner burned his remains; the ones who invaded this same Palacio de Oriente with ropes to hang the Desired One, and on the road to Cádiz obliged him to kiss the windows of his carriage so they could spit in his eyes. I recognize them, as any painter would recognize them, the cut of their features and that light in their eyes, resembling the gaze of Velázquez's dwarfs. I have seen them in the excursions and picnics on San Isidro, in church, at the bullfights, in roadside inns, in boarding houses, in taverns, at weddings, in fights, in brothels, in prisons. I heard them cheering the Inquisition, chains, freedom, the Constitution, the crown, the faith, the Revolution, death, prisons, the homeland, treason, vengeance, mercy, ignorance, absolutism, rebellion, the wild bulls, and the wine at Mass. They applauded not only the Prince of Peace, Fernando VII, Rafael Riego, and Juan Martín the Obstinate One, but also *Costillares*, *Pepe-Hillo*, Pedro Romero, José Romero, Joseph Bonaparte, Murat, the duke of Angoulême, the English, and the one hundred thousand Sons of Saint Louis. Now they will all go to the Palacio de Oriente to bid farewell to a dead man whom perhaps none of them has ever seen in the flesh. But at bottom they are not going to the palace, or anywhere, because as I always said to myself when I thought about them, they don't know the way and they don't know themselves.

THE MONSTERS

The Desired One

The Desired One was born in the Escorial, October 14, 1784. A document in the National Historical Archive says he was very ill at the age of four, with an ailment that was a corruption of the blood. A surgeon at the Farm of San Ildefonso, Manuel Olivares, offered to cure him with a tisane of his own devising; other patients, cured by the drink, testified to its virtues. In the end, his recovery was finally attributed to the miraculous intervention of San Isidro Labrador.

His first tutor was Fray Benito Scio, a learned Piarist who taught geography to his pupils by having them memorize the verses of the *Araucana* that describe the land. Fray Benito could recite the entire poem with his eyes closed. It is well known that one day, when the pedagogue was declaiming to the Desired One the verses that say "Like the hungry alligator when it hears / the school of fish noisily drawing near / as it cuts across the current," he fell down dead from a sudden inflammation of his pia mater. The Desired One, who must have been seven or eight years old at the time, did nothing but ring a gong for someone to pick up the remains of his teacher. No one knew how to interpret that sign of sovereign indifference to another person's death on the part of so young a prince.

Then the prince's preceptors entrusted the teaching of the Infante Don Carlos to Don Francisco Xavier Cabrera, bishop of Orihuela and a man very devoted to Godoy, whom he flattered shamelessly in the heading of all his letters: "My most loved and venerated Favorer and Prince . . ." Her Most Illustrious Majesty, who wrote with spelling mistakes, proposed a program of studies for the Desired One that would begin at six in the morning, from September 1 to April 30. After dressing, the prince would pray the *Te Deum* with his preceptor and the corresponding prayer, thanking heaven for having rescued him from the dark of night. The tutor would then propound to him some point of Christian meditation, government, or national politics.

At seven the Desired One would withdraw to study the lesson in Latin that his teacher would take up at eight, while the prince had breakfast. The same preceptor would remain with him until nine, explaining the following lesson and engaging him in a review of previous ones so that they would not be forgotten. Then, until a quarter past ten, the illustrious pupil would have his hair dressed in order to hear Mass and recite the lessons referring to the history of Spain. When hairdressing, Mass, and history were concluded, His Royal Highness would have a dance class for an hour.

At a quarter to eleven the Desired One would enter the rooms of his August Parents to render an account of his health, ask how they spent the night, and offer testimony to them of his filial love. Having returned to his own rooms, he would hear a lecture on Eloquence and Morality or preferably a sermon on Sacred History until it was time for lunch, which would always be served at twelve fifteen. After the meal he would take a siesta, without undressing, until two.

The afternoon schedule would be as strict as the one in the morning. From two to three the Desired One would study the Latin lesson indicated previously. Then he would have an outing with his August Brother Prince Don Carlos and the respective deputies of the tutor. On their return from the excursion, which could be forbidden by the princes' preceptors, he would go back to the royal chambers and repeat to Their Majesties his avowals of devotion. Having concluded this sacred duty, he would withdraw to review the lesson in grammar and receive thorough explanations of the next one. At eight he would pray the Rosary and the Litany, saving a few minutes afterward for an examination of conscience and to pray to God to forgive his defects. Finally the subchanters of the palace would read to him the saint of day from the Christian Year, instructing him in his virtues and advising him to imitate those moral qualities. At nine he would be served supper and could relax, spinning a top or playing cards, until he was sent for at ten or a little earlier. From the first of May until August 31, the prince would get up at five in the morning. During those months, morning exercises would take an hour and those in the afternoon would also take an hour.

As for the precept of confession, whose office Their Royal Majesties the king and queen entrusted to the bishop of Orihuela, he advised the Desired One to practice it on all the festivals of Our Lord Jesus Christ and His Most Holy Mother, as well as on the days of the apostles, Saint John the Baptist, his patron saint San Fernando, and generally every Friday in the event one of the aforementioned celebrations did not occur in that week.

At this time, when the Desired One was eleven years old, they named the royal chaplain and canon of the pilar, Juan Escoiquiz, as his teacher of geography, mathematics, and French. In his application, this ambitious ecclesiastic, a model of treachery, said he was the translator of Milton, Sabatier, and Cotte, as well as the author of an original unpublished poem in royal stanzas, *Mexico Conquered.* "In spite of being modesty itself, he should add that he was prepared to teach the proposed disciplines. He spoke and wrote French almost as well as Castilian and had knowledge of English and Italian." If so honorable a position were granted him, the canon would request complete instructions so as to always proceed according to the desires of his benevolent protector the Prince of Peace and duke of Alcudia.

Godoy, as poor a judge of his fellow man as he was of himself, erred when he selected Escoiquiz as an informer on his Royal Highness. The canon had hungers for power almost as fierce as those of the Prince of Peace and comparable scruples when the time came to satiate them. A good theatrical hypocrite because his manner was affable, he immediately gained the confidence of the Desired One.

It did not take him long to understand that the prince's hatred for Godoy and his mother exceeded only slightly his contempt for the king. More intelligent than all of them, and more vulnerable and rancorous, the Desired One despised them almost equally. Impatient like all Pharisees, Escoiquiz played his hand too quickly. He published his *Mexico Conquered* and dedicated it to the monarch. Then he proposed the heir's attendance at the meetings of the Council of Castilla, so that he would become accustomed to the business of government. At the same time, it should be remembered, Godoy sensed the worst of his enemies in the Desired One, and suggested the possibility of sending him to America to subject with a firm hand the viceregencies to the crown. Exasperated, Carlos IV exiled Escoiquiz to Toledo. Nonetheless, from there he maintained communication with his pupil by means of a ridiculous code in which the king was *Don Diego*, the queen *Doña Felipa*, Godoy *Don Nuño*, and the Desired One himself was called *Don Agustín*.

In September 1802 the Desired One married Princess María Antonia of Naples. Each of the illustrious consorts was barely eighteen years old, but they were far apart in their education and human profile. María Antonia was not beautiful, though she was much taller than her husband, with a good appearance, blond hair, and penetrating blue eyes. In addition to Italian, she spoke Spanish, French, English, and German. Her mother, Queen Carolina, would never forgive the French for the public execution of her sister, María Antonieta. Her hatred then centered on Napoleon, whom she believed was the legitimate heir of the Terror and all the revolutionaries. Austrian by birth, Carolina would always support England in the face of French ambitions. She was also a great admirer of Lady Hamilton, the wife of the English ambassador and soon to be known as the mistress of Admiral Nelson. She wrote her the letters of a schoolgirl with a crush. She called her to her chambers at any hour of the day or night so that she could sing for her the verses of Ophelia in her madness ("... *before you tumbled me, / You promised me to wed. / So would I*

ha' done, by yonder sun, / An thou hadst not come to my bed") or perform for her the dance of the seven veils. María Antonia participated
in her mother's politics and intrigues. From Spain she maintained a
secret correspondence with her, which French spies soon intercepted
and deciphered. Napoleon delighted in all those secrets of state and
of the bedroom, and then sent copies of the letters to the Prince of
Peace and María Luisa.

"I shall never forget *who Godoy is and who I am*," María Antonia
wrote to her mother, furiously underlining certain words. She thought
Carlos IV too naïve and the queen endowed with every defect. With
even greater wrath, María Luisa hated her daughter-in-law when she
read her confidential exchange of letters with Carolina of Naples.
"This bloodless little beast, all bitterness and poison, a half-dead frog,
a diabolical serpent," the queen offered Godoy her graphic sketch of
her daughter-in-law. She wrote these notes in bed while the king gave
her light, holding a candelabrum. At times she apologized for con-
cluding them in haste. The king dozed off and María Luisa decided
to extinguish the candles so they wouldn't set fire to the counterpane.
For an entire year she and María Antonia shared at least their contempt for the Desired One. As soon as she disembarked in Barcelona,
the princess wrote to her mother that she almost fainted when she
saw her fiancé. His ugliness far exceeded that shown in his portraits.
Besides, he was crude, uneducated, and completely different from
her. It took an entire year to consummate the marriage, to the delight of María Luisa. The Desired One had genitals of gigantic pro-
portions but suffered from psychological impotence, punctually re-
ported by his confessor, Father Fernando, who was a paid confidant of
the queen. Besides, the prince infuriated María Antonia, constantly
harassing her with his irritating company.

When the Desired One at last managed to perform, the tone of
María Antonia's letters to the queen of Naples would change radi-
cally. In her euphoria she fell completely into treason. "I do everything I can to hinder the alliance of the Spanish government with the

emperor of the French, and my dearly beloved Fernando helps me in this enterprise, which is also Your Majesty's." Napoleon was delighted to have achieved his intention of separating the Bourbons in Spain from those in Naples. The Desired One and María Antonia, now insatiable lovers, were for all practical purposes the captives of María Luisa and Godoy in the palace. The princess contracted tuberculosis, but even strolls through the gardens were forbidden to her. María Luisa's rage increased when the Neapolitan ambassador expressed the anguish his queen felt over María Antonia, and she repudiated the diplomat. Twice her daughter-in-law miscarried premature children, tiny and dead, an ironic comfort to María Luisa. After a long agony filled with coughing up blood and aggravated by dropsy, the first wife of the Desired One passed away in Aranjuez, at the age of twenty-two, on May 21, 1806. Her husband watched over her until the last moment, with a dedication and devotion he would not show again for any other human being.

As soon as the Desired One was widowed, his August Parents proposed that he marry again, this time the sister of the countess of Chinchón. Which is to say, Godoy's sister-in-law. They chose a bad moment to oblige him, for sorrow had humanized him to the point that he forgot his habitual intrigue and cowardice. "I prefer to become a monk or remain a widower for the rest of my life before marrying into the family of that swine," he responded with dignity. Then he left without kissing the hands of the monarchs or asking for his father's blessing, so enraged that he almost didn't give the servants time to announce him when he walked through the doors in a rush. That same week the marquise of Perijáa, another of the queen's spies, told the monarchs that their son was spending night after night writing like one possessed. The queen was alarmed but Carlos IV laughed at her fears, believing that the prince was busy with a translation of Condillac's *Course d'Études*, which His Majesty recommended to him as a way to distract his widower's grief in a Christian manner.

In a few days the sovereign himself almost swooned when he

discovered an anonymous sheet of paper on the desk in his office. "Prince Fernando is preparing an uprising in the Palace. Your Majesty's crown is in danger. The Queen risks being poisoned. It is urgent to stop these attempts without a moment's delay. The loyal vassal who sends this warning is not in a position or in circumstances to carry out his duties in any other way." Still doubting the veracity of the letter, but at the insistence of María Luisa, on October 28, 1807, the king personally entered the rooms of the Desired One in a way as abrupt as it was unexpected. On his personal writing desk and under a stone paperweight of green talc, he found the principal documents of the conspiracy. The monarch handed over the worrisome writings to the marquis de Caballero, minister of justice, instead of Godoy, sick in Madrid with autumnal dengue fever.

The pages of the charge in what was called the El Escorial lawsuit were as diverse as they were scandalous. A request to the king, dictated by Escoiquiz and written in his own hand by the Desired One, asked Carlos IV for the immediate detention of Godoy, accusing him of conspiring against the throne, without filing a complaint or subjecting his crimes to judicial trials "because of the dishonor to our Royal House that will result from juridical knowledge of the excesses of a man so closely joined to our house. Once Godoy has been arrested, it is absolutely necessary that Your Majesty permit me to remain at his side constantly so that my mother cannot speak to him alone." Another document, also the work of Escoiquiz, brought formal variants to the intrigue. A letter from the Desired One, dated the day of the proceedings but with no heading or signature, decided to entrust delivery of the accusations to a cleric and placed Fernando under the example and protection of Saint Hermenegild, even though the former confessed quite openly his scant talent for martyrdom. With the rebellion quashed, the proclamations would undoubtedly draw the entire storm down on the heads of Godoy and María Luisa, and exonerate the king, to cheers and applause.

Seized by panic, the Desired One denounced his associates and sent the king the most shameful of his letters on the third of November of that year. "My dear papa: I have transgressed. I have failed Your Majesty as King and as father; but I repent and offer my most humble obedience. I should not have done anything without notifying Your Majesty; but I was taken by surprise. I have informed on the guilty ones and beg Your Majesty to forgive me for having lied the other night, permitting your acknowledged son to kiss your royal feet." Heeding the pleas and petitions "of my beloved wife," the king pardoned the Desired One and returned him to his good graces, in the hope that his conduct would show proofs of true reformation in his loose behavior. The trial of his accomplices having been initiated, the Justice Ministry requested the death penalty for Escoiquiz and the duke del Infantado, and prison sentences for the count of Orgaz and the marquis de Ayerbe, as well as various sanctions for the servants and messengers of the prince. In the end, on January 25, 1808, the judges absolved everyone who had been tried. The king, perhaps surprised by so base a farce, banished the duke del Infantado to exile and Escoiquiz to a monastery.

The Desired One's vengeance, brief but complete, would come on March 18, when the Aranjuez insurrection brought down Godoy and dragged him to the feet of the Desired One. Slashed with knives and terrified, the Prince of Peace pleaded for pardon from Fernando, who allowed himself a touch of irony: "My dear Manuel, have you perhaps forgotten that my father is still king?" The next morning Carlos IV abdicated the crown in favor of the Desired One and left with the queen for Bayonne, where Napoleon had summoned the entire Royal Family. That first reign of Fernando VII, born in Aranjuez, would not last very long and ended in blood, but no other surpassed it in popular fervor. On March 23, Murat made his entrance into Madrid at the head of the Garde Imperiale and the Legion de Réserve. On the pretext of preparing for the invasion of Portugal, the emperor now had more than thirty thousand men in Spain; his intention was to take over the entire Peninsula in a rapid coup d'état.

On March 24, the Desired One arrived in Madrid through the Puerta de Atocha. In a kind of collective frenzy, a human tide rushed into the street as his horse passed, and they kissed the stirrups and covered him with early flowers. It took him three hours to reach the Palacio de Oriente, and from the balcony he greeted the people again, sobbing with happiness.

It was his last joy before history tragically made a headlong dash forward. Beauharnais, the French ambassador, and Savary, the emperor's personal representative, warned him to travel promptly to Bayonne, where they assured him that Napoleon was prepared to recognize him as king of Spain and the Indies. Escoiquiz, returned in triumph to royal favor, with great urgency advised him to go. At last Fernando left, filled with fears and premonitions. In Bayonne and in the Castle of Maracq, in the presence of his August Parents, the emperor treated him like a disobedient lackey and shouted his demand that he renounce the throne in favor of Carlos IV. Unexpectedly, the Desired One, in a rage, resisted the plundering. Carlos IV and María Luisa made common cause with Napoleon. In a fit of hysteria, the queen called her son a bastard. News of the events of May 2, in Madrid, had reached Maracq, and Carlos IV blamed Fernando for the bloodshed. At last the Desired One gave in and returned the crown to Carlos IV, who quickly passed it to the emperor so that he could present it to his brother Joseph. The Desired One thought that all was lost, forgetting his own capacity for survival. In the Castle of Valençay, where he spent the war, he embroidered, danced, rode horseback, and refused to read any book. With bitter fatalism he seemed to delight in his own baseness. He congratulated Joseph Bonaparte on his ascension to the throne of Spain and Napoleon on his victories over the Spanish. He even humbly solicited from the emperor the hand of his niece Lolotte. The despot did not even bother to respond. When the war ended in June 1813, with Wellington pursuing Soult into France itself, Napoleon had to sign the Treaty of Valençay and recognize Fernando as king of Spain and the Indies.

In Spain the Desired One refused to swear allegiance to the Constitution promulgated by the Parliament in Cádiz. He pursued, imprisoned, and exiled the liberals who dared to defend it. He reneged on a promise of amnesty made in Valençay, appropriated the property of those who had supported the French, and left them in exile. Half the ministers of the first absolutist government were imprisoned or confined for embezzlement. The real masters of the country were the old plotters from El Escorial, with Escoiquiz and the duke del Infantado at their head. New characters, the most unlikely ones, also entered the cabal. It was the moment of Antonio de Ugarte, the former porter, and Pedro Collado, an old water vendor from Fuente del Berro whom they called *Chamorro* and who diligently took on the duties of a royal buffoon. With creatures like these, from the lowest class, Fernando felt as comfortable as the duchesses of an earlier generation had with their bullfighters. He held a public audience every day and received everyone, including paupers and prostitutes. He conversed with beggars and ambassadors, wrapped in a threadbare dressing gown and smoking incessantly. A regular visitor to brothels, he found there one of the women with whom he would feel most in harmony from that time on: Pepa de Málaga. His second wife, mortally ill, found out about their involvement and angrily criticized him. The Desired One, beside himself, insulted, punched, and slapped her. Bellowing, so there could be no doubt concerning his intentions, he said he would not tolerate anyone's affronts to that illiterate Gypsy, whom he would esteem as much as he chose.

With slum dwellers he shared a taste for insults, obscenity, and cruel sarcasm. When the University of Salamanca granted a degree to Prince Antonio Pascual, whose stupidity was well known, the Desired One always referred to him as "my uncle, the doctor" or "my uncle, the idiot." Yet even when he was king, he never dared to smoke in the presence of that poor, senile, and cretinous old man. A group of Madrilenian noblemen, eager to improve their position through flattery, invited the Desired One and Don Antonio Pascual to enjoy a game of squash in the courtyard of the Royal Hospice of San Fernando. The August Persons accepted and went there, but a sudden storm drove them away in the middle of the game. They took refuge in a sitting room, where they were offered some refreshment; their hosts chatted awhile with the blue-blooded players, shirtless and with neckerchiefs tied around their heads. Suddenly the Desired One became impatient and requested that he be allowed to hide in a closet where balls and rackets were stored so he could smoke a cigar out of sight of his uncle, the idiot.

Unlike his brother, Don Carlos, he did not feel the messianism of power or attribute any meaning to it other than the pragmatic. "Spain is a bottle of beer and I am the stopper," he liked to say. "When that pops out, who knows where the spurt will land." If he retained absolute power, at times at the cost of the greatest infamies, he did so to quiet his great fear of physical pain and death. "His despotism is a form of weakness," Moratín wrote to Goya in the year they both died, in an unpublished letter that is now the property of Ramón Serrano Suñer. The attempts against his government began just a few months after his return to Spain. Mina rebelled in 1814; Porlier the following year; Richard, Lacy, and Milans in 1817; Joaquín Vidal in 1819. On January 1, 1820, Colonel Riego revolted in Cabezas de San Juan, at the head of the Battalion of Asturias when it was going to embark for America and put down the uprisings of the viceroyalties. Riego joined General Quiroga, and together they entered San Fernando, proclaiming the Constitution of 1812. This time the plot had been planned in the Masonic lodges of Cádiz and soon spread to El Ferrol, Vigo, Zaragoza, and Pamplona. Fernando VII entrusted the defense of Madrid to Count de La Bisbal, who quickly betrayed him, swearing his loyalty to the Constitution in Ocaña. The crowd attacked the palace and the soldiers on guard were friendly to the mob. The Desired One received a group of rebels and quickly swore his allegiance to the Constitution. "Let us march openly, and I the first, along the constitutional path." Then he withdrew to his rooms and wept with fury and shame. A few days later, Rafael Riego entered Madrid. The welcome the crowd tendered was as delirious in its enthusiasm as the one offered to the Desired One himself upon his return from Aranjuez twelve years earlier. And yet the king was now only a hostage, and Riego indicated that the constitutional monarchy was nothing but an obligatory transition to an inevitable Republic.

In Parliament moderate liberals like Argüelles and Martínez de la Rosa debated zealots from the ranks of Romero Alpuente. From San Lorenzo de El Escorial, the Desired One decreed the appointment of General Carvajal to lead the Captaincy of Castilla la Nueva without the countersignature of the government. It was an attempt at a coup by the monarch, which failed immediately as soon as the national militias disarmed the garrison in Madrid. When the Desired One and his family returned to the capital, the crowd insulted him and sang the anthem of Riego. Livid with terror at the passivity of his own escort, the sovereign tried to apologize through the window of his carriage. Riots ensued and the absolutists formed societies like The Exterminating Angel and Conception. In the countryside they moved on to armed conflict, with guerrilla bands like those of The Trapense and The Bearded One. The liberals formed other societies like The Maltese Cross, The Gold Fountain, The Landaburiana, and created parties in favor of the Constitution, like the Twelveyearist, the Carbonarist, the Communard, and the Ringkeeper, where they divided into moderates, realists, and radicals. On July 7, 1821, four battalions of the Royal Guard revolted in Madrid, under the command of a second lieutenant and to the shout of "Long live the absolute king!" Members of the militias faced them, cheering the Constitution; they pursued them down Calle de Arenal and surrounded them in the Plaza de Oriente, while Fernando VII, at a window of the palace, screamed hysterically: "Get them! Get them! Finish off the rebels!" The national militia paid no attention to him and the mutiny ended as a farce in one act. The officers conferred and embraced; the rebels returned to their barracks. Civil war, however, did not take long to break out. In Navarra the realists of Santos Ladrón y Quesada rebelled. In Urgel a regency was proclaimed. Through Vargas Laguna, his ambassador in Rome, the Desired One requested the assistance of the Holy Alliance. "You can believe, Vargas my friend, that the situation is very difficult and very distressing. Everything points to an unfortunate future if God does not help us."

In support of the Desired One, the hundred thousand Sons of Saint Louis arrived from France, though in reality they were sixty thousand, united with forty thousand Spanish absolutists. The Holy Alliance, meeting in Verona, agreed to support the campaign led by Russia, Prussia, Austria, and France, with sixty million francs a year. England opposed the intervention in vain. Spanish peasants, who fifteen years earlier had heroically fought against Napoleon, now welcomed the invaders enthusiastically, shouting: "Long live the absolutely absolute king!" and "Long live our chains!" The priests were in their glory, and the atrocities committed by the Fernandistas against their own countrymen angered and horrified the duke de Angoulême, who commanded the expeditionary forces of the Most Christian French Monarch Louis XVIII. "Wherever our armies may be, we make great efforts to maintain peace. Where we are not, they murder, rob, and rape in the most repugnant way. In this country of savages, the Spanish soldiers who say they are monarchists dedicate themselves only to rapine and plunder. What they fear most is, in fact, order."

Parliament approved the move of the royal family to Sevilla and then dissolved so that the executive power could be centered on the war effort. Once it had dissolved, Fernando attempted another coup, and by sudden royal decree unexpectedly replaced the entire government on February 19, 1823. Panic gave him the audacity needed for that act of strength, which was soon aborted. He wanted to remain in Madrid at all costs and wait there for the soldiers of the duke de Angoulême, from whom he expected liberation. When the decree was published, mobs assaulted the palace again. They beat the servants with clubs, destroyed mirrors and windows, broke furniture, and tore down hangings. Men crippled in the War for Independence displayed braided cords that they said they would use to hang the Desired One from a rafter. With studied delay the national militia intervened, and after long deliberations achieved the withdrawal of the masses. On March 10, early in the morning and escorted by a simple detachment of militiamen, the monarch and his people left for Sevilla. The French marched into Madrid, and the crowd offered them a reception comparable to the welcome they had given to Riego, and to the Desired One himself on his return from Aranjuez or from exile. In many churches they enthroned his image on the altar and the faithful prayed to him as if he were the Son of God. In Sevilla the sovereign attended the Holy Week processions. He gave public displays of great devotion, which in his heart he was far from feeling. In the meantime, he prepared an insurrection with the great Andalusian nobles, who would rouse the peasantry, led by officers of the Royal Guard, to restore absolutism. Their intrigues betrayed, and in the face of the advancing hundred thousand Sons of Saint Louis, who had already passed through Despeñaperros, the Parliament decided that the monarchs should flee to Cádiz. The city, guarded by the Trocadero garrison and accessible only by means of the isthmus, lent itself to a long defense. The Desired One, who feared prison and even death at the end of that exodus, refused to leave Sevilla.

An urgently convened Parliament declared the incompetence of the Desired One and the transfer of his powers to a regency council. The judicial reasoning that deposed Fernando was hurried, and for the most part as fallacious as almost all justifications of history. A monarch who preferred voluntary surrender to the invader over flight and resistance was a traitor or a madman. No one placed His Majesty's patriotic ethic in doubt, and therefore his intellectual incapacity was manifest. On the road to Cádiz, the Desired One and his party were subjected to all kinds of odious affronts. They were obliged to kiss the glass in their carriage and display themselves like captive beasts to the furor of the crowds of peasants. These were the same masses of olive pickers, reapers, and cattle herders, all of them slaves to the usual famine, who would have risen up, howling "Long live the absolute king!" if Fernando had triumphed in his conspiracy in Sevilla. A man hung from the carriage door, raised a tightly clenched fist, and shouted at the sovereign: "You're nobody anymore! You'll never rule again!" He was half wrong, because the constitutional regime would lead not to the Republic, as Riego had erroneously predicted, but to the most brutal of despotisms devised by the Desired One himself. Liberated by the French, who lay siege to Cádiz and easily took the Trocadero, Fernando disembarked in the Puerto de Santa María. He listened with a smile to the cheers for absolutism by the mobs that not long before had called for his eyes and entrails. The duke de Angoulême, who despised him now almost as much as he abhorred all of Spain, unwillingly ordered that homage be paid to him. "But, my dear Duke, didn't they say I was crazy?"

The executions began immediately. They killed Riego in the Plaza de la Cebada after a public Calvary that debased the regime. (The people shouted "Long live the Holy Inquisition!" and the Desired One shouted "Long live Riego and the mother who bore him" when he received the news of his death.) Disgusted, the duke de Angoulême left Madrid. The Holy Alliance was horrified, and Louis XVIII wrote an indignant letter to Fernando VII: *Un despotism aveugle, loin d'accroître le pouvoir des Rois, l'affaiblit; car si leur puissance ne connaît point de règles, s'ils ne respectent aucune loi, ils succombent bientôt sous le poids de leurs caprices.* The Desired One smiled and shrugged. No one had the right to give him lessons in good government. The absolutists hurled themselves into the field to exterminate the blackguards to the fourth generation. The rabble cheered him, just as they had adored him on his return from Valençay, and he felt much closer to those masses than to all the kings in the world. Wrapped in his threadbare dressing gown and smoking like a wagon driver, he again received beggars in his public audience. When a water seller told him that the magistrates had taken away his place on the Plaza de Oriente, he ordered it returned, and over the tap a sign was placed that read: "Water sold here by Royal Order."

The Desired One married three times after the death of María Antonia of Naples. In September 1816 he was wed to his niece Isabel de Braganza, daughter of Princess Carlota, whose hump Goya had hidden behind the prince of Bourbon Parma. Poor, a peasant, and Portuguese, as she was called by the people in some mocking, defamatory verses, the queen miscarried and died three years later, leaving no descendants. A sister of hers, María Francisca, was married to Prince Don Carlos. She became a mother before Isabel's death and boldly aspired to the throne for her husband and their heirs. In August 1819 the Desired One married Amalia of Saxony, almost twenty years younger than he. The new queen, very white-skinned and blue-eyed, like the porcelain shepherdesses of her country, wrote verses in the style of the *Fioretti* of Saint Francis and read the poets of the English Lake District who had been translated into German. On his wedding night, the Desired One surprised the entire palace when he left the bedroom red with rage and swearing like one possessed. Amalia, who had lost her mother when she was very young and grew up in a convent, felt a hysterical, violent repugnance to carnal relations with her husband. The Desired One petitioned for and obtained an intervention by the pope to bring the queen to reason. She ceded finally, more as a Christian than as a wife, but as it turned out, she was barren. She died on May 18, 1829, leaving the monarch no children.

Seven months later, Fernando married again. Like his old jailer in Valençay, the Desired One could state that he was looking not for a woman but a uterus where his blood could survive. The chosen one was María Cristina, his young Neapolitan niece, almost a quarter century younger than he. Princess Luisa Carlota, Cristina's sister and the sister-in-law of the king, her uncle, was the wife of Prince Don Francisco de Paula, and she arranged the wedding. Ironically, the Desired One would surrender his will to this final wife with the dark eyes and diminutive ears, as Villa Urrutia described her, whose faint smile and natural kindness were admired by the people and by the court. Even more ironically, a resentful Infante Don Carlos, who had opposed the marriage by all the means at his disposal, represented the king when he married by proxy in the chapel of the royal estate at Aranjuez. On March 29, 1830, the Desired One proclaimed the Pragmatic Sanction, reestablishing the Law of the Seven Parts and repealing an act of Felipe V that excluded females as heirs to the crown. Don Carlos and Doña María Francisca protested angrily, since they believed that the prince would have more valid right to the throne if María Cristina, who was pregnant at the time, gave birth to a girl. She was born on October 10 and baptized with the name María Isabel. On January 30, 1832, the queen gave birth to another daughter, María Luisa Fernanda. In September, severe attacks of gout brought the king to death's door. At the age of forty-seven he was an old man, and the doctors lost all hope. Pressured by the prime minister, Calomarde, and by the bishop of León, María Cristina gave in and permitted the Desired One to sign a codicil in which he revoked the Pragmatic Sanction.

Don Carlos, whose rights supported the absolutist Spain that was prepared to extirpate the blackguards down to the fourth generation, now believed his inheritance was assured. In La Granja, Princess Luisa Carlota chided the queen, who cried in her arms. (*Regina di galleria!*) She slapped Calomarde with all her strength. ("White hands do not offend, Señora.") She tore the codicil into a thousand pieces and established a cordon sanitaire around the dying man, which excluded visits from Don Carlos and from his wife. Unexpectedly, the Desired One, always cunning in the art of survival, recovered enough to publish a manifesto in which he denounced the stratagems of Carlism. "Perfidy finished off the horrible plot, begun by sedition." Don Carlos fled to Portugal and began the regency of María Cristina. On October 16, 1832, he decreed a broad amnesty and soon afterward granted a general pardon. On June 20, 1833, the Parliament swore allegiance to Isabel in the Church of San Jerónimo.

The king attended the ceremony, dragging legs that could barely support him. The interminable ceremony bored the little princess. She played with the lions carved into the arms of the chair, and the queen reprimanded her twice. The Desired One smiled. With death hovering over him, he stopped fearing it for the first time and found it difficult to recognize himself in that unexpected indifference. He too was bored in San Jerónimo, while the grandees of Spain, the nobles and the prelates, swore their allegiance. His head began to nod; fatigue overwhelmed him, and Spain inevitably approached civil war. Outside, in the bell towers, all the bells of Madrid rang out with glory.

Three months later, on September 29, he collapsed facedown onto the table when he finished lunch. Plates and crockery fell to the floor, where they clinked or shattered. An already clawed hand crushed the tablecloth. The queen stood up, screaming, while a chamberlain and two gentlemen-in-waiting rushed to help the king. His eyes were wide open and his smile, twisted in astonishment, was stained by a trickle of very red blood. Fernando VII, the Desired One, had just died.

November 21, 1975

Across a lake that would calm at a distance the waters of time, he heard the screech of his finger against the glass. He closed his eyes and saw the frozen lake where a pack of white bears with pink eyes, terrified by the screech that grew inside itself as it was repeated, like a spiral, were fleeing. In his fatigue, Sandro wanted to shout at them in vain that the ice of time would crack like mica, wounded by stridency. Beneath the ice spread nothingness, interminable and absolute, with no fish, no stars, no seaweed, no monsters: a nothingness that would devour the terrified bears as if they never had been. Suddenly darkness fell over his eyes, and the screech of the martyrized glass quieted, ending in a crash of crockery and forks scattered on the floor before silence fell. In that stillness, which seemed shocking because it was unexpected, he heard one of the voices he had learned to recognize in dreams. "Sleep if you like and go back to Bordeaux whenever you want to. I was hoping you would die here of old age, to give you a funeral worthy of Apelles. I would have had your body lying in state in the Puerta de Alcalá, watched over by the royal halberdiers and a troop of cavalry. In single file, all the way to the Ventas del Espíritu Santo, people would have waited all night to see you dead. The rabble attends executions as well as funerals. They're all part of the same circus."

Somewhere, perhaps in the book by Arzadin y Zabala, Sandro had read that after the war, when the Desired One returned, there weren't even chandeliers in the Palacio de Oriente. Everything had been looted by the invaders when they fled. Perhaps he hadn't read it in Arzadin y Zabala, he immediately said to himself. Maybe he had learned it in a much simpler but also a more inexplicable way. In any case, he continued to reflect, the palace without chandeliers would not have been the right place to receive Goya's remains on their return from Bordeaux. Better to display them in the Puerta de Alcalá, very close to where the old bullring had been and where Barbudo killed *Pepe-Hillo*. "Circus. I'll never go back to the circus on the Rue du Manège where I would take Rosarito to forget myself, watching the tumblers suspended for a moment between heaven and this hell we call earth. There the animals became buffoons and men played with wild beasts, as in the garden of earthly delights," the other voice continued, the one that Sandro knew, beneath his forehead, was his.

He became accustomed to the voices, as he did to their footsteps. Four or five years earlier, at Princeton, he had met Julian Jaynes, who spoke to him about a work of his, written over a long period of time, about the origins of the interior life. According to Jaynes, the human species developed language a hundred thousand years before Christ. But it did not discover consciousness and reason until some thousand years before the Christian Era. In the interim, men were guided by magical, mystic voices that advised them and filtered

through the right cerebral hemisphere, which still happens to para-
noids. Between the second and first millennia before Christ, vast mi-
grations, and the increasingly extensive use of the written word, created societies too complex to be governed by oracles and visionaries.
The species learned then to become absorbed in thought, and inside
itself it found knowledge. Sandro reminded Jaynes, who took hurried
notes, that Ortega had said that four centuries before our era, Socrates had discovered reason in the squares of Athens, although the pre-
Socratics used it earlier without reducing life to its format. Then he
added that in a sense the regime of sacred, inexplicable voices demonstrated its validity by surviving almost one hundred thousand years.
"Perhaps it wouldn't be a bad idea to go back to it and undo everything we have done in the course of three millennia." Julian Jaynes
shrugged and smiled. "You're killing my book, Vasari my friend." "No,
I'm simply proposing that you write another one with a totally different intention."

Now, with his eyes closed in his study, or rather, in R.'s study,
where Marina watched television in silence, Sandro said to himself
that the strange voice heard so often had eventually become his own.
"Whoever I may be, R.'s rough draft or a man of flesh and bone with
an inalienable identity, I'm also the one who speaks and agonizes inside me. The one who also listens to other beings inside me who speak
to him or rebuke him."

It was night on television, and the night was in Madrid. Franco
had died and his remains were moved from the Pardo to the Palacio
de Oriente. They watched over him there, in the Hall of Columns,
where, according to announcers, they had prepared the catafalque of
María de las Mercedes, the first wife of Alfonso XII. That room, decorated with Isabelline lamps, frescoes by Corrado Giaquinto, marble
floors, and funerary hangings brought from the Hieronymites and
the Royal Slaves, had been chosen because of its easy access and
two entrances. Endless lines, contained and flanked by low railings,
stretched toward the Plaza de España and were lost from view. They

spoke of hundreds of thousands of people prepared to spend the night and morning standing outdoors to bid farewell to the corpse. ("Their brothers are not unknown to me. I see in all of them the same crowds that cheered Godoy, the Desired One, the Intruder King, Riego, the Obstinate One. They're also the ones who dragged Godoy along the ground in Aranjuez, stabbing his legs; the ones who brought Riego to the scaffold in a charcoal seller's basket and then stoned the quarters of his body, hacked to pieces by axes and displayed on the pillars of twenty cities; the ones who gutted the Obstinate One with goads and razors when he was handcuffed in a cage, and danced with joy as the executioner burned his remains; the ones who invaded the Palacio de Oriente with ropes to hang the Desired One, and on the road to Cádiz obliged him to kiss the windows of his coach in order to spit in his eyes." Before the main entrance to the palace, the guards repeated unceasingly: "Remember that you cannot take in packages, handbags, or cameras. Remember that you cannot take in packages, handbags, or cameras. Remember . . ." Toward the end the column slowed and came to a stop. The ushers asked that they pass the coffin in fours; but no one wanted to find himself separated from the bier by other lines of people. The night was serene and icy.

Outside were first-aid stations, and from time to time bells struck the hour. The announcers counted the faithful who passed the cadaver, because that, as one of them said, was unforgettable history. Priests blessed the body lying in state and soldiers saluted it in military fashion. There were people who fell to their knees at the feet of the dead man, while others crossed themselves when they saw him. ("I have seen them on the San Isidro excursions and picnics, in church, at the bullfights, at roadside inns, hostelries, and taverns, at weddings, at brawls, in brothels, in jails. I've heard them cheer the Inquisition, chains, freedom, the Constitution, the crown, the faith, the Revolution, death, prisons, the homeland, treason, vengeance, mercy, ignorance, absolutism, rebellion, fierce bulls, and the wine at Mass.") "Do you think they'll let me give him a kiss when I get there?"

implored an old woman, wrapped up and sunk in a wheelchair. "Do you think . . . ?" Some Gypsies identified themselves: "We're the Gypsies from Pozo del Tío Raimundo. For us too he was a good man." A very old man rubbed his frozen hands and gave cavernous, intermittent coughs. "I've spent the whole night here, I haven't slept, but I'm not leaving without seeing him lying in state in the palace." Another shook his head, the lower part of his face and his ears wrapped in a scarf. "He was like a father to the country. He was like a father." ("They not only applauded the Prince of Peace, Fernando VII, Rafael Riego, and Juan Martín the Obstinate One, but also *Costillares*, Pedro Romero, José Romero, Joseph Bonaparte, Murat, the duke de Angoulême, the English, and the hundred thousand Sons of Saint Louis. Now they'll all go to the Palacio de Oriente to bid farewell to a dead man whom perhaps none of them had ever seen in the flesh. But at bottom they're not going to the palace or anywhere else, because as I've always told myself when I think of them, they don't know the way and they don't know themselves.")

In the Hall of Columns, Franco lay in his coffin in uniform. His endless dying, with its hemorrhages and surgeries, left no serious trace on the old man's face that the embalmers obviously remodeled with a master hand. Only on his upper lip, very close to the corner of his slimmed-down mouth, a wound similar to the mark of a pinprick was clearly visible on the screen. But nothing was left of the man who was Head of State, President of the Government, National Head of the Movement, and Generalissimo of the Armies, responsible only to God and to History. Nothing was left, Sandro repeated to himself, of the man who in his farewell address to the mounted cadets of the Military Academy of Zaragoza had said that there he had done away with officers who were puny weaklings; the man who prophesized in 1942 or 1943 that the world war would mean the end of one era and the beginning of another in which the liberal world would perish, victim of the cancer of its own errors, together with its imperialism, its capitalism, and its millions of unemployed; the man who at about the same time, or perhaps a little earlier, wrote to Hitler, Adolph, son of Hitler, Alois, an official of the imperial and royal customs house, and Hitler, Klara, *née* Pölzl, daughter of Pölzl, Johann, a peasant from Spital in Lower Austria, that he felt joined to him in a common historical destiny, whose abandonment would mean his suicide and that of the Cause he had represented and led in Spain; the man who ten or twelve years after the Second World War and the suicide of Hitler, Adolph, son of Hitler, Alois, an official of the imperial and royal customs house, would tell the representative of a French newspaper (*Le Figaro?*) that at absolutely no time during the conflict did he plan to place his country on the side of the Rome-Berlin Axis, and in a sense, Tokyo as well; the man who, at the end of that same worldwide conflict, would give the most negative of all the definitions of Constitutional Law after the final words of Carlos II, the Bewitched: "We are not on the right, or on the left, or in the center" (the Bewitched, on his death bed, "I am no longer anything"); the man who at about the time of the interview granted to the French paper (*Le Figaro? Le Matin? France-Soir?* No, it definitely wasn't *France-Soir*) would say it was completely absurd and malevolent to call him a dictator, since his prerogatives and powers were very inferior to those of the president of the United States, at that time Eisenhower, the former general; the man who, in the middle of the civil war, assured the correspondent from another foreign paper, this time Japanese, that once his mission was concluded, he would retire to the country and lose himself in private, domestic life; the man who twenty years later, specifically and precisely on November 22, 1966, on the occasion of the introduction in Parliament of the Organic Law of the State, would speak of the familiar demons of the Spanish nation: an anarchic spirit, negative criticism, lack of solidarity, extremism, and enmity; the man who, four years before his death, four years almost to the day, affirmed that as long as God granted him strength, life, and clear judgment, he would remain at the helm of state in the service of the unity, greatness, and liberty of his people.

Sandro did not allow himself to be carried away by easy emotions. The ones that, in the name of obvious truths, tolled for the dead man from the depths of the past. Those that oppressively reiterated the perishable nature of power: as transitory, or even more so, than men themselves. The winds of time carried away the ashes of empires and of slaves. Because it is mortal, in the end there is nothing more human than history. El Greco survived Felipe II, who did not like his art; as Velázquez survived Felipe IV, who sincerely admired him; as Goya survived Fernando VII, who feared and respected him in so evident and enigmatic a manner. All of that became insignificant through repetition. ("I would have displayed your body lying in state at the Puerta de Alcalá, watched over by the royal halberdiers and a troop of cavalry," repeated one of those voices deep inside him that had become inseparable from his deepest being. "I would have displayed your body lying in state . . .") The television screen looked like a dark aquarium where images trembling in the depths of night slipped away. Far away, in a genuine, inalienable distance, Sandro again heard the strident wail of a wet index finger caressing the rim of a glass.

In the Grande Chartreuse of Bordeaux the inscription on the tomb that Goya shared with his son's father-in-law was mistaken. *Hispanienses Pertisimus Pictor,* who they said passed at eighty-five and not eighty-two, his age when he died. If they noticed the error, Xavier and Mariano Goya never cared to correct it. It was likely that they had forgotten the precise age of their father and grandfather. Alfonso XII was the first to propose the transfer of Goya's body to Madrid, soon after the restoration of the monarchy. However, as usual, Spanish administrative functions bogged down and took too long. The king died before the remains were exhumed. In 1888, during the regency of María Cristina, the recovery of the bones was brought up again. As Saint-Paulien so aptly put it, Sagasta had recognized civil marriage and promulgated universal, though *restricted* suffrage, and there was no reason for the liberal remains of the painter of San Antonio de la

Florida to remain in exile. On February 25, 1889, the city council of Bordeaux authorized the prefecture of la Gironde to perform the exhumation. The boards of the coffins had rotted and the remains of Goya and Goicoechea mixed together. Amazingly, even though the grave offered no signs of having been violated, the authorities found only one skull: the one belonging to Goicoechea. *Les verifications ont permis de constater que le corps que l'on croit être celui de Goya n'aurait pas de tête . . .* Those in charge of the exhumation vacillated over the mystery. They requested instructions from Madrid, but Madrid, disconcerted, decided to forget about so irritating a case. After a year the bones of the two men returned to their grave. Goya, dead, patiently continued to waste away in exile.

The enigma of the missing skull would not begin to be clarified until eighty years later. Apparently, in 1846, it was removed by a French phrenologist, the painter Dionisio Fierros, and the marquis de San Adrián. Three years later, Fierros painted in oils and dated a canvas, on the back of which the marquis de San Adrián wrote in his own hand: *The Cranium of Goya Painted by Fierros.* Fierros felt a "strange tenderness for that skull," according to his widow, and kept it under a bell jar in his study. Later, the painting was lost in Zaragoza. In 1911, one of the artist's sons, a medical student in Zaragoza, took the skull apart and divided the pieces among his friends after letting them in on the secret. He kept a piece of the parietal bone as a kind of relic, which his grandson still had in 1961, when he revealed the entire story to *Mundo Hispánico.*

That was the fate of Goya's remains, on the interminable barren plains of death, where Franco now accompanied the painter of the shootings of May 3 in Madrid. The remains in San Antonio de la Florida and the splinter of the parietal, the private and, until then, secret property of Dionisio Gamallo Fierros, was also all that remained of the painter of four kings, the deaf lover of María Teresa in Sanlúcar, the close friend of *Costillares*, Pedro Romero, and *Pepe-Hillo,* the most truthful and implacable witness to his time, and the man who had descended down to the deepest interior chasms and found there abysses and spaces as immense as those that separated nebulas and constellations, among which a terrified humanity trembled. But the pilgrimage of Goya's remains was not over yet. In 1899, on the brink of another century that in Spain would see all the horrors of *The Disasters of War* exaggerated, and the stupidity and irrationality of *The Caprices* and *The Absurdities* magnified, Goya's remains, confused with Goicoechea's, returned to Madrid. There the cemetery of San Isidro gave them shelter, expecting a monument that was supposed to honor them along with the remains of other exiles like Moratín, Donoso Cortés, and Menéndez Valdés. The monument was never built. Finally, on November 29, 1919, they found rest beneath the frescoes of San Antonio de la Florida. Goya's final burial did not move the Madrid of the period to any great extent. The country that prayed and charged, as Machado had written a little earlier, destroyed and forgot with identical celerity. *La Esfera*, for example, did not even mention the ceremony at San Antonio. The decapitated skeleton of Goya now slept in a metal coffer beneath a stone slab. ("At nightfall everyone leaves and the winter stars begin to light up above the lantern. Only the moon and the presbytery lamp illuminate that chapel, where a play of mirrors in the corners multiply my paintings and the shadows. Suddenly, without raising latches or pushing doors on their hinges, the four couples of *Blind Man's Bluff* pass the walls, and holding hands, form a circle around my tomb.") Ramón Gómez de la Serna, who was present at Goya's last burial so far, observed in astonishment the small size of the case. It is distressing and shocking, he thought to himself, to see how the greatest men diminish.

All at once and always with movements that seemed measured and thought out, Marina turned off the television. Then she sat down on the rug, next to Sandro, and lit a cigarette.

"All this," she said in a hushed voice, "has already happened."

"It's very possible," Sandro agreed, "though no demographic or historical document exists that indicates the death of any other Galician."

"You didn't understand me, or you don't want to. In any case, it doesn't matter."

"I'm making an effort to understand you."

"If that's so, you forgot who we are or, more to the point, who we aren't. We and everything around us, including the vigil for Franco in the Palacio de Oriente, exist only in R.'s book. Nothing is ours, Sandro, not the history and not the chimeras. Everything we saw on television is as unreal as the phantoms of *Blind Man's Bluff* dancing in the meadow, because we ourselves are another man's dream or fairy tale."

"Then why did you say that all this had already happened?"

"Because this is true. In real time, the time in which R. is truly alive and is writing our lives, it's been a year or two since Franco died."

"R. was the one who called us from the United States to tell us he had just died."

"He called us in his book. How many times do I have to repeat it before you begin to listen to me? By then, in reality, months or years had passed since the death of that man, who so many believed was immortal."

Two dawns before, at about five in the morning, Sandro dreamed that he was dreaming. In the dream he could make out a man, prematurely aged and poorly dressed, playing with some children in a public garden, which then disappeared in a thunderstorm. Then he dreamed that he awoke and saw a woman, not Marina, naked and sleeping facedown beside him. In his memory now he saw again her very dark hair, a brilliant black, spread over her shoulders and the sheets. On the other side of a window a storm was clearing. A rainbow appeared in the sky, and, passing through the glass, flashed on the woman's back, setting it aflame with all the colors of the prism. Sandro woke her then and said: "I dreamed I saw Godoy in a park where I had never been. He was very old, but I recognized his features, because I've never forgotten a face. Sitting on a bench and dressed like someone unemployed, he was talking to other grandfathers as poorly dressed as he. At times the children approached him and he gave them his cane so they could ride it around a pond. My dream melted away in a storm. I don't understand it, but I'm afraid it's a bad omen." At that moment the ringing of the telephone really woke him. The window, the morning, and the rainbow disappeared. It was Marina sleeping now beside him, on her stomach, and naked. He picked up the phone in a daze and heard the voice of R., as close and distinct as if he were speaking to him in the same room. "Sandro, do you want to witness the fall of the last Empire raised to God, like the Tower of Babel?" His spirit brightened when he heard the news. He was completely lucid when he asked if they had published the news in the United States. "American television just announced it. It's eleven at night here, Eastern Time," R. specified. "I'll leave you now in the company of a more or less uncertain history." It wasn't until the next morning that Sandro realized that R. hadn't told him exactly where he was phoning from (Eastern Time) or asked about his book on Goya. He also never found out whether when he referred to a more or less uncertain history, he was talking about the past or the future.

"If two years really have passed since the death of Franco, and we are nothing but fictional beings lost in a book where R. struggles in vain to give us life, what's really going on in the country now? Do you happen to know?"

"How would I know if R. didn't want us to see the future in his work? As for the rest, I also don't know what that question's about. You always said that living here is seeing the same thing over again, and that the future of Spain is doubtful because its present tends to resemble its past."

"I said only the last part," Sandro gently defended himself. "The rest is from Azorín, though that seems a lie."

"It doesn't matter who it's from." He was astonished at the impatience in Marina's voice. "If we never were really alive, if we draw breath only in the mind of a flesh-and-blood man, then this country never really existed either."

He admitted to himself again that Marina had lost her mind. Yet her dementia revealed an intrinsic consistency whose internal logic ("the logic of dreams or of literary characters, these fictional beings that she claims we are") seemed both brilliant and compelling. As he had done six days earlier, faced with the phantoms dancing in the Prado disguised as flashy young dandies, he affirmed his belief that madness was the most convincing of certainties while the remaining realities, of knowledge, sentiment, and the senses, were always relative and negotiable. In that case, why not accept Marina's nonsense and willingly make it his own? After all, the important thing wasn't existing or not existing but learning to know oneself, Sandro said to himself, never knowing whether that idea was his or R.'s and he had plagiarized it without realizing it.

"Goya did exist," he affirmed in a quiet voice, avoiding Marina's eyes.

"He existed and said that the dream of reason produces monsters. Creatures like us conjured up by R.'s reason, unless he's crazy and we're creatures not of his reason but his delirium."

"In any case, if he were mad and we were his phantoms, we'd never know about his insanity either."

"Oh, he's crazy! Don't doubt that for a second!" Marina repeated, excited now, tossing her lit cigarette onto the smoking logs in the fireplace. "Who but a madman could have imagined people like us to give us the absurd destiny it was our luck to fall into? Think of your dead children and mine who will never be born. Think of the ghosts in the painting. Think of the painted bull when it appeared alive at the foot of the window. Think of our unlikely meeting and the fact that now we find ourselves together here, in R.'s house, not really knowing whether we love or hate each other . . ."

"I suppose you're thinking too about my book on Goya," Sandro said, controlling his expression and lowering his eyes.

"I wasn't going to forget it, because in a sense it's the most senseless of R.'s deliriums. Your book exists only in his, the one he's writing about us. You'll never finish it, because R. planned that you wouldn't. Just for that reason he made you responsible for it. It will be left endless in R.'s work, which among other things will be the story of this frustration of yours."

"Perhaps you're right about that . . ." Sandro murmured, his gaze fixed on the flickering fire.

"Of course I'm right! You must think I'm talking nonsense and even feel tempted sometimes to infect you with my madness. Don't try to deny it, because I see it in your eyes." In silence, Sandro continued to contemplate the flames. "At first I supposed that my ravings were R's punishment, the torture imposed gratuitously by a sadistic author on one of his creatures. Now I know, however, that my madness is only the reflection of his: the living image of the insanity of someone who at the same time imagines himself as reason and as our reason for being."

His hands crossed beneath his chin, his elbows pressing against his knees, a motionless Sandro studied the fire in the depths of the fireplace. Very far away, in the final abysses of himself, he heard again the interminable moan of the glass rubbed back and forth by a damp finger. He wanted to tell Marina that this wasn't the complete summary of the drama and the condition of the two of them. Even in the case that he and Marina were both only chimeras in the book R. was writing in his own image and likeness, another man and other voices were insistently making themselves heard deep inside Sandro, obliging him to identify with a dead painter in exile a century and a half before Franco lay in state in the Royal Palace. The invisible glass was squeaking now like a rusty blade against a whetstone. ("Señor, I beg you!" "Ah, forgive me! I thought you heard absolutely nothing." "I do hear this screeching. And sometimes thunderclaps too, when they sound very far away.") Yet he said nothing about all that. Without looking away from the logs and the tripod, he murmured as if to himself:

"Godoy too, in a letter written two nights before he died, said he sometimes believed he had lived someone else's dream: actually, the dream of reason. Perhaps it isn't necessary to add that the letter is unpublished and belongs now to R. He gave me a photocopy."

"Very good! If the dream of reason produces monsters, let's see now if the dream of monsters like us conjures up our reason for being!" Kneeling next to Sandro, Marina pressed his palms between her cold, trembling hands. "R.'s book is almost finished and at any moment, whenever he decides, we'll disappear into the void. I want to live and I want to live with you! Just like the damned country, as you call it, wants to live in peace and harmony after the great absurdity ending now with the death of Franco."

"Marina, for the love of God, try to calm down . . ."

"I don't want to calm down and I don't want God's love. I want to survive with you and I want your love, even if it belongs to a phantom as maddened and crazed as I am! The phantom of a drunkard who killed all my children in my womb before I could conceive them! Well, whatever, let each person have his leprosy and his weeping, as whoever it was who said that, said!"

"Marina, I beg you . . ."

"I beg you, help me to summon R. Let's force him to appear here, in the middle of his own dream, and oblige him to keep us alive in his book! Together we're as strong as he is, or perhaps even more powerful. Even though we may be figures in an unfinished fable and R. may be flesh and blood, we can survive him. Isn't it a natural law, after all, that characters outlive their authors? Is it or isn't it?"

"Yes, it is," Sandro murmured very quietly. "San Manuel Bueno, the priest who didn't believe in immortality, has outlived Unamuno. But Unamuno will outlive Franco. Only the feigned is true."

"In that case, we can invoke R., here in his own house. What better place to request his presence? He's the one who arranged the stage and the actors in order to make his entrance at the last minute. He was incapable only of foreseeing our rebellion, which would compel him to continue our lives when he's prepared to abandon us. If we call him now, he won't be able to resist, because when all is said and done, he's only a mortal man who needs his ghosts as much as we need him."

"We in order to keep living and he in order not to lose his mind," Sandro specified, almost without realizing it. "Yes, it's very possible that all this is very true."

"What are we waiting for, then? If we both invoke him he'll find himself obliged to appear, because our power will be that of the communion of the saints. Or, perhaps, do we have to wait here forever, in fiction and in reality, for the right to exist with dignity as human beings? Or do you possibly think I'm the victim of the strangest madness, that of a living woman, though incapable of giving life, who imagines she is a literary character in someone else's book?"

Sandro did not answer immediately. In spite of himself, he indulged in thinking about a sudden though not unexpected appearance by R., summoned by him and Marina. He would come, he thought, like Satan or the Great Goat, appearing in the oak groves of Biscay at the spells and commands of Goya's witches. He would come if Marina was right and they really didn't exist, to give an account not of having granted them a fictitious life ("only the feigned is true") but of having denied them a very real freedom. Perhaps he would appear almost thirty years younger, the way he was that spring in 1947, when he introduced him and Marina beside the pond with the water lilies in the courtyard of Letters. (*"How beautiful these flowers are! I wonder what they're called"* Villaespesa had exclaimed in the Retiro, according to R. *"Don't be an idiot, Villaespesa. These beautiful flowers are white water lilies that appear every day in one of your poems."*) In front of the bulletin board Falangist and Monarchist students were slapping one another. Some defended the manifesto of Don Juan de Bourbon in Estoril, which the others had not been able to rip off the board yet. "What the country desires is to emerge immediately from an increasingly dangerous temporariness, without understanding that the hostility the nation finds all around it is born for the most part of General Franco's presence as Head of State." Almost thirty years later, during that autumn, the nation knew once again that it was surrounded by a worldwide enemy, as a result of the five political executions in September: the last Francoist executions before the death of Franco. On the balcony of the same palace where he now lay in state, a man shrunken and cracked by age greeted with a trembling hand the delirious crowd that shouted its loyalty to him and its repudiation of the world for condemning him. For thirty-six years he had dictatorially and for life governed that country where he always found hundreds of thousands of people to applaud him. The same hundreds of thousands who would forget him very soon, as if he had never been born. When he thought of the old man and his people, Sandro told himself that neither he nor the people could be right. Their common history was a delirious dream that by contrast gave the appearance of reality to fits of madness and fictions. No one with any knowledge of those true years could accuse Marina of dementia for believing herself a character in the book of a madman.

"No, Marina," he said finally, "I wouldn't imagine you possessed by the strangest kind of madness when you claim to be a phantom imagined by a man. In the final analysis, the greatest insanity will never be literature but history. On the other hand, our condition as dreamed beings is as impossible to prove as our reality. In any case, nearby or from a distance, fictitious or real, we live always governed by R. It isn't a matter of summoning him to demand an explanation, but simply that he free us."

"How would we free ourselves from him? Do you know?"

"I think so."

"How? For heaven's sake! How could we do it?"

"By making an effort to live our own lives, in the same way that this country, as true or as unreal as we are, will have to do now. Our freedom, Marina, is the measure of our existence. If yours is far from me, you can leave me tonight. I won't try to persuade you or hold you."

"I have no place to go. I'll disappear with you as soon as R. finishes his book."

"Perhaps the book will disappear, its destiny to remain unfinished, like the history of this country of ours, where nothing is completed and we always go back to absolute zero. In any case, whether he abandons or continues his work, a work that perhaps doesn't even exist, I have to conclude mine."

"The life of Goya, which R. made you responsible for. We're still caught in the same vicious circle."

"No," Sandro replied very slowly and in a very quiet voice, "it isn't a matter of the life of Goya that he made me responsible for. It's a matter of writing my own life, as if I were Goya, or as if Goya were me. Tonight, when Franco is lying in state, every Spaniard is in a certain sense Goya, because we're living the end of an *Absurdity* and beginning a *Caprice*, where our duty is the search for ourselves."

"Don't forget *The Disasters of War*."

"I haven't forgotten. Just as I remember very well that all of our contemporary history begins on May 2, 1808, under the sign of the bull. Come, help me, sit down at the typewriter."

Marina obeyed slowly, as if each of her steps and gestures were obeying a specific, inalienable decision. Outside, the gale grew stronger and the trees moaned and shook above the sound of the torrent and the howl of the north wind. Standing at the window, Sandro dictated in too loud a voice, as if he had become deaf. Marina hesitated for an instant, surprised in part by his voice's timbre and tone. Then, suddenly forgetting her surprise, she began to type a dialogue that on Sandro's lips seemed like a confession.

"And His Majesty the king said to me:
" 'What is your idea of happiness on earth?'

"'To die before my son Xavier,' I replied immediately. 'My wife and I had already buried the other four before I buried her too, during the starvation in the war. I don't want to lose this one.'

"He started to laugh without letting go of the lit cigar between his teeth, as yellow as a ram's. He was approaching forty, or already was forty. Only when I painted him then, for the last time and by his request, did I really see how deformed his face was, heavy jawed, fat cheeked, and uneven beneath his large, deep-black brows. But his eyes, regardless of whether he had a squint, shone with a malice that was in no way dim-witted. He had been the most loved man and was the most detested, in this country that always charges when it is time to kill or reproduce . . ."

TIMELINE

Goya

Timeline of Goya's Life and Work

March 3, 1746 — Francisco de Goya Lucientes is born in the village of Fuendetodos, Saragossa.

1760 — Joins the studio of José Luzán as an apprentice. He will leave it four years later.

1763 — First trip to Madrid. Meets and works for the brothers Bayeu, Ramón and Francisco.

1770–1771 — Trip to Italy. In the summer of 1771 he is back in Saragossa. He is contracted to paint the vault of one chapel of El Pilar.

1773 — Marries Josefa Bayeu, the sister of Francisco and Ramón Bayeu. She will bear five children, though only the last one, Xavier, will survive his parents. All the others die in infancy.

1774–1778 — Paints cartoons for tapestries in the Real Fábrica de Santa Bárbara.

1779 — Meets His Majesty Carlos III and the so-called princes of Asturias, Don Carlos and Doña María Luisa. He is utterly charmed by the encounter. Eventually two of his portraits of young princes, in hunting attire, will be donated to the Prado by Fernando VII.

1793 — On a trip to Andalucía falls gravely ill, probably with a first attack of syphilis. The doctors save his life, but he will be stone deaf for the rest of his existence.

1795, July or August — Probable beginning of his amorous affair with María Teresa de Alba, duchess of Alba.

1796 — Nominated president of the Section of Painting at the Academy of San Fernando. He will renounce the position in April of the following year because of his deafness.

1797—In Sanlúcar depicts the duchess of Alba wearing mourning for her husband the late duke, and showing two rings named after her and Goya.

1797–1798—Composes his *Caprices* or *Caprichos*. With the help of Godoy the album is published in 1799. Two other series of engravings— *The Disasters of War* and *Los Disparates or the Absurdities*—will be printed and distributed after the artist's death.

1798—In five or six months, with his aide Asensio Juliá, completes the frescoes of San Antonio de la Florida, where the painter's decapitated vestiges now rest.

1799—Elevated to the position of first painter of the royal chamber.

1801—Paints the family of Carlos IV.

1802—Sudden death of the duchess of Alba.

May 2, 1808—From one of his windows, and with the help of a telescope, watches the fight of the Madrileños with the Mamelukes of Joachim Murat, marshal of France and Napoleon's brother-in-law. In the early hours of the following day, accompanied by a young male servant, the painter sketches recently executed Madrileños at the foot of Príncipe Pío Hill. After the French defeat at Bailén, July 16–19, and the temporary lifting of the siege of Saragossa, Goya is invited to visit the city. On his trip from Madrid he sees vestiges of the atrocities committed by the invaders and the guerrillas. Added to the executions of May 3 at the foot of Príncipe Pío Hill, the crimes exposed on the road to Saragossa probably mark the beginning of *The Disasters of War* in the artist's tireless creative consciousness.

1812—In the famine of Madrid, under siege by the guerrillas, Josefa Bayeu de Goya dies. Her husband and her son Xavier attend the wake. Three years later Goya paints her portrait from memory.

1808–1813—Though he once tries to escape to Portugal, Goya remains in Madrid almost all of this five-year period. He has a good friendship with Joseph Bonaparte and paints his portrait. Nevertheless, in 1813 he also paints the *Second* and the *Third of May, 1808*, his major masterpiece among all masterpieces, to celebrate the return of Fernando VII.

1816—*The Tauromachy* appears in Madrid and sells out in a short time.

1819 — Buys the so-called Quinta del Sordo, and almost immediately
   begins to decorate it with the *Pinturas Negras* or *Black Paintings*.
   Once again contrary fate crosses his path, and another syphilis attack
   nearly kills him. A grateful Goya paints his self-portrait, attended by a
   certain doctor Arrieta.

May 30, 1824 — Fernando VII permits Goya a trip to Plombièrs "to take
   its medicinal waters," though the king knows only too well that the
   painter intends to leave Spain for good.

July–September, 1824 — Visits Paris and meets many old friends who dwell
   there in exile. September 1 he travels back to Bordeaux, where he had
   briefly stopped on his way to Paris. In Bordeaux he is joined by his last
   mistress, Leocadia Weiss, and her daughter Rosarito, who is rumored
   to have been sired by Goya.

1826–1827 — Briefly travels to Madrid twice. He intends to solicit a
   retirement annuity and to add a clause to his will leaving Marianito,
   his grandson, la Quinta del Sordo. The annuity is immediately
   granted. Leocadia and Rosarito are not even mentioned in the
   painter's last testament.

April 16, 1828 — Dies in Bordeaux.

Franco

Excerpts from a Timetable of Franco's Last Days

November 7, 1975 — With the patient suffering a gastric hemorrhage
   and unresponsive to medical treatment, a new operation is decided
   upon. (Franco had been operated on at El Pardo in deplorable
   circumstances. In the midst of a furious storm, even the electricity
   went off, and it took a long while to come back on.) His Excellency
   the Chief of State is moved to "La Paz" Hospital Complex and
   immediately placed in the care of surgeons, anesthetists, and four
   cardiorespiratory supervisors. The operation reveals many ulcers of
   the stomach, which were bleeding profusely. The gastric surgery lasts
   four hours, and requires five more liters of blood. The vital signs are
   normal, but the prognosis is very grave.

November 8, 1975 — At 8:30 a.m. the clinical evolution of His Excellency the Chief of State is as follows: he has slept almost through the night, though he awoke from anesthesia at 3 a.m. and was sedated to avoid any pain. His vital signs, his cardiocirculatory situation, and the thrombophlebitic process in his left thigh remain normal. From the beginning of yesterday's surgical operation to this moment he has received seven liters and two hundred milliliters of blood by transfusion. (It was said that by the time of his death not a drop of Franco's own blood was in his body.)

November 14, 1975—At 3:30 p.m. His Excellency the Generalissimo presents acute arterial hypotension, an increase in venous pressure, and an abdominal distension, caused by a probable deficiency in suturing. After a decision for immediate intervention, a recent dehiscence, related to shock, is confirmed at the gastrojejunal anastomosis. After the dehiscent zone is sutured again, drains are placed in the abdominal cavity. The intervention lasts two hours and is satisfactorily tolerated, but the prognosis is extremely grave.

November 15, 1975—At 9:00 a.m. arterial and venous pressure is constant, rhythm and frequency of the pulse are acceptable. The pulmonary situation remains stable, with respiration assisted. A session of hemodialysis is well tolerated. The prognosis continues to be extremely grave.

November 20, 1975—Franco dies. Multiple causes of death are listed as peritonitis, Parkinson's disease, renal dysfunction, stomach ulcers, heart stoppage, etc., etc. His perishing is attributed to almost any mortal illness except cancer, and a cynical joke adds that he had killed his cancer when he was in the throes of death. *Poor cancer!*

CARLOS ROJAS is a novelist, an art historian, and since the age of fifty a creator of visual works of art. He was born in Barcelona and came to the United States as a young man. In 1960 he joined the faculty of Emory University, where he is now Charles Howard Candler Professor of Spanish Literature, Emeritus. He has received numerous important Spanish literary prizes, including the Premio Cervantes. He lives in Atlanta.

EDITH GROSSMAN has translated major contemporary and classic authors, including Carlos Rojas, Gabriel García Márquez, Mario Vargas Llosa, Carlos Fuentes, Álvaro Mutis, Luis de Góngora, Sor Juana Inés de la Cruz, and Miguel de Cervantes. Both Carlos Fuentes and Harold Bloom have praised her version of *Don Quixote* (Ecco, 2003) as one of the best in English.